Souls of Three

The Starseed Trilogy

Ashley McLeo

Meraki Press

"Do not feel lonely, the entire universe is inside you.

Stop acting so small. You are the universe in ecstatic motion.

Set your life on fire. Seek those who fan your flames."

— Rumi

Contents

Returning Cast

Lily Whiplark - Firstborn of the three, triplet, earth witch, healer, runner, and Terramar commune resident.

Evelyn Locksley - Second born of the three, triplet, water witch, siren, ceremens, and New York resident.

Sara McKinney - Third born of three, triplet, fire witch, ex-military brat, currently on sabbatical from her studies at Princeton.

Brigit McKay-Clery - Lily, Evelyn, and Sara's mother, earth and fire witch, blends amazing tea with herbs from her garden.

Aengus Clery - Lily, Evelyn, and Sara's father, non-wizard, and deceased.

Gwenn Dolan - Brigit's older sister, earth witch, Rena's ex-girlfriend, runs an internet business, and is a dead ringer for Lily.

Mary O-Byrne - Brigit's younger sister, water witch, siren, midwife, dresses eclectically, and is a dead ringer for Evelyn.

Aoife McKay - Brigit's youngest sister, fire witch, ceremens, runs Aoife's Apothecary in town, and is a dead ringer for Sara.

Fiona Fallon - Brigit's cousin, earth witch, healer, Lily's healing instructor, and college friend of Sonja Locksley (Evelyn's adoptive mother).

Nora McFadden - Brigit's best friend since childhood, skilled witch, prodigious ceremens, and Terramar intermediary.

Morgane Murphy - McKay family friend and triplet tutor, octogenarian, academic, and has a healthy disregard for societal restrictions. Brought Sara to her first adoptive mother and father, who perished in a car fire.

Rena Whiplark - Lily's adoptive mother, witch, Taurus, and matriarch of Terramar commune.

Annika Karlsson - Rena's partner, Terramar resident, witch, Swedish by birth, and dedicated yogi.

Selma de Avila - Terramar resident, married to Richard, chatterbox, Spanish, and siren descended from the sirens of the Odyssey.

Emily Harp - Terramar resident, empathetic witch, Texas born, and deceased at the hands of Amon, Empusa, and Lily.

Empusa - Oldest vampire in the world, daughter of Noro and Seraphina, twin to Amon, and deadly.

Amon - Oldest vampire in the world, son of Noro and Seraphina, twin to Empusa, and deadly.

Noro - Fata sent to Earth to prepare it for the arrival of the fata.

Dimia - King of the fata on Hecate, Lilith, Eve, and Seraphina's father.

Lilith - Sister to Seraphina and Eve, fata sent to scout Earth, mother, and first wife of Adam before his betrayal.

Eve - Sister to Lilith and Seraphina, fata sent to scout Earth, mother to Aya, lover of Noro, and second wife of Adam.

Seraphina - Sister to Lilith and Eve, fata sent to scout Earth, mother to Empusa, Amon, and Esther (the keeper of Seraphina's tale).

Hypatia - Guardian of Seraphina's tale before her abrupt death at the hands of Amon. Constructed a prophecy and re-wrote Seraphina's tale then hid it in space and time until the arrival of the three destined to save Earth from the fata.

Spells of Potential Interest

This list is for those readers who are curious about the spells used in *The Starseed Trilogy*. Most of my spells are based off the Basque language, which is a language isolate having little to no similarities with other known languages. This list is not in alphabetical order, rather it is in the order in which the spells appear in the series.

- Solvo - Unbinds magic previously bound in a person.
- Hebeto - To dim, reduce, weaken, or blunt.
- Arma - Produces a shield charm.
- Flamarba - Produces a flame shield or gate.
- Flampila - Produces a fireball.
- Cludo - Closing or a barrier in mind magic.

- Inruo - Breaking in/intruding when using mind magic.
- Inruo ego - Sending memories into another's mind (Aoife's speciality).
- Candeo - To create a glow/light.
- Resipisico - To revive, regenerate, resurrect, reappear (waking the dead).
- Salus - The general healer's spell for health, welfare, and fixing of small injuries, can be additive but only to a certain degree. Does not work with every injury-vampire or werewolf bites for instance.
- Dedisco - Erases a person's memory.
- Volavari - To Fly/raise someone/something in the air.
- Islatu - To reflect.
- Aberro (for a person) - To deflect or throw back a person.
- Impingo (for an object) - Impinge, strike, dash, inflict, or throw back.
- Lotu - To bind a person.
- Dantza - To make someone dance.
- Birarazi - To make spin .
- Murr - To reduce or crush.
- Cogerba - "The ground-kissing curse" Forces people to the ground.

- Caeliter - Astral travel or space travel if you have a pneuma. :)
- Lascero - To tear, rip, break, claw, or mangle.
- Lascarma - To destroy a shied or other protective casing. Rip, tear, break, claw, or mangle.
- Clostium - To unlock.
- Pream - Blowing up something
- Serostium - To lock (a door).
- Dionean - A stunning spell.
- Mahasoka - Creates vine ropes.
- Benda - Like a bandaid spell it keeps wounds from getting infected. Preventative healing magic.
- Hercapto - Plants capturing a person. Ex. grass wrapping around a leg.
- Eginura - Conjures water.
- Finium - To halt your own spell (not someone else's).
- Argibeltza - The black light curse. Specific to fighting daemons because it swallows up the energy they've collected.
- Elkartaire - To pull air together, thickens the air. If the witch/wizard was strong enough (usually an air witch/wizard) this could create a shield of sorts.

- Homaire - To produce a compression wall of air.
- Motus - To move something.
- Bratu - A rotation charm that can rotate in any medium.
- Arimegin - A fata curse to rid the world of a fata pneuma who has done wrong for good (means "soul ceasing" in basque).

The Siren's Call
Evelyn

MUSIC PULSED IN HER BONES, winding its way through the gyrating crowd into her body, swaying and shaking alone on the edge of the dance floor.

It had been months since she'd felt so alive, so like her old self. Miles from the stone cottage where her life, the entire world, had changed forever. In this moment she wanted nothing more than to forget all that and get lost in her old New York City persona. To be the old Evelyn Locksley, heiress to a billion-dollar empire, business mogul, expert sailor, and man-eater. She wondered if she could still count the last two as characteristics as a part of her previous life. Did they not fall under the umbrella of water witch and siren?

Screw it. Life will never be the same no matter how much I want it to.

She tossed out a new blend of siren and witching magic she'd been playing with. The potent hormones mixed with a mind stimulating spell did their work and Evelyn caught the spectacular specimen of a man she'd sensed watching her. He heeded her call and approached her, his dark eyes hungry.

Two strong hands cupped her lower back and she allowed herself to be pulled into his hard chest until the space between them was nonexistent. The man beamed down at her. He smelled vaguely like the salty canvas sail of a sailboat and looked like a young Enrique Iglesias, but more macho.

Much hotter, Evelyn thought. She bit her lip and looked up at him through lowered lashes. He ground against her in response and she pushed her breasts front and center, showing off her excellent cleavage.

Time for some fun.

She took it slow at first, commanding small bursts of estrogen into her bloodstream. The hormone emerged from Evelyn's body seconds later, encased in the golden-hued sweat of a siren. Perspiration glistened on her skin momentarily, like a full-body halo attracting its mate before evaporating into the air to capture him.

At least a dozen male faces responded to the biochemical change. Their faces turning away from their friends or potential partners to stare at her.

Evelyn's dance partner's arms gripped her tighter as he protected his prospective mate.

Evelyn chuckled to herself.

Her arms rose to cup her partner's neck, twisting the ends of his thick, black hair.

His eyes widened, and a bulge pressed against her thigh.

She smiled wickedly. Then she turned to face the rest of her audience.

Her partner's breath covered the back of Evelyn's neck as she grabbed his hands and pulled them to her waist. She swayed her hips from side to side and smiled at the men who watched, enraptured, from the bar. At her command estrogen leapt off Evelyn's skin, spraying all within a twenty-foot radius with a potent dose of fertility and sexuality.

Evelyn's dance partner's hands inched up and she allowed him a light brush of her breast before commanding them back down, one mind to another.

Let's not get too fresh here, buddy. This isn't your show.

The Enrique look-alike shivered against her, placed his hands back on her rounded hips and squeezed.

Their audience had grown to at least fifty men and a few women, all staring at her. Evelyn repressed a shudder of excitement as the power of captivating so many rushed through her.

One glance into the crowd confirmed she had started a few arguments. A leggy redhead grabbed her man by his collar, forcing his eyes to hers. Other women had stormed off, leaving their love interests with their mouths hanging wide open.

Time to finish this.

Evelyn blew her partner a parting kiss over her shoulder and disengaged her body from his, leaving him wanting in her wake. Bodies parted before the curvaceous blonde as she sashayed deeper into the throng of partygoers, to a premeditated cleared circle, her stage, in the precise center of the dance floor.

Evelyn ran her hands down her torso, reveling in the contrast of bare skin and silk, twisting and turning as easeful as water with the beat. A vision of a snake emerging from a basket to dance for onlookers came to Evelyn, and she shook it from her head. Reminders that she was the snake, powerful, seductive, the original sin, were the last thing she wanted to think about right now.

Arms flung wide and head thrown back, she twirled to the music, glorying in the space she occupied and claiming more with each heartbeat. Her hair whipped around her, tossed high in the current of air she called to her aid. Though air was her weakest element, it was worth it to put in a little extra effort sometimes for dramatic effect. As she grew in presence the men under her spell pulled in, creating a tight circle that shielded her from the rest of the bar.

She caught sight of her Enrique look-alike dance partner in the passing swirl of faces, sweating a bit but otherwise fine. *I chose well. At least he's holding it together.* Others had not been so lucky, squirming and trembling uncontrollably. One man was clutching his groin like a child trying not to wet himself.

Evelyn pulled her arms and the energy pulsing around her in an inch closer. She gasped. A flood of power stormed through her, lighting her blood, her mind, her very soul on fire. With the combined sexual energy of so many at her fingertips she felt like she could fly away at any moment.

The song was ending, a perfect natural finale to her own performance. Evelyn followed suit as the beat faded: her rotations growing smaller, her speed slowing, her golden glow dimming. She was coming back into herself, releasing her hold over her prey's bodies and minds, her body filling with what she'd come here for.

Power.

The music fell into a momentary silence and Evelyn stopped, yanked her arms to her sides, and flung her hair back.

The man grabbing his crotch moaned. A dazed look came over the rest. They stared first at her and then each other, wondering why they were standing highly aroused, shoulder to shoulder with other men. Or where their partners were.

Not my problem.

Evelyn shivered as the raw, animalistic energy of a crowd of men and two women pulsed through her. The exchange of energy, their sexual energy for her magic, had been just what she needed. Her power had been pent up for too long. It was exhausting, *stifling* to live like this between her two worlds, unsuspecting human and witch.

Her partner stood at the edge of the circle, eyes crazed with desire. Evelyn made her way over to him, stood on tiptoe, and kissed him on the cheek before extracting herself from the circle.

"Dedisco," she whispered, spreading her arms wide. She bid the spell to jog around the bar and wipe the memories of everyone in it.

"Thanks for the good time, handsome," Evelyn called over her shoulder and disappeared into the crowd and out onto the street.

"Morning, Vici," Evelyn said, skipping into the kitchen and inhaling the scent of espresso.

"God, you're up early. Didn't you go out last night? How do you always look so damn good?" Vicencia Del Sarto asked as she hovered over the espresso maker for her daily fix.

"I left early. Dad asked me to attend a meeting today and I want to be at my best. He thinks I may help seal a big deal he's been working on."

"Hmm, did you tell him you're going back to Ireland yet? What if he tries to bring you into something and you can't finish what you started? How will that affect the account?" Vici asked, the concern in her voice unmistakable.

That was why Evelyn and Vicencia were best friends. As daughters of the CEO and COO of Locksley Enterprises, they both valued and respected the company that gave them a life most others only dreamt about. If anyone had cause for concern over her leaving, it was Vici. As Evelyn's counterpart, Vicencia would take over Evelyn's obligations in her absence.

And Evelyn anticipated being gone for a long time. It could take years to fight the supernatural war fate had chosen for her. It was why Evelyn had yet to tell Vicencia the truth of her trip. Or about herself.

What would down-to-earth Vici say when Evelyn

admitted she'd be running around with a bunch of witches to save humans from being enslaved by magical aliens for the foreseeable future? It sounded ridiculous. Especially here, so far away from the rolling green hills and mystical mists of Ireland. In the concrete jungle of New York City it was easy to discount the reality of witches, vampires, and any other creatures that went bump in the night.

Unless you were one of them.

Evelyn sighed, "I'll tell him today, Vici. I'm sorry you got stuck with my work while I was gone. I didn't expect to meet so many people, and we had a lot to catch up on. I won't let Dad do that to you again."

It was her driving reason to go in today. To tell her father, James Locksley—her mentor and the most important man in her life—to put her position up for grabs. He wouldn't like it. Hell, *she* didn't like it, but it was the right thing to do. She'd put Locksley Enterprises in a bind these last few months, forcing Vici to fill in the gaps that she'd left while Evelyn traipsed off for magic lessons.

She should have told them earlier that she would need an extended break, but she loved working with her father, and Vici, and getting shit done. The power that came with running a boardroom never failed to entice her. Though she had to admit the thrill was less now that she'd experienced the flow of magic in her veins.

"Thanks," Vicencia said looking relieved. "It's not that I don't want you to spend time with your birth family . . . God, it still feels wrong to say that." She studied Evelyn's heart shaped face, "But not for you . . ."

"I've come to terms with it."

"Right. Well, you were with them a while. Getting to know your sisters must have been fun." Vicencia said the words cheerily, though Evelyn heard the drip of jealousy in them. *If only I could tell her what our relationships are really like.*

"It's just that, well, I want to move forward, too, and it's hard to do when I'm at the office fifteen hours a day, seven days a week. I think Michael is going to propose soon. Then we can move in together." Excitement twinkled in Vicencia's large brown eyes.

Evelyn sucked in her breath. "How do you know?" she asked hoping Vicencia hadn't seen the hurt flash across her face. It wasn't right to feel left out when she'd abandoned her best friend for three months. Vici deserved to be happy and if that meant moving in with Michael the first chance she got, so be it.

I won't be here anyway, Evelyn reminded herself.

"I saw him looking in my jewelry box. He had one of those ring sizing things in his hand." Vicencia smiled at the memory. "My dad will have no reason not to let us live together after Michael proposes. Engaged couples live together in Italy all the time. That's when my cousin convinced her dad to let her move in with her man. And we'd get to plan a wedding, Evie!"

Evelyn's heart burst as happiness for her friend overtook the pain of losing her. "Of course, Vici! I can't wait to go dress shopping with you." *If I'm still around*, a small voice in her head amended as Evelyn beamed at her oldest, dearest friend.

Vicencia sipped her coffee, her stress lines softening at Evelyn's response.

"Do you want to share a car to the office today?" Evelyn asked. She was desperate for neutral ground where neither of them felt hurt or left out.

"Michael will be here soon. He rented a car to go upstate today. He said he'd drop me by the office on the way. Thanks, though." Vici dropped her espresso cup into the sink where Evelyn knew it would sit until the cleaners came on Thursday.

The clean kitchen Brigit, Evelyn's biological mother in Ireland, kept flashed through her mind. Though tiny, cluttered, and sometimes annoyingly cramped Fern Cottage—where Evelyn had spent the last three months —was, at the very least, always sparkling clean.

"I'll see you there. My meeting with dad is at nine. Let's do lunch later?"

"Text me when and where," Vicencia said as she waved her way from the room to complete her beautification rituals.

By the time George, Evelyn's driver, arrived, Evelyn had given herself a headache considering how her father would react to the news of her leaving Locksley Enterprises.

I hope Mom isn't there, too. Evelyn sighed, knowing her wish was fruitless. *Why wouldn't Mom be in the office on such a huge day for the company?* Sonja, even more so than Evelyn, was James Locksley's deal sealer. It would be stupid not to have her there with such a big client on the line. *Should I rethink using mind magic on her?* Though she'd like to, especially since she would be delivering bad, potentially world-shattering news, Evelyn knew she could never use her ceremens powers on her adoptive parents. If she started down that line with people she loved where would it stop? *No way can I use magic on them without them even knowing I'm a witch.*

Evelyn puffed out her cheeks and released the air slowly. That was another secret she had to unveil today. The holes in her story were growing too big to miss. Her father had already commented three times on how strange she'd been acting and she'd only been home a week and a half.

I hope they don't look at me differently. Or think because I have magical powers I can't be trusted.

"We're here, Miss Evelyn," George said from the front seat.

Evelyn jumped.

"Uhh, thanks, George. Sorry, must have dozed off," she said, thankful that the loyal family driver did not ask questions.

She stepped out of the car into a swarm of people: coming and going, all fast, most staring into their phones, going about their business. This was New York. This was where she thrived. The sensation of purpose. The smell of asphalt and bodies crammed together. The gloomy darkness and chill of the late fall morning. The movement of the city air around her as she weaved her way through the crowd to push open the modern brass and glass doors of Locksley Enterprises.

The difference between the lobby of Locksley Enterprises and outside world never ceased to amaze Evelyn. Here, inside her family's empire, there was space. White, well lit, and smelling of pine cleaner with touches of copper and sage, the offices were a stark contrast to the city. Her father had made sure of that.

"We want our clients to believe they've entered a

sanctuary. A place where they can relax. The city, while exhilarating, is not the best place to do a deal. It's too rushed, too anxious, and too dark. Our clients need light, space to think, and time if we are to succeed. They will find it here," James had explained when they remodeled the building years ago.

Everyone in the business world thought her father was crazy then. They asked dozens of times why would he waste money creating a beautiful office when it could be put in shareholders' pockets or reinvested? But James Locksley had a knack for power dynamics that the doubters had failed to see. It was why at only forty-nine years old James was where he was.

"Good morning, Miss Locksley," a pretty girl with a posh English accent at the front counter smiled at her. "Might I send you up a coffee once you're settled?"

"Morning, Rose. That would be great. Thanks."

Rose nodded, the phone already in hand to call in the order.

Blessedly, the elevator ride up to the fifty-first floor was nonstop and quiet. Evelyn loved that. A bit of quiet before what was sure to be a storm. She was going to need it today. The elevator dinged, and she stepped onto the executive floor.

The top floor of the building was like the entrance but on steroids. Floor to ceiling windows provided the executives with a stunning view of the city. It gave their clients the impression that all was possible with Locksley Enterprises.

Cubicles were forbidden. Instead, there were spacious offices with doors made of translucent Japanese paper framed in bronze. As a modern shoji, the doors provided enough material to give one privacy but still exude a sensation of lightness. Lush, leafy plants in warm copper pots lined the hallway, providing fresh air and color.

This may be the only place in the city, besides the park, where Lily would be happy. The thought struck her out of nowhere and Evelyn sighed. *For now, witches, mysterious ancient books, and other families don't exist.*

She was about to open her office door when she glimpsed movement in the conference room. Stretching her neck, Evelyn peeked down the hall. She caught sight of her father and mother inside the glass enclosure at the end of the hall, opposite of her father's office.

James ran his hands through his dark hair and smiled sheepishly at Sonja, who was fixing James's tie. The gestures were so familiar it made Evelyn's heart swell.

How did I not know they weren't my biological parents? Evelyn's sapphire eyes flitted over her mother's petite frame, dark hair and eyes, nestled in a beautiful olive complexion. Evelyn looked nothing like James either. His chestnut brown hair, slitted gray-blue eyes, and thin frame gave an impression of a nimble wolf. None of her light coloring, curvy frame, or sensual features were in these people, yet she'd never doubted they were her blood. *Did other people wonder? I guess it would be difficult not to.*

Evelyn had stayed with her parents in their Hampton home for a couple of days after her return from Ireland. She'd wanted to hear their side of the story and what they knew of the McKays, her biological family in Ireland, before retreating to the city apartment she shared with Vici.

It was as Brigit said it would be. James and Sonja knew almost nothing of the McKays. To them, Evelyn had been a godsend for a young, hardworking power couple plagued by infertility. Even all those years ago they preferred to work with people they had a history with, and Sonja trusted few more than her college friend, Fiona Fallon. Sonja had thought it lucky that Fiona, Evelyn's second cousin by blood, had taken a senior position at an Irish adoption agency. Lucky that there was a baby girl recently born and waiting for them. Lucky, that the birth family's stipulations could be easily met.

"We were the luckiest couple we knew," Sonja had claimed when Evelyn asked of her adoption story.

But Evelyn knew better.

There had been no luck involved. Just as there had been no adoption agency, only a family of witches hoping to hand out three daughters to people who could provide well and keep them safe. Evelyn found herself wanting to correct her parents. To inform them on who they were in partnership with. How most of what they believed about her heritage, and the world in general, was one big lie. But first, she had to out herself as a witch. *Soon,* she thought as she made her way to her desk and extracted a slim gold notepad from her brief-case before heading down the hall.

James opened the conference room door at her approach.

"Evelyn. Come in," he said, his gray eyes crinkling at the corners. "Now that we're all here, we can begin." James motioned down the long table.

Evelyn twitched as she took in the figure in the room she had not seen from the hallway. He was young, only a few years older than her, though his stance suggested otherwise. Tall, slender, and well-built, the man filled any space in the room not taken up by the large personalities of Evelyn and her parents. He looked up, saw her standing in the doorway, and with a closed-lip smile walked forward and extended a hand.

Evelyn slammed down sturdy mind barriers—it was a self-imposed rule she'd devised for business interactions to keep them fair—before clasping his hand. Their skin touched for only a second before she pulled away.

What was that? She caught the man's playful blue eyes.

"Sorry about that," he said shaking his hand and extending it once more. "I'm Roman. Roman Simons. Didn't mean to shock you. It's a surprise anything can carry electricity in here, what with all the glass and paper decor."

Evelyn nodded and took his hand again.

"Evelyn Locksley." She tried to concentrate on Roman's strong handshake rather than the alluring, peppery scent of cloves.

"Evelyn recently returned from a trip to Ireland. We're so glad that your time in the city overlapped. We think you two will find much that you can agree on," Sonja said taking her seat, her eyes trained on Evelyn.

"Ahh, Ireland. A charming country. I have familial ties there. Dad and I try to get back at least once every year, go hunting, feel the blood of our forefathers pound in our veins. You know, manly bonding. Too bad we haven't made it yet this year, what with the company growing so fast and all." As Roman spoke a slight twang arose, and Evelyn's ears perked up.

"Where are you from?"

"Nashville," Roman admitted, a blush accentuating his high cheekbones. "But don't tell my father when you meet him that you caught onto the accent. He tried to train it out of us as kids. He likes to put on the big city persona. Thinks somehow losing the accent makes us appear to be better businessman. Truth is, he has a harder time covering up his accent than me."

Evelyn stifled a giggle. "Fake it till you make it."

The words escaped her before she could catch herself. *Where is this shit coming from? And did I just giggle in a meeting?* An unfamiliar heat crept up her neck and Evelyn realized she was blushing. She looked at her father, hoping he'd be able to set the meeting back on track.

The grin on James's face said it all. There was a reason he had wanted her here, and it wasn't all work related.

"Well, now that everyone knows each other, what do you say we get on to business?" James said correctly interpreting her glower.

They emerged two hours later, having achieved more than Evelyn expected despite her humiliating performance. She couldn't think of a single other meeting where she'd added less value. Reading figures off charts was about all she had been good for. Probably because she didn't have to make eye contact with Roman or her parents.

How could they embarrass me like that? She slammed her notebook on her desk. She hated being out of control in the two arenas she excelled at: business and men.

Don't they realize I have more to worry about than men?

She shook her head at the absurdity of her own question. *Of course they don't. I still haven't told them my plans to go back to Ireland. Or the reason why.* With that she turned and strode out the door to her father's office.

Her steps softened as she drew closer and peeked in. Roman was gone. They were alone.

"Evie! That went well, didn't it?" James jumped from his seat as Evelyn slid his door open.

"Depends on what your meaning of well is. Why didn't you tell me this was some type of weird setup?"

James and Sonja locked eyes and Evelyn read the

words that flowed between them as clearly as if she'd been reading their minds with her mind magic.

Guilty, guilty, guilty.

"To be fair, darling, we didn't plan it this way. Roman's father was set to come instead."

"But you would have known days ago. Yesterday, at the very least, when you three went over the preliminaries."

James winced.

Guilty again.

"You're right," her mother said, leaning back into her chair, her fingers tented beneath her chin. "We should have told you we found Roman extremely charming and the type of man we want you with. Probably that he was young, and handsome, too, but when has that ever mattered?"

Sonja raised her eyebrows. "You always have the upper hand with men. I see it at every society function we attend. After I spoke with Roman yesterday I'll admit, I hoped you'd take to him. Even date him once we finalized his accounts and set them to automation so it didn't violate company protocol. But I wasn't about to make a big deal over something that may be nothing."

Evelyn studied her mother. No doubt Sonja was telling the truth. It didn't make Evelyn feel less humiliated, but at least the air was clear now.

"Alright," Evelyn said dropping into a chair next to her mother. "As long as we're being honest now, I have something to say."

Her parents nodded.

"I have to go back to Ireland soon. I'm not sure for how long and it's not fair that Vicencia gets bogged down with all my work. I'll be there for the foreseeable future so you'll have to hire someone capable to help." Her heart hurt saying the words.

"What do you mean foreseeable future?" James asked, his eyes hardening.

"Are you moving there?" Sonja bit her lip and drew her brows together.

"I . . . no. There are things I have to work on with my family there. Things I can't do from New York." *Why can't I say it? I'm a witch and I have to train to save the world. How hard can it be?*

She opened her mouth, but the words stayed lodged deep inside.

"That complicates things," James said leaning forward in his chair. "Your advancement within the company, for one thing. Especially if you don't know when you'll be back. And that's not even taking into account our current situation."

"What situation?"

"The one where Roman has asked to work with you

as his lead account manager on this project. I hope he'll still be amenable to working with us once he learns you're exiting. It's a large deal for Locksley Enterprises."

Evelyn's stomach hardened. She'd seen the numbers and knew how large a deal it was for them. If Roman's company kept expanding at its current rate, it meant hundreds of millions to billions in added revenue every year.

A battle broke out inside Evelyn. The business woman in her jumped at the chance to prove herself. To grow her father's company in a way that with their average clients could take years. To be the one who took Locksley Enterprises to the next level.

The witch was cautious.

From what Brigit told them after the battle in Alexandria, the triplets were nowhere near as prepared as they should be to face their foes. Evelyn knew she should be in Ireland training and learning magic. She didn't want to fall behind in her training and be the weakest of the three. Especially, now that they'd lost the element of surprise and secrecy.

Evelyn shivered as Brigit's ominous words of warning that they should be battle ready at any moment came rushing back to her. That Brigit had only been willing to give them two weeks with their adoptive families before returning to Fern Cottage spoke volumes.

And Evelyn was all too aware her time in New York was almost up. *Brigit probably wouldn't have let us leave Fern Cottage at all if Lily hadn't been so deep in mourning. Not after the horrors they saw in Alexandria. But I don't want to disappoint Dad either . . .*

She hated letting her father down. James Locksley, the man she had looked up to all her life. A man who had given so much of himself to his company and yet always managed to put Evelyn and Sonja first. A father who was annoyingly supportive when it came to Evelyn becoming acquainted with her birth family. The one person who helped them get to Alexandria to try to save Lily's kidnapped family member from the vampires, no questions asked, when it seemed impossible. *I can't do that to him.*

"I'll stay to help with the Simons account, but only until we get the initialization plan off the ground and running. A month, two at the absolute most. After that, someone else will have to take over for the next few months before automation. It will take at least that long at their current growth rate to stabilize. And *it can't be Vici*, she's already got enough. Hire someone. I can supervise remotely until they are comfortable taking the reins."

James smiled, "That's our girl. Roman will be pleased. He took a liking to you."

"And us trying to set you up is a moot point, now that you're taking an extended break. You won't have time to fall for him," Sonja teased, though Evelyn could tell she was trying to put on a happy face at the news of her daughter leaving again.

Evelyn returned her father's smile as her stomach flipped uncontrollably. *How am I going to tell Brigit? And, even worse, Lily? We've finally gotten on semi-even ground and now I'm abandoning her for two months? And I still have to tell everyone I'm a witch . . .*

Evelyn closed her eyes briefly. *One thing at a time.* "Thanks, Dad. Have Natalia send Roman my information, will you? I'm late to meet Vici for lunch." She turned to leave, feeling even more confused than when she'd arrived at the office that morning.

Tradition and Troubles
Lily

"You're back!" Sara cried, engulfing Lily in a hug tinged with the faint scent of the sage bundles Sara burned during meditation. "It was so weird here without you. Our room felt too big."

Lily smiled at her sister's crooked grin and bright copper eyes. *I didn't expect coming back to feel this good.*

"How are you? I bet you were happy Gwenn picked you up instead of Morgane. Less chatter after such a long flight." Sara winked and took Lily's small duffle from her hands and guided her down the hallway.

"Feeling a little better, thanks. And as much as I like Morgane and know her picking me up would have been more convenient, I agree Gwenn being there was a pleasant surprise. It was nice to have another earth witch in the car, sensing that I needed quiet. Gwenn has always been so in tune with my needs."

Sara nodded as she pushed open the door to their shared bedroom.

Lily stopped dead in her tracks.

"Do you like it?" Sara whispered, brows knitted together.

Their room had undergone a complete renovation in the two weeks Lily had been recovering and healing with her adoptive family in Oregon. She gawked at the sage duvet, warm cherry wood side table and dresser, and reupholstered green wingback chair that sat next to its tartan twin. The old carpet was gone, replaced with shiny wood floors and sheepskin rugs below the beds.

Walking to her side of the room, Lily felt the warmth and love that had gone into creating the space. The soft green of moss and swaths of naked wood put her at ease as if she was sitting in a forest. A photo collage of her Oregon and Irish family hung in a place of honor above her bed. Best of all was the decorative divider running the length of the room creating the illusion of separate living spaces.

"How did you manage to get all this done?"

"It was Mom's idea. She thought our room should reflect our personalities a bit more. We didn't get as much studying done as I thought we would while you were gone. We mostly did this."

Lily tilted her head trying to discern how she felt about Brigit's title change in her absence. She had no qualms with Sara calling Brigit, Mom. She was after all their biological mother, and Lily could even see why it would feel natural to Sara.

As a child Sara hadn't had the traditional, loving mother figure. As a result she'd bonded to Brigit and Brigit's three sisters, Gwenn, Mary, and Aoife, faster than Lily or Evelyn had.

Mom. Lily closed her eyes and repeated the word three more times. To her surprise, both Rena's, the woman who had raised her, and Brigit's images arose. She opened her eyes again and smiled. The brief exercise had told her more than weeks of internal debate could have.

Sara's right. We may have only known each other four months but they've been intense and unlike any other months in my life. All the women here have literally put their lives on the line for me. Brigit feels just as much a mother to me as Rena. I think it's time to let her know.

"That's so thoughtful. Thank you. I love your side, too," Lily said finally.

She crossed the barrier into Sara's half of the room

where warm reds and oranges dominated what looked to be a mash-up of a yoga studio and bedroom. A large mandala hung above Sara's bed. In the corner between the dresser and the tartan chair was a small mat, cushion, and low bench. The bench was decorated with candles of all shapes and sizes and photos of the McKays, Lily, Evelyn, and Sara. Lily recognized it as a meditation alter, much like Rena's partner Annika's at home.

"Why'd you keep your chair tartan?" she asked, walking over to drop into the new plush velvet covering her chair.

"Tradition. Something had to stay the same, and I kind of like it. Plus since the divider doesn't extend that far it goes better with your chair than red or orange. That would look too Christmasy." Sara wrinkled her nose.

Lily nodded in agreement.

"We did Evelyn's room, too. Very posh, blue and gold tones, but not too gold. I think she'll like it."

"Sounds very Evelyn. I'm sure she'll like it way better than what she had," Lily grinned thinking of the plain single room the heiress had occupied before.

Sara lowered herself into her tartan chair as Lily set her bag on the bed. The room fell into an uncomfortable silence and Lily knew exactly why. *May as well get this over with . . .*

"It was so weird, being home without Em. Knowing she'll never come back and that I was the one to make it final," Lily said without looking up.

Sara let out the breath she'd been holding.

"I needed the time to mourn Em but I'm glad to be back. If I'm being honest, it was a little overwhelming, so many emotions running high and nothing I could do about it but talk and listen. At least here I can do something, learn more, and fight again to avenge Em's death. Most of the time, I just felt sad at Terramar."

"You know a little bit of that sadness will always be there, right?" Sara asked, the concern evident in her voice.

"I know, but it will dampen. And it will be easier here than there. Did Brigit tell you that Rena, Annika, and Selma are coming here to visit?" she asked, careful not to drop the 'M' bomb with Sara before Brigit heard her say it.

"They want to see where I'm living and meet you and Evelyn. Selma is especially excited. She doesn't get to socialize with others that have siren powers often." Lily stifled a laugh as a vision of Selma, the Spanish Siren of Terramar commune, chatting Evelyn's ear off rose in her mind. "I'll have to warn Evelyn that Selma can be a chatterbox."

"That's great," Sara beamed. "I can't wait to meet them. Two sirens in one little cottage? Good thing there are never any men here."

Lily nodded in agreement. "When does Evelyn get back?"

"Mom talked to her yesterday and said she was planning on telling her parents after work today that she need to return to Ireland. Evelyn will bring the family jet over and hire a driver so we don't have to worry about making arrangements to get her all the way out here. I think she's trying to avoid any of Morgane's wacky conversations. She'll show up sometime next week."

"What a life."

"Seriously."

The sound of the front door opening traveled down the hall.

"Sara? Is Lil here yet?" Brigit called from the entryway.

Now's the time. "Hi, Mom!" Lily yelled. Out of the corner of her eye she saw Sara's mouth fall open and then snap shut and widen into a smile.

Brigit had barely kicked off her rain boots when Lily pounced on her. Hugging and breathing in her mother's scent of cinnamon and lavender, a profound sense of coming home washed over her.

Nearly two weeks in Oregon had been more than enough time for Lily to consider what she thought of her new family and what she found surprised her. So far from the anger and denial she felt when they'd first met, now there was deep love for the family that gave her up so she could live in safety and love another.

"You've no idea how happy that word makes me. Thank you, Lil," Brigit said hugging her daughter tight. "I'm so glad you're back."

"Did you—?" Brigit asked, her brown eyes latching on Sara's copper ones.

"Yup. She loved it."

"Good. Something a bit more personal and new. You three deserve it after all the work you've been putting in. Mary's been trying to get me to redo those rooms for years. Wanted to try her hand at interior deco-rating, but I was waiting until I met you," Brigit pulled away and smiled at the pair of them. "Would anyone like a cuppa? I'm desperate for one. The Gallagher birth was quite problematic. I may even need something a bit stronger."

Sara and Lily glanced at each other and raised their eyebrows. Mary, their blonde bombshell aunt, had eclectic taste and Lily could only imagine what a room she decorated would look like. *Probably sequin curtains and all sorts of crazy colors.*

"How's the new baby?" Sara asked as they followed Brigit into the kitchen.

"She's fit now. Mary and I have been up since dawn hoping to pry her out. The wee thing was a bit willful. A lot like a few other wee ones I knew." Brigit winked and set the kettle to boil.

"That was your last birth for a while, right?"

"Aye. I thought it best not to take on any new clients while you three are studying. Mary will take on the excess and I'll help when I can. Gwenn will step in if Mary really needs help and I can't. Gwenn hasn't attended a birth since she started her internet business but she knows the basics. We think it best that one of us is always here in case of a new development. We can't predict when a babe comes and goddess knows we may need to be ready at a moment's notice should anything arise in the supernatural realm."

"Are we going to resume our studies again soon then?"

Lily smiled at the excitement in Sara's voice. *Two whole weeks without lessons must have been torture for her.*

"I'm thinking we could start you two tomorrow or the next day. I'm still waiting to hear from Evelyn as you know. Can you believe she's been working the entire time she's been home? Child must not like rest. No idea where she got that from, certainly not me."

Brigit placed three tea bags in mugs and began filling them with her homemade cinnamon and spice loose leaf mix.

"It's Thanksgiving tea," Lily said as the smells of the holiday wafted over. Back at the start of summer, before she'd found out she was a witch fated to rescue humanity from an ancient magical race, she'd been looking forward to a home-cooked Thanksgiving dinner.

"Oh my gosh! It's Thanksgiving isn't it?" Sara looked stunned. Apparently, she'd forgotten about the holiday.

"Yup. In Oregon everyone's at Selma and Richard's. Rich is cooking a huge turkey, Annika is making the vegetarian version plus sides, and they'll all indulge in homemade mead," Lily said with a sigh.

"You know I kind of miss Thanksgiving, too. It's been years since I celebrated with a full dinner. I never go home for holidays anymore. Hey! Maybe when Rena, Annika, and Selma visit we can have a late Thanksgiving! What do you think, Mom?" Sara asked her eyes shining with the thought.

Lily's eyes popped open. *That would be perfect.* She held her breath for Brigit's answer.

Brigit tilted her head in consideration and her auburn hair fell over her shoulder. "I've never cooked an American Thanksgiving—being Irish and all it's not done here. But since you three celebrate, I suppose we must. Aye, when your family visits would be best. I'll need help preparing such a large feast."

Lily smirked imagining Rena and Selma in the kitchen. Neither of them had the culinary skills to fill a teacup. "Sure! Annika is a great cook. Healthy, too."

"Well that'd be grand. We need more healthful food and activities about here don't we, Sara?" Brigit teased the petite redhead. "You wouldn't believe what this one here had me doing while you were gone, Lil! I couldn't walk normal for days."

"It was only a few sun salutations." Sara waved off Brigit's playful jab. "I could teach you too, Lily."

"That sounds awesome! Maybe before classes?" Her mind always felt clearer after her body had been worked.

"That's the spirit! I bet Evelyn would like them, too. I heard her talking with Mary about Pilates once. Yoga and Pilates aren't that different."

Brigit deposited two steaming mugs of tea in front of them. The aroma of cinnamon permeated the kitchen and Lily relaxed back in her chair. It felt good to chat easily again.

Though she'd done a lot of catching up at Terramar, the conversation always turned back to Em. There was no way Lily could deny the people who loved Em the story of her death. She wasn't the only one seeking closure for a loved one lost. The entire community had been grieving with her. At least at Fern Cottage it would be easier to bury her grief in work and the comings and goings of family. Things were rarely slow at the cottage.

Lily sipped her tea. Warmth slipped through her and the hearth fire, so large it separated the kitchen-diner from the sitting room, burned hot at Lily's back. Lily's muscles loosened and a weariness overtook her.

"Did you put a sleeping draught in this tea?" she joked.

Brigit shook her head. "I expect that's the travel catching up with you, love. Did you sleep at all?"

Lily laughed at the question. For weeks sleep had felt impossible, and on a good night she'd manage four hours. She hadn't even closed her eyes on the flights over.

"Not a wink. You're probably right. I think I'll finish this in my room and then lie down. Is anyone coming for dinner?"

"Your aunts will be here at six." Brigit's voice brightened as it always did when she spoke of her sisters.

Lily rose with more effort than she felt should be

necessary. *God, I am tired.* She was about to round the hearth when the question she'd been dying to ask for weeks, but somehow had forgotten the moment she'd seen Sara, popped into her mind. "Hey, did anyone find anything else in Hypatia's book?"

"I expect your aunts will want to be here for that chat. Especially Mary, she's been studying that thing obsessively. Go get some sleep, Lil. We'll wake you for supper."

SHE AWOKE to a soft knock on the door.

"Lil? Everyone's here," Sara said peeking into their room.

"I'll be right there," Lily answered, throwing her arms into a wide stretch and flexing her long legs.

Despite many hours in bed since Em's death, she hadn't slept so hard in weeks. At Terramar lying in bed equated to thinking and second guessing herself until daylight approached.

Being back at Fern Cottage is like taking a sleeping pill. She rose from bed and opened her drawer, a sense of purpose she hadn't felt in weeks budding within her.

Five minutes later she strolled into the bustling kitchen and was pulled into a bear hug by her curvy, blonde aunt Mary and a smaller, toastier hug from her fire witch aunt Aoife.

From Aoife's arms Lily grinned at her look-alike aunt Gwenn, who had picked Lily up from the airport hours earlier.

"Alright. Alright, you lot. Break it up. The girl just woke up from a sizable nap. She's probably starving," Brigit said, guiding Lily to the table and setting a plate of roasted chicken, vegetables, and potatoes in front of her. "Eat up, Lil. We need to beef you up, make you three big and strong."

Lily grinned impishly. Eating was the one thing she'd never had trouble doing.

"She's been saying that to me ever since you two left," Sara said, nabbing the seat next to Lily, her own plate heaped high with food. "There must have been some hulking vamps in that mansion."

Lily stiffened at mention of the mansion. *Here we go.*

"Most I saw were slight and beautiful. They were still super strong, though," Lily said, trying to act normal and breathe through the tightness in her chest.

"They always are. That's one thing popular culture gets right. You will never find an ugly or weak vampire. Even the few I've seen that were turned in their mature years are still lovely looking. Something in the blood makes them that way, irresistible to their prey." Aoife's voice was tight as she pulled up a chair next to her fire witch mentee and doppelgänger, Sara.

Lily's nostrils filled with Aoife's spicy ginger and pepper scent as she took in her aunt's words. *Well, that does explain a lot.* An image of Em's cruel red eyes surrounded by wrinkle-free, lustrous skin flashed in Lily's mind. She felt everyone's eyes on her, taking her measure. Lily wasn't ready to talk about Em again yet, but she knew that wasn't likely who they were thinking about, anyway.

"Like Amon," Lily said.

Brigit's mouth flattened into a thin line and Gwenn's shoulders tightened, but no one spoke.

"I'm sorry I didn't tell you before I left. Everything hurt too much." Lily took in the solemn gazes of her family. "Amon and I dated during my last year of college. He was my first boyfriend and, I thought, my first love. I went to Bryn Mawr so the fact that no one knew him didn't seem strange to me. He went by Liam there."

"Bryn Mawr is an all-girl college," Sara explained as confusion clouded Aoife and Gwenn's expressions.

"I have to ask, Lily," Brigit said, looking afraid to hear the answer, "Did you sleep with him?"

"No. He's the first guy I ever dated. I've . . . I'm still a virgin," Lily admitted, her face dropping to her plate.

"Thank the goddess."

Lily's head shot up. "Why?"

"For one thing it took extreme force of character not to give into Amon's seductions in the first place. I do not doubt he was working his vampiric charms to get what he wanted. Vampires exert their strongest emotional powers over those they've mated with. It's an intense bond and one Amon would have loved to exploit. I'll wager it made him right furious that you weren't completely in his thrall," Brigit explained, a smug smile growing on her face.

Lily nodded remembering the feel of Amon's arm gripping her shoulder as his parting words rang in her head.

"You're hiding something. Rest assured, I'll uncover your secrets. You can't remain silent forever. You'll slip up soon, I can feel it. If you don't give them to me, I can force them from you."

"He was furious one night, the last night I spoke with him before we met again in Alexandria. We didn't even officially break up, I just left in the middle of the night and drove home to Terramar. He talked about forcing secrets out of me. I thought he was crazy."

"Leaving like that was the best thing you could have

done." Brigit said the words without a hint of doubt. "I'd wager Amon thought you'd come back. He would have been sure of his sway over you. But you felt something in him that was off, didn't you? Something that scared you more than even his words?"

"His presence that night was animalistic. Terrifying. Almost as terrifying as when I found out what he truly was."

"That's the one good thing about vamps. They'll charm the pants off you but can never hide their predator side for long. Makes them easier to weed out once you know what you're looking for," Aoife's voice became more gravelly than normal as she stabbed a piece of chicken with her fork.

The sound of forks scraping plates and throats gulping down water filled the conversational lull until Lily couldn't take it any longer.

"Did you find anything about Hypatia's book?"

"Was wondering when you'd want to talk about that." Mary's soprano voice was muffled through a mouth full of food. She swallowed and took a swig of her wine.

"We've each read through at least a half dozen times," Mary continued. "It's been subjected to many magical tests to reveal any secrets that may be hiding in the ink or even the fibers of the paper itself. Bahati visited while you were away. She read it, too. For her, the book appeared in Egyptian so we compared notes to see if anything was lost in translation. Not a single detail was altered. That means the text had been written in lingua primum, the first language of magic—which makes sense, considering its ancient origins. Seraphina and her daughter Esther could not be sure that their language would be around by the time the second coming of the three occurred."

"Any other spells or enchantments?" Lily asked, her breath tightening in her chest.

Mary shook her head. "We found nothing magical in the text to indicate it was more than a story or history. No hidden magical properties or underlying text."

There's nothing magical about the book we risked our lives for?

"So we began reading for information we didn't know of that negated common folklore. Like, for instance, how a fata can die." Mary's blue eyes glimmered with the thrill of discovery, reminding Lily that while Mary might be a midwife by training, she was a researcher at heart and the primary reason they knew anything about Hypatia, the prophecy told at the triplets' birth, or fata.

Lily's ears perked up.

"What? There were no instructions. I'd remember

that!"

"Instructions no," Mary continued, "But Seraphina died, right? Her soul leaked from her body, Lil. If we can puncture through their skin all the way to an inner membrane to their soul, or pneuma as they call it, the fata will die."

"Alright. Maybe Noro knew how to do that because he was a fata, but how do we do it? And what if it was just because Seraphina was transforming?" Lily asked, her voice dripping with skepticism.

"We're still working on that," Sara said. "But it's a start isn't it? It gave me hope that if we come into contact with a fata, we'll stand a chance. Better than going in completely blind."

"As none of us are experts in fata, or any other magical creatures really, we've been chatting with witches and wizards who know more about the specifics of other species," Gwenn jumped in. "We're hoping to find commonalities between species that may be little known among other magical creatures. For example, everyone knows silver is fatal to vampires and fae can't touch iron. There's speculation in reviewing the few folklore tales Mary came across that fata could be sensitive to iron as well. What if we learn most daemons, elves, and incubi are sensitive to it, too? Then it's a good guess that the folktales are right."

Lily nodded. "Speaking of vampires. Empusa and Amon were Seraphina's twins, weren't they? That's what Amon meant when he said they were our kin."

"We think so, but of course there's no proof except their word. It's not like we could perform a DNA test. Hell, we don't even know if fata have DNA," Aoife trailed off, looking amused.

"But the eyes match perfectly with Seraphina's description. I noticed how green Empusa's were right away and Amon's"—Lily flushed—"well, I know for a fact his eyes are gray flecked with violet. Seraphina called them gray-violet but human eyes change all the time after birth. Couldn't a vampire's eyes?"

"And they drank blood," Sara added, diverting attention from Lily. "So if that's true, not only are they our distant kin, they're also the first vampires."

"Did Noro know they would come out vampires and not fata?" Lily asked.

"No. Noro said 'I wonder' when they were born. There was no way he could have known what a fata-fata mating would produce on a planet that wasn't Hecate, but that doesn't mean he wouldn't take advantage of a new species to mold." Mary answered. Her cherubic cheeks were pink now, whether from the wine, the fire at her back, or the rush of talking about her research, Lily wasn't sure.

"But how did that happen? Like two fatas had sex and then a different creature pops out? I don't get it."

"Experts Gwenn spoke with agree that the magic of the planet Earth versus the magic found on Hecate has something to do with the child's development," Mary answered.

"So let me get this straight once and for all: Human DNA combined with fata genetics to produce baby witches? Then the magic that witch children inherited from their fata ancestors was passed down through the generations even if they mated with humans because it was already a part of their genetic code?"

The McKay women nodded in unison.

Lily shook her head to clear it. "Alright, so I get the witches part but now I *have* to ask. All the magical variability on Earth can't just be the product of Noro and Eve, right? I'm assuming Noro stayed here because how would he get back? He was too weak to bring himself to Earth, he was probably too weak to get back to Hecate alone. Maybe he's still here! Who knows? Anyway, even if you add Lilith in for genetic variability, assuming they ever found her before she died, which she had to have died because," Lily pointed to herself, "the original three have to be dead if we're here to fulfill a prophecy. Well, there's a lot of different magical creatures! That makes me think Eve must have succeeded in bringing over more fata after Seraphina died. Either that or she and Noro were *really* busy making all sorts of supernatural creature babies. But even then there'd have to be some incest and I know that doesn't end well for humans."

"That a few more fata made it to Earth is the consensus of the magical diversity experts Gwenn talked to. It would explain nicely the magical variability and the lack of weakness over time that incest would create," Mary answered simply.

"So, what do these experts think happened when the children of fata-fata pairings mated with humans? I mean it had to have happened, right?"

"Quite a bit, I'd guess," Mary said, looking thrilled at where the conversation had led them. "Any humanoid creature you can think of was likely a product of a fata-fata parentage subsequently mated with humans. Fae, for instance, have the look of a human, magical powers resembling witches, and abnormally long lifespans like fata. We believe a new magical creature was created with fata unions and then it took on a human form and minor human characteristics with subsequent human matings. Less mating with humans means stranger-looking creatures like djinn, which look kind of like ghosts or wind."

Lily sighed. *We could be up against any number of magical creatures and the only one I know how to fight is vampires. And I sucked at that. How were we ever going to win when I'm so far behind? I need to change the subject before I lose my mind . . .*

"Did you ever find out who was staying in that first room we walked into in Empusa's mansion?" Lily blurted out the next question she'd been obsessing over.

Brigit shook her head. "But we're sure it was a witch or wizard. The room had the feel of witching magic. Whether they were on our side or not, we may never know."

"Can I read Hypatia's book again?" Lily had saved her biggest question for last. She needed to get her hands on that book again, to examine it herself.

"I'd have been shocked if you didn't ask." Mary pulled the book out from a beaded purple satchel hung across the back of her chair. As she handed the book over, Lily caught whiffs of Mary's grapefruit and rain scents. *She must have been examining it nonstop for her smell to seep into the old leather.*

Here it was, in Lily's hands. Thirty-three pages of roughly bound, thin paper. So small and potent. She knew she would obsess over it until all its secrets were plunged. *There has to be something we're missing.*

"Thanks, Mary," Lily said, her hand shaking as she placed the book on her lap, away from any liquids or food on the table.

"We hear there's a chance your family is coming to visit soon?" Gwenn asked, sensing Lily's need for a lighter subject.

Lily nodded, "Brigit said we could have them for a belated Thanksgiving."

"Brilliant! That'll be a real treat," Aoife said, grinning her lopsided grin.

"As long as Annika can cook it well enough," Gwenn's comment was spoken with such familiarity that it turned Lily's head.

"I forgot you knew Rena." The fact that her adoptive mother had dated her aunt seemed so minuscule after everything else Lily had learned that she had never asked about it.

"Aye, we met in a bar after a Cher concert. We were arguing over our favorite song, if you can believe it!"

Lily rolled her eyes. She could so believe it—Rena was nothing if not serious about Cher.

"Well I suppose you can, then," Gwenn laughed and ran her hands through her brown hair. "Rena was different from anyone I'd ever met. We started dating shortly after, then road tripped around the states. We stopped in Nashville and met Emily. Rena learned of Terramar from Emily. We had a bit of an adventure in Nashville with a so called rogue fae and a fractionated coven. It was a summer I'll never forget. Rena told me all about Terramar when she moved there. It's how we knew where to send you."

Lily's eyes were wide with discovery. She'd known Gwenn and Rena had dated but that they'd both met Em at the same time was new to her. *How much else do I not know?*

"And what about Selma? Nora seemed very familiar with her when we had our first ceremens class." Lily tried not to sound bitter about the day Evelyn had broken into Nora's head and discovered her ceremens talents.

The way Nora had spoken about her family—condescending but with assured familiarity—before she'd been reduced to a terrified pile on the grass still irritated Lily. *I can see why Rena and Nora don't get along.*

"Who doesn't know Selma de Avila?" Mary said as if Selma were the Queen of England. "Not everyone can claim to be descended from the sirens of the Odyssey, now can they? Selma and I have known each other for years. We spent months gallivanting all over Spain. I even stayed with the notorious de Avila women in Menorca."

Lily blinked. Her head felt like it was about to explode. Every day she learned some new, extraordinary fact about her life. Like how intertwined her two families were.

"I told you, we couldn't give you and your sisters to any old family," Brigit came up behind Lily and rubbed her shoulder. "There had to be a personal connection. People we could rely on to do right by you. Those we knew would not deny us knowing you later in life."

"They didn't talk to you about any of this when you were home?" Sara asked, copper eyes wide.

"Most of the time we grieved and talked about Em . . ." She trailed off, wanting more than anything to avoid talking about Em.

"There's no need to rush anything. We'll all be around tomorrow if you want to talk," Gwenn jumped in. She reached out to grab Lily's hand and Lily felt calming earth magic, like walking through a quiet forest on a spring day, pulse beneath her aunt's palm.

"Yea. Thanks. I think I'll go relax in my room. I'm pretty sleep deprived and this would all be easier to take rested," Lily said standing to rise.

"Sounds good, honey. We've set a couple lessons for you and Sara tomorrow, a few warm-up drills mixed in with a couple new things. We'll wait 'til Evelyn arrives to get going on the more difficult work. Wouldn't want her to feel left behind."

"Sounds good. I'll be ready," Lily said and waved herself out of the room.

The Spark Ignites
Evelyn

"How do you keep this pace up?" Roman asked, shutting his laptop.

Evelyn, determined to finish the last few points of the extensive business plan they'd been crafting the last two days, continued to type. "I told you, I can only work with you for two months tops. I have personal obligations I'm putting off overseas. It's imperative we get all your accounts, projections, assets, and plans up to date so I can be sure everything will run well in my absence."

"Couldn't you be available by phone? I don't mind doing some of this with you working remotely if you need to leave now. I can manage most of the basics and you could come back once I've implemented the initial steps."

Evelyn turned her back to him. "I can't guarantee it.

Where I'm going cell service is spotty and I'm not sure how long I'll need to be gone. I'm sorry, but it has to be this way. My father is working to find a competent replacement to take over your accounts. That way we won't leave you in a bind." Her tone was as firm as she dared.

The last thing she wanted was to discuss with a client why she was leaving her powerful, sought-after position for an undetermined amount of time. *I wish he'd just stop with the all the questions.*

"Alright, but I can't keep up with these big city hours without some fun. What do you say we go grab a drink? I like to know more about the people I partner with than how they take the dozen cups of coffee they inhale every day. If this were Nashville, we'd already have bought each other a couple beers by now."

"We've only known each other three days." Evelyn hoped he was joking.

"Southern charm, Miss Locksley. We like to get real personal down home."

I shouldn't but a martini does sound amazing. She closed her eyes and rolled her neck, which crackled with tension. When she opened her eyes again the piles of paperwork on her desk leapt out at her and her decision was made. "Only one. We have another big day tomorrow."

Roman grinned and opened the door to the conference room with a flourish that despite herself Evelyn found amusing. "To the point. I like how you big city girls operate."

"Uh huh."

They rode the elevator in silence. Roman scrolled through the messages on his phone while Evelyn compiled a mental list of where not to take him. *Somewhere with food is good—I'm starving. Definitely not any of the clubs I played siren at, though. That would be too weird.* The list of acceptable places was dwindling fast.

"Are you hungry? What kind of drinks do you prefer? It will help me decide where we should go. I'd prefer to go somewhere where I know the bouncer and we don't have to wait to get in," she said as they strode into the empty lobby.

A look of amusement crossed Roman's face. "I was thinkin' a beer and burger sounded dandy. Have any of those joints 'round here?"

A dive bar, Evelyn refrained from rolling her eyes. *I should have seen it coming.* "I'm sure I can find something," she said, pulling out her phone.

Thirty seconds later she had the name and address of a place touted as the best dive bar on the island. *It'll have to do.* "Found a place. Let me call George. He can drive us."

"How 'bout we walk?" Roman said, touching her wrist as she raised her phone to her ear.

She shivered. There was that spark again. The one she tried to ignore every time their hands reached for the same paper or exchanged cups of coffee after Rose mixed up their order.

"Walk?"

"Sure. It's a nice night, and fresh air would do us good after being cooped up inside all day. Knowin' you as I do, this place is efficiently close anyhow."

He was right. It was three blocks away.

Ten minutes later they walked into the most disgusting place Evelyn had ever seen. Tall tables lined the edges of the room shrouded in the neon glow of beer signs that hung above. Smaller tables dotted the middle of the room haphazardly. There was a minuscule dance floor that looked as if it hadn't been polished in as long as Evelyn had been alive. The clientele was even worse. Cheap suits, tight flannel shirts, horn-rimmed glasses, and dresses too short to be decent lined the bar, their feet precariously close to dipping into the old-fashioned trough at its base.

"Is this good?" Evelyn's torso was already angling toward the door.

"It's perfect," Roman said, his grin wide as he grazed her shoulder with his fingers.

The spark and an unfamiliar wave of tingles raced up Evelyn's arm as Roman pulled her to one of the high top tables by a window.

"This reminds me of my favorite places back home. Take a seat, Miss Locksley. First round's on me."

<hr>

THREE HOURS later Evelyn was still sitting in the same dirty bar.

I haven't laughed so hard in years. She fanned herself as Roman regaled her with stories of his life back in Tennessee. *It feels good to not be so serious and have a release that's not all about my power.*

An image of Lily and Sara practicing spells and brewing potions back at Fern Cottage flashed in her mind. Evelyn pushed it back. Roman was surprisingly intuitive and she didn't need him asking more questions than he already did.

Instead she focused on Roman's charming smile and longish sandy blond hair. He wasn't her usual tall, dark, and handsome type at all. Yet, after hours of sitting with the man in a dirty bar, she had to admit he had grown on her. *Must be that southern charm he's always talking about. Either way I can't deny he seems to get more attractive by the minute.*

It pleased her that Roman seemed interested, too, even though she hadn't used her siren or ceremens powers on him. While Roman had no problem flirting with her, he was still, first and foremost, a client of Locksley Enterprises and therefore not to be blasted with magic. Though she had to admit, Roman had been making that rule more difficult to follow tonight.

Roman left to get them another round of drinks. Evelyn watched him walk away savoring the outline of his tall form and broad back. Women and men parted for him like they often did for her. The man oozed charm and confidence. *No wonder his family has risen from dirt poor to soon-to-be billionaires.*

She spun her finger around her martini glass. Free of any distraction for the first time in hours, the question of how Brigit would react when Evelyn told her she was delaying her return to Ireland pinged in her head. Evelyn sighed. She'd been dreading the call so much she'd managed to put it off for two days. She could handle Brigit, who would be disappointed, and Sara, who wouldn't like her decision but would understand, but Lily was a different matter entirely.

After a rocky start Lily and Evelyn had finally achieved level ground. Had even felt like sisters for a moment. Now though, after Emily had met a tragic death over a book that as far as Evelyn was concerned seemed largely useless . . . *Lily's going to be pissed at me for abandoning her after everything she went through for the rest of us. I can't say I blame her either . . .*

"What's got you down, Miss Locksley?" Roman said, his face concerned as he set what Evelyn had deemed a surprisingly good martini before her.

Evelyn shook her head. Bogging a client down with personal issues was going too far. Not to mention she couldn't even tell him most of it. There was no way she was telling Roman Simons she was a witch before her parents or Vici.

Or ever.

"It's nothing. Personal drama."

"If you need an ear you can use mine. Even if we are business partners. I not only like to know the people I'm working with can hold their martinis, I like to know they're human too."

Evelyn smiled a thin-lipped smile as Aoife's remark of fata-human unions producing witches surfaced in her mind. *If he only knew.*

"Aw, now don't go gettin' even sadder on me! I'm serious. Now I feel responsible," Roman's accent had thickened with their drinks and Evelyn leaned back as he cupped her shoulder and looked deep into her eyes.

It was a gesture meant to comfort but the effect it had on Evelyn was anything but comforting. She sucked in her breath as a wave of heat washed through her. *What is it with this guy?* Their eyes locked and her heart started to race. *I guess it couldn't hurt to tell him about the adoption . . . I bet he's wondering why I don't look like my parents anyhow.*

"I'm thinking about my family."

"Did something happen? Should we leave?" Roman sat up straighter.

Evelyn couldn't help herself; she smiled. Not everyone would feel the need to insert themselves into family drama having just met the family that week.

"Not my mother or father here. They're actually my adoptive parents. I have a biological mother, aunts, and sisters in Ireland whom I met this summer. My sisters, Sara, Lily, and I are triplets and I'm supposed to meet up with them again soon. We have this whole bonding thing planned. I'm nervous about how they'll take the news that I'm staying here. Especially Lily. We haven't quite clicked yet."

"Well . . . that's amazing," Roman put his hand on top of hers and beamed.

Her mouth went dry.

"Now I understand why you want to get moving as fast as possible. You want to spend time with people you've reconnected with."

"Thank you. I guess I just feel guilty," Evelyn

glanced down at where their skin met. This man was so curious. With a simple look or touch he made her want to do far more than she'd ever done on a first date. *Hell, this isn't even a date,* she reminded herself.

Roman followed her gaze and blushed. "I'm sorry, I got so excited for you. I come from a touchy family, especially when we like the person." His bright eyes sought hers, searching for an indication to how his feelings were received. He made a move to extract his hand and the pleasurable flutter in Evelyn's heart retreated.

Instinctively, Evelyn grasped his hand tighter.

Roman's charming smile morphed into a small smirk and he leaned in closer.

The scent of cloves intensified and Evelyn felt a little woozy. Outwardly, she held it together except for the slight widening of her eyes. *How unprofessional,* she thought though she knew professionalism was the last thing on her mind anymore.

She hadn't felt so free, so unworried, so happy for months. She felt like her old self, before she learned she was a witch. There was something about Roman that made her feel that way, and she didn't want to pull away from that. The fact that she hadn't used any magic to ensnare him was almost as appealing as her attraction to Roman. No one could claim this feeling was a result of a leaky binding or blatant display of siren power because she had control over her power now. Nope, this was pure lust and it was long overdue.

For once Evelyn didn't want to learn some man's—her business competition's—secrets. She wanted to smell Roman's hair, whisper in his ear, and feel his skin on hers.

What's the harm in pursuing a fling?And I never made any rule about good old fashioned human flirting. I'll just keep my magic locked up tight. Desire pulsed through her as Roman's eyes burned into hers. *I'm gone soon anyhow. As long as we keep it quiet around the office it should be fine. Mom and Dad were trying to set us up after all . . . They can't get too mad about it . . . I hope. Whatever. I'll take the risk.*

She softened her gaze and looked up from under her lashes. "My family wasn't touchy feely but I'll admit, I like you, too. What do you say we finish these drinks and grab a late dinner?" She leaned forward to give him a full shot of cleavage and her thumb caressed the top of his hand in soft, smooth strokes.

Roman gawked. He'd been flirting with her all night, but he clearly hadn't anticipated she'd return the sentiment.

Victory bloomed in Evelyn's chest and she beamed as she took in Roman's wide blue eyes. *God, I love being on top.*

"Sounds great. I could sure use some grub," Roman said regaining his confident persona and smiling back at her. Evelyn noted he hadn't taken his eyes off her for a second.

"I agree. I'm starving, too," Evelyn purred, reclaiming her hand and lifting her glass to cheers his.

The Great Schism
Lily

"Arma!" Lily screeched, darting behind her shield to avoid Sara's tickling charm. A faint sensation of feathers rippled across her skin and she forced herself to stay rigid, hoping not to give herself away. *Too slow again.*

Aoife smirked. "By the looks of it, Sara grazed your heel. If you'd have moved a second sooner, you'd have been in the clear."

"Good to know," Lily panted, frustration rising in her for what felt like the millionth time today.

"It should be. Sara is fast on the draw and most importantly practices everyday. You're not doing bad, Lil. You're just out of practice."

If I had expected being drilled to death on my first day back, I would have practiced more. Lily struggled to keep the words in her head. Apparently what Brigit meant by a few warmup drills was combat-like training where they hexed each other without the safety of their aunt's sturdy, ever present shields they had been allowed in their earlier magic lessons.

Now, they were expected to create their own means of protection and fight back at the same time. It took more mental energy than Lily was used to and although all the spells Sara had used today were harmless, she couldn't help but feel attacked.

So far, Lily had spent the entire day on the receiving end and suspected her abysmal performance in Alexandria had everything to do with it.

She cringed as a memory of her bringing her hands to her face to block a man rushing toward her and Brigit in Empusa's mansion swam into the forefront of Lily's thoughts. Brigit had sworn it was natural to forget how to defend yourself during your first altercation, but she clearly didn't want it happening again.

"Want to switch?" Lily asked Sara, desperate for a breather.

"Sure," Sara said, crouching into a defensive stance.

"Remember, Lily, in battle scenarios we have no time to weave together numerous spells or concoct novel enchantments as is oft done in healing. Short, fast spells are best. It needs to be as automatic as possible. Trust your intuition," Aoife said, then turned to Sara. "Your shield is quite good enough already. Why don't you work on deflecting and reflecting a bit, Sara? That should make the scenario a wee bit more interesting."

Lily rolled her eyes. As if she wasn't exhausted enough after hours of defensive practice, now Aoife wanted her to play both offense and defense. When the recipient of the spell reflected, it meant possible double duty for the attacker, who could find herself having to ward off her own spell and the incoming spell of her opponent.

Backing away from her sister carefully so as not to trip over the furrows and roots poking up from the uneven ground, Lily wracked her brain for any spell Sara might not know. She came up empty and pivoted to her other strength. Physicality, the only arena she reliably topped Sara in besides healing, was her best chance.

Lily charged, closing the fifty feet between her and Sara with exceptional speed. What she had lost by not practicing magic during her two weeks home, Lily had made up for by regaining her strength.

Miles and miles of running each day had been a meditation for her and the only way to separate herself from the sad looks. Now, she hoped it would help her get a few good jabs in, or at least save her from being impaled by her own hex.

"Volavari." Lily's levitation charm shot toward Sara, and Lily zagged left in case her sister deflected the spell back at her.

Sara had nimble reflexes for someone who spent so much time perched on a meditation cushion. She flung her body to the right, landing on the ground with a thwack as Lily's charm missed her by inches.

Lily feinted two feet away from Sara, who threw up a proactive shield with a grimace.

"Forget the shields. Reflect or deflect only, Sara! Come on, get up!" Aoife's voice rang out from the sidelines.

Lily smiled. Having the upper hand, even if only for a moment, felt damn good.

Sara jumped to her feet, arms outstretched and ready for whatever Lily might throw at her.

Lily circled her, weaving in and out of the now naked orchard bordering their grassy battlefield with the ease of a deer running through the forest. She felt Sara's copper eyes tracking her, waiting for her to make her move.

Lily made it, peeking her head just beyond the tree line she murmured, "Lotu." And then for good measure, "Mahasoka." Her new favorite spell erupted from her fingertips, light transforming into vines that flew right at Sara.

Sara's body stiffened as the body bind curse hit and her legs and arms snapped together, immovable, as if they'd been sealed in invisible plastic wrap. Two seconds later, the vines from Lily's second spell wound their way around Sara.

"Brilliant, Lily! Gwenn knew you'd enjoy that vine rope spell." Aoife clapped her hands together and the vines loosened in the same instant that Sara was released from Lily's body bind curse.

"But I couldn't see her! She hid in the trees. How is that fair?" Sara asked, unable to keep the tone of annoyance from her voice.

"How is it not?" Aoife asked. "We may duel out in the open, enabling us to not only see, but hear, and predict our opponent's next moves. But as Lily already knows, that is not the true way of battle. Make no mistake, our enemies will have no qualms about hexing or attacking you when your back is to them. Lily is forcing you to step up your game."

"Yea, step it up, Sara!" Lily taunted leaning against a tree, unable to hold in her mirth as a look of incredulity passed over Sara's elven features.

The apple tree bark behind her grew hot and Lily jumped forward, "What the hell?"

"You ready for this, Lil?" Sara teased back, her crooked grin growing wider.

Crap. Now what have I gotten myself into? Lily wondered, walking back to the dueling circle and racking her brain for a spell to end all spells. Two charms came to her and she went with it, hoping at least one would hit its mark, as she weaved and darted across the uneven ground.

"Dantza! Birarazi!"

"Islatu!" Sara cried, reflecting both spells with a wide sweep of her arm.

Lily tripped as both her tripping jinx and dancing spell rebounded to hit her and her feet began twitching like rubber chicken legs against the damp grass.

"Finum," she whispered, halting her own spells and jumping to her feet in one smooth motion before Sara countered. Something orange caught her eye and Lily realized countering was the last thing on her sister's mind.

A circle of flames hotter and higher than the one Lily had conjured in Alexandria rose up around Sara. *Damn, her flame gates are on point,* Lily thought, circling closer to the gate as she assessed her options.

Should I try to conjure up a little water or wind? Can spells move through elements like fire?

"Eginura," Lily muttered, pointing at a section of the flame gate as water gushed from her outstretched palm. The fire drowned for as long as she kept up the flow and replenished itself from the sodden ground once the stream ceased. A thought struck her and despite Aoife's prior restrictions, she acted on it, instinctively weaving together a new stream of water with a collapsing curse. She watched in awe as the concept unfolded. The water flew through the gate straight at Sara, who collapsed face first. Her flame gate followed, falling to the ground in defeat behind its master.

"I'd say Lily's gaining on you, Sara."

"Herbcapto!" Lily, still high on adrenaline from sparring, turned and flung the spell in the direction of the new voice.

Oops, she thought as she caught sight of Nora at the edge of the orchard, trying to kick free of the grass Lily had enchanted to wrap around the invader's feet and legs.

Nora looked as glamorous as ever, clad in a sheath dress and stylish knee-length boots, if a bit too skinny.

Must be one of those people who forget to eat when she gets busy. Wonder what that's like? The questions breezed through Lily's mind before she realized Nora was glaring at her. *Oh yeah, I should call off my spell.*

"Finum." The spell ceased and Nora stopped kicking. "Sorry, Nora! You caught me off guard!" Lily called across the clearing.

"Don't ever apologize for quick reflexes, Lily. You're

in training!" Aoife said with a wide grin before turning to Nora. "And Nora! What a surprise. Brigit will be right pleased." Aoife jumped up from the stone bench she'd been perched on to meet her old friend.

"I negotiated a week home, thought I'd stay the night to see how you all were progressing. We're all overdue for a long chat. Am I right?" Nora said, holding up a weekend bag.

"Aye, you can have Evelyn's room." Aoife clapped her hand to Nora's thin shoulder, "Why don't we all go inside? I sense that you girls have had enough?"

Lily nodded. Despite her stroke of luck she could feel the exhaustion deep in her bones. Ending on a high note would be best.

"I don't mind sleeping on the couch. That room's a bit cramped for the both of us, and I doubt Evelyn will take to being put out," Nora said, looking uneasy.

Lily used the pretense of grabbing her sweater off the ground to hide her grin. *Is Nora still afraid Evelyn will break into her mind? Even I have to admit Evelyn has been pretty respectful in that arena. As long as you don't make it too easy.*

"She has yet to arrive. You'll have the room all to yourself," Aoife said, waving her hand and breaking the protective enchantments of the dueling circle.

"Oh. Right then."

"Good moves back there. Sneaky as hell but good," Sara said joining Lily.

"Thanks," Lily replied, her easy tone belying the immense pleasure she felt at beating her sister. For once she was on top, a feeling she could get used to, though with Sara she felt no need to rub it in. Every victory of her own was a victory for the team and vice versa.

In the past, her competitive nature honed from years of athletics had made it hard to see things that way, but she was getting better at it. Sara's laid back nature made it easier. The pair walked in companionable silence, content to listen to Nora and Aoife chatter at their back, as they followed the path through Brigit's garden to Fern Cottage.

They were emerging from the herb patch, still thriving in mid-November thanks to Brigit and Lily's earth magic, when a shout came from the stone cottage.

"Was that Mom?" Sara asked, red brows pulling together. She glanced at Aoife, who ran toward the door, leaving Nora standing alone looking uncomfortable.

The intensity of Brigit's shouting grew as the cottage door flew open and Aoife rushed in.

Lily sucked in a breath. She'd only ever heard Brigit raise her voice during extenuating circumstances involving magic or a battle. She sincerely hoped neither was happening in the cottage.

"I hear you, but do you hear yourself? This is serious. It's *real*. Your actions could set us back months. Goddess knows, it puts you at great risk and could cost others their freedom!"

"Should I leave?" Nora squeaked, her body already pointed in the direction of the enchanted hedge that hid Fern Cottage from the road.

"No, stay. You're her best friend; Mom needs you. I've never heard her sound so furious," Lily said grabbing Nora's hand.

Nora winced and Lily loosened her grip, glancing once more at Nora's thin, delicate frame. *She's as weak as a bird,* she thought, only belatedly remembering Nora's prodigious ceremens talents when she shot Lily a look.

"Sorry," Lily mumbled, reactivating the spell that kept her thoughts in her own head. The mind barriers were difficult to keep up during the stress of their mock battles and she often let them fall. Not to mention, Lily had become out of practice at Terramar, where her family was not composed of strong witches who could read every thought from her leaky mind.

"Who do you think she's talking to?" Sara whispered as they tiptoed into the entryway.

"No idea," Lily answered, biting back the name on the tip of her tongue as she undid her laces and sat on the couch across from the hearth. She pulled her legs to her chest and glanced at Nora who seemed to have lost all the blood in her face. *Mom becoming this upset must be a rare occurrence if Nora looks that anxious.*

"Get off the phone, Brig. You need to calm down before you say something you don't mean," Aoife's gravel and sandpaper voice carried through the heavy stone fireplace to the sitting room.

"There's nothing I can do anyhow to change her mind, Aoife! She's acting right thick, choosing money and prestige when so much, including her own safety, is at stake," Brigit snapped. She stopped talking and Lily got the distinct impression whoever was on the other end of the line was firing back.

"You know why I did what I did when you were babes. I care about your safety more than anything. I love you three and want to make sure we have a future together! It's why I want you here, practicing and preparing, I—" Brigit stopped short again.

"Well, I hope you realize that the size of the account won't matter if we do not succeed." Brigit's tone calmed slightly, like she was trying to reign it in. "While helping your family is noble, I'm sure others are more than capable of the task your father has set you. You know where to find us when you've come to your senses. *Please*, try and stay safe."

Nora leapt from her seat.

Lily turned to see a cordless phone soar through the entryway to the other side of the sitting room to collide with a stone wall. The plastic cracked and the phone fell to the ground.

"I know, I know, Aoife! I let me fire get to me, but can you blame me? How fecking reckless and short-sighted! I thought we had made progress with her. And now I won't be able to stop worrying about her halfway around the globe doing who knows what." Brigit stormed out the kitchen into the sitting room and stopped at the sight of them.

"Oh. Hello girls. Nora," Brigit said, her voice unnaturally high.

"Who was that on the phone?" Sara asked in little more than a whisper.

Aoife, who had followed her sister in, placed a hand on Brigit's shoulder.

Brigit softened at the touch and bit her lip.

"It was Evelyn, wasn't it?" Lily asked, sparing Brigit the duty of voicing what she clearly did not want to admit. "She's not coming?"

"Not yet," Brigit answered, her tone dripping with disappointment. "She took on a task at her father's company. One she needs two months to complete and then she'll join us."

"Two months? But that isn't that long."

Lily swung her head to look at Sara. *Not that long? Does she not realize that the first attack, Em's kidnapping, happened only four months after we found out we were witches? Em died because we, I, wasn't fast enough. Does Sara think the other side is going to wait until we're trained up to make it a fair fight?*

"No," Brigit agreed. She bit her lip again and shot a look at Lily. "In the large scheme of things it's not, but we can't count on having loads of time now, can we? Who knows when our enemies may strike next? And I worry about Evelyn not being here, away from our protective enchantments, though I doubt she felt that the way I spoke to her." Guilt clouded Brigit's face.

But Lily wasn't having it. *It's like Evelyn doesn't even care about what we went through three weeks ago. I killed someone I loved but she can't turn down a business deal?*

"Don't feel bad about yelling at her!" Lily said indignantly. "She deserves it for thinking she can abandon us like that. Like we don't even need her! She heard Seraphina's tale and the prophecy! I can't believe this. I was just starting to trust her . . ."

"Who knows? Maybe she'll finish earlier and come to join us. Business people always set long deadlines so it looks better when they meet them. I bet she'll be back in a few weeks. Evelyn wouldn't leave us like that, Lily," Sara said, her voice small.

"How do you know that?" Lily asked, her tone mocking as frustration bubbled into anger inside her. *How can she take Evelyn's side when she's ditching us?*

"Evelyn hasn't lost anyone. Didn't have to kill them and see them die right in front of her. I bet she thinks she can go back to her glittering life. I mean who walks out on people who have given up everything to save humanity with them? What kind of person does that? As far as I'm concerned, I've been right to keep my guard all these months."

The couch shook and Lily looked down to see her hands clenching the fabric, glowing blue with rage. Small ripples of blue were radiating out and down into the floor which shook below them. She let go, allowing the rage to dissipate and create ripples in the air all around her.

"If you'd have opened up to Evelyn, maybe you'd trust her more," Sara replied.

"Oh whatever!" Lily threw her hands up.

"Even Nora knows Evelyn better than you do, Sara. Why else do you think she hardly ever comes around? Why she doesn't want to stay in Evelyn's room? Nora doesn't trust Evelyn either after she broke into her head! Not everyone is as shiny and good as you make them out to be. You should lay off the meditation. I think it may be making you a poor judge of character." Lily clapped her hands over her mouth, instantly regretting the words.

"Just because I want to trust Evelyn doesn't make me blind," Sara said leaning away from Lily. "She has faults. We all do. But I know we work better together than apart. I wish you'd see that, Lily."

"I wish I could, too." Lily turned to Nora. "You can have my bed. I'll take Evelyn's room, seeing as you didn't want to. Evelyn won't be using it anytime soon."

With that, Lily turned on her heels to storm down the hallway before she said something else she'd regret.

Business and Pleasure
Evelyn

Is this even real? Evelyn wondered.

She watched Roman Simons breathe next to her, his head on the pillow. *How did this happen? In less than a week I've gone from dead set on returning to Ireland to . . . whatever this is?*

She couldn't deny it, even to herself. She was falling for Roman. Falling hard. A client she didn't want to take in the first place. A man she'd seduced into her bed that same night for fun and met at the office the next day to work out the kinks in his business plan without her parents being the wiser. Evelyn grinned; those weren't the only kinks they'd been working out.

In all their days and nights together, Roman had proved himself to be nothing short of amazing. And yet even with the head rush that accompanied Roman's alluring scent and the jittery tingles she got every time she looked at him, Evelyn had her reservations. It was a weird feeling. So unlike the Evelyn of six months prior, before she knew she was a siren.

Back then Evelyn had blurred the lines of dating and business by asking out eligible men in positions of power at competing companies and blasting them with her charm to get the inside dirt. All with zero reservations.

But it wasn't really charm that hooked them, it was my magic.

She could no longer deny she'd probably been using her magic all along. Likely some mix of siren power and ceremens that no man could deny. *How could they when I had the ability to manipulate their minds and blast them with a cocktail of pheromones so intense most guys could hardly keep their shit together?* Almost all of them had given her what she wanted as soon as she asked.

The consequences, which often involved them losing their high-powered positions, be damned. All for so little: a touch, a smile, and if she'd received something particularly promising, a kiss. Never anything more, definitely not anything serious. Her father had always wondered how she'd played the market so well.

But she'd never done this. Slept with a client of Locksley Enterprises. A big client. Four nights in a row!

Like they were a couple. *Holy hell, are we dating?* The thought was as thrilling as it was terrifying.

Evelyn hadn't dated, *really* dated, anyone since high school. In the back of her mind there was always that niggling thought that her potential love interests were using her for her money or power. It's why her closest friends had been the same for years. She'd gone on dates, yes, most of them for the sake of Locksley Enterprises or to satiate carnal desire she could no longer deny. But they'd all seemed as if the spark was too easy, too one-sided.

Dating a siren would tend to do that, she supposed. But whatever was between her and Roman didn't feel that way—not now that she could choose when to use her powers. Evelyn thought back to her siren performance the other night at the club and winced. For the first two days of their fling Evelyn couldn't stop wondering if Roman had been there for her escapades. He didn't seem the type, but still, one never knew. She'd slipped in a few of the club's names when they were deciding where to grab a drink their second night together, after another twelve-hour day, and did a mental jig when Roman said he'd never heard of any of them.

She'd always been careful to wipe the memories of the club goers but that didn't change the fact that if there had been even the slightest chance Roman had fallen prey to her powers, Evelyn wouldn't be able to take him or his attraction to her seriously. But there wasn't and since they'd met she'd barred even the slightest bit of her siren magic from leaking out even before it became clear they were attracted to one another.

It was a matter of professional etiquette. Roman was a client, not competition like all the men before.

Besides being a paying client, Roman was also, quite possibly, the sweetest, sexiest, most in touch with his feelings man that Evelyn had ever met. Unlike all of her previous flings, there was no denying the tingles she felt when they touched or how Roman seemed to see Evelyn better than people she'd known her entire life. She couldn't help but want him for herself.

It was a foreign feeling but one Evelyn found herself enjoying.

"I see through your hardcore city girl, business mogul exterior. I can tell, deep down you're sweet as sugar. But don't worry, I won't tell anyone. We all have to keep up appearances, am I right? We won't even mention the name of this place, it would tarnish your rep. Wait, does it have a name?" Roman had laughed when they left the dive bar their first night together.

A beam of sunlight shot through her blinds, falling on Roman's high cheekbones.

"Well, well, it seems I have an admirer," he whispered, his cool blue eyes cracking open. "How long you been starin' at me, sweetheart?"

"Just counting the pillow lines on your face," Evelyn teased, less mortified than she would have imagined being two weeks ago if a man woke up to find her staring at him.

"You should get a new hobby. Want me to show you one of mine?" Roman asked.

The hem of her silk nightgown rose up her thigh as he pulled her over to him. Evelyn's breath shortened as Roman's hands caressed her arms, along her collarbone, and up her cheek. The kiss he gave her was smooth, skillful, and full of need, like the first one they'd shared. The strap of her nightgown slid down her arm and Roman teased it down further.

Evelyn came up for air. "I think we may find some common ground here," she said, before diving back into his lips.

"So when do you think we should tell your father?" Roman asked, pulling a tailored jacket over his broad shoulders as Evelyn watched from bed.

"Tell him what?"

"That we're dating."

Her heart stopped. *So we are dating. Well, isn't that a development.* She wrapped the sheet around her and made her way over to her new boyfriend.

"Is that what we're doing?" she asked, coming up behind Roman and wrapping her arms around him, knowing the tension in his body would belie any falsehood or misgivings he might have.

He swirled in her grip, pulling her so close she felt the soft sheets in places she never had before.

"It's what you want, isn't it? I know I do." His voice was a low whisper, edging on a growl.

Roman's aroma of cloves swirled in the air and Evelyn nearly swooned as she took in the peppery scent before shaking her head to clear it.

"Yes. I want it, too." The admission spilled from her lips. "Well, I won't lie, my parents have already told me they thought we'd be good together. But I doubt they thought it would happen so fast. Definitely not while you were still on my client list. This isn't a scenario that's ever come up before."

"I should hope not," Roman whispered, nibbling at her ear.

"What if he takes me off your account? I know Dad and Mom were angling for this, but it's against company policy to date a client and way too soon for me to hand your account over to anyone else. That's what happened before when someone at work fell for a client. We had to take them off the account to keep the interests separate. And this project is the only thing keeping me in the city." She felt guilty saying it, knowing she'd prefer to be here, with Roman, rather than in Ireland. *But who could blame me? I mean look at him.*

"Let me talk to your father," Roman said raising his eyebrows as if he could hear her thoughts.

Evelyn raised her eyebrows in reply, "Won't that be weird?"

"Trust me. I'll persuade him. I'll talk to him tonight. Man to man. Our account is so important to him that I doubt he'll deny us being together if I insist you continue as account lead, but you can't be there. I don't know your father well, but if he's anything like mine and this was either of my sisters dating a client, well . . . one strict look from my dad and that relationship would be over."

She cocked her head. "You have sisters?"

"Two," Roman answered with a grin. "Both still in

school. Lacy is a business major and Rita's in finance. I have a brother in high school, too. Lucas is the star of the football team." He paused to assess her.

"Have you been having second thoughts about staying? Do you want to go back to Ireland sooner to be with your sisters?" His grip tightened on her and she felt a wave of tingles rush through her.

She sighed. *Not if you're here.*

"It's fine. I've already spoken to Brigit, my biological mother. They totally understand what's happening," she fought the natural wince that accompanied the lie. "Besides, Dad and I already have a plan in action. The Locksleys are my family, too, and I'm not sure I can trust anyone else with your accounts right now. Not until they hire someone spectacular and they're trained up a bit."

He bent down to kiss her and her lips burned. It was all Evelyn could do not to gasp. *How is he such an excellent kisser?*

"I'd be lying if I said I wasn't relieved. I want you here, too. It's decided then? I'll speak to your father tonight, and we'll keep working this insane schedule so you can take off when we're done. Leaves us with seven weeks to get to know each other better. We can continue that exploration tonight after I have drinks with your father. See you at the office?"

"I'll be in around ten, but Dad should be there already, and Vici, too. She can help you with anything you need if Dad isn't there."

"Ahh, I'll get to talk to Vicencia alone for once."

Her best friend had been absent the last few days, staying over at Michael's and stopping at the apartment only for clothes.

Vici claimed it was because Evelyn needed privacy with her new male suitor. They both knew it had been ages since Evelyn had liked a man enough to bring him home but Evelyn recognized Vici had another motive.

Vicencia was using this time to give her own relationship a little nudge. If Vici was right, and she usually was, Michael was going to propose soon. Vici was using Evelyn's man-candy distraction as an excuse not to hurt her best friend's feelings and trying to give her boyfriend ample incentive to propose all at once.

"Remember . . ."

"I know, I know I won't tell her I'm your mystery man. Or the one that left the toilet seat up in the hall bath."

Evelyn smiled and stood on tiptoe to kiss him. "How about I tell her tonight while you're out with Dad?"

"Sounds perfect. See you soon, babe." Roman returned her kiss before walking out the door.

She exhaled. *Only one more day.* The uncertainty

between her and Roman mixed with his big shot client status had made easy conversation with her parents more difficult these past few days. Evelyn had been all too aware that one slip up and the Simonses' account would have been taken away from her and reassigned.

But Roman was right, if he was the one to request she stay on Roman's account James would be more likely to allow it.

The client is always right.

One problem off her chest, Evelyn found herself pivoting to one of the many other issues in her life. Like how she was going to practice magic with a new boyfriend around all the time. No doubt she would confess her witchy status to him if they stayed together. She just needed time to work her way up to it.

But Evelyn would get rusty without practice and the magical tension in her body was growing unbearable. The water surrounding Manhattan called to her as soon as she stepped out of the door every morning, begging her to use it, to transmute it and let it flow from her fingers in the flashiest way possible.

Instead, she ignored it.

She'd considered practicing ceremens a few times, though that too was risky. What if she accidentally tried on another witch and blew her cover?

She'd managed a few minor rounds on Rose, but

those were limited to her time to and from the office door to the elevator. Evelyn would need more than a few minutes if she was going to strengthen her skills and not fall behind her sisters.

Sara had been the only one who'd bothered to reach out since the disastrous phone call with Brigit, when they'd both said things they didn't mean. She wasn't surprised, but it still hurt.

Sara assured her that all was well in Ireland, that she should finish her work and hurry over as soon as possible, and that Brigit was more worried about Evelyn than mad—a story Evelyn found hard to believe considering the guilt trip she'd laid on Brigit.

I still can't believe I threw her putting us up for adoption in her face. Especially now that I know everything she said about the fata and the prophecy is real. I would be mad at me if I were her.

It hadn't escaped Evelyn's notice that Sara had provided updates on every witch that frequented Fern Cottage except one. But then, Evelyn had known Lily would be pissed at her and probably would continue to be so long after she returned to Fern Cottage, tail between her legs.

The worst part was, Evelyn couldn't blame her. In the few moments she and Roman weren't together having the time of their lives, Evelyn had experienced severe pangs of guilt at her capacity to abandon her family in Ireland when so much was at stake.

But there are numerous types of abandonment, aren't there? And I've been a Locksley longer than I've been a McKay. And I'm coming back eventually. I'll fix everything then.

Her head began to pound and she turned to her closet, welcoming the frivolous distraction dressing for the day brought. She settled on a low-cut white blouse and dark blue pantsuit, a striking combination with her eyes. The suit was tailored to her exact measurements, and it screamed power, authority, and sex.

Roman wouldn't be able to keep his eyes off her.

A quick turn of the curling iron, a few swipes of her mascara wand, dabs of concealer to mask the nights when guilt stole her sleep, and one espresso later Evelyn was out the door, ready for whatever the day would bring.

"WHAT DID HE SAY?" Evelyn asked later that day as Roman walked through her apartment door reeking of cigars and whiskey.

"Easy, darlin'! No need to worry, we have your father's blessing."

Evelyn gawked. The entire day had been one long emotional roller coaster. Mundane tasks like walking into her dad's office to drop off reports had her nerves jumping. Sitting across from her boyfriend, feeling the pull of his eyes and tingle of his skin when their hands touched was nearly impossible.

It was only when Roman left with her father for the club that Evelyn felt she could breathe again. That was, until she remembered what he was going to do. Since then, she'd been checking her phone every ten minutes for a text from her father, demanding they talk.

"But what about you being a client? Our *huge* client! Am I off the account? I can't believe it. That's so unlike Dad."

"Your father seemed to think you were more than capable of separating business and pleasure. He has a point. I mean we've been dating for days now and no one's noticed. It's like you said, they wanted us together. He seemed happy about it."

"I still can't help feeling a little surprised. And relieved. And happy. We're breaking company policy, which my parents are total sticklers about, but I get to have my cake and eat it, too!"

"I hope to get you used to that feeling," Roman smiled at her and grabbed her hips. "To be honest, I wasn't sure I was going to be able to wait to tell your father. Seeing you today, in that power suit, all work, work, work; I got a little worked up myself."

Evelyn grinned wickedly, "I thought you might." She lifted onto her tiptoes to kiss him.

"So worked up in fact, I thought I'd like us to get to know each other in a more personal environment." He quirked an eyebrow. "Somewhere where we can be alone—not your apartment or my hotel but neutral ground. I'm not free this weekend, I have to make a trip to the home office, but what do you say we go away next weekend or the weekend after? You and me darlin', all alone."

Her sapphire eyes grew wide. "You want to go on a vacation with me?" She'd never gone anywhere with a boyfriend before.

"One tiny weekend away," Roman took her mouth in his and kissed her breathless. "I didn't want to book a week and scare you off. And you don't have to answer me now if you don't want to. I have a few places in mind I can reserve last minute."

"Wow. I mean, I'll think about it." She licked her lips, savoring the essence of cloves he left there.

"Wonderful. How'd Vicencia take the news?"

"Pretty well, actually. Especially when I promised her, yet again, that she wouldn't have to take over your accounts while I'm gone."

Vicencia hadn't even blinked when Evelyn told her she was having an affair with the company's largest client. She'd admitted preferring that her best friend date someone, rather than Evelyn hitting up the club all night long, but Roman didn't need to know that.

"Now that we're out we should celebrate!" Roman rubbed circles on her back. "I took the liberty of making a reservation, if you're up for it? It's one of those fancy places you're always gabbing with your Mom about, not any of those dives I've been lucky to get you to step foot in. You've been so accommodating I figure I owe you at least a dozen high class dates."

Her heart leapt. *No more dive bars and shabby all night diners! How does he always know what I need to hear? He's a miracle.*

"I'll grab my coat."

Uniting

Lily

WATER STREAMED into the coffee pot as Lily finished prepping the first of what was sure to be many pots of coffee for the day. She pressed the on button and stretched her arms wide.

Vertebra after vertebra popped up her spine, a testament to her sleepless nights that had caused her and everyone else in the house so much frustration. The three weeks since they'd received word that Evelyn would be staying in New York for two months had been some of the hardest Lily had endured at Fern Cottage.

Not only did Lily dislike the posh gold and blue tones of the room she'd confined herself to nearly as much as the person it was custom decorated for, she also couldn't manage a full night's sleep in it. Lily knew she would sleep better in her own bed, but she still couldn't bring herself to be alone with Sara, who would force her to talk out feelings that Lily knew were irrational but could not shrug off.

Every time Lily thought of Evelyn sitting behind her desk working as if nothing in the world had changed, as if Em hadn't died for their cause, Lily wanted to punch something.

If that wasn't bad enough, her frustration and anger had become heightened by what she considered Sara's betrayal: taking Evelyn's side in the matter, as if it were fine to run out on the responsibilities you committed to when others were dying for you.

The coffee pot beeped and Lily poured the coffee into her mug, adding cream until the black gold transmuted into the perfect paper bag hue. She added a tablespoon of raw sugar to cut the bitterness and took a sip.

Ahh, perfect. The caramel taste of the brew ran over Lily's tongue. Not so intense that she'd have the jitters, yet strong enough to last until the others woke up, which she knew wouldn't be for a couple hours. Hours Lily would spend with her current obsession, Seraphina's tome.

Since returning to Ireland, she devoured Hypatia's recollection of Seraphina's words at least once a day, looking for a gem of information the others had missed.

So far, she hadn't found anything new but at least the hours spent with the small book were a distraction—a way in which she felt she was doing something useful, and a small step in the direction of avenging Em's death.

Lily settled herself onto the loveseat. Here she had a view of Brigit's garden, where a fair number of hearty plants flourished despite the frost that had rampaged the Irish countryside a few days ago. She set her coffee on the side table and pulled a blanket over her knees before extracting Seraphina's tome from her robe's oversized pocket.

It was as she'd seen it a dozen times before. No larger than a birthday card, thirty-three pages of papyrus roughly sewn together with a string of leather. Despite its age, it was undoubtedly one of the most immaculate ancient volumes ever found.

Mary and Aoife attributed the book's pristine condition to its being preserved in time and space where temperature, humidity, fire, oils, and even pollutants in the air would not act on it. Most of what little wear showed on its pages had occurred only in the weeks since its discovery. A light differentiation of color on the leather string and pages where the witches bent it open, a faint oil mark from someone's fingerprints and a page with a tiny tear were the marks of the McKay witches. Lily had learned that even the way Hypatia had bound the volume, as one would a modern book, was remarkable and against the painstaking tradition of rolling papyri into scrolls.

Practically everything about this book is remarkable. Too bad it isn't easier to discover why so many people thought it was important.

Lily opened to the first page, what she'd come to think of as the foreword by Seraphina's daughter, Esther. She often lingered on this page. She thought it was because she could relate with the daughter, a woman discovering the truth of her family's lineage. She sympathized with Esther learning that her entire life, the family she'd grown up with, was not what she thought. That Esther's mother and aunts were sent to change Earth in ways Esther could not possibly imagine. And that Esther had been handed a huge responsibility to pass on the story, selectively and carefully, until the destined three arrived.

The destined three? More like the destined two, Lily thought with a huff, *and even those two are not a united front.* After a few days of stewing Lily had been inclined to forgive Sara's gut instinct to defend their sister. Looking back she even thought Sara's easy forgiveness of Evelyn's poor choices was kind of noble.

But then she discovered the phone calls.

Phone calls Sara hid from Lily. The ones where

Sara comforted Evelyn and rejoiced in her easy life in New York. In Lily's opinion it was one thing to defend a person. It was entirely another thing to allow them to believe their poor choices were acceptable. To make matters worse, Lily had overheard enough of one specific call to know that Evelyn had a boyfriend and they were going on a trip together today.

A trip together! While we sit here, broken and sparring our asses off every day. Evelyn has a private jet at her disposal. She could come to Ireland for the weekend to practice with us. At least then I could get some anger out in person.

Lily sighed and reached for her coffee. It was stone cold. She glanced up at the clock and saw an hour had passed.

Seraphina's tome has a way with time, that's for sure. She flipped to the second page and began to read in earnest. She was halfway done when Brigit appeared in the sitting room, rubbing sleep from her eyes.

"Care for a cuppa? Or would you fancy more coffee?" she asked before bending down to the hearth and murmuring a few words. A fire sprang up, high and hot, to chase the chill from the room.

"Coffee, please. Mine was cold before I got to it." Lily shut Seraphina's tome and followed her mother into the kitchen.

"Find anything new?" Brigit asked, gesturing to the book.

"Nope. I always seem to get stuck on the first page and then speed read the rest. Something's there, I know it is. I'm just not finding it."

"Hmm. I suppose it will come when it's supposed to," Brigit said unhelpfully and poured more coffee into Lily's mug.

Silence hung in the air. Easy conversation between Lily and those who frequented Fern Cottage had vanished in the weeks since Evelyn announced her decision.

For the most part Lily didn't mind. It meant she had fewer outbursts to apologize for later, but today was different. Today was special, and might be what she needed to turn her attitude around.

"Sooo, who's picking up Rena, Annika, and Selma?"

"Aoife volunteered. They should be here a little after eleven."

Lily's heart squeezed. Having a small part of her Terramar family here would be the medicine she needed. Even if Sara and Lily would be crammed into Evelyn's tiny room to accommodate them.

"The turkey's thawed, right?"

"Aye. Even if I don't know how to make a Thanksgiving dinner, I know enough to thaw a twenty-pound bird ahead of time. All is in order. I've given everyone their grocery lists. Nora's picking up most of the ingredients for sides. She's been to the States during the holiday and knows what they ought look like."

Lily nodded.

"You'll need to clean up Evelyn's room before they arrive. Make some space for Sara's things. It'll be a full house for the next week, and we need to make it as pleasant as we can for everyone." Brigit's voice was even though Lily discerned a tone of anxiety beneath the calm.

"I'll go do that now," Lil said hoping to avoid another 'you should talk to your sister speech'. She sped out of the kitchen and down the hallway, doing her best to ignore the pull of the old room she shared with Sara.

"Holaaaa! Where's my chica?"

Lily jumped up from the supine position from which she'd been examining the ceiling of Evelyn's room and ignoring the sound of laughter in the kitchen.

"You're here!" Lily cried running into the sitting room and throwing her arms around Selma, Rena, and Annika in turn.

"Aye, would have been here sooner, if some ninny of

a farmer hadn't left his cows out to graze on the motorway. Would have been easy to coax them off the road with a spell, but non-magic folk were already there." Aoife's ginger and pepper scent preceded her as she walked up the stairs.

By the looks of it, Lily's Oregon family, probably Selma, had let themselves in. As if to confirm her suspicions Brigit emerged from the kitchen with Sara quick on her heels, wiping her hands on a towel and looking at a loss.

Lily held back her laughter as Brigit watched Selma show herself around the sitting room, marveling at the triquetras and intricate blown glass pieces that adorned the stone walls.

"Hey Sel, come here. You still need to be introduced," Lily said, saving Brigit from having to corral the wild Spanish siren threatening to wander down the hallway.

The introductions were quick as everyone present had already heard of each other, if not met, long ago.

"Where are Gwenn and Mary?" Rena asked, reminding Lily that Rena knew her aunt Gwenn on a very personal level.

I wonder if things will be a bit weird between them?

"They'll be 'round for dinner. Mary's tending to a birth and Gwenn had a few business calls today. My cousin Fiona and Nora will be joining us, too," Brigit said as she guided everyone from the small entryway to the sitting room.

Annika spun around and admired the stone cottage. "This is a lovely place you have Brigit. We don't have many stone homes in Oregon. It's a treat to stay here." She gestured to the triquetras on the wall. "I have to say I just love your decorations. So very Irish, and that garden! I can't wait to practice yoga in it. You'll have to teach us a few things about tending a garden like that. Em wasn't an earth witch, but she had a way with plants that we will miss."

"One of the many things we'll miss," Rena added, sitting down on the couch.

"Of course," Brigit replied with a small smile, "I'd be more than happy to."

"Please let's not be so dour. Now's not the time. We're in Ireland with our Lil and her family!" Selma beamed and sat in an armchair. "Tell us what you all have been up to! What kind of lessons have you been doing, chica? Sara?"

Sara's eyes sought Lily's, as if asking permission to speak and Lily looked away to lock eyes firmly with Selma.

"We've been dueling a lot, and we're both getting pretty good. Or at least improving. I know a few dozen spells by now, all of which should be useful in a fight. Especially once we get to the point where we know what other creatures are susceptible to and can tell them apart by sight. So far all we've worked on is vampires. Daemons and fae are next. Potions and healing are going well, too. Tell them what you've been up to, Sara." Lily felt her nonchalance undermined by Sara's eyes growing wide at her inclusion.

She's surprised that I spoke to her. Lily tried her best to ignore the guilt that arose with the thought.

Thanks largely to Selma's loquacious nature, the conversation flowed easily from that point on.

"Shouldn't we get dinner started? The bird takes hours right?" Lily asked when Mary and Gwenn arrived an hour later, arms laden with groceries and wine. She shot a glance at Annika, the only one she was sure had ever cooked an entire turkey.

"Well of course it takes hours, look at the size of the thing! No wonder so many Americans are overweight. Though of course you lot all seem to be outliers." Aoife stood up with gusto and slicked her short red hair into a ponytail. "I'll help out. I'm not much in the kitchen but I can do prep work."

Mary volunteered to help, too, rolling up the sleeves of her midnight blue jumpsuit as she led Annika to the kitchen. Gwenn chatted with Rena a few minutes more before joining the cooking crew, which left Brigit, Rena, Selma, Lily, and Sara in the sitting room to enjoy a glass of the French burgundy Aoife had brought over.

Lily's shoulders tensed as she watched Gwenn disappear into the kitchen. She wondered if Gwenn and Annika working together in the kitchen would be weird. Both had appeared happy to meet each other, and Rena had acted normal when she met her old flame. Lily supposed the years apart had a lot to do with it.

"No need to worry about those two, Lil," Rena said, correctly interpreting Lily's body language. "Neither is the jealous type, and Ann can charm anyone. She has so many great stories to tell. On the flight over she was telling me about the yoga retreat she just got back from. Five days in a Costa Rican jungle listening to a bunch of wackos who think their souls have been waiting for them on the moon for centuries. Her roommate was particularly interesting . . ."

Laughter exploded from the kitchen and Rena grinned as if her point had been proven.

Lily's shoulders fell. *Rena's right, they'll be fine.*

"Thank the goddess Mary's in there, too," Brigit whispered in mock conspiracy to Rena, though the words were loud enough for Sara and Lily to hear. "Aoife, despite her strengths in choosing a perfect red wine, is a right laugh in the kitchen."

Lily giggled as Rena and Selma pinked. Their own culinary skills also left a lot to be desired.

"That reminds me," Selma said, clearly keen to change the subject. "We come bearing gifts." She unzipped a large suitcase and pulled out three bottles of what Lily knew to be a pricey pinot noir and two bottles of barbera, a Terramar favorite.

"That's too kind of you," Brigit said, accepting the bottles. "What do you say we save them for dinner? I'll take them into the kitchen. Lily and Sara, could you show Rena and Selma the cottage and put their bags in their bedroom?"

"I'm sure you'll be dying to get back in here, Lil. Brigit and Sara did an excellent job decorating to your tastes." Rena noted as Lily showed them to the room she used to share with Sara after touring the rest of the cottage.

"Sara, your side is nice, too," Selma added putting her suitcase on Sara's bed. "Red is my favorite color."

Sara smiled, pleased by Selma's compliment.

"Once Evelyn arrives that little single room will be tight. Or is one of you moving out onto the couch?" Rena asked opening her bag and pulling out her toiletries.

Lily stiffened and went to set Annika's yoga bag by Sara's meditation altar. So much had happened in the last three weeks that Lily hadn't called home more than once, to confirm their trip here. She hadn't told them about Evelyn's two-month absence, how she felt about it, and the aftermath of those feelings. And now she had to do it in front of Sara.

"She's not coming back any time soon," Lily said, staring deadpan at the altar.

"What Lily means is, Evelyn had family obligations to take care of before she returns. She should be back in about a month," Sara said.

"If by family obligations you mean going on a trip with her new boyfriend," Lily snapped before she could stop herself.

The guilt that clouded Sara's face gave Lily the tiny bit of ammo she needed to speak the words that had been itching to spring out of her all day.

"Yea, I overheard that phone call, Sara. I mean this place is minuscule, how could I not? So while we're here, working our asses off, Evelyn is laying on a Caribbean beach or wherever the one percent spend their vacations? How are you fine with that? I mean, Em *died* for this cause, one each of us agreed to, and Evelyn is taking a vacation?"

"Evelyn deserves a break from time to time, too, doesn't she? We're taking time off from lessons while your family is here. Why can't Evelyn?"

"She's already had a three-week break and doesn't plan to be back for another month! Who the hell knows what could happen in that amount of time? Em was fine at the beginning of the week and an undead vampire *I had to freaking kill* by the end of the week! I'm sorry but the way you are defending her is ridiculous. You know she doesn't deserve it."

"Well, I'm sorry if I want to see the best in people. If I don't want history to repeat itself and I want to stay close to both of you. If you'll excuse me, I need to move some of my stuff into our room." Sara hefted a pile of clothes and books from atop her dresser and stalked out of the room.

"So," Rena's eyebrows knit together as Sara slammed the door, "I see things have been a little rocky?"

Lily slumped to the ground by the door. She'd been dying to say the words for days, ever since she'd over-heard the conversation through their bedroom door. *So why do I feel worse now?*

"Is this really about Evelyn not returning when you did, Lil? Or is it something else?"

Lily sighed. Leave it to Rena not to beat around the bush.

"Of course I'm mad that Evelyn is not here, but I'm more mad that I can see her abandoning us for good. She hasn't lost anything, probably never has, and now she's going off on some fancy vacation with a new boyfriend. Doesn't sound like she's very tormented by her decision, does it?"

"No, but then you can't know that for sure, can you? What if she's wracked with guilt but knows you don't want to speak with her? Sara seems like a peacekeeper. I bet if you cared to ask Sara she'd tell you how Evelyn is feeling."

Lily nodded. Probably talking to Sara would ease her frustration, but Lily couldn't shake the notion that much of what Sara would say to her would be sugar coated to appease her. *Do I want to feel better? Or do I want to rage for a bit? Isn't that the next step in grieving or whatever?*

She fingered the pages of Seraphina's tome in the oversized pocket of a knit cardigan she'd thrown on to keep the book close. The old pieces of paper rustling over her fingers brought comfort even if they brought few answers.

"What's that, chica?" Selma asked gesturing to Lily's pocket.

"Is that the book you told us about? The one Empusa and Amon wanted?" Rena asked, her dark eyes growing wide as Lily pulled Seraphina's book out. "And why do you feel it is appropriate to keep it in your pocket?"

"I wanted to be near it," Lily shrugged. "Usually we keep it tucked away in a drawer in the sitting room."

Rena raised her eyebrows. "May we?"

Lily handed over the book. She watched Rena's and Selma's expressions morph from awe to sadness, incredulity, and finally anger, reflecting what Lily felt each time she read the book. They were only missing one emotion in their progression: anxiety. But then they hadn't read it dozens of times and still come short of what they were seeking.

"This is amazing. What a piece of history." Rena closed the book and handed it back to Lily.

"Not only history but it confirms where magical creatures on earth came from. It gives credence to the flimsy theories based on a few myths. It's the beginning of a magical lineage written down for all to see. My mother always wondered where we came from. Now I know if the fata made vampires, we are likely of them, too." Selma's eyes were shining with tears.

"What did your mother think sirens were descended from?" Lily asked, curious.

"A fish and a man," Selma said and Lily giggled. "My mother was never a believer in aliens. It was not fashionable in the nineteenth century when she grew up."

"I'm sorry, did you just say the nineteenth century?" Lily's mouth gaped.

Selma grinned mischievously. "There are many things you have not learned about sirens, chica. And I have been careful not to express my true influence around you."

"Okaaaaay, like what?"

"To start with, my true age is much higher than I've told you. I turn one hundred and five next June."

Lily gawked, her eyes roving over Selma's dewy, wrinkle-free skin.

"Being in a small, mostly female community that understood the true nature of our world, was a deliberate choice. I, like most sirens, thrive where we can rely on bonds of friendship, sisterhood, to keep us safe, from others and ourselves. Living in such a way hides our otherness. If I were to live in a city with thousands of men, most of which I do not know, I would not be able to walk down a street without harassment. Only when I am in a community I trust can I keep my power in check; otherwise it begins to get away from me. It is," Selma paused, searching for the word, "a bit like being mad."

"But you lived in New York."

"Si, a turbulent period in my life. It was a time when I had less inclination to control my power. I wanted attention as many young people do. Unfortunately for those in my wake, my magic made attention easy for me to acquire. So many people under my control. Accidents and broken homes occurred because of my selfishness. I am ashamed of that time."

"Is that why you're the only one in your family to leave Menorca?" Lily asked recalling Richard's stories of Selma's hometown on the tiny Spanish island. How her family, largely female, ran the town and the men in circles. To hear Richard speak of it, the Avila women were celebrities there.

"It's safer for them there. The tiny town knows us to be different, but most have married into our family at one time or another. Our blood bonds keep us safe."

Lily jumped as something heavy fell to the floor outside the door. She cracked open the door to find a lemon and a can of green beans outside her bedroom door. Fiona stood arms laden with three overflowing grocery bags in the entryway.

Lily picked up the lemon and the can and rushed down the hall. "Here, let me help you."

"Much appreciated," Fiona said, passing off a bag. "That's Nora's contribution. She called me this morning. She sounded terrible and asked me to swing by her place and pick up her share. Poor lass felt so bad she left it on the front step."

"Can't say I'm upset about not seeing her," Rena grumbled, coming up behind Lily. "You must be Fiona? Brigit's cousin and Lil's instructor in healing, right?"

"Aye. And you must be Rena. Lily has told us much about you. Welcome to Ireland. I must say I'm looking forward to an American Thanksgiving. A chance to be gluttonous and not feel bad about it for a change, am I right?"

Lily laughed at Fiona's blatant honesty, "That is pretty much what we use it for."

They made their way into the kitchen, which smelled heavenly. Brigit had gotten roped into the task of chopping vegetables with Aoife, who had been working too slowly for Annika's liking. Annika, Gwenn, and Mary were preparing three different pies. Sara, Lily noticed with a pang of guilt, was nowhere to be seen.

"It smells about right in here," Rena said inhaling deeply.

"We're making good time. Aoife is helping move things along quite nicely. It's good to have a fire witch around when you're starving and want to cook the bird a bit faster. I'm guessing it will be done in less than two hours," Annika said, a wide grin on her face.

Lily's stomach voiced its approval.

"I heard that," Rena and Brigit said together.

"What can we do to help?" Lily asked after the

laughter that enveloped the room had died down. "Nothing too complicated—we don't want Rena or Selma losing a finger trying to cook their first holiday meal."

A zap of electricity caused Lily's butt muscle to seize and she whirled around to face the culprit.

"Watch your words, child. Remember, we're free to do magic around you now," Rena said with a smirk.

Lily gaped. *My own mother used magic against me?!* A snort of laughter caught her ear and Lily swiveled her head to find Brigit barely holding in her mirth.

Hmmm, seems like this Thanksgiving will be more authentic than I thought it would be, Lily thought, sticking out her tongue and turning to peel a pile of potatoes.

Heiress Down
Evelyn

"WHEN YOU SAID A WEEKEND AWAY, I'd assumed you meant somewhere warmer." Evelyn stared out the window of the Bentley and shivered. "I packed too light for all this snow."

"Who says we're doing anything outside?" Roman replied, his sandy eyebrows raised roguishly.

Evelyn grinned and shoved his arm. It was nice to be taken somewhere, treated, and surprised. Roman had arranged everything. He'd even requested they both leave their cell phones at home, an idea Evelyn did not embrace, but she did consent to meet Roman halfway. The phone would remain off from the time they got in the car to the moment they returned home, with the exception of one check-in a day.

She couldn't remember the last time she'd been

without a cell phone. Even at Fern Cottage she'd kept it close by though the reception there was awful. She had to admit, with all the pressure she'd been feeling it was nice to be cut off from the rest of the world for a short time.

Evelyn suspected Roman needed a break, too. He'd been acting strange, sadder, and a bit frustrated since returning to New York from his home office earlier that week. *Something must have happened with his family.* She wasn't about to push him; after all, she had secrets, too.

She swept the worry from her head. *Stop thinking of all that. Stay positive and this weekend will be what we both need to get on track. He's just a boy and I'm just a normal girl. We're as carefree as can be.*

"I don't think I've ever been this far north. It's too remote for everyday living for my tastes, but there's no denying it's beautiful."

"The remoteness is my favorite part. The seclusion reminds me of our cabin back in Tennessee. You can do anything there and no one will care, or even know. Not like the city where everyone knows every time you take a breath."

He had a point. Evelyn could appreciate a little privacy from all the comings and goings of city life, for a short period anyway.

"How did you even find this place?"

"A friend told me about it. She stayed here once with her family. Said it had every luxury you can imagine. I for one can't wait to take a soak in the hot tub."

She shook her head, only half listening as Roman continued to list the amenities the rental property boasted. *How on earth did I land a man so wonderful?*

Aside from the sadness he'd been trying his best to conceal from her, Evelyn had yet to find a single flaw in Roman, and as for their sex life . . . well, she'd never been so turned on by anyone, ever. If she didn't know any better, she'd guess Roman was the siren and not her.

She also loved the fact that her parents liked Roman almost as much as she did. So much in fact, that since Roman told James they were a couple Evelyn's parents had asked how things were going every day. If Evelyn visited her parents' city apartment, they insisted she bring Roman. At work James latched onto her boyfriend so often Evelyn was finding it impossible to talk to her father alone. It was for this reason that Evelyn still hadn't told her parents about her being a witch. She wanted more than anything to tell them, but didn't think it was time to tell Roman yet. She wasn't so overconfident to assume he'd be into the whole supernatural thing and she couldn't bear the idea of them breaking up. It gave Evelyn a new appreciation for Brigit's story about telling the triplets' biological father, Aengus Clery, that she was a witch. *Telling the truth is harder than I thought it would be.*

"There's the drive," Roman said, his voice cracking weirdly as he squinted at a sign coming up fast on the secluded country road.

The sign proclaimed they were at Peacock Manor and was decorated with some of the most amazing metal work Evelyn had ever seen. A dozen peacocks in copper, silver, and gold stood with their plumage spread wide below a full starry sky. A large gate loomed behind the sign, resolutely closed.

"Is someone here to let us in?" Evelyn asked squinting through the ironwork.

"They sent me a code," Roman replied inching closer to the sign and rolled down the window.

Cold air gushed into the car and Evelyn shivered. She noticed Roman's fingers trembling slightly as he punched in the numbers onto a keypad and the gate swung open to allow them entrance. He pushed the button to roll the window back up but stopped short, leaving it open an inch.

Evelyn glanced at the gap in the window and rolled the scarf in her lap around her neck. *I guess it is a little stuffy in here.*

They continued down a long drive lined with

skeletal trees. *This property would be gorgeous in summer or fall, when the trees are full of color. I wonder if they actually keep peacocks here? That'd be amazing to see them running around.*

"Is that an archery range?" she asked pointing to what looked like targets in the distance.

"Oh, yea, I forgot to mention that. Too much snow for our interest, but still pretty cool, right?" Roman undid the top button on his shirt and cracked the window open further.

"Very. I've always wanted to get into archery, but sailing took up too much of my time. Would you believe I've never even shot a gun?" Evelyn pulled her scarf around her tighter. *How is he hot? It's freezing out.*

Roman smiled a tight-lipped smile. "You mean you're an heiress that grew up in Manhattan and you're not trained to defend yourself? I hate to say it, sugar, but that's pretty believable."

You'd be surprised at what I've trained for, even if I am a little rusty. Evelyn smirked and watched the lights twinkling down the long, secluded drive draw closer.

The drive ended in a circle, abutting one of the most impressive homes she'd ever seen. Larger than her family's ten bedroom Hampton home, the building looked like an old English manor house, but more chic. The massive windows revealed that the lights had been left on to welcome them.

"Do you like it?" Roman asked as he bit his lip, his eyes fixed on her.

"Like it? It's gorgeous. I'm tempted to ask Dad to buy it."

"Good," he paused and drew a long breath. "Evelyn?"

"Hmm?" Evelyn asked flipping down the visor mirror to reapply her lipstick.

He didn't answer, only stared at her before sighing and popping open the car door. "Never mind. Let's get our bags and head in."

I hope he tells me soon what happened when he was home. Evelyn dabbed her lips with a tissue and followed Roman.

The winter air hit Evelyn full in the face as she opened the car door. A patch of snow fell from an old-timey decorative street light above, landing on the top of her head and sliding down her cheeks. Evelyn shot an embarrassed glance at Roman, who had his head buried deep in the trunk. *Thank goodness he didn't see that.* She waved her hand near her face and the snow vanished, leaving behind a coiffed chignon once more.

Roman's head flew from the trunk, his face pale against the backdrop of snow and eyes wide.

"What's wrong?" Evelyn watched his bright blue eyes dart from her to the house to the woods that surrounded them.

"Sorry. I thought I heard . . . a bear."

"Don't worry, I'll protect you," Evelyn said, sidling up to him as he shut the trunk and hefted both their weekend bags over his shoulders. She noticed his was much smaller than hers. "I guess you weren't joking about not going outside. Did you even pack a jacket?"

"I'll be warm soon enough," Roman answered avoiding her eyes as he made his way toward the steps without waiting for her.

She wracked her brain. *Okaaay . . . Cue inexplicably frustrated Roman.* She jogged to catch up.

"How are we going to decide which room to stay in?" she said as they reached the top of the massive staircase. "This place is huge. There must be at least twenty rooms to choose from." She spoke lightly in an effort to cheer up his sudden moodiness.

Roman shrugged and entered the code on the keypad.

WARM AIR RUSHED to greet them, inundating Evelyn's frozen hands and face with welcoming heat. She sniffed and caught the faintest whiff of smoke on the air. *At least part of this trip will be warm.*

She glanced at Roman who stared icily in front of him and shook her head slightly. Hoping if she stayed positive she could lift his sour mood, Evelyn revolved on the spot to better take in the ambiance of gold gilding upon creamy white walls, the gleaming marble floors, the intricate stained glass above the front doors, and the grand staircase that spiraled delightfully from floor to floor.

"Dad would love—" she jumped as two figures emerged at the top of the staircase. There was one male, one female, both stunning and intimidating. "Who are they, Roman?" Evelyn asked backing into Roman, who dropped their bags to the floor, ready to defend them.

"You mean you don't recognize us, dearest Eve?" the woman asked in a faint French accent.

Evelyn's blood ran cold. *Eve?* She studied the pair as they started down the staircase in perfect unison. Their skin was the color of lightly burnt caramel and even from the bottom of the staircase Evelyn could see the woman's eyes were a startling bright green, and the man's a mercurial gray. The man smiled and Evelyn's heart stopped short at the sight of their sharp, shapely canines.

"Now she knows who we are, sister!" Amon cried in

delight.

Fuck! Evelyn whirled around and ran straight into Roman's chest. "We have to get out of here. Hurry, I'll explain later." She grabbed his hand and pulled but he stayed rooted in place.

"Roman," she hissed. "I'm serious!"

Roman's eyes, trained on the vampire twins, shifted to Evelyn and softened. "There's no way out. You can't outrun them. They're natural predators and will hunt you down in a second. I know. I've seen it."

Evelyn's mouth fell open. "What do you mean you know?"

"Our old friend Roman here has been—how should I put it?—in our employ for some time now. We helped his father out of a bind a while back. Incubi cause an ungodly amount of trouble! They're so egotistical, always putting images of themselves in dreams that make them prime suspects of later crimes. Though I must say, we never imagined Roman would be able to repay us so thoroughly," Empusa purred as she reached the bottom of the steps.

"I'm *not* your friend, I . . ." Roman's whispered words died in his mouth when Evelyn spoke.

"What?! You're an incubus?" Evelyn's mind reeled trying to filter through her supernatural knowledge and come up with what the hell an incubus was.

"Tsk, tsk. Brigit isn't up to snuff when it comes to teaching you girls, now is she? First Lily and her abysmal fighting and now you don't even know what an incubus is?" The twins were before her now and Evelyn stood paralyzed with fear as Amon grabbed her arm roughly.

"Careful, brother, we don't want to harm her. How will she do what we want her to if she's battered and bruised?"

Empusa's emerald eyes shifted from Amon to Evelyn. "I'll admit, it was difficult deciding how we would convince one of you to come visit us next. Lily's guard was sure to be up and rumor has it Sara remained safe and sound with Brigit. You were the obvious target, free roaming around New York as you were. So independent and arrogant. But how to ensnare a powerful water witch and siren? That was where Roman came into the picture. Most creatures are susceptible to sirens, but not incubi. As you are aware from your many nights together, Roman has immense talents with the opposite sex, sirens included. We postulated you two might balance each other well." She wagged her eyebrows.

"It was simpler than we dared hope. Roman was already growing rich, and he owed us a favor for saving his family's reputation. He knew the consequences would be *dire* if he did not make good on that favor.

Siblings lost, a father back in prison . . . The plan fell into place like that," Empusa snapped her fingers.

Roman is an incubus. He betrayed me. And I slept with him!

Evelyn's face grew hot as she turned to look at the man she'd thought of nearly every waking minute for the last three weeks. She wanted to cry and have him tell her it wasn't true, to throw herself in his arms.

Instead, her blue eyes narrowed into a ferocious glare.

"When I get out of here, you better believe I'll come for you." Evelyn's hands grew warm as her power, neglected and rusty, rose to the surface. She concentrated hard, hoping to conjure up the fireballs her family had used in Alexandria. A bead of sweat trickled down her forehead and she grunted weakly as she glanced at her hands.

Amon laughed at her efforts. "You think we wouldn't seal the manor from your magic before letting you in? This house is under our control and recognizes other, far greater powers." Amon's hand gripped Evelyn's bicep tightly, and he pulled her down the hallway after Empusa.

She glanced back at Roman as if he would tell her what these "greater powers" were when he'd betrayed her. He followed behind the vampires, head hanging low and tears streaming down his face. She softened for the space of a heartbeat before coming to her senses.

Dammit! No! He sold me out! I probably wouldn't even like him if he didn't use his incubus woo-woo on me. Evelyn scowled and turned around, determined not to look at Roman again. *But I'm one of "the three," what could another witch do that I can't break? It may take a few tries but I'll get out of here . . . sooner or later.*

She shifted her attention to Amon. The guy was tall and cut, but not in a too-muscly sort of way, and handsome. Maybe one of the most handsome men Evelyn had ever seen. She had to admit Lily and Amon would have made a striking couple if he hadn't turned out to be a psychopath vampire. Despite having just failed at performing magic, Evelyn called forth her inner siren, the goddess that made all men fall at her feet.

"Didn't I say your powers won't work?" Amon scowled at her. Up close his gray eyes were even more stunning, flecked with violet. "Not only is the house in the grips of magical wards, we've tailored the wards to your particular strengths. Any magic you attempt will simmer in your blood. If you continue, it may even drive you insane." He looked intrigued by the idea.

Evelyn stopped trying to call forth her magic. *If I go crazy, I'm never getting out of here.*

They were almost at the end of the hall when

Empusa took a hard right down a staircase and Amon followed. Evelyn's senses tickled as they descended the stairs. *What is that?* Her hands itched to run along the wall to uncover the magic within them. But it was too risky with the twins watching, so she settled for sniffing the air softly as she'd seen Aoife and Brigit do before.

"Are you crying little siren," Empusa taunted, her voice high, like the clicking of her stilettos on marble.

Evelyn ignored her, focusing instead on the air she inhaled and the static-filled memories that pushed against the recesses of her mind before falling into oblivion. *Something about this magic just feels so familiar. . .*

They reached the end of the stairway and Empusa extracted a set of keys from a hidden pocket in her skirt. *How did she even wiggle into that thing?* Evelyn wondered staring at the provocative, skin-tight outfit.

The door opened and a stale breeze flew at them. Empusa stepped down and the tonality of her heels deepened and echoed as the marble roughened to stone. They had reached the basement.

Evelyn shivered.

"Is this necessary?" Roman asked, his voice small as he followed the group into a dark, damp hallway.

"No one asked your opinion, incubus," Empusa snarled, her lips curling up and giving Evelyn a view of her canines.

Not super long but they look sharp as hell. The thought did not comfort her.

"Would it be so hard for the witch to put her spells over a room that's nicer? Or at least not as cold? It's freezing down here."

"The siren has gotten to you, incubus. A few days apart and you will be back to your senses and invading the dreams of your little southern belles back home."

Empusa continued down the hall, not caring to hear Roman's response.

Well, that blows. Evelyn had half hoped the vampire would listen to Roman, though she would not give him the honor of knowing that.

They'd gone forty feet down the dark hall when Empusa came to an abrupt stop.

Evelyn jumped as a large figure appeared from a recessed doorway to Empusa's right. *What the hell?*

"This is Felix, your guard," Amon grinned wickedly.

Tall and muscular, the man, Felix, had an extraordinary amount of body hair. He was filthy and his clothes carried weeks worth of dirt.

Evelyn sniffed and the rank odor of sweat, unwashed body parts, and metal made her woozy.

"I wouldn't get too close if I were you," Amon whispered in her ear. "Felix only bathes once a month, after the full moon. If you saw him after he spends the night howling at the moon, you'd understand why. So much blood and mud. Werewolves are disgusting creatures— useful, but disgusting. We'll have someone else guard you that night."

An incubus and now a werewolf? What else am I going to see that I don't understand?

"Stand aside," Empusa ordered Felix.

Felix grunted and shifted to reveal a door behind him. It was of the design of an old German castle, older than Evelyn could date, with intricate wood work and long metal slats running the length, width, and edges. Evelyn judged it would be impossible to beat down or penetrate without magic. Even for someone like Felix.

Empusa selected an ancient-looking key off the key ring, iron with three notches and a large loop at the end. It slid into the door and clicked loudly. The door opened and a stench like old socks worn for a marathon and rolled in urine crawled toward them.

Evelyn gagged.

"Does the room we chose offend you, princess?" Empusa mocked.

She wasn't sure what it was about the remark that hit her so hard, but fury flooded Evelyn as it never had before. She lifted her gaze to stare into Empusa's amused eyes and her own eyes narrowed. And then,

Evelyn did something she'd never imagined she would do.

She spit on Empusa's stilettos.

The repercussion was instantaneous. A hiss and a hard slap across the face. Stars shown in Evelyn's vision and she blinked rapidly. Her hand lifted to cradle her cheek.

"Mind your place, witch. That may be all the discipline I'm permitted to impress upon you, but that doesn't mean I won't slip one day." And with that, Empusa began walking the perimeter of the room, heels clicking on stone, checking that all was secure.

Amon shoved Evelyn into the room with a chuckle.

The room was a large rectangle, with damp stone walls and a rough stone floor. A pile of hay lie at one end topped with a thin blanket. The end closest to Evelyn contained a variety of instruments she had little knowledge of. A metal piece with two opposed, bi-pronged forks attached to a small belt, two slats of wood as tall as the cross she imagined Jesus was hung on but in the shape of an "X", dozens of disposable scalpels, and a small saw stood out to her.

She cringed.

"We know it's not much, but this environment will be most conducive to your training. If you show promise you'll move into the rooms above, where the other

Acolytes of Hecate stay. For now though, this is how you will show your penance."

Training? Acolytes of Hecate? Despite her ignorance Evelyn stared Empusa down unwilling to show how little she understood.

"This one is strong sister. The defiance radiates from her," Amon said, pushing Evelyn toward the hay.

"We'll see how strong she is. Tomorrow we begin conversion therapy," Empusa sneered, as they backed out of the room.

Evelyn walked to the hay, knowing it would be fruitless to attempt escape right then, with no access to magic, two vampires, a very scary werewolf, and a traitorous incubus on her heels. The sharp bristles of hay poked her skin as she laid down. Evelyn considered laying the blanket on top of the hay, but had a feeling she wouldn't last without it covering her, protecting her from what was sure to be a frigid night.

She was about to turn her back to the door and release the tears that had been building behind her hard exterior since she'd realized Roman's betrayal when she heard a chuckle.

The twins were still there, watching her, smiling at her pain and humiliation. She lifted her chin and stared back through the dark, defiant, unwilling to show weakness while they watched.

"This one will be fun to play with," Amon said.

Evelyn caught one last glimmer of Empusa's brilliant smile as the door shut behind them, trapping her in darkness.

A SCREECH SHOT through Evelyn's nightmare. She jumped and an uncomfortable prickling punctured her side. *What the hell?* The stiffness of hay in her hand brought her back to her terrifying reality. A voice she did not recognize echoed through a slit at the bottom of the heavy wood door, followed by the sound of metal skidding on stone.

"Breakfast."

Breakfast? At least I won't starve to death before I figure out how to get out of here.

She looked up. A metal box lay on the ground five feet from her bed, filled with two pieces of toast, an orange, and a bottle of water. *Maybe I spoke too soon . . .*

Evelyn picked up the box and brought it to her bed of hay, the only semi-comfortable spot in the room. She bit into the toast. It was dry and burnt but dammit she would eat it. She would need every ounce of energy she could muster to plan her escape. Also, she was ravenous.

Dinner last night had not gone as planned. No

candlelight, no wine, and no romantic dancing in the snow followed by a dip in the hot tub after dinner. *Roman, that bastard! I can't believe I was so stupid. It's the worst time in my life to fall in love and I fucking went and did it.*

Evelyn cringed, but couldn't take the words back.

Yes. She'd been in love with him, even if he hadn't known it. *Hell, I barely knew it.* Even now, the memory of him kissing her neck sent chills up her spine.

She supposed it was the incubus in him, a creature she took to have powers similar to a siren over the opposite sex. *I didn't use my powers on him, but he used his on me.*

She slammed her fist into the hay as she recalled the initial spark of their touch and how she'd been drawn to him, despite many good reasons not to be. Evelyn suspected even her father's quick agreement to their relationship had been fabricated by Roman's powers. She couldn't trust any of her feelings from the last few weeks.

The uncertainty was terrifying.

She took another bite of toast. *Is this how people feel around me? Is this how Lily felt around me? Uncertain of how they feel, like I'd mess with their mind whenever I want?*

Without warning, the door swung open and Evelyn jumped.

Felix, brawny and intimidating as ever, stepped aside to reveal the curvy, lovely figure of Empusa.

The vampire sauntered into the room and Evelyn's shoulders lowered an inch into relaxation. At least this time Empusa was wearing wedges. The sound of stilettos on stone had plagued her nightmares.

Evelyn sniffed. Empusa smelled of espresso. *I wonder if vampires only drink blood or if they eat other things, too?*

"Ah! Someone fed you. Roman's idea, I'm sure. Neither Amon nor I would even consider doing such a thing, not having eaten food in years ourselves."

Well, there's one question answered.

Evelyn shoved the last bite of toast into her mouth and downed her water in two consecutive moves, in case Empusa decided to deny her the rest of her meager meal.

"I suppose you'll be needing a chamber pot, too," Empusa wrinkled her perfect nose. "I would hate for it to stink in here while your lessons are occurring. Your teacher would certainly take offense."

"And who would that be? I assume two vampires would have little to teach a witch," Evelyn said, her curiosity and ego getting the best of her.

"Ahh, well, you are right in thinking my brother and I will not be teaching you magic. Although you are wrong in thinking we have nothing to teach you. For one, we could teach you not to lie to our faces as your mother did in Alexandria. It's clear you do not have it with you, but be sure we will procure it from your family soon enough."

Evelyn rolled her eyes. "You'd think after thousands of years of being alive you'd be less cryptic. What the hell are you talking about?"

"Seraphina's book, you imbecile! The same thing we've been seeking for centuries. Our spy informed us you found it."

Evelyn twitched, taken aback. *Their spy knew Lily had found the book? How could that be? No one except the McKays knew . . . And why the hell do the vampires even want the book so badly?*

"I see our spy was not lying. Well, well. This is good news. It will only be a matter of time before my brother and I have it, then." Empusa smiled a malicious smile and Evelyn shuddered. "I must go. Until next time, witch. Felix!"

Felix lumbered in with a gait that reeked of wildness. He leered at Evelyn and she realized that he must have heard her crying last night, heard all the pain, fear, and sorrow she was trying to hide now.

"Position the witch on St. Andrew's Cross. Make sure she's bound well but not too tight—wouldn't want discomfort to hinder her lessons today." With that Empusa turned on her heels and strode out of the room.

Evelyn's eyes swung to the "X" shaped cross on the other side of the room. She rose, hoping to avoid Felix's hands on her and retain whatever dignity she could as she made her way to the cross.

Felix growled behind her, but he kept his distance, apparently content to bask in the fear radiating off of her.

As Evelyn drew closer to the cross and the instruments around it her eyes bulged. A side table adorned with a feather duster, a rod with leather tassels, and a sharpened stick tinged an ominous shade of rust sat beside the cross. The cross itself had patches of lighter wood the same shade of rust-red as the sharpened stick. And old, dried blood wasn't even the worst of it. The leather straps where Evelyn deduced her hands were to go had indentions in the wood attached to them, small cuts the exact size of a person's finger nail.

While she wasn't sure torture was the cross's intended purpose, that was certainly what *this one* was used for. Evelyn gulped as she stepped up to the cross and turned to face Felix.

His smile had grown impossibly more lascivious.

And as his feral eyes raked over her, Evelyn knew, even without her mind magic, what he was thinking.

"I swear if you touch me," Evelyn started, her voice sounding stronger than she felt.

"You'll do what?" Felix cut her off. "You're as powerless as a human down here." He shoved Evelyn into the cross and bound her hands first, then her feet. On his way back up, Felix's face paused inches from Evelyn's groin, and the werewolf inhaled deeply.

She made to kick Felix in the face but her feet jerked to a stop inches from the cross and Felix laughed a low, rumbling laugh.

Evelyn clenched her hands and jaw in rage as Felix took the liberty of sniffing her in all the parts of her body she never wished anyone to smell. He stopped the longest at her armpits, which Evelyn was aware had soaked through the thin shirt she wore.

"Adrenaline," Felix said, as one would say "delicious" when enjoying a decadent dessert.

Evelyn closed her eyes, not wanting to see what Felix planned to do next, and was astonished to hear the soft sound of predatory footsteps withdrawing from the room. Only when the door creaked closed was she sure she was safe, at least for the time being.

She exhaled, trying to regain control of her heart rate. Minutes passed like years as she ran through the possibilities of what could happen. Being in a basement with no exterior light, even for a night, had given her a profound sense of disorientation. *Is it really morning, or did they feed me breakfast because I woke up? Or is bread, a bit of fruit, and water all I'll ever get?*

More questions spiraled through her mind, exhausting her with all the uncertainties and fear that came with them. Her head had just started to droop—sleeping in a bed of hay was more romantic than it was practical—when the door flew open once more.

Her eyes narrowed and her hands burned, begging to release a flame, the tiniest spell, with which to punish the man she saw. But her magic would not come. "Get the hell out of here. I don't want to see you," Evelyn growled.

Roman dropped his chiseled face to the floor and it became further illuminated by the flashlight he carried.

Evelyn squinted. Her eyes, now accustomed to darkness, were having a hard time adjusting to the sudden influx of light. *Why does he look so dark and fuzzy?*

It was only when Roman shifted to the side that Evelyn saw the ghostlike figure floating before Roman's solid body, obscuring it. The figure was opaque navy except for the eyes which were two solid spots of black above the mouth, another black spot in what Evelyn assumed to be the ghost's face. The ghost had limbs, though they looked amorphous, like the amoebas she'd seen under a microscope in high school, growing and shrinking at the creature's will as it moved. *What the hell is that thing?*

The ghost approached at a leisurely pace. Evelyn thought she saw the black, iris-less eyes looking her up and down, assessing her. The ghost was ten feet from her when it spoke. Its voice, airy as its form, reverberated off the stones in the room.

"It's true," the dark ghost began circling the cross, examining her from all angles. "I feel the power of water, untethered and relentless, flowing through your veins. I can taste the magic of home radiating from you, from the very center of you, begging to burst from your frail human casings. I see the passion in your eyes, through your fear. This time will be different my love. This time we will work together to build a better world. *This time* we will be together, forever." The strange ghost came full circle to stand before Evelyn, and suddenly she knew who he was.

Evelyn shuddered as the three black gaping holes in Noro's face dilated to the size of large, round saucers.

"My Eve has returned to me."

Thanksgiving
Lily

Lily leaned back in her chair. She was stuffed and more relaxed than she'd been in weeks. Thanksgiving dinner had turned out better than expected with only one small mishap involving the gravy. Luckily, Brigit had purchased such an enormous bird that Annika whipped up a second batch with ease.

Despite having seen multiple films and photos of a traditional American Thanksgiving, the Irish among them had goggled at the amount of food they'd made once it was all on the table.

"It didn't seem like so much when I was writing the grocery list," Brigit's voice rose into a squeak as they'd sat down to eat among the scent of fresh rolls and cheesy green beans. An hour later there was substantially less food, and everyone looked ready for a huge nap.

"The wine was superb, ladies. Thank you for bringing it all the way from Oregon," Aoife said, tilting the remainder of her glass at Selma before downing it.

"Agreed. If it wasn't so bloody hard to find I'd switch out my French wines for Oregon pinot any day," Mary lamented, the apples of her cheeks tinged a pretty pink.

"I suppose all that's left is to clean up then? Lily, Sara, and I can do the bulk of it. We didn't travel today." Brigit rose from the table.

Lily shot a glance at Sara who stood to help, eyes glued to the floor.

Was I really that harsh? Lily sighed as she rounded the table and picked up plates.

Sara hadn't come out of their room until the meal was on the table. Even then only at Selma's asking, as Sara had taken a strong liking to her. She'd been silent most of the meal, speaking only when spoken to, and downing two glasses of wine.

Lily made her way across the sitting room, the only space large enough to fit their extended table, toward the combination kitchen-diner, wondering if she should say anything to Sara to lighten the mood.

Her answer came as she rounded the hearth and ran into Brigit, one hand on Sara's shoulders, the other on a chair next to Sara.

"Set those dishes in the sink and take a seat." Brigit motioned to the chair, and Lily realized she was having an intervention.

Maybe it's best this way. At least I don't have to pluck up the courage to make the first move when we're trapped in the same bedroom, she thought setting the plates in the farmhouse sink. Admitting she'd behaved badly had never been Lily's strong suit.

"What's all this about?" Brigit said, as Lily sat down. "I know you two haven't been getting along these last couple weeks but not a single word to each other at dinner? Not even 'pass the gravy'? What else happened that I don't know about?"

"I said some hurtful things after I found out that Evelyn was going on a vacation with her boy toy this weekend."

Brigit's eyes widened, but she remained silent, a cue Lily took to continue.

In for a penny . . . Lily thought hurling herself into a web of thoughts she'd been considering over dinner.

"I'm sorry I hurt you, Sara. It wasn't my intention. I'm just so mad at Evelyn I could explode, and it's seeping into all my other relationships. I know you want to keep your ties to her open, and I can't blame you for that. I would've responded better to the weekend away thing if the phone calls between you two weren't hidden from me. I'll probably still be a little mad until Evelyn comes back and I can take out my anger in person. But I don't want to lose you in the meantime. Can we start over? Pretend today, at least, didn't happen?"

Sara gave Lily a watery smile. "I'd like that." Her voice was rough from what Lily assumed was a day of crying. "I didn't like hiding that I was talking to Evelyn. It felt wrong, deceitful even, but you were already so angry at her. I didn't want to make you madder. As long as you don't mind that I talk to her, I can forgive everything you said. But I'm not going to hurt one sister to appease the other. That's not how I want my relationships with my sisters to work."

There was truth there. Lily knew it. No one at the cottage would intentionally hurt her, and it was time for her to reciprocate that example. To let go of the anger that had simmered beside her sadness since Em's death and use it for something greater.

And how selfish of me to want Sara to not talk to Evelyn! What kind of person thinks like that?

Lily shook her head at her own childishness. "Deal. Talk to her all you want. Evelyn and I will sort out our differences whenever she returns."

"Aye, there we are. That's the sisterly love I'd hoped to see my first Thanksgiving. What do you say you two hug it out and then we'll get to work? I wasn't kidding about all those dishes," Brigit said, leaving them to finish their kumbaya moment.

"Thanks for forgiving me so easily. I don't know how you do it. You're always so willing to see the best in people," Lily said, extending her arms for a hug.

"I've had a lot of practice," Sara muttered, and Lily's heart ached for the loveless childhood she knew her sister had experienced.

"At least sharing a bedroom tonight won't be so awkward now," Lily said squeezing her sister tight.

Sara squeezed her back.

They split and rose to help Brigit. Constant sounds of merriment floated in from the sitting room and Lily grinned. It was nice to have her family here and the interactions between old and new feel natural. Like her entire life was finally melding together. *Almost . . .* Lily amended, as an image of Evelyn popped into her mind.

Sara hung back, clearing the mountain of grocery bags and general debris thrown in a haphazard pile near the hearth to maximize space for food prep. Lily rolled up her sleeves and made her way into the kitchen. They cleaned with a renewed sense of peace as laughter and chatter filtered in from the sitting room to weave with Brigit's low humming, the anthem to their work.

Brigit was drying dishes and Lily was wiping down

the last counter when she noticed Sara, standing with her head cocked to the side by the fire, a folded bag in one hand, a piece of paper in the other.

"Alright, Sara?" Brigit asked, noticing Lily's sudden pause and following her gaze to Sara.

"This fell out of one of the grocery bags I was folding up. It's for you, Mom, but I don't recognize the handwriting." Sara held out an envelope.

Brigit wiped her hands dry on her apron and glanced at the handwriting. "That looks like Nora's writing. I'll bet it's instructions on how to prepare that sweet potato dish she always raves about after being in the States. She always worries, but we managed without her pretty well." She took the envelope and ripped it open.

Brigit's hands stilled as she unfolded the paper. "It's . . . it's a letter," she said, brow furrowing in concern, her eyes moving rapidly down the page.

A letter? Why wouldn't Nora just call? She can't be so sick she can't talk on the phone. "What does it say?" Lily asked, her interest piqued.

"Goddess be," Brigit whispered, the fear in her voice undeniable.

"What's wrong? Is Nora alright? She said it was only a flu," Sara asked rushing to catch Brigit as she fell against the counter.

"The fecking spy. Nora . . . Evelyn . . . she's in

danger." Brigit seized a handful of hair before swiveling around as if in search of something. She jerked to a stop and covered the length of the room in seconds, grabbed the phone from where it sat on the windowsill and punched in a number.

"The spy? Which one's in danger? Both?" Lily gasped.

Brigit said nothing. The ringing on the other end was audible from where Lily stood, and Sara and Lily waited with bated breath to see who would pick up. A voice answered. Lily thought she heard the word Locksley Enterprises and then a beep.

Brigit slammed the phone in the cradle. "They have her. They took my daughter." She swept into the sitting room without another word.

***

SHE'D SEEN THE NOTE, passed around the room to everyone present at least twice, and still Lily couldn't fathom how it came to be that Nora, Brigit's best friend since childhood, was the spy.

Nora had been the one to give up Lily's identity. The one who stayed in the room with the tunnel in Empusa's Alexandrian mansion. She was responsible for Em's death. Even worse, Nora felt justified in her decisions. The note Nora had written made that clear. It passed into Lily's hands once more and she looked down to read it again, hoping to find some semblance of a joke or even that she'd hallucinated the blue swoops and soft lines.

Dᴇᴀʀᴇsᴛ Bʀɪɢɪᴛ,

You are my oldest and best friend. It is because of our history that writing this letter is not easy. We've grown together from young witchlings with no power to speak of into women grown. It is amazing how we have changed. In truth, I'd never expected such power to come from you when we were younger, but you surprised me, in more ways than one.

The biggest surprise of all was the birth of your daughters, and how you chose to interpret it. Your decision to hide them away has flabbergasted me from the start though I tried to trust your judgement in the matter. Later, your decision astounded me for other reasons.

Now I know better and I can no longer try and make sense of what isn't sensible. It is time for me to make my feelings known and with that my place in the battle between our world and the world of our magical ancestors. I'll admit I didn't believe in fata for the longest time. Like most witches I thought of them as little more than a myth, but these past few years have opened my eyes.

I was approached and shown all that our kind will soon be capable of. How we will grow in power and status under the new regime. We, as witches, will acquire special rankings above the humans and will learn fata magic. From what I've heard, once a fata acclimates to Earth, the fata is as powerful as ten strong witches. Though there are not many here yet, they will come and when they do, you will want to have been on the right side of history. You will not want to feel their wrath, dear friend, and I do not want you to. I beg you to change your stance. We are all from the same line, best friends and family. Family shouldn't fight.

With that news, I want you to know that we have detained your daughter, Evelyn. I've spoken well of her power, how well rounded she is, and while Evelyn is not the most skilled of your daughters, she may have the most raw magic. Water witches are lucky to live on Earth and experience much raw elemental power to pull from.

I'm hoping that as a pragmatic businesswoman she will see the benefits a new regime on our planet can bring. The benefits you closed yourself off from. I for one see little that humans have done right with our world and am sure the fata can do better.

I urge your daughters to see the light too. Lily and Sara, if you are reading this, know you may be instrumental in changing the fate of all supernaturals on Earth. Noro (on behalf of Dimia, future King of Earth) is willing to spare your loved ones from any of the lower-ranking tasks they have deemed appropriate for less-fortunate souls. You may keep them as your personal entourage as reward for a job well done. In this way all you love will be cared for.

I beg you to join myself, other witches, and creatures who have seen the light as an Acolyte of Hecate, our ancestral home and magical mother. While Evelyn will be of some help, we will need you, too. I sincerely hope I have helped sway you to the side of our ancestors. We will be awaiting your arrival in the city where dreams are made true.

Your friend,

Nora

Acolyte of Hecate, First Order

Lily looked up from the letter. Brigit was weeping uncontrollably, her sisters gathered round her trying to comfort Brigit, though they didn't seem much better off.

Lily had a few close friends, but none she counted as family, not like Nora was to Brigit. She had no one her age she'd grown up with, went through the toughest of times with, and leaned on through it all.

And that wasn't even factoring in the fear and guilt Brigit was feeling from Evelyn's abduction. Her daughter was abducted and her best friend had made it happen, Lily thought watching Brigit's trembling body.

Her mind swung to Evelyn, taken, held against her will by Noro and his Acolytes.

At least Nora's letter answers one question. Noro is still here. The pit in Lily's stomach deepened. No matter how mad she was at Evelyn, or how little she trusted her at times, blood recognized blood. Especially when that blood had been abducted by aliens. *We must find her.*

She tore her eyes from the McKay women and found Rena staring back at her. Hard lines fell deep in the dark skin of Rena's face and her generous lips pulled tight at their corners. In that moment, it wouldn't have surprised Lily if Rena ripped off her shirt to reveal the intricate girdle of an Amazon, one breast bared. She was a warrior queen.

"What are we going to do?" Lily asked the mother she'd known all her life.

There was a pause, a moment between them, and

only the far off echo of a crow cawing in the woods was able to penetrate it. Lily shivered and Rena exhaled deeply.

"We're going to find your sister and kill the bastards that took her."

Burning Blood
Evelyn

The door opened slowly and with a prolonged creak.

Evelyn crouched, hidden at the side of the door, ready to ambush Noro.

All I need is a tiny opening and a good shot. She extended her hands out as best she could without ripping open the long gash that ran down her right triceps.

She'd taken the hits for a day, been Noro's plaything, and attempted the fata magic he forced her to try or face the punishment, but Evelyn didn't plan on doing it again.

"Good morning, Eve!" Noro called out, his voice jubilant as he floated through the door.

Evelyn pounced.

"Lotu! Dionean!" She forced the body binding spell out of her, followed a heartbeat later by a stunning spell for good measure.

To Evelyn's horror, the spells rebounded back inside her. Her body stiffened and then collapsed against the wall as her first spell hit and she became a victim of her own magic. Her brows knit together. *How am I still standing if my stunning spell rebounded back inside me?*

Then a heat surged through her arteries and veins as her blood began to burn inside her.

"Ah! Ahhh!" Evelyn squeezed her eyes shut and wished for nothing other than the blackness of unconsciousness.

"My children told you that would happen and yet, you still thought it prudent to try. Did you think I'd forget to reset the enchantments on this room? I would never forget such a thing," Noro's voice simmered with anger.

Evelyn flew twenty feet backwards through the air and slammed against a wall.

The naked skin on her back split open, slowly releasing the magic burning in her blood into the air. Her blood cooled and her body loosened, no longer bound or stunned. *It figures that injury to myself is the only way to find relief here.*

"I love you, Eve, but I will not tolerate this type of disobedience. Do you understand?"

Evelyn sat up and a sharp pain shot from her tailbone to her skull.

Noro was there, inches from her, looking her in the eyes, his navy hue dark and furious. His form was stretched out, making him feet taller than he'd been just the day before, yet still amorphous, as if fata skin was not solid enough to confine a fata's insides to a shape.

A stray rock found its way into her hand and Evelyn swiped at Noro. Her expression faltered when the fata flowed out of the way of her loaded hand, like a water balloon that hit the ground but would not break.

Noro retaliated, his airy limb hardening in an instant to match the texture of stone.

Her jaw cracked and Evelyn screamed.

Noro, not wasting a minute and uncaring of her injury, levitated her to the cross she'd hung upon hours before.

Glass, Copper, and Hysteria
Lily

THE CROWDS at JFK International Airport parted before the witches rushing through the terminal as if engineered by magic. It had been two excruciating days since the witches' Thanksgiving celebration ended in the worst way possible.

Unable to reach Evelyn or her parents and beg access to the Locksley's jet, the McKays, Rena, Annika, and Selma were at the scheduling whims of international airlines, a conglomerate so large and complicated even magic was little help. To make things more difficult, Brigit—who'd become short and emotional with anyone who crossed her—insisted they all fly together.

Only Fiona stayed behind to look after two of her terminally ill clients until another witch could make the journey to their remote village and act as healer in her stead.

"I would have bet everything I owned that Nora was a trustworthy, steadfast friend. But I was wrong and I refuse to give the Acolytes of Hecate any way to weaken our position further. An Acolyte could be anywhere, waiting to pounce when one of us strays. We stick together," Brigit decreed when Aoife dared to suggest that Brigit go ahead with Mary and Gwenn to scout out the New York scene.

Lily, for one, was relieved that Brigit had put her foot down. She felt safer traveling in a larger group, though none were sitting next to each other on the flight. The situation suited Lily, allowing her time alone to think without the insecurity of being completely alone. And she had a lot to think about.

Lily had been furious with Evelyn these last few weeks, but now her feelings were more nuanced. Could she still be raging mad at Evelyn after her sister had been abducted and forced to perform magic Aoife repeatedly proclaimed was beyond her capabilities?

The answer, Lily decided as they were flying into New York Harbor, was no. She couldn't be mad when her sister's life was in danger. Yet, she still found herself blaming Evelyn for everything that had happened.

How dare Evelyn put us in this predicament? she asked herself for the hundredth time.

Evelyn had known it was too soon for the triplets to be left to their own devices in the world. They didn't know enough magic and with Nora's betrayal had lost their veil of anonymity, giving the Acolytes a clear upper hand. Their cover was totally blown, and the Acolytes had only been able to exploit them because Evelyn stayed in New York instead of returning to the safety of Fern Cottage.

And though anger simmered in her skin, Lily knew she couldn't hold on to it. *I wish I was more naturally forgiving, like Sara was with me. I guess now is the perfect time to practice . . . I just hope I don't lose anyone else because of Evelyn's poor decisions.* Her heart heavy with the memory of Em's death, she glanced over at Rena, Annika, and Selma, each of whom had insisted on joining the McKay's to save Evelyn.

"Where to first?" Mary asked, her voice hushed as the group assembled at the end of a long cab stand line.

"I called the largest New York covens during our layover in France and asked if they had any knowledge of the abduction or any sort of funny business." Gwenn answered, shuffling forward with the line "Seeing as Evelyn is not yet a registered witch, none of the covens except one knew who she was and that's only because of the Locksleys' prominence in New York. The Sisters of Salem are allowing us refuge in their safe house. They'll listen to our case in person and decide whether or not to get involved after."

"We should go to Locksley Enterprises first," Sara said, astonishing everyone.

"And why is that, Sara? The Locksleys have no connection to the supernatural world besides Evelyn and Fiona." Gwenn's brows were furrowed over her bright green eyes.

"That's true, but they may know Evelyn's last whereabouts, and who she's been hanging out with. Don't you find it telling that this was the weekend she went away with her new boyfriend? Maybe they have info on the guy. Evelyn was very vague about him, never even told me his name, but they'll spill if we tell them what's happening."

Brigit let out a long whistle, earning her dirty looks from all the cab drivers waiting to pull up to the front of the line. "You're bang on, Sara. We have to go there first. I'm wishing Fiona was with us right now. Sonja's never met any of us but she trusts Fiona."

"Hey lady! You want a cab or not?" a cabbie yelled from the front of the line.

Lily looked up to see the crowd of people before them had vanished. *What the...?*

"What's the use of being a ceremens if you can't use it to your advantage every now and again?" Aoife winked as she strode toward the waiting cab.

Lily's head craned upward as the cab pulled to a stop. She'd known Evelyn came from wealth, but to have a monstrosity such as the gleaming building before her shoved in her face put into perspective just how wealthy her sister really was.

Stepping out the cab allowed Lily a full view of the modern steel, brass, and glass front of Locksley Enterprises. It looked entirely chic in a sea of concrete and dingy art déco buildings, and though it wasn't quite her style, it still drew the eye.

Two cabs filled with the remainder of their rescue party pulled up. Each person's face held a look of awe that mirrored how Lily felt. Once everyone had arrived they huddled together in a tight circle confined by the glass exterior of the building and the pulsing crowd on the sidewalk.

"This place is mad," Aoife said, her copper eyes darting around as she ran her hand through her red hair in agitation. "How people can live like this, right near on top of each other, is beyond me."

"But you have to admit, Aoife, it's exhilarating!" Mary's blue eyes danced and her smile widened as she watched the crowds of people surge past them like river water. Aoife shot her blonde sister the side-eye.

Lily smirked. While she found herself agreeing more with Aoife, it didn't surprise Lily that Mary, a social butterfly and most like Evelyn, was thrilled to be here. *In a way, I can see the appeal, too.* Lily watched a woman in high heels and a long fur coat stride down the sidewalk as if she owned it.

Yes, the city was crowded, loud as hell, and it smelled a little, but beside the reek of urine and exhaust hung the undeniable thrill of life invading your every sense. It was an adrenaline rush just to stand on the sidewalk. Evelyn would thrive here, on the tiny island surrounded by water, inundated with powerful men and filled with minds that whirred nonstop.

"So what's the plan? I doubt we're going to be let up to a billionaire's office without some sort of appointment or explanation. And I don't think we should tell anyone beside Evelyn's parents about her abduction," Gwenn said, pulling them back to the issue at hand as was so often her task as eldest McKay sister.

"Aoife, can you use ceremens to find the office location and get us up there? In a place such as this there ought to be a lobby desk with a couple of people working," Rena said, revealing a plan far better than the one Lily had been composing in her head. Her plan consisted of nine women running like hell to the elevator as security chased close behind.

"I can manage about three people at a time. If there's any more at the desk someone else will have to help dissuade them from calling security." Aoife surveyed the group, which Lily knew had no other strong mind witches. "Sara, it looks like you're up next. Then Brig if there's more. Hopefully that will be enough."

Sara beamed with pride as the group streamed through the huge, reflective glass doors of the building.

Wow, it's white in here. Lily took in the airy spaciousness, white marble, clean lines of the building, and the single woman behind the front desk.

The woman was talking on the phone in a crisp English accent with a frantic look in her eye. The desk attendant didn't even blink when nine women, who looked like they had no business being there, approached the desk luggage in tow. The witches and one siren stood there for a second, waiting for Rose Wellington—as indicated by her nameplate—to acknowledge them. Lily's ears perked up as they over-heard bits and pieces of her conversation.

"No, Mr. Locksley is not taking any calls at the moment. Yes, we are aware there has been a glitch in the system. We are working to resolve it. Yes. Thank you." Rose hung up the call. "Locksley Enterprises, this is Rose how may I—Oh good day, Mr. Allamud. No, I'm so sorry, Mr. Locksley is not available at the moment. Yes, I'll have him call you." She switched to the next blinking light without so much as a glance up.

Lily looked down at the phone board and saw two dozen red lights blinking. *Something's going on.*

"Come on, let's move," Aoife whispered and pulled Lily's arm. The witches left the desk and went to the elevator.

"Looks like we're not the only one in a crisis," Annika said as the door closed. "Aoife, did you even—?"

"Not at all," Aoife answered, anticipating the question as she studied a gold-plated directory by the elevator. "The poor girl was so frantic her mind was going in all sorts of directions. I don't think she even registered we were there."

THE ELEVATOR SHOT up to the executive floor in less than a minute. It was, Lily supposed while placing a hand over her stomach, something one had to get used to.

"Dios mio, that's what I'd call one hell of a ride."

Selma closed her eyes and took a deep breath as they stepped out.

Lily gawked as people ran by, phones attached to their ears. The chaos did not jive with the light and serene atmosphere the office so obviously tried to promote with the help of light colors, lots of negative space, and flourishing green plants. *It even smells calming up here,* Lily thought inhaling the scent of sage just as a man with one phone cinched between his ear and left shoulder, another phone in his right hand, and a laptop held open in his left hand, nearly bowled her over.

He scowled at Lily as he hopped on the elevator, punched a button with his elbow, and disappeared behind the doors.

Gwenn twitched. "It feels as if everyone in here could use a good calming spell." Her hands rose slightly as if preparing to gift her speciality spell to anyone they passed.

"Don't even think about it, Gwenn. We don't have time. We've already spent too long getting to the States. We have to be smart, figure out where Evelyn is, and find her as fast as possible, not help a few worker bees," Brigit said, pushing her sister's hands down.

Another smaller directory hung at the entrance to the hall telling them which office was Mr. Locksley's.

The witches made their way down the hallway, unimpeded, checking numbers and peeking into any open doors, which inevitably held a man or woman in a state of panic. No one seemed to notice the nine-woman mafia as they made their way deeper and deeper into the heart of Locksley Enterprises.

Brigit held her arm out to stop the herd at her back as they approached the end of the hall. "It's got to be one of those two," she said in little more than a whisper. "Hang back a second." She approached with the care of someone walking on eggshells, peeking first left then right. She froze.

"Come on, girls. Brigit needs support," Annika said, taking in Brigit's shock with her sharp, ice-blue eyes and nudging Lily and Sara forward.

Approaching wordlessly, Lily squeezed next to Brigit to peek through an open door crack into James Locksley's office. Her heart cracked in half at what she saw. James sat at his desk, hands tented with his forehead against them and shoulders trembling.

Brigit pointed into a corner that Lily, from her position, could just make out. Her breath caught in her throat, as Lily caught sight of a woman, petite with olive skin and long black hair, sitting in a cream tufted chair and sobbing into her hands. *That must be Sonja.*

"Ready, Brig?" Aoife whispered, moving around the

group to be by her sister and putting her hand on the door.

"I think so," Brigit's voice was barely more than a breath.

Aoife slid the shoji door open and the witches poured into the room.

Neither James or Sonja even glanced up.

Well, this is awkward, Lily thought as Aoife cleared her throat, startling both Locksleys out of their misery.

"Oh!" Sonja exclaimed, wiping her fingers beneath her eyes and smudging her mascara.

"Who are you? How did you get in here?" James looked torn between anger at having a horde of strange women enter his office and curiosity.

"We're sorry," Brigit smiled weakly, "We walked up ourselves. The rest of the office seemed a bit . . . busy."

James snorted. "What an understatement. So who are you and why did you barge into my office uninvited and unannounced?"

"I'm Brigit McKay-Clery. These are my sisters, daughters, and friends."

Sonja paled at the name. "You're Evelyn's biological mother?" she asked, her voice trembling. Brigit nodded, "And these two are her sisters, Lily and Sara." She pointed to the girls in turn. "I'm not sure if Fiona told you, but Evelyn is a triplet."

"No, she didn't. Evelyn didn't mention it either," Sonja knit her brows together increasing the tension in her face. "Why are you here?" She looked pained, like a person who wanted to admit something but couldn't.

Brigit cleared her throat. "We received word that Evelyn has disappeared. We came to help find her. We're hoping you may have information that will lead us to her."

"But how did you find out? We've only now realized it!"

"What sort of information?" James interrupted his wife, his mouth set in a hard line.

Brigit walked closer and the rest of the group followed. Neither James nor Sonja protested. "Like who Evelyn has been hanging around with since she's been home. Her last known whereabouts. And if you've heard of any other strange happenings since Evelyn's come home, besides the obvious ones stemming from the change in Evelyn, of course."

The Locksley's exchanged looks.

"What do you mean by strange happenings and the change in Evelyn? She's been a little on edge, but other than that everything seems fine. Is there something wrong with her?" Sonja said, her perfect brows knit so close together now they were almost touching.

"That's to be expected, what with everything that's

going on. Specifically, we're wondering if anyone has been following Evelyn. Or maybe she told a friend she was a witch and now they're estranged? Things like that," Brigit explained.

Silence hung in the air, reverberating off the walls and through Lily's bones. James's mouth opened so wide Lily was sure his jaw would fall off his face any second. *Something's not right here.*

Finally Sonja spoke. "Did you call our daughter a witch?"

"Bloody hell," Aoife muttered.

Mary's hand flew to cover her bright red lips.

Everyone else gaped.

Evelyn hasn't told them! But . . . she's been home for a month! Does that mean she was never planning on telling her parents anything? I can't believe this.

"Should I ceremens them, Brig?" Aoife whispered.

"Or a calming spell?" Gwenn added, her green eyes darting from Brigit, to Aoife, to the Locksleys.

Brigit shook her head. She looked at a complete loss for what to do next.

To everyone's surprise Sara sidestepped out of the group and made her way toward the large wooden desk. "We're all witches," Sara held out her hand in which hovered a blazing blue ball of fire with two smaller golden balls circling it.

James leapt back and Sonja cursed.

Sara extinguished the flame. "Don't worry, I have complete control over my powers and would never harm Evelyn's parents. May I sit?" she asked pointing to the large leather chair on the other side of the desk from James.

He nodded and watched as the tiny redhead lowered herself into the chair with authority.

"We've only just met, but please be assured I love your daughter. I found out a few months ago I had two older sisters. I also found out that Evelyn, who I'm lucky to call one of those sisters, was brought up very differently from me. With the love of a family and the security of a bright future. My childhood wasn't filled with either. I didn't get amazing adoptive parents like you and I'll never tell my own adoptive parents our story, the story of my sisters and me. Would you mind if I told you? I'm sure Evelyn will want to talk to you about it when she returns, but it might be nice if you had a baseline already."

Holy shit. Lily released a breath she hadn't known she had been holding. *Sara doesn't look at all fazed sitting before one of most influential couples in America.*

James and Sonja turned to each other, eyes wide.

Then, without a word, they both sat down to face Sara and nodded.

Everyone listened as Sara told their story. The past, present, and supposed future. She told the truth, even if she hadn't been present for it. Lily kept waiting for the shoe to drop. To hear Sara tell Evelyn's parents about the estranged relationship between their daughter and Lily. She waited to see James and Sonja's gaping mouths close and have their accusing fingers pointed in her face.

But none of that happened.

"What you said explains so much. Why Evelyn's been so distant since returning. The thorough questioning about exactly what we knew when she returned. And why she needed the jet so quickly," James mused, his face paler than before Sara shared their story. "I thought Alexandria was an odd choice, but we own a couple jets so . . ." he raised his shoulders as if to say 'why the hell not?'

Sara nodded as if the logistics of owning multiple private jets was second nature to her. "So as you see, Evelyn has undergone a major life change, and there are very dangerous people out to get her. We need any information you can give us if we are going to find her."

"Shouldn't we call the police?" Sonja wiped away the tears that had started flowing again when Sara spoke of their unbinding and hadn't stopped since.

"They'd be clueless with a case like this one," Brigit cut in. "Evelyn is in great danger. Supernaturals took her and only supernaturals can find her, but we need your help. You're the ones who know her best."

Her final words seemed to hearten the Locksleys, who for the first time since the witches' arrival smiled.

"Her boyfriend's name is Roman Simons." Sonja launched into an information dump without further prodding. "He's the oldest son of an energy industry tycoon in Tennessee. We acquired their account out of the blue a month ago. Roman and Evelyn hit it off right away, that much was clear. She went out of town with him this weekend. I haven't heard from her in two days. Except for when she was in Ireland, with you, I talk to Evelyn once a day. Your group showed up shortly after James received the message that explained why I haven't heard from her."

"Message?" Rena asked, leaning forward.

"An email," James answered. "Few people know my personal email so whoever sent it got it from someone I trust.

"Mind if we read it?"

James turned his oversized monitor around and the witches inched closer to read.

• • •

GREETINGS JAMES!

You're probably wondering who I am to have your email. Let's say I have insider information. I have taken someone very dear to you. If you ever wish to see your little Evie again, make a transfer of one hundred million dollars to the following account:

LILY LEANED back when the email tapered off to list a long string of numbers, a bank name, and a sign-off from Acolyte of Hecate Number Two. *Two guesses who that is,* she thought sourly. *So the other side needs money and lots of it. But why? If they can do magic, why do they need so much?*

"As soon as I read this I tried calling Evelyn. When there was no answer, I filled Sonja in. We checked around and none of her friends have spoken with her in over a day. That never happens. She's very communicative, our daughter."

Are we searching for the same person? Lily frowned, remembering all the days when she and Evelyn had barely exchanged a word.

"So no leads, but we can guess that this Roman Simons is in on the abduction," Brigit mused.

James and Sonja nodded. Despite having learned

some serious truths about their daughter, they looked less fearful than when the witches had arrived.

"Well, I suppose our road is clear then. We need to get in touch with the supernatural community. We'll ask if anyone has seen this guy and knows of his whereabouts. I'll keep in touch with you two and inform you as soon as we find Evelyn. If you give us a number we can reach you at directly, we'll be on our way." Brigit rose, ready to get down to business.

"Actually," Aoife said, "I have one more question. What's going on in your office? I find it hard to believe you told your entire staff about your missing daughter .. . am I right?"

Lily's eyes grew wide. Aoife was right. There was no way James and Sonja had sent out a call about their missing daughter. They hadn't had the time. They had been wracking their brains to digest the message when the witches arrived.

"Oh, that." James collapsed in his chair with a wave of his hand, as if the chaos in his business empire was of little consequence. "There was a security breach last night. Someone hacked into our system and accessed a number of our clients' accounts. All in all, about two million dollars disappeared from our books."

"Can you imagine being so nonchalant about losing two million dollars?" Lily asked, pressing the elevator button for the lobby.

"Aye. It's a pretty penny," Aoife nodded. "His reaction speaks to his character. He's letting others figure out the business mess while he brainstorms a way to save his daughter. Didn't even balk at having to shell out one hundred million for her. That's a dedicated da if I ever saw one. Reminds me of Aengus."

"Me too," Brigit agreed. "I only hope we can find her, for his sake as much as ours."

"So, onto the Sisters of Salem safe house?" Mary asked. "We can make calls to the local community and get intel on this Roman Simons character from there. They're one of the largest covens in the world with lots of eyes on these streets. Maybe someone saw Roman taking Evelyn somewhere."

Everyone nodded, unable to come up with anything better.

We're going to need help if we're going to find her fast, Lily thought, recalling the panoramic views of the city out James Locksley's window.

The elevator door opened. They strode past Rose, who looked more bogged down by phone calls than an hour ago, and out the front door of Locksley Enterprises, arms readied to hail the first cabs they saw.

Broken Soul

Evelyn

Evelyn's broken body curled in on itself for protection as another day dawned and metal scraped upon stone.

Noooo. Evelyn buried her face in hay and winced as her nose collided with the cold stone below her bed of hay, which had flattened under her weight as she slept.

"Good morning, Eve darling!" Noro called out. "Rise and shine! I have another full day planned for us."

Her body rose and floated to the other side of her cell unaided by her muscles and bones.

A couple days in the dungeon had taught Evelyn there was no use in fighting the fata. He was the strongest creature she'd ever met. She hoped this was only because Noro had been on Earth for millennia and been able to build his magic in that time, as Seraphina had spoken of in her tale.

Noro lowered Evelyn's body onto a narrow metal table resembling ones used for gynecological exams. The table was covered with a threadbare towel and shackles were welded to the sides where a person's hands and feet would lay.

Evelyn's feet fell like bricks into the stirrups as her bruised arms rested protectively over her internal organs.

"I hope you slept well, Eve, for today is a big day. Dimia is anxious for progress and has commanded we open a portal today. I negotiated for you, I really did. Tried to buy you another day or two of training. You are not as strong as I would like you to be for this task. I'll be honest, he didn't appreciate the news, but I made sure he knew your weakness was all down to your human blood. Still, I suggest you try your hardest to open the portal, my love. Dimia has waited many years and has grown impatient. It is not in our best interests, yours especially, to fail him. As long as Dimia makes it to Earth, he will be more amenable to wait a few days for another to open for his subjects."

Noro landed next to her and his mouth opened wide as he took in Evelyn's body. "Of course, it would please me, too, if you succeeded. I have waited thousands of years for this, to see your lustrous power emerge again in such a glorious manner. I'll admit, you are not what I expected being so—human. Yet, what you lack in the fata magic of your ancestor, you make up for with relative submissiveness. It's a trait I find attractive in my partners."

Evelyn shuddered. While the torture had been bad, Noro's insistence that they were together as "partners and lovers" was far worse. She hoped being a lover meant something different to a fata, because picturing Noro's gaping black hole of mouth on her mouth was almost more than she could bear. And as Evelyn had learned since her abduction, she could bear a lot more than she'd ever thought possible.

For two days a tray of bread, fruit, and water slid into her cell at an unknowable time and Evelyn bolted down the food, knowing it was the last sustenance she would see for the day. Then she laid back down on her bed of hay to wait. Noro arrived minutes or hours later, there was no way to be sure, and Evelyn's fata magic lesson began.

The navy fata expected Evelyn to replicate his magic mere minutes after he taught it to her. Apparently, these were the same high standards thrust upon Dimia's daughters when they'd trained on Hecate. The difference was that the original triplets succeeded, whereas Evelyn failed to meet most of Noro's expectations. A single failure meant enraging Noro and hours of torture.

And Evelyn had the marks to prove it.

Scalpel lines ran the width of her belly, back, and other parts of her body not covered by the scraps of what Noro deemed vile human clothes. The scraps remained only because of Evelyn's insistence that she'd freeze to death at night without them.

On her inner right thigh two new marks glowed, one a white spiral, the other a navy eight pointed star. Evelyn had received both Dimia's and Noro's brands the day before. Contrary to her expectations, it hadn't hurt when Noro branded her with his magic, but the fact that he'd marked her, claimed Evelyn for himself, infuriated her.

"You will receive your own symbol with which you may claim human slaves once the fata have taken over. I'm sure Dimia will approve you anything you'd like. He would not dare deny you that basic right, Eve, but everyone, the king excluded, must have superiors, am I right? And who better to be your superior than your lover?" Noro had insisted as his navy star appeared on her skin along side Dimia's spiral.

Other marks Noro left deep inside her. Like the time he twisted Evelyn's intestines into knots when she failed to levitate more than a few feet across the room in the graceful fata manner. The pain had been excruciating, and it was the only time being deprived of food seemed a bonus. Or the time he'd attempted to force Evelyn to pull the life force from a kitten. She'd been pleased when she'd failed that one. But Noro hadn't, and in the end, Evelyn was forced to watch the kitten die, his little eyes blinking up at her as he crumpled to the ground. Evelyn moved its tiny body to the opposite side of the dungeon and hid it from sight beneath a bloody rag. For once she was grateful the dungeon was cold; the corpse hardly smelled at all.

"Does that sound amenable to you?"

Noro touched Evelyn's arm, and the sensation reminded her of a small tornado of air hovering and whirring on top of her skin. His dark eyes stared at her and she realized he was waiting for her to respond to some asked question.

She nodded, wondering why he bothered to ask her opinion. *It's not like I have a choice in the matter if I want to survive.*

"Perfect," Noro squealed and pushed his dark, sausage-resembling limbs together in a soundless clap.

"Skipping levitation practice will allow you to conserve your energy for the opening of the portal. I realize it will be embarrassing that you have not mastered levitation and must walk on the ground when

Dimia arrives, but I'm glad you recognize the predicament we are in. The king's wishes must always supersede our own vanities."

Evelyn barely repressed her eye roll.

"Now then, Eve, we shall first review what the Ancients—the oldest and most powerful fata on Hecate—and I believe are the basics of how to create a portal. To our best knowledge, this has to do with distorting space-time. The Ancients have been trying to work out how Dimia's daughters managed to open a portal for thousands of years. As you can imagine, many attempts were made after Lilith, Eve, and Seraphina left. None succeeded but their failures were useful as teaching tools."

There it is again. Evelyn's mouth flattened in annoyance. Noro was always referring to the "human part" of her genome. No matter how much she insisted that after so many generations of human ancestors it was unlikely she had anything but a human genome with magic-giving witchy genes mixed in. *I suppose learning science is beneath a fata.*

"The Ancients' current hypothesis is that the original portal was more a *loss* of magic and energy than a use of magic. Meaning Dimia's daughters expended all the talents they had on Hecate to gain new ones on this planet. Powers that do not exist on Hecate, such as the ability to manipulate fire magic. They traded the magic Hecate gifted them, as the planet does with each newborn fata, for magic they could reap from Earth." He gestured to the ground as if one could easily visualize lush greenery beneath the stone. "My powers, on the other hand, have only grown since coming here as I have been able to access some of Earth's magic while my magic from Hecate never left me. I believe this to be because Eve created the portal that brought me over. Therefore, I did not need to expend my own power. Are you following?"

Evelyn shrugged. *What does it matter? I doubt this will work anyway.*

"Very well," Noro eyed her suspiciously before continuing. "We believe one way for Lilith, Eve, and Seraphina to have expended so much magic is to have undertaken the enormous task of bending space-time in the opposite way it wishes to be bent. It would have taken a staggering amount of power, but I can assure you Dimia's daughters were no normal fata. They, like you, were stronger than all others."

Noro's mouth twisted into something resembling a frown. "Of course, they benefited from the best fata tutors their entire lives and knew how to leverage their powers. Had your stupid mother not hidden you from me, you would perhaps be the same and I would not have to fear for your life as you undertook this task."

It's like he actually cares if I can handle this, Evelyn mused.

"Once Dimia's daughters succeeded in bending space-time and it created a hole through space, they used what was left of their power to travel through the hole or portal to Earth. The closest thing I've heard a human do is hedgecrossing, which is analogous to my own talent of sending my pneuma through space separate from my body. Alas, all humans who had accomplished hedge-crossing have died, their souls lost somewhere in the space or time between your world and others."

A conversation flashed in Evelyn's mind: Mary telling the triplets about hedgecrossers, witches with immense power whose souls traveled out of their bodies not just on earth as witches more commonly did during astral travel, but also in space. Mary had spoken of how other supernaturals had desired to use hedgecrossers for their own means, which led to many suppressing their talents or ignoring them.

But Mary said it took years to develop the talent and . . . Didn't she tell us a story about Empusa and Amon hunting hedgecrossers to use them? Evelyn eyed Noro warily.

"I see you are familiar with the term," Noro said, assessing her reaction. "Fear not, my dearest Eve. Those other humans did not have a fata's help. More to the point, they were not *you*. I realize it will be farther than you've ever allowed your soul to travel, but with a fata's guidance and access to our magic, the magic of your ancestors, it is possible."

But I can't even astral travel! It was too ironic for words. The one skill Evelyn needed to appease Noro, save herself another round of torture, and possibly negotiate a way out of this basement was a branch of magic she had never had any success with. She sighed.

"So let me get this straight. You want me to bend space-time in a way it doesn't want to be bent, then send my soul through it? What if it kills me? You said it depleted Dimia's daughters' power. And that all the hedgecrossers who have tried to travel have died. The odds don't seem too good."

Noro's black eyes glimmered as if stars were twinkling in and out of sight within them. "After you open a portal, you *will* be depleted. You may even, as you have guessed, die. A fata's pneuma is more robust than a human soul, after all. However, I will do everything in my power so that you may live, Eve. And as you know, I hold much power. Tell me you will try, my love. I have already promised our king. If I have to tell him other-wise, I will be most unhappy."

Holy shit! He's batshit crazy for thinking I can do this! I'll have to trick him into thinking I'm trying hard. Or maybe I should try really hard until I become depleted in magic and can't do any more? Then he'll have to leave me alone until my power returns. Hope-fully, that will be long enough for someone to come looking for me.

The Locksleys may have already called the police, but Evelyn knew the police would be useless in this scenario. Only the McKays could get her out of here. She thought of Brigit, her aunts, and sisters at Fern Cottage and how they weren't expecting her for a month. It wouldn't be Lily who called to check on her.

Sara would, but how long would that take? Why do my only options suck?

Evelyn lifted her eyes to find Noro's level gaze on her, waiting for her reply.

"So how do I bend space-time?" she asked, settling on option one for the time being.

She listened as Noro related all the possible ways the Ancients had postulated to bend space-time. Every-thing he said sounded complicated and unnatural, so unlike her lessons with Brigit. Witches needed only spells, incantations, willpower, and intention to work magic. Fata needed something else, something Evelyn felt sure she didn't have.

Hours later Evelyn's head hit the cold metal of the examination table with a thud and a groan escaped her chapped lips. She was as close to bending space-time as she was to sprouting wings, though she thought she had noticed the air before her shimmer a bit. Once.

Her inability to pull off the impossible had become increasingly infuriating to Noro. While he had yet to cut or manhandle Evelyn, she sensed a punishment building as the fata's navy body grew darker and darker. By the time he called off their session he was bordering on black, a shade Evelyn had yet to see him achieve.

"This did not go as I had hoped, Eve. Not at all. You leave me with only one choice. A choice I was hoping to save as a reward for after you constructed the portal. But now . . . now I see your human shell limits you more than I thought. You must be stronger to negate that shell. My children will not like this one bit, but your weakness leaves me with little choice." Noro floated toward the door. "Felix!"

The door squeaked opened. Felix peered in and

smiled at the sight of Evelyn lying half naked on the table.

Her blood froze. *Please don't let him in here.*

Noro waved his arm and cold encased Evelyn's ankles as the shackles near her feet bound her to the examination table.

"Shut the door and lock it. Eve is weak but the wards on this room remain down. I will return," Noro instructed Felix.

Evelyn exhaled when the door closed, grateful for the barrier between her and Felix, even if it was keeping her from her freedom.

She took advantage of the fact that Noro had only bound her feet and combed her hands through her hair. She shuddered and willed herself to ignore the parts of her usual silky blonde hair that had been hacked or burned off. The gesture almost made her feel normal. And if she closed her eyes she could imagine herself elsewhere, like getting ready for a party or work. Too soon, the hard note of stilettos hitting stone cut through the silent basement dungeon and Evelyn's fantasy dissipated.

Noro is bringing Empusa? Evelyn had seen the vampire only twice since Empusa had tossed her in the basement. Both times the purpose of Empusa's visits seemed to be to remind Evelyn how helpless she was.

Empusa's favorite topic was what she and her brother would do to James and Sonja if Evelyn didn't help their cause.

But why does Noro need her help? He's more powerful than a vampire.

The door flew open, flooding the room with blinding beams of light. Evelyn squinted and saw Noro hadn't only brought Empusa. Amon stood behind his sister as did creatures holding the flashlights that blinded Evelyn.

Roman's tall, muscular stance was absent but that was no surprise. No one had even mentioned the incubus since the night Roman brought her to the manor. The closest thing to an interaction she'd had with Roman was his voice, arguing with Felix in Evelyn's dreams the night before.

Evelyn's fingernails dug into her palms. *I bet he's already crawled back home. Or is hiding out somewhere.*

The Acolytes filed in behind Noro to form a circle around Evelyn. It was only when her eyes had readjusted that she saw all the faces of those Noro had called to assist him.

Evelyn gasped.

Nora, Brigit's best friend, stood to Evelyn's right, smiling wickedly.

"Nora? What are you doing here? How did they—?"

But her questions were cut short by Noro, who threw his arms wide in a gesture of grandiosity. "Eve, darling, you've met Empusa and Amon, my children. Everyone here has vowed to assist me in our shared goal of bringing the fata to Earth. They are the inner circle of the Acolytes of Hecate, a group of revolutionaries with a vision for a better Earth."

Holy shit. Nora's the spy! An Acolyte of Hecate! It all makes so much sense! She hardly ever came by Fern Cottage after I broke into her head. She must have thought I saw something that would give her away or that I would peek inside her head. And she's the one who gave Lily up. What a bitch.

"Eve darling, each of these Acolytes are familiar with human anatomy, in case you have a negative reaction to our next step in unfolding your potential as humans have in the past. I'm sorry to put you at risk but I feel strongly that this is the only way."

What the hell was he talking about?

"Empusa, come."

The vampire moved to face her father, her mouth tight. Stiffly, Empusa extended her arm.

Evelyn watched in horror as Noro's right limb elongated and sharpened into a sword and swiped a large gash across Empusa's forearm.

Blood, black as night, poured from the cut.

Amon stepped forward to catch the blood in a juice glass before the wound could stitched itself together.

Oh, hell no. Evelyn fought her gag reflex. *He has got to be kidding.*

But she knew better than that. Noro didn't joke around, and as Amon approached her with the glass, she knew there was no getting out of it. Even if she vomited the blood back up Noro would continue cutting his children until she drank what he deemed enough.

"Take your juice, princess," Amon said, yanking Evelyn's torso up and presenting her with the glass.

"And you'd better not spill a drop," Empusa hissed, her green eyes narrowed. "My blood is more valuable than gold. Be grateful you get to drink it."

The pungent scent of metal and something far more ancient swirled below Evelyn's nostrils as she took the glass.

She looked down and a vision of Empusa swam up from the dark liquid. The vampire, looking gorgeous as she stalked a man down a cobblestone street in . . . Spain? Evelyn watched, her throat closing in on itself as Empusa pounced on the man and ripped into his jugular. The scene switched to Empusa running through a jungle with Amon, a panther between them. It changed again, to a nameless modern city with Empusa pressed against a wall by a man who ground his body into her.

"Hurry, witch," Empusa's French accent flared and she clenched her fists.

Evelyn's hands were shaking now. *What the hell just happened? Was that me? Or does her blood have magic?* Before she had time to get her thoughts straight an ice-cold hand pushed the glass to Evelyn's face and tipped it into her mouth.

The liquid crawled over her tongue like thick molasses. Evelyn imagined she could feel the lives of thousands of humans in the blood. She closed her eyes and drank faster. With her visual stimuli gone, her taste buds seemed to amplify. Underneath the undeniable tang of blood were hints of cinnamon, clove, sugar, and fennel.

Focus on those flavors, Evelyn thought tipping the glass back further.

"You better have enjoyed that, witch, because you won't be getting any more," Amon said, his face stony as the last drop disappeared down Evelyn's throat and he wrenched the empty glass from her hands.

Evelyn wasn't sure she'd enjoyed it, but she was sure about one thing. Vampires did not like giving up their blood. *I wonder . . . Oh!*

The temperature of the room shot up twenty degrees. Beads of sweat began forming on Evelyn's forehead and rolling down her face. Evelyn lowered herself back down onto the freezing table, desperate for relief from the sudden heat overtaking her.

"It's working. Bind her hands," Noro commanded and cold metal wrapped around Evelyn's wrists.

Evelyn's brows furrowed in confusion and she cranked her neck back to find Noro standing at the head of the table, his face millimeters from her own. *Why is he binding my hands now? Like I can do anything with all these people around . . . What the hell?!*

Her arms and legs began to tremble and strain against their bindings. The metal chains filled the dungeon with a clattering noise as they pulled and shook against the table. Evelyn's muscles popped out of her clothing in a way she'd never seen happen despite thousands of hours in the gym and astronomical personal trainer bills. Something in her chest fluttered wildly and she gasped.

Am I changing into a vampire? No, that can't be it, a vampire can't open a portal—otherwise why would they need me?

"Yesssss," Noro whispered. His eyes were lighter, more starry than Evelyn had ever seen them. "The blood, it's working, she is becoming stronger. This is what we've been missing the entire time. You are so beautiful, my love."

Bile climbed up Evelyn's throat at Noro's compliment.

Noro glanced around at the circle of faces that awaited his word. "No medical intervention will be necessary. The blood has taken well. We will allow Eve to rest and gain as much strength from Empusa's blood as she can. I will call you back when she is ready to open her first portal. Until then, leave us."

A dozen creatures filed out the door, only one of whom turned around. Nora, her eyes full of envy, glared at Evelyn.

What is she jealous about? That I drank vampire blood? That piece of scum can have it.

The door slammed shut and Noro turned his attention back to Evelyn. "If only you could see yourself, my love. One of your traitorous sisters has finally helped our cause. Your fata self has prevailed at last and it's glorious. You shine with the power you had thousands of years ago before you gave it all up for the greater good and met your end. Please know, my dearest Eve, your death was not in vain. We are still here. Myself and the seven other fata you brought over, one by one, working in the shadows for your father's mission. Recruiting creatures for our new realm. I know you likely wish to proceed right away now that you are released from your human bindings, but please forgive me for my selfishness. I wanted a few minutes alone with you before we perform the greatest work of our lives." His arms crept up to cradle Evelyn's face before moving down her body.

Bound by chains Evelyn could only watch, her mouth open in a silent scream, as Noro levitated off the ground to land his body on top of hers.

***

EVELYN DID NOT MOVE when they unshackled her.

She was numb. Dead inside from the hours Noro spent touching her, manipulating her body, pushing power into her for his own pleasure while assuring her that next time she would enjoy it more.

"Now that we have coupled, your fata instincts and capabilities are finally free. They will grow stronger as Empusa's blood strengthens you. Soon, my love, we shall be together like old times."

Evelyn shuddered as she recalled his words, his body like a cold gel, rushing over her, suffocating her as she lay bound to the table. Whenever Evelyn managed to get enough air into her lungs, she used it to cry out in protest, hoping Noro would listen to her pleas. From the moment he'd landed upon her Evelyn had closed her eyes, but it wasn't enough to ignore the sensation of

Noro's body on top of her, hollowing her out with a foreign magic.

When Evelyn showed no inclination to rise on her own, hands lifted her from the table.

"Noro wants her here," Empusa demanded, an evil smile on her lips as she pointed to the center of a circle of Acolytes.

A memory of another day flew through Evelyn's mind. The day she'd stood in the center of a different circle and called forth a long dead ancestor, surrounded and supported by family and love. That Samhain night their circle performed the first calling of an ancestor that had worked in over a hundred years. *How was that only a month ago? It feels like a lifetime.*

"How dare you look so miserable when you've been blessed?" A familiar voice whispered in Evelyn's ear.

Only then did she notice Nora was holding up her right side. A woman Evelyn would have grown up calling an auntie had circumstances been different studied Evelyn's face with equal parts awe and jealousy. Evelyn let her head fall, unwilling to spare energy for the woman she hated more than any other.

"Any Acolyte would give all their powers to be in your place." Nora's tone was accusatory, disbelieving. "A mistress of Noro himself. I'll never understand why he chose you when he could have so many."

A mistress of Noro? Oh, hell no. Evelyn would find a way to kill herself before anything of the sort happened again.

Nora and a scrawny wizard carried Evelyn to the center of the circle before removing their support.

Outwardly, Evelyn radiated strength. Empusa's blood had wrought undeniable changes in her body, yet she'd never felt more defeated. She considered allowing herself to collapse to the ground before deciding that was no good either.

All that would do is incite them.

So she stood, alone and shivering, in the middle of the room.

The Sisters of Salem

Lily

"What part of New York is this?" Lily asked, as the cab pulled to a stop next to a coffee shop.

The shop boasted dozens of men growing groomed beards or ironic twirled mustaches and women decorated head to toe with tattoos, donning all black ensembles. There was an old-school record player in the front window next to a mannequin with a unicorn head. It was the most hipster place she'd ever seen.

"Brooklyn," Selma said, a bemused smile on her face. "It is unrecognizable from when I was here. Younger, trendier, and much cleaner. That place is the same, though." She pointed to a dingy single family home wedged between two high-end condo complexes.

Yikes. I wonder why the owner didn't sell to a busi-

ness or contractor once their home became boxed in by those condo monstrosities.

Aoife paid the cabbie, and they exited following her aunt across the street. Lily slammed into her aunt's back when she stopped in front of the shabby house.

"Wait. This is the safe house?! But it looks like a shack!" It was impossible to keep the tone of incredulity from her voice. *It's even smaller than Fern Cottage and that's tight with four people living there and three constant visitors. This coven must be teensy.*

"One of the best I've been to," Aoife grinned at Lily's gaping mouth. "Only supernatural creatures that have been here previously can see the place as it is. Regular humans can't see it at all. Creatures who have not gained entry see the same rundown home you are seeing."

"It looks different to you two?" Lily asked.

"Ahh, yes, I forgot about that clever bit of sorcery!" Selma chuckled. "How hideous it looked the first time I saw it, all peeling paint, shattered glass, and rotting wood. I nearly turned away standing at the gate but I'm thankful I didn't. This is where my life changed for the better. The Sisters of Salem saved me at my lowest low. They took me in and protected me from myself and others. I will be forever grateful. Did you know that they are one of the few covens in the world to accept non-witch members? Now that I am back and well, I may have to inquire."

Lily cringed as Aoife pushed open the rusty, screechy wrought iron gate. They waited in the yard and Lily tried her best to avoid peeking in the welcoming condo windows next door, opting instead to watch the variety of people traipsing down the sidewalk.

"This city and it's fecking traffic," Gwenn grumbled as the rest of their group climbed the stairs to join them. "I'll be happy to be in the quiet of the safe house."

Quiet? With all this noise on the streets? Yea right, those walls look like they'd be paper thin.

Aoife rapped on the door and they waited as an ambulance and five police vehicles drove by, sirens blaring.

They waited so long that Lily was about to ask if the Sisters of Salem were in fact expecting them when the door cracked open. Lily peered around Aoife.

No one was there.

"Good day to you, Sisters. We've been waiting for you. Especially you, Gingy. Please, come in," a high-pitched, musical voice rang out of the nothingness.

Aoife chuckled, her eyes firmly on the ground before her. "Aye, good to see you, too, Griselda. How I've missed you."

Lily followed Aoife's gaze and sucked in her breath.

A woman, no more than three feet tall, stood holding the door. Griselda had the general shape of a human yet Lily found she could not place her in any of the few supernatural categories she knew.

Griselda's long, needle-like nose protruded from a thick, heavyset skull. Her ears, pointed at the tips and bottoms, stuck out inches from her face and reminded Lily of an elf. Griselda turned at Lily's intake of air and Lily averted her eyes.

Griselda sniggered. "I see one of your young ones is green. You can ask girl. I won't take offense."

Lily's face burned, "I—I'm sorry, I've never . . ."

"You've never seen another magical creature like me, am I right? Well, you won't be finding too many that look like me anyhow. Dad was a leprechaun and Ma was an elf. I'm one of a kind."

"To be fair, Griselda," Brigit said patting Lily on the shoulder and smiling down at the tiny woman, "Lily hasn't met many creatures other than witches yet. She's seen vampires, and a few daemons, though I didn't have the luxury of standing around and pointing them out at the time. Might we get moving along? We're in a bit of a hurry to speak with Jane and your council."

Griselda let out a loud bark of laughter, "Damn vamps, how can anyone go through life not seeing one? I wish I'd been so lucky." With that she whirled about and led them down a long hallway lined with heavy, dark wood doors.

Lily let her eyes wander, glad to have Griselda's prickly attention off her. *It looks like a wreck outside, but inside it's a legit mansion.*

The aroma of leather, wood polish, and baked bread filled the air, subverting her assumptions further. Lily shook her head in disbelief as they passed doors adorned with crystal doorknobs, chandeliers dripping with crystals that gave off a prismatic effect like a muted disco ball, and gold framed portraits that spoke of wealth and a respect for the past.

"They're the coven leaders dating back to the time of the Sisters of Salem's inception. Right after that insane witch hunt in Salem. Most of the real witches in Salem saved themselves before the hunt gained steam. They moved south and settled here. Been here in this very house since 1695," Griselda said, catching Lily's questioning gaze as she stopped before a door.

"In this house? But why haven't you moved? Hasn't the neighborhood changed a lot?" Lily asked thinking back to Selma's earlier remark.

A grin grew on Griselda's wide face, "Everything changes. We like the neighborhood; it keeps us central and is convenient for our members. I'll admit the house has undergone a few magical remodels and expansions to accommodate our growing numbers and visitors, but other than that this house is perfect. Quiet in here, isn't it?"

Lily cocked her head. Not a single honking horn or siren met her ears.

"Silencing charm," Griselda said. "You get good at those in the city. And you can bet we alter the scenery outside our windows. There's a rotation of landscapes depending on who's around that day. I prefer the Japanese gardens myself, but Toshi hasn't been by to indulge me in months." Griselda glared at Lily as if she had been responsible for keeping Toshi, whoever he was, busy.

Lily held up her hands as if to say 'whoa, you got the wrong girl.'

Griselda turned back around with a snort. "In the end, contractors paid us well to develop the land on either side of the house. The coven couldn't say no but you're right to think it would have been awful to look at those hideous condos every day." Griselda paused before a door and knocked.

The door opened and a tall, beautiful Indian woman wearing an ornate orange sari stood before them.

"Selma," the woman exclaimed peering into the hall with her enormous brown eyes and spotting the petite siren in the middle of the group. A smile spread across the woman's face, raising her cheekbones to unbeliev-able heights.

Selma shimmied to the front of the line and threw herself at the woman. "Shefali! Girl, it's been way too long!"

"Indeed it has, sister. We have a lot of catching up to do," Shefali said, putting an arm around Selma's shoulders and waving for the rest to follow her through the door.

The room Shefali led them into was larger than the entire outside of the house appeared. Fifty feet wide with fifteen-foot ceilings, the considerable wall space was covered from top to bottom with books of all shapes and sizes. An antique globe dominated the center of the room, surrounded by plush brown leather couches and chairs. A fire burned in a magnificent marble fireplace opposite the door, around which a delegation of seven stood.

"Selma!" two women who looked like sisters cried and rushed over to hug Selma.

Lily held back and watched as Brigit spoke hurriedly to a regal-looking woman with dark thin braids peeking out of a bright head wrap. Aoife, Mary, and Gwenn knelt to hug a tiny creature with a booming voice while Annika and Rena shook hands with a wizened old man who remained seated near the fire.

"It still feels like we know nothing about this world, doesn't it?" Sara asked, sidling up to Lily.

Lily watched the interactions in the room, conversations flowing, partners changing, hugs exchanged, and hands shook. "I understand that Mom wanted to start us with basic magic and learning how to defend ourselves. Let's be honest, that part alone took forever. But I can't help thinking if we knew more people, had more exposure to other creatures, this would be easier."

"Lil! Sara! Could you come over here?" Rena called from across the room. "I have someone who wants to meet the two of you."

The old man watched their approach with such intensity that Lily looked away, discomforted by his stare. *Who is this guy?* It was only when she stood before him that she felt safe enough to look him in the eye.

He was older than she'd guessed from across the room. At least in his nineties, and while his body appeared frail, his eyes shone with all the vitality of youth. A futuristic looking wheelchair sat beside the old man along with a pile of books. Peeking at the spines Lily saw she recognized none of them. From the titles she assumed they were all books on history and magic.

"Girls, this is Alistair Levi, an old friend of Terramar commune and one of the Sisters of Salem's most prestigious members."

"Don't say that too loud, Rena. Elections are coming up and we wouldn't want Jane to think an incubus is trying to take her spot as high priest, now would we? That would break the all-female winning streak," Alistair chuckled good-naturedly, his entire body shaking from the effort.

"Hello, Mr. Levi. I'm Sara McKinney. Are coven leaders always women, then? I've never heard of a man leading a coven. Granted, I haven't met with many covens, but it seems the witching world is the reverse of the rest of the world."

Lily stifled a laugh as Mr. Levi's eyes grew wide.

"Well. Well. I like you. Not afraid to question the status quo, are you? If you're Sara, you must be Lily. It's good to meet both of you. And as for your question, Sara, the answer is no. Coven leaders are not always women, but they are usually witches or wizards, which I am not."

Sara nodded. "Is that because there are more women witches, Mr. Levi? We rarely ever meet men. Maybe it's who our family knows but I don't think so."

"Please call me Alistair." His gray-blue eyes twinkled as he grinned. "As for the witches and wizards, there are about equal number born. The real catch is that women tend to take to magic more. Perhaps it is a stronger calling in them, or perhaps it is the way our societies value that a man be level headed and go work somewhere traditional like a law firm or factory. Whatever the case, wizards ignore the magic in their blood often." Alistair gave a great sigh.

"For other types of creatures, such as werewolves, that would be impossible. The werewolf population has a more equal gender split. Sometimes a wizard's ignorance or refusal to be what he was born to be results in anger issues, but more commonly they simply fail to become the great man they dreamt of being. Women find it harder to ignore their magic, and if they do the consequences are dire. They often become depressed, shells of what they could be. It is a sad thing to see either gender ignore their power, for one is witnessing a life half lived."

Lily wondered if that would have been her, living her life half-way, had Brigit never asked to meet her.

"You're right to think so," Alistair said, turning to Lily. "From what I can read of you, the both of you would have plunged into a deep depression."

Lily reinforced her mind barriers. *Travel is making me careless.*

"It's not that. Your mind barriers are sufficient. Excellent even." Alistair paused to take a sip of water, "Like I said, I'm an incubus, dear girl. It's one of my greatest powers to get inside a woman's mind and give her what she desires. I'm sorry to say it, but as I was just telling Rena I fear you may be here because of me. You see, I taught Roman Simons all I know about being an incubus."

Rena nodded and put her hand on the old man's shoulder. "I'm glad you're here, Alistair. Lil, Sara, will you help get everyone's attention so Alistair only has to tell his story once?"

"As soon as Jane mentioned you were arriving because your daughter—a water witch and ceremens with siren magic—was missing, I had an inkling Roman might be involved. Not many creatures could abduct a ceremens and siren and get away with it, strong incubi being one of the exceptions. I'd say there are only two incubi on this continent strong enough to charm such a woman: Roman and myself." The incubus pointed to himself for emphasis.

"It is why Stephen Simons, Roman's father and an incubus, approached me to be the boy's tutor when he started showing the sway he held over the women in their town. I agreed and instructed Roman for many years. Our lessons began well before puberty and may have saved Roman from becoming a complete monster.

Puberty is difficult for humans. If you're an incubus striving for morality, it is torture. And that is what I sought to teach Roman: how to control himself and be moral when he must hunt. Never to take too much of the human's essence, or to stalk, and never, ever to assault. I can say with all confidences in the man that I am sure he is still this way."

"But how can you be so sure, Alistair?" Brigit asked, looking skeptical. "By all accounts Roman helped take my daughter, and her siren capabilities are as strong as a full-blooded siren."

"Roman has done wrong, I make no qualms with you about that, but I am sure he did not want to. You see, I received news months ago that the Simons family had fallen into a bit of trouble. Stephen, once a moral incubus, had succumbed to the temptations our kind always fights. He became obsessed with a powerful woman from a Nashville dynasty who sought vengeance as soon as she came to her senses. The woman turned the whole city against the Simons family. She labeled Stephen a criminal, and rightly so. Stephen had put her in his thrall, manipulated her mind, used his powers to gain her consent falsely, and raped her."

"That incubus deserved his time in jail," Shefali said, her lips pursed and arms crossed over her sari. "It's selfish creatures like Stephen who break the rules and overextend their powers that put us all at risk."

"I'm not defending Stephen, only telling Roman's story." Alistair lifted his hands in mock surrender. "Roman is Stephen's son and couldn't bear seeing his father rot away in jail. Even worse, Roman thought Stephen might get the death sentence, a suggestion the woman Stephen seduced threw into the legal ring every chance she got. Roman couldn't bear to see his father killed or what little money and reputation the family had left drained. So he sought assistance from creatures known for their cunning and power over humans: vampires."

"Goddam vamps sticking their noses in others' business," Griselda grumbled from her spot near the fireplace.

Alistair gave Griselda a small smile. "The vampires Roman went to make a practice of it. It was Amon whom Roman chose to approach. Why the boy asked him instead of a less notorious vampire, I'll never understand. Their arrangement involved the woman becoming enthralled by a vampire, recanting her accusation, and dropping the charges. This, of course, ruined the woman's reputation but did wonders for the Simonses' business. Empusa and Amon could not have calculated that beforehand. However, when it became clear the Simonses' company was now a top-tier organization, they undoubtedly made the connection to Locksley Enterprises. A business relationship as a ruse to get a powerful incubus before an unsuspecting siren. They'd have to be idiots not to call in the favor."

Alistair turned to Brigit. "I've never met your daughter, but I have read several interviews she's granted, and as an incubus I'm well versed in reading between the lines of what women say. I'd be shocked if Evelyn stooped to using her powers on Roman. Her family's business ethics are far too strong and *that* was likely her downfall. That and not knowing the tells of being in an incubus snare."

"No doubt you are right." Mary twirled her blonde hair nervously. "We didn't often have other creatures at the cottage when the girls were training. They've only been with us four months and we've focused on witches' magic and basic defensive spells. It's a failing on our part as their teachers, one we will have to remedy quite soon. You say Roman is a good person—do you think he's remorseful for what he's done?"

The old man cocked his head. "I have no doubt about that. I met with the boy for lunch not two weeks ago. He couldn't stop talking about the girl he was seeing. I'd say Roman has fallen for Evelyn. I'm sure he saw no way out of helping with her abduction. His family was at stake and we all know how vampires, Empusa and Amon in particular, can be when you are in their debt. But I believe, if we make contact, Roman will help get Evelyn out."

"Well, it's something," Mary replied grimly.

The same regal woman with the head wrap Brigit had been speaking to earlier stepped forward, her full lips pulled tight.

"Brigit, because of your family's reputation, we have allowed you into our coven headquarters without question. Now as high priestess I must ask: Why have we never heard of your daughters before, and why are they popping up now? Why have Empusa and Amon schemed to take one? It is clear these two have raw power, perhaps more than anyone in this room." The woman gestured to Sara and Lily, eyes roving over their bodies before they locked on Brigit's once more.

"It seems the McKay clan is going to ask the New York community to fight for you, are you not? To fight creatures known to be dangerous. Tell us why we should risk our lives for a cause we have little knowledge of, and for a family that has a reputation for keeping secrets." The woman quirked a brow. "We are intelligent enough to infer this is not only an abduction. There is something more going on here. As high priestess of the Sisters of Salem, I am formally requesting you reveal some of your secrets. If my coven is to fight with you, we deserve to be told the truth."

Everyone in the room held their breath, waiting for Brigit's reply.

"While I respect your opinion, Jane, I must ask for a room where my family and I can discuss this in private. I want to make sure my inclinations are amenable to everyone."

"I'll show you across the hall," Jane said, as if she'd anticipated the move.

The McKay women, including Lily and Sara, fell into step beside Brigit, who glanced back when they reached the door. "Aren't you coming, Rena, Annika, and Selma?"

THE ROOM across the hall was as large as the library, a feat that judging by the outside of the house should have been impossible. It was a meeting room, boasting a twenty-person table surrounded by heavy, high-backed chairs and a large fireplace. A wall of photographs depicting groups of people from different eras staring back at her from around the same paper-strewn table confirmed Lily's suspicions.

"Well, this is official," Brigit said claiming the head

of the table. Her lips pursed with amusement as she lifted a gavel for inspection before tapping it on the table.

"I say we tell them, but only the bare bones of it," Aoife launched into the meeting without preamble.

"Thought you'd say that," Brigit nodded, "It's in our witches' blood to keep our secrets, this family more than most. And it certainly would be quicker. Every minute that passes is another where Evelyn is in danger. Now, anyone else have an opinion?" She leaned back in her chair, opening the floor.

The room exploded with voices.

Lily listened as everyone, excluding Sara, Brigit, and herself, attempted to talk over each other.

The consensus seemed split down the middle. Half wanted to tell the Sisters of Salem everything. The other half opted for a limited rendition—enough to get them on their side without revealing the true, dire nature of their situation. Each person had a point, and each was looking out for the triplets' best interests. After a few minutes of debate, Brigit tapped the gavel onto the table, bringing the group to silence.

"I get the feeling that we are evenly split." Brigit twirled the gavel in her hand. "Half of us want to protect our secret, while the other half want to be open. We don't have much time for debate. We need to get the

Sisters of Salem on our side and mobilize a force quickly to save Evelyn, but I noticed two important voices missing from the fray. I would like to withhold my own opinion until they give us theirs. Lily? Sara?"

The sisters glanced at each other. As their eyes met, Lily was sure they were on the same page. She bowed to Sara, her younger, far more articulate sister, granting her the lead.

Sara stood and all eyes latched onto her. "I heard a lot of what you all said and can't argue with most of it. There's danger in outing ourselves, there's no doubt about that. And if these last few weeks have shown me anything it's that trust is a fickle thing," her eyes flicked to Lily and Lily smiled to assure her there were no hard feelings. Sara stood taller.

"But the one thing I know for sure, and I think Lily agrees, is that we can trust everyone in this room above all others. Thank you for always making our safety your top priority. It's an honor." She paused and bit her lip.

Lily, sensing her sister's hesitation, reached for Sara's hand and squeezed it. *I'm with you. I want this, too.* She lifted a small corner of her mind barriers and pushed the thought toward Sara.

Sara squeezed back, straightened her shoulders, and continued. "That being said, we don't want to keep our secret any longer. We need to learn more, from as many people as possible, and that can't happen if no one is allowed to know about us and what we're meant to do. If we don't succeed in our mission, there will be another altercation. It seems our enemies, the Acolytes of Hecate, have no issue with recruiting people, whether through force or a promise they tell their followers of greater power to come under a new realm. We need help, too, but we should be better than our enemies. We should be honest with those who help us. Give them the choice to fight for the future of our planet. *Ask* if they want to help us instead of demand it. We're in New York with a global platform outside the front door. Let's not waste it."

Lily stared around the table, her heart beating hard and fast in her chest. It wasn't until she turned to Brigit, the gavel spinning between her fingers and a smile split her face, that she relaxed.

"I was hoping you would say that. As I always say, magic is about choice and intention. So is life. I always wanted to leave the decision up to you, and you're more than ready to make it. I think you've made a fine choice. You won't be safe, and you will attract a degree of celebrity, but I agree we will need help in the battles to come, and many more creatures than just witches to win this war. That being said, there's a lot to do and we should get to it. Is everyone ready to spread the word?"

The Traveler
Evelyn

Noro entered the dungeon with Amon.

Evelyn whimpered and Empusa glared at her.

Not again. Evelyn's eyes latched onto the cup and blade in Amon's hands as the pair approached her. Noro looked jubilant and a shade lighter than his typical dark navy hue. In contrast, Amon was a walking storm.

"Eve, my love. I hope I find you restored after our morning session? I believe I've allotted enough time for your transformation? For your basest human parts, Empusa's blood would have trouble penetrating to become stronger? Shall we test my theory and see if you are capable of opening a portal?" Evelyn flinched as Noro caressed her cheek.

Gasps of arousal arose from the crowd. It was all Evelyn could do not to vomit.

"Dimia will be waiting for a portal to open at The Crystal Palace. I know you have not seen it, but the Ancients assure me that knowing the name of the place is enough. The part of your soul that clings to your fata ancestry should hone in on your ancestral planet once you've begun the process." Noro gazed at her with his round, bottomless fata eyes.

She had to work to suppress a shudder.

"First, you must open the portal here by bending the surrounding space-time," Noro continued. "Then, you will project your soul and the name of the place you wish to visit into the portal. Trust in the ancient fata wisdom persisting within you and you will find it. Hold the portal open for as long as you can but certainly until Dimia comes through."

Right. Evelyn inhaled and closed her eyes briefly. "And how, if this even works, will I know which one Dimia is?"

"His color is a golden opalescence. I remember it well despite all my years on Earth. It is a glorious color."

"And what if I still can't do it?" Evelyn asked, raising her chin in the most overt gesture of defiance she dared.

A hiss arose from the crowd.

Noro floated closer until his dark face was only inches from Evelyn.

It took all she could not to jump back and scream.

Instead, she straightened up and stared into his eyes, unwilling to show him how much he terrified her. As she searched Noro's eyes, familiar white dots popped into the dark, black recesses in his face. Evelyn watched as the beams of light twisted and rotated through the space in Noro's head, like constellations in the night sky. *I never noticed the stars moved before. How did I miss that?*

Noro's mouth opened wide and completely round into a fata smile. He moved to whisper in Evelyn's ear. "My eyes contain a map of all the planets my pneuma visited to find this one. I do not always reveal them, but they have traveled with me for thousands of years. All that work. All the ridicule I endured from fata who did not understand my gift. The ones who thought being born with only one talent made me less of a fata. I've waited *years* to show them how strong I've become thanks to Earth's magic. I endured millennia of ridicule on my home planet just to please my king. You understood this once as you sought to please him, too." Noro darkened as he relived his past.

Evelyn leaned back as far as she could.

"I will not travel again to find a new planet. You *will* open this portal, Eve. Perhaps not today, it is all too likely that you will need a few more *lessons*. However, I urge you to learn, for no matter how much I love you, neither Dimia nor I will remain patient for forever. Your actions have the power to influence many you love. Keep that in mind."

Evelyn hated herself for believing him. The only negotiations she could think of sounded weak, so unlike her typical strong-armed deals. The scales of power were tipped significantly out of her favor for the first time in her life.

Maybe if I let a few fata through I can negotiate my way out of this dungeon and then find a way to escape? Once I reunite with my family I'm sure we could deal with a few fata.

"Now then," Noro turned, flung his arms out wide and raised his voice so all could hear, "Witches."

Half of the circle stepped forward.

Evelyn studied the woman to her right and wondered what she was. If Empusa and Amon were any indication, this hunch-backed and pock-faced woman was not a vampire.

She sighed. *Even if I escape, I'll have to fight off witches, vampires, and who knows what else? I wish we'd spent more time learning about the greater magical world.* Even as she thought the words, she knew they were unfair.

Brigit and her aunts had worked them nearly to death, cramming twenty-one years of magical education and self-defense into three months. The next logical step would have been a crash course in creatures, especially after Alexandria.

Why didn't I go back? None of this would have happened . . .

"Lift the enchantments on the manor," Noro instructed.

Evelyn's eyes widened and she blinked.

"The entire manor, Master?" a man with a long white beard asked.

"That was my order."

"But what if she escapes?"

"How do you expect Eve to create a portal from this house, through space, and to the motherland, if her magic is bound to this room?" Noro's voice boomed in the cavernous space. "She shall be under my watch. Now do as I command, half-breed!"

The man cringed and hunched his shoulders like a beaten dog.

Half-breed, is it? How did Noro get these people to follow him if he treats them this way?

A sea of words flew up around her as witches undid their spells. Most used wands, whereas Nora and a couple others performed magic with only their hands, as the McKays did. Evelyn listened carefully, and though she did not understand everything, she found she recognized about half. *Good, if I can just remember how to counter all of those spells then I have a chance at escape later.*

"It is done, Master," Nora's tone was eager to please.

Noro nodded at her, and she blushed.

Evelyn rolled her eyes. *Oh, how disgusting.*

"My dearest Eve, it is time to do as we discussed earlier. Remember, you must bend space-time in on itself. To do so will take a true hollowing of yourself. Do not fear for your own well-being. I have Amon waiting to donate blood. His blood, a derivative of my own, powerful, immortal essence, will keep you alive. Give this everything you have. I shall know if you do not."

Well crap. Evelyn racked her brain. How Noro wanted her to do something she'd never done, that *no witch* had ever done, was beyond her. She stood in the middle of the circle with two dozen pairs of probing eyes on her. Evelyn shuddered and closed her eyes.

Bending space-time in on itself, Evelyn thought, hoping that simply thinking the words enough would bring an epiphany. *Space time, bending, hollowing herself, hedgecrossing . . . what does it all mean?* She huffed a breath of air through her nose.

Start with baby steps. Maybe astral travel will work this time. It can't be any worse than all that weird fata magic shit.

Expecting nothing to happen as it had every other time, she thought the spell for astral travel. *Caeliter.*

Her magic electrified her fingertips and Evelyn's lips curved up. Then she jumped a foot high as something thumped hard against her chest.

"A half-hearted attempt," Nora sneered. "She's only using the spell we taught her. If astral travel was the answer, the fata would have been here long ago."

Evelyn scowled and pushed Nora from her mind. She hadn't even noticed the witch was there, but then Nora had always been a skilled sneak.

Once Evelyn was alone in her mind once more she considered the situation. *It may have been half-hearted, but something actually happened,* Evelyn marveled. *Wait, doesn't Aoife always lie down when she travels? I should look like I'm making every possible effort.*

"I need to lie down," Evelyn said staring into Noro's black eyes and ignoring the guffaws and snickers that arose from his minions.

Noro nodded, and the sniggers ceased.

Evelyn lowered herself to the floor, trying not to think of the kitten that had died there. *Concentrate, Evelyn, concentrate. You'll have even less room to negotiate if you don't give him something.*

Closing her eyes, Evelyn envisioned her soul floating above her body. A vague feeling of déjà vu came over her, as if somehow, somewhere, part of her had done this before.

"Caeliter," she whispered.

She gasped as something within her pushed hard against the confines of her skin and a sapphire blue light burst out of her hands to hover above her. Her heart raced in her chest. *Did it work? Is that my soul? But Aoife said she could never think inside her body without her soul. Why is it just floating there?*

The blue light shimmered high above her but made no move to go further.

Maybe it needs instructions. You're supposed to go to The Crystal Palace, Evelyn pushed the thought out.

Suddenly, the blue light formed arms that reached out toward Evelyn.

Evelyn blinked.

Noro swooped down close to her. He too seemed unable to take his eyes off the blue light. "Tell her where she must go and give her a piece of you so she can find her way back."

Give the freaking light a piece of me? Like a toenail?

The blue light shook from side to side, and her stubby arms touched the top of her.

You want a piece of my head?

The sapphire light moved up and down.

That thing just wants me to toss a piece of my . . . Oh! A memory of Evelyn's first ceremens lesson surfaced.

"Toss your mind out like a fishing line and wait for it to catch on another's mind," Morgane, their crazy octogenarian teacher, had instructed months ago.

Evelyn's heart seized as she realized what she had to do. *I have to separate my mind like Aoife does. My soul is going to catch it and take it with her through space. I have to give her instructions when I toss it. Well, this should be interesting.*

Before Evelyn could talk herself out of it, she closed her eyes. She imagined herself wrapping up the words "The Crystal Palace" in paper so they stayed together and threw the words toward the shimmering light, attached to a bit of her mind.

And then, Evelyn saw massive rocks hurling past her in her mind's eye. She dodged and whirled around them, gleeful for the familiar feeling freedom of flight. Turning, she saw a circle with rings around it and waved.

Evelyn sucked in a breath and gripped the floor. Sweat began pouring from her forehead. *I like flying? No, not me . . . My soul likes flying. And was that freaking Saturn?*

She kept her eyes closed for fear of losing sight of

what she was seeing in the portion of her mind her soul carried with it. Or worse, losing her soul.

Noro moved closer to Evelyn. "It's working," he whispered, millimeters from her ear so that only she could hear. "You're no longer part fata. I sense only your witch's soul still inside you. Your pneuma, your pure fata soul hidden beneath the mire of human flesh and blood, is seeking its home."

MY PNEUMA! Holy hell that's what he was always gabbing on about, saying I was part fata. So I have a pneuma—a freaking fata soul living inside me—and now it's in outer space. My witch soul is still with me so I can think and feel the room I'm in. Despite the insanity of this idea, Evelyn forced her mind to quiet so she could focus on following her pneuma's procession through space.

It was the strangest sensation. Sensing the rough, uneven stone against her flesh *and* a trickle of stardust that brushed her pneuma's cheeks at the same time. Through her pneuma's eyes, Evelyn moved faster than she ever had bodily, covering thousands of miles in seconds. She looked up in time to see Pluto zoom by. In no more than a minute she was farther than any man had ever traveled, in a different galaxy, or as far as she knew, none at all.

Evelyn felt a faint pressure on her chest as her

pneuma pulled closer the words Evelyn had wrapped up and tossed to her. Her pneuma glanced at the package against her chest and Evelyn saw that what she had envisioned as a plain brown paper package containing the words "The Crystal Palace" was actually a glowing silver ball. Evelyn examined the ball through her pneuma's eyes and realized the ball was growing larger the farther her pneuma flew. *What the hell?*

As if she'd heard Evelyn's question, her pneuma glanced behind her and Evelyn's heart stopped. A string, glittering with the brilliance of a thousand stars, was attached to the ball. It was like a ball of yarn except as the string lengthened behind her pneuma, the ball grew larger, not smaller. Evelyn's mouth fell open as she witnessed the sparkling string opening into a void in space as it trailed her shimmering blue pneuma.

Holy shit. That string is space-time. My pneuma is pulling space-time in on itself and winding it into the package of words I gave her as she flies! This is insane! A sudden stab of fear overcame her excitement. *I hope she can make it back. Will I go crazy if she doesn't? She has a portion of my mind.*

Evelyn gripped the ground beneath her so that her nails broke against the stone as her pneuma nearly collided with an asteroid and brought her attention back to the moment.

Now I know how Aoife felt when she had to split her consciousness to show us our birth. It's enough to drive a person mad, having two minds, two inputs of sensation, all at once. She let out an exhale and inhaled slowly, trying to calm her racing heart. A constricted stream of air passed through her nostrils and into her lungs. Breathing was growing more difficult the further her pneuma traveled from her body.

"There it is!" Noro shrieked in glee.

The surrounding witches gasped and shuffled their feet in excitement.

Evelyn's eyes popped open.

A hole, blacker than the blackest black and no larger than a doughnut, hovered at the end of her feet in the dark cellar room.

"Make it larger," Noro instructed.

But Evelyn no longer needed Noro's instruction. Her pneuma was in charge now.

Her pneuma flew faster, past stunning celestial bodies Evelyn could not name and entire fields of asteroids. Evelyn's human eyes remained trained on the black hole before her, now the size of a kiddie pool. *How big will it get? Is the basement large enough to accommodate it?* A vision of Noro, Empusa, Amon, and Nora disappearing through the black hole swam up, and she nearly smiled. *Well, that wouldn't be so bad.*

And then, a red planet was upon her in her mind's eye, only seconds away. An alien spring of happiness arose in Evelyn. Her pneuma was celebrating, far away in space.

She's found Hecate.

Dark red mountains and forests came into focus through her pneuma's eyes. It was a strangely familiar and totally alien sight. Her pneuma raced through the bulbous trees with square leaves the size of car windshields and flew over a canyon hundreds of miles wide.

Evelyn watched as if on a split screen, her pneuma shooting through a wooded area and the hole in the basement growing ever larger and closer to Evelyn's feet. *I hope she finds The Crystal Palace soon. I don't think I'll survive slipping into that hole after her.*

A second later a glittering brilliance filled the dark basement, blinding everyone in it.

Evelyn blinked rapidly and focused on her labored inhales and exhales as she stared into the black hole in amazement. There in the center of the black hole was a palace, shining bright in the distance and growing larger with every second.

In no time at all her pneuma was at the palace gates and up the steps. For the first time since leaving Earth, her pneuma paused.

A wheezy gasp escaped Evelyn's lips. The Crystal

Palace was the most beautiful place she had ever seen, honed of diamond-like stones with smaller colored gems resembling rubies, emeralds, and sapphires bordering the large windows and doors. Light shone through the stones creating a prismatic rainbow effect on every surface. Before she had time to take it all in, Evelyn was on the move once more as her pneuma opened the heavy palace door and zoomed down the hallway, slower than she flew in space, but still fast.

Evelyn was grateful for her pneuma's speed. As much as she would have liked to stare at the palace in wonder, she was fighting for every breath she took. *Is my pneuma sensitive to what I feel? Or is she just happy to be home and rushing? What the—holy hell!* Evelyn's gut dropped to her feet as two large doors at the end of a long hallway flew open at her pneuma's approach.

Thousands of fata floated before her.

THE FATA in the crowd murmured in an unintelligible language as they caught sight of Evelyn's pneuma. Fata parted, creating an aisle for her to pass. Evelyn's pneuma locked eyes with a fuchsia fata whose gaze flowed down her pneuma's sapphire body to the blackness, the thread of space-time, that trailed Evelyn's pneuma like a never-ending blanket. The fuchsia fata met Evelyn's pneuma's eyes once more and Evelyn thought it looked hesitant, scared even.

Dimia was easy to spot due to his positioning in the room, though he looked nothing like Noro had described. Flat white, with a faint shimmer of gold around his dark eyes, he resembled a ghost well past his prime. The fata king's eyes locked on Evelyn's brilliant sapphire pneuma and he rose from his throne.

"Come, daughter," Dimia instructed.

Dimia speaks English? Well, I guess Noro has been on Earth long enough to teach him . . .

Evelyn's pneuma floated forward, clutching the words that led her here now wrapped in layers of glittering strings of space-time.

"I always knew you would come. My most loyal daughter. I see the portal trails behind you. Will you not open it and let your people join you? We have waited a long time."

Evelyn closed her eyes, trying to block out the whispers of onlookers and concentrate on her obstructed breathing. Noro's panting was particularly distracting.

Why is he panting? He doesn't even breathe, Evelyn wondered with a stab of envy over Noro's heavy breaths.

"Set your parcel down," Dimia instructed, gesturing to the ball and string Evelyn's pneuma carried.

Her pneuma set the ball of words wrapped in space-time upon the glittering floor. The words and string her pneuma had carried for light-years opened into a tunnel, a portal connecting Hecate and Earth.

The instant the portal opened on Hecate, Evelyn let out a blood-curdling scream, expelling what little air was left in her lungs. Her body pulled into a tight ball. Her head pounded in agony. *No. NO!* Evelyn attempted to draw in a breath and received only a small, merciful sip.

She yearned for her pneuma and her bit of missing mind almost as much as air. The act of her pneuma setting down her bundle of words and opening the portal had made one thing clear. The bit of her mind Evelyn had tossed out and the words her pneuma carried through space were still attached to each other. Both now rested on the floor of a palace in Hecate. Evelyn's mind was now on two planets at once and dangerously close to snapping.

She needs to pick the package back up. We need to be touching through my mind or else my mind will break, Evelyn realized with terror.

Come back, Evelyn commanded.

But, as Evelyn saw through the black hole, her pneuma had eyes only for Dimia, who was making sweeping proclamations a galaxy away. "This is the moment we have been waiting for, dear subjects. Follow me to our new home, Earth! A home where we will once again become powerful." With that, Dimia leapt into the void.

Now! He's through. Pick it up now! Come back! Evelyn shouted, hoping the half of her mind laying on the floor of the Crystal Palace would project her thought to her pneuma, as a sensation of a thousand knives plunging into her skull washed over her.

This time, her pneuma looked around as if bewildered.

A rainbow of fata approached the void and two dozen followed their king without ceremony.

Pick up the words and leave. Or I'll die. You won't have a body to come back to. Only as Evelyn said the words did she register the choppiness of the voice in her head and how her vision had dimmed.

Her entire body trembled against the cold stone as Evelyn drew in another tiny sip of air. She would pass out from lack of oxygen soon if something didn't change. Her eyes trained on the black portal before her and an idea appeared from its depths. She knew it might cause her to pass out and likely die right then and there if she used too much magical energy. *But it's my best hope. I have to get her attention.*

Using only as much magic as she dared, Evelyn called forth a stream of air and molded it into a ball the size of a golf ball above her prone body. She cupped the ball in her shaking hands and brought it to her lips.

"Come back. I'm dying," she whispered into the ball.

And then, she hurled the ball through the portal.

Her arm hit the ground with a thunk and Evelyn lay there, waiting, hoping, sure if the ball didn't get through in time or her pneuma came back too slowly, those would be her last words.

A small reassurance came seconds later when Evelyn heard her own voice trumpet forth, out of the black portal on Hecate and vibrate off the palace's jeweled walls. The crowd of fata around her pneuma paused and stared down at the black hole in wonder.

Evelyn waited, breath tight in her chest to see what her pneuma would do. *Come on, pick it up and leave!*

A heartbeat later Evelyn forced out an exhale as her pneuma sprang into action, picking up the word bundle and string and disappearing the way she came.

The portal followed, sealing itself in her pneuma's wake.

Shouts in an alien tongue arose as a stampede of fata followed Evelyn's pneuma through the halls and out the doors. But they were weak from millennia of living on a dying planet, and Evelyn's pneuma escaped them with ease, clutching her package of words to her body as she fled.

The sapphire pneuma flew at a dizzying pace over mountains and canyons as she retraced her exact path and launched herself back into space. She flew without marvel or awe past planets humans had yet to discover, racing back home to where Evelyn's body lay.

Vaguely, Evelyn felt the ghostly impression of the package her pneuma clutched grow smaller as the string of space-time unraveled and the portal closed in her pneuma's wake.

On Earth, green, yellow, and purple spots popped into being before the gaping blackness of the portal in the basement—a blackness that was shrinking with every mile Evelyn's pneuma flew through space. *Maybe if she hurries it will trap the king in there and he'll never be able to get out. This can all end here.*

Not a second later Evelyn's heart stopped as a faint glimmer of gold emerged from the shrinking darkness and stole what remained of her breath.

Plans and Pancakes
Lily

Lily slumped in her chair. Her brain felt sluggish, taken over by a fog, and they weren't even close to done. By the time they had finished explaining the triplets' strange birth, the prophecy, Hypatia's reproduction of Seraphina's tome, what had happened at the Battle of Alexandria, and finally the finding of Seraphina's tome, they were well into the small hours of the night. After hearing the triplets' story and reading Nora's letter, which Annika had had the foresight to grab, the Sisters of Salem agreed to help them.

Jane, the Sisters of Salem high priestess, proclaimed they would spread the word in their coven, city, and from there the world. Everyone agreed that the triplets' tale and destiny would only be told to those with supernatural blood and only if the coven members trusted their confidant without fail.

"No point in involving anyone who may root for the other side," Aoife pointed out.

"Or anyone who has no chance of standing up to witches, vampires, weres, and other supes. Not to mention possibly Noro," Annika added. "Humans have no place in this war, even if they benefit from our fighting it."

Over two dozen local coven members had joined them in the library, now fitted with a meeting table and chairs like the one across the hall, to devise a plan of attack.

Lily soon realized that the diversity of creatures she had seen when they walked into the safe house was only a tiny representation of the members of the Sisters of Salem. So far, she'd been introduced to at least three elves, two dwarves, a fairy, and a vampire. She'd jumped as the vamp entered the room, unused to seeing them in non-threatening situations. Jane, who'd spotted Lily's reaction, made a point of introducing her to the vampire, Celestine, who had once been a witch.

"We've got a sizable group, so let's get down to business. Anyone have any ideas on how to rescue Evelyn? Bonus points if it's easily implemented. The sooner we get to her, the better." Brigit spoke from her half of the head of the table she shared with Jane.

As the official leaders of the movement, Brigit and Jane were tasked with the job of keeping everyone on track and as civil as possible.

Alistair raised his hand, and Brigit raised her eyebrows. "You don't have to raise your hand, Alistair. What's your idea?"

"Forgive me. I thought it wise." The room burst into nervous giggles recalling the stringent magical threats Brigit and Jane had employed five minutes ago if the crowd didn't settle down and use their inside voices.

"Ha. Ha. I take your point," Brigit smirked.

"I called Roman's mother during your family's meeting. Roman has not called home nor returned to the hotel where he is staying in the city for three days now. This, for a man who speaks to his family daily, is as you may guess . . . distressing. When I last had lunch with him two weeks ago, he mentioned a weekend getaway at an upstate mansion surrounded by woods to woo his lady. Knowing what I know of Evelyn, the home would have to be quite impressive to get her to agree to go, would it not? While New York has many such homes, how many are rentals? Perhaps they are even advertised online? It's not concrete but I suggest we should start there."

"Excellent idea, Alistair," Jane said.

She pointed out five Sisters of Salem coven members and instructed them to find such a home. "Search for a luxury rental that goes for thousands of dollars a night. Even better if it's secluded. Why else would they have stolen money from the Locksleys already? Make calls to the landlord. Make up any story you must to get information on if it's rented out this weekend and the renter's names."

"I think next we should start a list of the skills everyone here can bring to the table," Brigit said. "That way our attack squads will be well-rounded and equally powerful. We'll need diversity of power. I'm positive Empusa and Amon will have more fighters than they did in Alexandria and they'll be more diverse in their strengths and weaknesses."

A coven member rolled a double-sided whiteboard in from the meeting room, and two lines formed.

Jane, who knew her coven members' primary powers, dug a bit deeper for more nuanced magics they could leverage in a fight. Brigit took down only people's strongest magics. Mary, Gwenn, and Aoife took those already assessed, situated them into three large groups, and asked them to demonstrate their powers so they could evaluate relative strength of skills. Rena, Annika, and Selma made a food run to fuel all the people that had shown up and would soon need energy to fight.

Lily watched as lists overtook the front of the white board, forcing them to use the back. She read words like therionlogy, enerkinesis and elenchus. She saw a man transform into a rat and back again in the space of thirty seconds and a witch cast the strongest abbero charm Lily had ever seen, tossing a full grown man the length of the long room with ease. She shook her head. *My world is so small compared to this one.*

"It's overwhelming, isn't it? I guess it isn't helping that we haven't slept either."

Lily nodded. Sara was right. She doubted she could string two intelligent sentences together at this point. Making sense of what everyone was saying around her was out of the question. "Wanna lay our heads down? Rest our eyes a bit? We're going to need energy for a rescue mission. I can't fight like this."

Sara complied without a word, her copper eyes closing before they disappeared into the folds of her arms.

<hr>

Lily's loud snore awoke her hours later. Lifting her head from her folded arms, she stretched and completed a few neck circles to loosen up. Something moved out of the corner of her eye. She turned to see Sara, pressed up against the wall and floating in a perfect half moon pose. Passed out supernaturals on cots littered the room. It seemed that once the assessment was complete, everyone had turned in for a much needed nap.

What did they decide? Have they figured out where Evelyn is being kept?

Lily searched for Brigit and found her passed out in a chair by the fire, her mouth hanging wide open. The whiteboard with four neat columns of names sat to her right.

A loud rumble disrupted the sound of wheezing breath and shifting bodies. Lily clenched her stomach and realized she was starving. *I wonder where the kitchen is? There's no way I can wait to eat until all these people wake up.*

She stood gingerly and tried to find the best possible route to the door without disturbing anyone. *Mom told me not to waste my magic but . . .* She glanced at Brigit to make sure she was still soundly sleeping. *Oh screw it! What good is it being a witch if I can't use my magic for fun sometimes? And it will be faster . . .*

"Volavari," Lily pointed at herself and her body rose in the air.

"Motus," she whispered and swept her arm in a path toward the door.

She flew slowly and a bit shakily, above the sleeping bodies to the door. Her eyes latched onto a young man with chiseled cheekbones, raven dark hair, full red lips, and brown creamy skin sleeping peacefully on the floor.

Whoa, how did I not see him before?

Lily dipped a foot lower as she levitated above the man and he rolled to his back. She looked away quickly, not wanting to be caught and urged her body forward through the air. *Clearly, doing magic and hot guys don't mix. Good thing I don't see hot guys that often . . . Or ever.*

"Finum," Lily muttered when she reached the edge of the room. Her body fell through air and she landed clumsily but with a proud grin on her face. *Not bad for my first try! I could probably have managed at least twenty more feet.*

Sara eased the door closed as she joined Lily. "Showing off a little, I see?" Sara teased.

"I couldn't wait until I found my way out of that maze. Are you as hungry as I am?" Lily whispered, hoping Sara hadn't seen her checking out the guy and nearly falling out of the air.

"Starving," Sara agreed. "I was waiting for you to wake up, I didn't want to go wandering around alone."

She could see why. Lily wouldn't want to be wandering in a strange coven safe house alone either. *Who knows what other types of crazy we may find?*

The pair crept down the hall listening at doors and opening them softly. There were a few offices decorated with heavy wood desks and huge bookshelves and a small gym but most were guest bedrooms filled with slumbering supernaturals. The only empty bedroom Lily found was the one boasting two hospital-style beds with IV hookups next to it. *I suppose we are in a safe house,* Lily raised an eyebrow and closed the door. *Accidents and fights are sure to happen in the magical world. Especially in a city the size of New York. I bet supernatural creatures would go to any length to avoid a human hospital.*

Sara stopped and sniffed the air, "Do you smell that?"

Lily sniffed too and nearly began drooling. *Bacon! And . . . pancakes? Oh please let there be pancakes.*

They followed their noses to a door at the end of the hall.

"Hello, girls," Celestine called out over the kitchen island as they opened the door. "Come! Come! Have a seat. There's food ready, but I've got a lot to do before the army arrives."

"You made all this?" Lily asked, staring at the piles

of pancakes, heaps of bacon, and mounds of sautéed veggies on the white marble counter.

"Well of course I made it! Everyone else had to sleep, but I was wide awake. Perks or curse of being a vampire, depending on how you look at it."

"But I thought vampires only needed blood to survive? Why would you bother learning how to cook like this if you don't eat?" Lily asked staring at the perfect golden pancakes.

"As I said last night, I wasn't always a vampire. In my first life, I was a witch. There are many like us, turned witches. We tend to run together or with other witches, or both. There are five of us in this coven alone, a high proportion, but this is New York, so I suppose that fits." Celestine shrugged.

"When I was a witch, I owned a little bakery in Toulouse, France, where I grew up. I lived for my bakery. I was also a healer so I often put medicinal herbs and tinctures into my bakes when I knew illness was going around. You are right in thinking that food, especially cooked food, does not hold the same pull over me. I will eat in the company of humans so I appear normal but I get no nourishment from it. However, I still find the act of cooking and baking a pleasurable way to spend the hours."

"Wow," Sara said, hopping onto a stool and helping herself to a plate.

Celestine grinned and went back to work, assembling and mixing a new bowl of pancake batter as if on autopilot. Behind her the curtains blew inward with a warm breeze to reveal a bright, sunny day with palm trees blowing outside.

Lily froze, momentarily perplexed and snorted when she realized she was staring at the scenery of the day. *Whoever put that one up has a sense of humor. I bet it's freezing outside. I wonder if every room is the same?*

She was just easing into a chair tucked beneath the island when the phone rang. Celestine and Sara looked at her expectantly. One had her hands covered in batter, and the other's face was already stuffed with food. Lily sighed and walked to the phone hanging on the kitchen wall.

"Hello?"

"Good morning. Is this Miss Berghert? The one who called about Peacock Manor for rent on Wooster Lane?"

Lily racked her brains. *Which one is Miss Berghert?*

"Yes," she lied, unwilling to go searching for the mystery woman.

"This is Marty Mindel, property manager of Peacock Manor. Sorry to call you so early, but you said it was urgent and I'm an early riser. Anyhow the manor house is in use this weekend to the next, but if you can put off your elopement another week, it's all yours."

"Oh, um I wonder if I could reason with the people staying there? Did the renter leave a name or number that I could call? Perhaps we could share part of the property? I'll make it worth both your time," the lies slipped off her tongue, leaving Lily impressed with herself.

Marty paused on the other end of the line. Lily pictured him working out if the monetary gain would be enough to give up client information. He decided it was.

"I don't usually do this but it's a vast property and there's only supposed to be two people there this weekend. The guy who rented it is Roman Simons. Seemed like a nice guy. I don't see him turning down a couple that's been through so much like you two. You got a pen handy for his number? If it's fine with Mr. Simons, it's fine with me."

"I'm ready." She memorized the number as he gave it to her. "I'll call you back if he says yes and we'll work out the fee. Thank you." Lily hung up and walked to the fridge where a scribble-filled grocery list hung and jotted down the number.

Oh my goddess!

"Was that another of Shefali's friends? I swear she must know half the witches in India with the number of calls I've picked up this morning offering to help," Celestine asked, pouring another round of batter onto the griddle.

"I know where they're keeping Evelyn. The property management person gave me the property name and Roman's phone number . . . what should we do?" Lily asked wide eyed.

Celestine wiped her hands in her apron, a steely glint in her eye. "Go wake the others and tell them breakfast is ready. Then we fight."

Black

Evelyn

THE BLACKNESS ENGULFING Evelyn lifted slightly, though the energy to open her eyes remained elusive. A profound sense of aloneness punctuated by curious stabs of envy overcame her and she gave up trying to pry herself from the depths.

But Evelyn wasn't alone.

The voices closest to her were congratulatory, overtaking the whispers of those that surrounded them.

A whimper.

A moan.

A deep, thoughtful sound.

In bits and pieces, words began to make sense.

"You will move her. Now that I am here, I will see to it she cedes her power. I can already feel the magic of this place strengthening me. No doubt I have many hard days ahead, but shortly I, and all other fata, shall be strong once more. We will be as we were thousands of years ago during the rise of the Ancients, before Hecate denied us her magic," a regal voice echoed off stone.

"Yes, your highness. Truth be told, I doubt she'd survive down here anyhow."

Evelyn would have shuddered in revulsion at the second voice, Noro's voice, if only she had the energy.

"Witch!"

"Yes, Master Noro?" a person who sounded like a mouse squeaked.

"Take Eve to a more comfortable room so she may heal."

"Should I put her with the other? The one we caught down here?"

"The other? No, you idiot creature. His conditions are scarcely better than hers. Upstairs, near Empusa and Amon's quarters. You three help. See to it Eve is handled gently."

The only response was the shuffle of feet and hands on her skin. Rough calloused hands. Hands with long, dagger-like nails. Soft, smooth ones. Thin, bony ones.

Evelyn's body lifted from the cold, damp stone, bolstered by hands that dare not let her drop.

A door creaked, and she was moving, air flowing

over her swaths of naked skin and rags. Footsteps rang down a corridor, and the hands grew rougher.

Evelyn groaned.

"The witch is waking up," a high, eager voice said.

A pair of hands stiffened beneath her.

"Don't you dare give me that look, Alma. Noro will know if we hurt her," another voice said.

"How? He's too busy with King Dim—what the hell?!"

A loud pounding upon wood trampled their whispers and the dagger-like nails dug into Evelyn's back. Her eyelids fluttered, sending her body into spasms of pain. She began slipping back toward the dark. Toward peace.

"Quiet! It's the incubus. I bet he can sense her or something. Incubus are freaky like that."

And the night reclaimed her.

Alpha, Beta, Gamma, and Delta
Lily

Lily turned to check that the caravan was still behind them. Growing up in a part of Oregon that got little snow, she'd always dreaded driving in the stuff. Even after four years of college on the East Coast, visions of cars flipping into mounds of packed snow had Lily wringing her hands and turning in her seat so often that Aoife had offered her a compact mirror.

"They'll be fine, Lil," Brigit said from the other side of Sara. "They live in New York and know how to handle snow. We'll all get there in one piece."

Lily recognized how laughable it was to be so concerned over a possible car accident when they were literally driving hundreds of miles to fight other supernatural creatures.

All in all, thirty-five people had arrived at the safe

house and stayed to fight, a few of them slipping in only moments before they were set to leave. In fact, the largest challenge they'd faced in regards to their army was not convincing anyone to fight, but rather finding available cars and drivers. Who knew only a small percentage of such a large city could drive?

"The rest stop is a couple miles away on the right," Jane said from the driver's seat. "Aoife, would you instruct the others to turn in there? And I know we're in a hurry, Brigit, but we need to go over the plan once more. Most of the latecomers only heard it once. These people are risking their lives; the least we can do is make sure they know where to be."

Brigit's mouth flattened but she tamed the mother lion within. She'd grown increasingly frustrated with how long it took to form an army and at one point uncharacteristically threatened to go save Evelyn on her own. It was only Gwenn's level-headed insistence that they needed each and every fighter there if they were to save Evelyn from the Acolytes that kept Brigit at the safe house.

"Roger that." Aoife punched a text into her phone.

Five minutes later, Jane turned into the rest stop. They parked far away from the two other vehicles in the lot, one of which looked abandoned.

"Follow me," Jane said, opening her door and disappearing into the woods surrounding the parking lot.

The sounds of cracking branches and dead leaves filled the afternoon silence as they walked through the woods. Other footsteps and soft voices trickled in behind them, one small group at a time. It was all part of the plan to appear as nondescript as possible. Obviously fifty people all taking the same hike on a frigid winter's day was not at all normal, but it was the best they could do. They were counting on the remoteness of the location and cold of the season to make up for what they lacked in discretion. Lucky for them, they'd passed only two other cars on the remote country road off the highway.

"I remember coming to these woods alone as a child and playing with my magic," Jane said as she came to a stop in a clearing off the main trail and looked up at the naked, frozen branches on the trees around them. She paused and the sound of a brook chattering somewhere in the distance and crunching snow filled her pensive silence.

"I didn't know what I was doing, but I realized I had to keep it a secret. If only I'd known how helpful this spot would become years later." As Jane spoke plumes of white air blasted out of her nostrils and mouth.

Lily shivered at Jane's words as much as at the cold.

She couldn't imagine growing up in the situation Jane had shared during their drive. What would she have done if she'd showed signs of magic, even as her devout evangelical family denounced witches as unnatural, evil creatures at the dining table? Lily imagined generations of lone witches, ones of no magical lineage, retreating to the forest to hide, to be free.

"That's everyone," Mary's soprano voice called out from the trees, barely visible in the winter camo gear she'd picked up that morning before they left.

That's Mary—always has to have the perfect outfit for the occasion, Lily thought, watching her aunt's blonde head bob up and down as Mary jogged to meet them.

Jane's clap rang out through the clearing. "Can everyone please find their assigned squadrons? If you can't remember, Brigit has the list."

Lily watched four groups form out of chaos before leaving Brigit's and Jane's side to join Gamma Squad.

"There's our star!" a woman Lily vaguely recalled meeting cried as a half dozen other hands belonging to people she hadn't yet met stuck out to shake her hand.

She jumped as she clasped hands with a woman who introduced herself as Jo.

"Oops! Sorry about that," Jo said, holding up her hands in apology, "Enerkinesis witch. I've been trying to save it all up for the battle but when I get excited the excess leaks out."

"No worries," Lily said, smiling weakly at the witch whose flyaway gray hair gave the impression that electricity *never* stopped leaking out of her. She noticed her sister was receiving a similar exuberant welcome from Beta Squad.

"And I'm Alfred," a young man said and waved enthusiastically from the back of Lily's group.

Lily peered past Jo and the hottie she had shamelessly checked out while levitating herself over a room of sleeping supernaturals gave her a confident wink of a velvet, dark brown eye. She pinked and turned with little more than a wave back.

Now is not the time for flirting. Just my luck Aoife would claim him for our squad. She clearly didn't see how distracting he could be.

"It seems everyone has assembled, so let's begin," Jane clapped again. "You've been placed into your squads for the diversity you could add to the group. No one else in your squad can do exactly what you do. Therefore, it would be ideal if you stuck together as long as possible."

A plump man in Sara's group interrupted to voice his concerns about the long walk.

Jane frowned. "No, Roger, we cannot drive up to the

end of the driveway. There's an intercom there with a passcode—how do you expect us to get through? Do you really think driving up in twenty cars brimming with witches wouldn't look suspicious? You'd have already realized there was a hike in if you were awake during the briefing." It sounded as though she'd tried to keep the annoyance from her tone but failed.

"When we arrive at the property the squadrons will regroup near their specified entry points. A member of your squadron has been designated to send up a single fireball when your team is ready. Then, wait there, until Aoife gives the final signal."

Aoife raised her hands, releasing a shower of sparks and smaller balls of fire that flew up before landing on the ground and rolling about like golden golf balls, melting the white snow beneath them.

"Thank you for the demonstration. Of course the signals will be much higher in the sky and the balls larger than Aoife's display, but you get the point." Jane nodded, as if daring anyone to claim differently. "Once you see Aoife's shower of fire, it's time to leave the woods. We will then split for good, half of us flanking the building's two back entrances, the other half coming from the sides. Photographs online show the front entry being up a long set of stairs, ending in French doors made of glass. Avoid that area, it's by far the most vulnerable and exposed point of entry. Not to mention it's likely weres or other shifters will be guarding it. Rumor has it packs of weres from the rougher neighborhoods along the Eastern seaboard were hired en masse a week ago as guards. Felix Krimena's gang was one of those packs."

There was a collective sucking in of breath. Lily looked around to see pale faces and nervous glances all around.

"Excuse me," Lily said as she raised her hand like a schoolgirl. "Who is Felix—?" The name sounded ridiculous, like a cartoon character's, coming off her tongue.

"Only the most notorious werewolf in North America," a man in Alpha Squad said. "Nasty piece of work, he is. He hunts year round and chooses the prettiest girls in towns to maul and change. The men he kills unless he thinks he can use them. He's even gone after a few children."

"What do you mean by hunts year round?"

"Well I'm not a shifter of any type," the man pulled back his long hair to reveal pointed ears, "But from what I've heard there are two lifestyle ideologies for werewolves and to a lesser extent other shifters. Weres are either feral weres or city weres. Most feral werewolves hunt every full moon, maybe more in the winter when there's less chance a human hunter will kill them or if they're feeling their wolf side needs the hunt to stay sane. They say it keeps their wolf self sharper and healthier. But the Krimena gang takes it to the extreme. They hunt as often as they can, every night if possible, both animals and humans."

"The elf is right," Caleb, a young man in Rena's group Lily had met just before they left said. "I'm a city were. We don't hunt much. Usually just go buy steak and eat it raw during the full moon or whenever we feel the urge to hunt. There are many of our kind who find our behavior unnatural, Felix being a strong proponent of that belief."

Lily gulped, "So there's a whole pack of werewolves on guard duty?"

Jane nodded. "Weres have the second best set of senses in the supernatural community, after vampires. Most vampires don't take kindly to guard duty, though. They think it's beneath them, so it's likely weres are the first line of defense we will come up against."

"It'll be fine, Lil. Stay in your group. We've put people in each group who are talented in handling various sorts of supernatural attacks." Brigit's voice wafted through Lily, easing her fear.

"Once we're inside, the werewolves have less of an advantage. They can't rely on a pack formation in smaller spaces," Jane added, glancing at Lily before returning her gaze to the crowd.

"If their reputation and pride are anything to go on, I doubt Empusa or Amon will deem it necessary to assign many guards to the servants quarters we plan on entering through. The entrances will likely be shielded, but breaking separate shields only helps us. We'll be sounding various alarms simultaneously and breaking up the bulk of the were guards. Everyone enters on the ground level and infiltrates up. Once your team is inside and has disabled the first round of weres or Acolytes, you can split off into smaller groups, but stay close enough to hear the rest of your squadron. Also, a witch or elf with fire power should always buddy one without." She held up leave fingers and brought them together to illustrate her point.

"Fire magic worked for the McKays in the Battle of Alexandria and vamps aren't the only creatures who burn. Now let's see . . . Alpha Squad?"

A group of witches including Gwenn, Rena, and Annika—who had refused to separate—two elves, Selma, Caleb, and Celestine raised their hands at Jane's back. The elves hefted large metal clubs. Shefali, unable to come herself, had given Selma a dagger which sat on her hip, and Annika's wand poked out of her pocket.

Lily eyed the weapons thankfully and wished Rena hadn't been too proud to carry one.

Jane turned to face them. "Your goal is to scour the basement for clues and other prisoners. Look for locked doors and don't forget to run your hands along walls. Though it's unlikely, they could have built passageways in only two days, you never know. Once you've scoured the basement, ascend the stairs until you find where you're most needed. Now where's Beta Squad?"

Sara's group took a collective step forward.

"Each of you has a degree of fire power to fight vampires with. We can assume Empusa and Amon would take the largest, grandest rooms for themselves. Those are on the top floor and that is where you will aim to be. Though we doubt they'd want to do the work of caring for Evelyn, they may have opted to put her close to them for safekeeping. Your primary objective is to take out as many vampires as you can while looking for Evelyn. Key targets are Empusa and Amon themselves."

Sara and the rest of Beta Squad nodded.

"That leaves Gamma and Delta squads," Jane glanced around at her own group and Lily's.

"Your primary objective is to find Evelyn. It is most likely that they have hidden Evelyn in the maze that is the middle two levels. That's where the original servants quarters and hallways lie. These were, to say the least, poorly planned and littered with doorways that lead to other hidden rooms. Evelyn would be easily guarded by lackeys on these floors, which seems like Empusa and Amon's style. The extra rooms feeding into each other and the sheer inconsistency of the layout could lock a person in if they didn't know where they were going. They're perfect for hiding someone. Gamma, you take the second floor; Delta will take the ground level."

Jane drew in a deep breath. "Does anyone have questions?"

The ominous cawing of a crow in a tree above filled the silence hanging in the cold winter air. Everyone glanced up warily. The crow's interjection felt like an assertion of death.

Lily closed her eyes and inhaled. The scent of earth, pine trees, snow upon the ground, and somewhere in the distance smoke from a fire rushed in to fill her nostrils, calming her nerves slightly.

How many of these people have been in battle before? Or ever seen one? I hope more of them than I think.

"Let's get moving, then," Brigit said, turning and leading the army through the trees to her daughter.

You're Different

Evelyn

EVELYN SHIFTED her arm an inch and gasped as her neurons caught on fire. *Smaller. Start smaller.* Hesitantly, she opened her eyes and let out the breath she'd been holding. No pain, but her eyes were so blurry it was impossible to see anything other than the blinding white of the room she was in.

Wait . . . white? She blinked a few times to clear her eyes. *Ouch. Ouch. Ouch.* Evelyn made to push herself up and felt not damp hay or cold stone, but soft feathers beneath her. *Was it all a nightmare?* She sat up, her body popping and cracking in ways she'd never heard before. Looking around the well-lit room, she caught sight of an en suite bath and sighed. *No more bucket.*

"Good, you're awake."

Evelyn turned to find Nora sitting in a chair beside the door with a novel closed on her lap.

"What are you doing here?" Evelyn asked, her voice cracking from disuse, though she hoped Nora still sensed the anger she intended.

"Waiting for you to wake up. We've been taking turns—well the witches have, no vamps or werewolves. Noro deemed both too untrustworthy. The only thing they love to taste more than a witch with siren abilities is an empath."

"Why am I here? How long have I been out?"

Nora smirked. "Dimia insisted that you, his favorite daughter as he keeps referring to you, be moved from the basement. At least while you continue to cooperate. You've only been out for a little over a day."

A day! But that would mean I've been hostage for . . . three days? Four? The dungeon-like basement had no access to natural light so it was impossible to be sure. *Shouldn't three days be enough time for someone to come looking for me?*

"You would think, wouldn't you/" Nora said with a smug lift of her eyebrows. "But no one's breached our perimeters. It seems your decision to stay in New York has changed how your family thought about you."

Evelyn flailed, trying to secure her mind.

Nora let out a bark of laughter. "Don't bother. You're so depleted that you barely have control over your body's basic functions. There's no way you have control over your magic. As much as I hate to admit it, that was an impressive display of power. I've never seen anything like it before. But that's no surprise, you've always been different."

I have no control over myself, my magic? Evelyn's stomach sank. *How am I going to escape without magic? Wait . . . Maybe . . .*

"Not even control over my pneuma?"

Nora balked. "What are you going on about a pneuma? That was your witch soul that traveled to Hecate, stupid. I know it's unbelievable considering neither you nor your sisters even managed to astral travel a meter outside your body before but it finally happened. Really . . . A pneuma . . . Ha! Like you could just grow a fata soul! You're not lucky enough to be a fata," Nora sneered.

Evelyn blinked unsure how to respond. *I know I did not make up that blue glowing light . . . Did I?*

"I'll tell Noro you're up. He wanted to see you as soon as you woke." Nora let herself out without another word, locking the door behind her.

Evelyn leaned back into the pillows wondering what

had happened after she passed out. Fuzzy memories of a grayish-white-gold figure appearing from the black hole emerged. Either her vision had been crazy blurry by that point or Dimia looked far less grand than Noro described. She hoped it was the latter. If she had to bring fata over, it would be best if they were weak and sickly. *At least then we have a chance at fighting them.*

She lifted her arm to brush a chunk of burnt hair from her eyes and stopped suddenly. Her hand was glowing. Evelyn squinted and brought both hands closer to see a familiar symbol glowing white against her palms.

"The triquetra," Evelyn whispered.

The symbol had been all over Fern Cottage and though she'd never paid it much mind before, now she wished she had. Unlike the brands that marked her inner thigh, the small triquetra on each of her palms shimmered welcomingly. *My pneuma must have made these. I knew I didn't make that shit up. There's no way I'm that creative.*

The lock clicked on the other side of the door.

Evelyn pulled the covers up and shoved her hands under, instinctively hiding them though she wasn't sure why. It was only then she realized she'd had been stripped naked and bathed sometime during her unconsciousness. While it felt good to be clean, she'd rather not think of how it all happened. Or who had bathed her.

The door flew open and Noro entered the room, followed by Amon holding a glass. Nora slunk in behind them.

Not this again. Evelyn's stomach clenched and rolled.

"Eve, my love, you have no idea how happy it makes me to see you. We were wondering how long it would take for you to regain consciousness. Rest assured with each dose of vampire blood you will become stronger so the recovery shall be less."

Evelyn scowled as Noro floated to her bedside.

"Now that you are awake, we will continue. I'm pleased to see our training *familiarizing* you with fata magic has worked. When given a difficult task a human could never complete, you managed to access your true potential beneath your filthy human genetics. I can sense the fata power in you growing and thriving within." Noro's eyes grew round as they ran up and down her body.

Evelyn's muscles tightened. *I'd rather die than let that monster touch me again.*

"As we suspected, Empusa's blood was the key,

allowing you to actually use your deepest powers. It gave you strength enough to create a portal between Earth and Hecate when you were weak from training. No matter how short lived, Dimia, myself, and all fata kind consider this a great success. Therefore, keeping up your strength is our first priority, so that you may try again. Amon?"

Amon scowled at Evelyn, as if she had been the one to force him to give up his blood, before lowering his head and biting into his own arm. Black blood tinged red welled up at the site. Amon held the cup below the bite mark and allowed the dark liquid to flow. It took less than a minute for the wound to heal, but in that time enough blood seeped out to fill almost half the glass.

"Why does it look different? It's redder," Evelyn asked as Amon, unable to give Evelyn the glass directly as her hands were still hidden beneath the blanket, shoved the glass at Nora who took it grudgingly.

"It's fresh. I fed this morning, so you'd receive the best."

Evelyn gagged, unable to hold back her repulsion.

Noro ignored her outburst. "This will be your new regimen. Empusa and Amon will alternate daily so each can keep up their blood supply. I will accompany them each day to see to it the plan is carried out. You will perform no other magic unless I instruct you to, so as not to drain your powers. We are hoping you will be able to create another portal in a matter of days."

Evelyn stared at him, "And what if I don't want to keep drinking their blood?"

"Do you like your new accommodations?" Noro asked.

Evelyn's sapphire eyes narrowed.

"If you prefer this space," Noro said, taking her silence as compliance, "you will do as we say. We are all working to make room for fata-kind in this new world, Eve. If you wish to continue being hailed as the savior of fata-kind, you will do the same." He turned and floated toward the door.

Projecting much? I never said I wanted that.

"See to it Eve drinks every last drop."

Evelyn watched Nora clutch her heart as Amon and Noro disappeared into the hallway. "You're pathetic. You know that, right? I can't believe Brigit never—"

"Drink the blood, siren," Nora interrupted, spitting out the words with malice as she turned to face the bed. "Be blissful in your ignorance as to what his kind can do. How witch magic is nothing in comparison. How we, those who serve them, will be rewarded in Earth's new realm."

"And that's why Noro needs me, then? When their

kind is so much more powerful? I don't see any of them being able to open their own portal."

Nora's eyes narrowed, "You know nothing of what they can do, girl. Still, I stand by what I said earlier, what I've known from the day you were born. You're different. Your sisters, too. Not entirely a witch, nor a human, nor one of them."

Evelyn's hand shook under the covers as Nora forced them out of hiding with her magic. Evelyn looked down hoping to hide the triquetras glowing in her palms with a discreet flick of the wrist.

She gasped. The triquetras had disappeared.

"But that doesn't mean you get everything you want." Nora placed the cup in Evelyn's hand before shoving the glass to Evelyn's lips and tipping blood into her mouth.

***

"You MADE that harder than it needed to be," Nora said, picking up the cup from where it had fallen empty onto Evelyn's chest.

Evelyn glared at Nora, unable to move, or even speak from the binding spell Nora had placed on her as soon as she finished drinking Amon's blood.

"I'm not lifting your bind," Nora said walking back

to the door. "At least not until the danger of you vomiting it all back up has passed. It's difficult getting a vampire's blood from them, even for Noro. It would make them angry if they had to donate again so soon. As they can't punish you, I'd be the obvious choice. I'll be back in a few hours to lift the bind. Don't worry, I'll spell you up safe and sound behind me so there are no surprise visitors." Nora disappeared through the door.

Seconds later, the stiff cocoon of a sanctuary charm washed over Evelyn. It was uncomfortable, as if a cactus had wrapped itself around her, so unlike Brigit's charm over Fern Cottage, which had been soft and comforting.

Still, Evelyn found herself the tiniest bit grateful for Nora's foresight, even if she'd only done it to save her own ass. For all Evelyn knew, Felix or someone worse roamed the halls. She hadn't needed her ceremens powers to read what had been on Felix's mind during the days he'd stood outside her cell. In her current state, Evelyn was better off in here. Even if she could only blink, swallow, breathe, and think.

Of course the instant she was immobilized she developed an insatiable itch on her foot. Evelyn sighed.

Is this how my life will be until I let an entire planet of magic aliens onto Earth? Lying in bed, drinking repulsive vampire blood every few days until I'm strong enough to force another portal open. Faint. Repeat. Should I let myself die?

She dimly recalled the image of her pneuma fleeing back to her body on Earth. Evelyn was sure she would have died already if she hadn't called her pneuma back when she did.

My pneuma.

She considered the word again, letting it roll around in her mind. Though she'd known of her pneuma's presence in her body for only a day, it felt as familiar as her heartbeat. She recalled Noro's words, unforgettable as they were revolting, after he molested her.

"Now that we have coupled, your fata instincts and capabilities are finally free. They will only grow stronger as Empusa's blood strengthens you. Soon, my love, we shall be together like old times."

Evelyn had to admit that a fata waking up powers and even a fata soul within her with his own magic made sense.

But why didn't my pneuma show itself to me before I opened a portal, then? Maybe it wasn't strong enough until I drank vampire blood? I wonder if there's an expert on pneumas somewhere in the world? Nora didn't seem to know a thing about them.

Nora had thought the blue light was her witch soul.

And Amon hadn't mentioned her pneuma or acted like it was anything out of the ordinary.

But it is out of the ordinary. I have two freaking souls inside me—how can that not be strange?

The answer hit Evelyn like a freight train as her first clear memory from the night she opened the portal came rushing back. Noro swooping in, millimeters from her face, to whisper in her ear. Him telling Evelyn she had a pneuma and her subsequent freak out.

It was a secret! Noro is a secret keeper!

Noro never actually announced it, he just let everyone *believe* it was her witch's soul. Aoife and Brigit had always said astral travel was difficult to master. The witches in the room probably hadn't know enough about it to understand otherwise.

So, is Noro the only one with answers? Her heart raced at the idea and her fight or flight response kicked in.

Goddess be. The witchy words rolled through her for the first time in her life. *Please let Brigit or one of my aunts know about pneumas.*

A sharp pain shot through Evelyn's gut at the thought of her biological family. Her stomach clenched, and she fought against Nora's bind, desperate to double over in pain. Her pelvis started to pulse, a rhythmic, alien uproar that started in the center and wound its way clockwise and out, until it was skating along the outer rim of her pelvic bowl. Each sensation felt how she imagined childbirth contractions, shattering and all encompassing. She made to grit her teeth but her mouth held fast in its bound resting position, her teeth hovering millimeters from each other, stealing the small comfort clenching her jaw would give.

This must be the vampire blood working, Evelyn realized. *But it wasn't like this before.*

She quieted and concentrated on the life blood of another supernatural being weaving through her gut, her bloodstream, and into the muscles and organs it supplied, strengthening her in an accelerated way, vibrating her body with energy no living being should be allowed or expected to endure. It was the magic of the vampires that flowed through her, and the very reason they were so reluctant to give their blood up. Her muscles hardened, and her pneuma fluttered deep within her, re-energized by the blood.

Evelyn's arms quivered, each muscle cramping and loosening one after the other. An overwhelming sensation came over Evelyn as her muscles knotted, organs spasmed and tickled, bones hardened, and her pneuma raced up and down the length of her spine. She wanted to vomit, but of course, even that had been denied her. She needed a release. Any release. An idea hit her as her pneuma flew up again toward her heart, causing the organ to skip a beat.

Alright, pneuma, Evelyn thought, ignoring the pain as best she could. *You can be free now. I need less sensation and you're the only part of me that can leave so . . . go?*

Nothing happened.

How did I do it before? Evelyn's mind raced back to the seconds before she opened the portal. The whole event blurred further as pain overtook her. A blue light, a black hole growing at her feet, and flying through space. Other fragments came at her as various combinations of colors and light, making little sense. Air forcing its way through her as her air tubes tightened and then suffocation. She remembered standing in the circle, cruel faces around her, and laying on the ground. A sensation of thumping against her chest, her pneuma.

But how did I let her out?

Her pneuma flung itself against her skull and the spell for astral travel popped into Evelyn's head as though her pneuma had given it to her.

Of course! Um, thanks. Now let's see if it works.

Unable to speak, Evelyn said the spell in her mind, doubting it would work, doubting that she was strong enough.

She was wrong.

Space opened within Evelyn as her pneuma crawled past her organs, through her throat, and out of her mouth. Pleasure at the small release coursed through Evelyn and she closed her eyes slowly. When she opened them again her pneuma, a brilliant sapphire light, was hovering before her. She watched as its arm moved up to the space between her eyes and caressed it gently.

What the hell? Why is it touching me?

A second later, without explanation or even a parting wave, Evelyn's pneuma shot up through the ceiling and away.

Evelyn gasped as once again she was seeing double. The nice, normal room she was lying in was visible with her eyes, while the larger world outside flashed by in snippets supplied by her pneuma. Frigid air brushed against Evelyn's cheeks, traveled through her nostrils, and froze her lungs. Sunlight momentarily blinded her. The taste of a winter day stole the moisture from her tongue.

It's taking me with it, Evelyn realized and though the experience was not helping her nausea, she was grateful not to be left totally alone.

Wind sprayed across Evelyn's face as her pneuma flew higher toward the sun, which was descending in a spray of pink and orange. From her pneuma's vantage,

Evelyn saw the house her body lay trapped in and the miles and miles of sparkling snow covering the surrounding forest.

She felt a single tear slide down her cheek as she took in the surroundings where her body lay confined to a bed, all too aware that it might be the last time she'd ever be free.

The Blue Beacon
Lily

The sky darkened as the witches' army of creatures trudged through the woods. Jane estimated the journey to be five miles as the crow flew but the snow-pack and general fitness of the group made it seem far longer.

Even Lily, a distance runner who rarely went two days without exercise, felt the strain. It was because of this, the hindrance of having to check their compass often, and the fear of losing a single person in the remote wilderness that they were progressing at a crawl.

"Ready for this?" Rena walked up on one side of Lily and grasped her hand as Selma took the other. Annika strode alongside Rena, her ice-blue eyes boring into Lily.

Lily nodded and forced herself to smile. *At least Mom put them all in Alpha Squad.*

Lily knew Brigit had placed her Oregon family in the squadron with the "safest tasks" to help Lily's peace of mind. She'd even added Gwenn and two other vampires to the Alpha Squad for added muscle. It was an arrangement Jane had questioned, as both the vampires and Gwenn would have been more useful on the upper levels, but Brigit did not budge.

She's trying to protect me as best she can, even through all these shitty situations. Mom knew I'd probably lose my mind if I lost another person I loved.

"As ready as I'll ever be. At least this time I know what to expect and won't freak out when someone comes charging at me," Lily replied.

Selma squeezed her hand.

"We'll all be behind you, Lil. Judging by how huge this place is, you might not see us, but we'll be there," Annika said smiling at her.

"Thanks, Ann." She wanted to say more—to beg them to leave, to not fight for her, to tell them she couldn't bear it if they lost their lives for this cause—but she knew they would not accept her wishes. Her family would never allow her to fight alone. She knew it because it was what she would do if the roles were reversed. So she stayed silent.

The conversation dropped, and they continued the miles with their own thoughts.

Lily was guessing they had gone about four miles when a gasp rose from behind her. She stiffened and crouched low, her stance wide and arms outstretched for battle.

"What is that?" she heard Sara ask.

Lily turned and saw her sister pointing up. Her gaze followed the trajectory of Sara's hand and Lily's breath caught in her throat.

One hundred feet in the air a bright sapphire light pulsed against the darkening sky. Lily didn't dare to blink as she stared at the light that was familiar and strange all at once. The invading army watched from the cover of leafless branches as the ghostly light floated, spun, expanded, and shrunk on the spot before dropping out of sight.

Lily shuddered and her muscles tightened.

"Was that a lookout? Do they know we're coming?" The man named Roger broached the question Lily was sure they'd all been wondering.

"I don't think so," Aoife said, walking up to stand by Jane at the head of the army.

"How can you be sure?" Jo, the enerkinesis witch in Lily's squad, asked.

"I can't but as someone whose soul has traveled from

my body, I can guess. That . . . thing looked how I look when I travel astrally, although I will admit it was brighter and more colorful. I'm opaque and a wee bit white, which I've always heard was normal, but perhaps not everyone's the same?" Aoife looked at the group, most of whom stared back blankly.

"Aye, I'm whitish, too," Brigit said. "Can anyone else here say different?"

The crowd quieted.

"I've never met *anyone* who could travel," a wizard admitted.

Two others, then three, four, and soon the entire group shook their heads. No one in their coven had the ability, and most had never come across a witch who could do it.

Lily's mouth hung open. She'd heard the McKays were special dozens of times from dozens of witches, but only now, as their small army stared at her mother and aunt gobsmacked and nervous over the strange event they'd just witnessed, did she understand just how special the McKays were.

"What if it wasn't a soul? I don't like the idea of fighting something I don't know about," a voice called from the back of the army and other voices rose all around, questioning, whispering, glancing back the way they came.

We're losing them. Lily watched hysteria creep through the crowd.

"I think it's safe to say no one has seen the likes of whatever that was." Gwenn detached herself from Alpha Squad to join her sisters.

A faint, covert sensation of calm brushed over Lily and she smiled. Gwenn was implementing her specialty, a calming charm, to counteract the hysteria.

"But does it matter what we've seen and what we haven't when so much is at stake?" Gwenn asked, her green eyes leveling the skittish crowd. "Like as not we'll be seeing more of the latter in that manor anyways, so you all best prepare yourselves. Remember, you're walking into battle to help save humanity. What's the difference if it starts now, in another mile, or in a year?" Her words flew through the woods, amplified by the empty spaces between the leafless tree limbs.

"Gwenn's right," Jane said, standing up straighter. "Turn back now if you want, but I'm moving forward, end of story. With any luck that wasn't a lookout. If it was, and *if* it saw us, they'll send weres. At least then we'll have a heads-up; weres are shit at stealth attacks." With that she resumed her slow march through the snow.

To Lily's surprise no one turned around and the crowd followed, albeit more hesitantly than before.

That was close.

"It must be something, learning you're a part of a powerful family like yours," Alfred said, falling into step beside her and raising a dark eyebrow at Lily.

He smelled of cedar and soap. Lily sighed, *I can't escape him or the McKay reputation.*

"You have no idea. Shoot, most of the time I have no idea. I didn't know astral travel was that rare. Aoife has been trying to teach us how to travel for months. Now I don't feel so bad for not getting it."

Alfred laughed a deep, warm laugh, "I'm no wizard but I'm sure a few months is nothing. It took years for my powers to come to full strength, but I needed the extra time. I wouldn't have known what to do with the electricity in the city, not to mention natural forms of energy."

"So . . . Um . . . What are you, anyway? I can tell you're not a vampire but we haven't gotten around to learning much about other creatures. Sorry if that's offensive. I'm not well versed in supernatural etiquette." Lily pinked slightly at her admission.

Alfred's red lips parted to reveal a white smile. "I thought you'd never ask!" he teased and nudged his shoulder into hers, causing Lily to stumble and land face first into the snow.

"Oh shit! I'm so sorry. I didn't mean to knock you

over. Are you hurt?" Alfred extended his hand to help her up.

Lily glanced away, hoping to avoid Alfred's gorgeous, concerned eyes as he helped her up and saw Aoife watching them, a wicked grin on her face. Lily glared at her aunt, who turned around with a soft chuckle.

"I'm fine, let's go. We don't want to hold the group up." The words came out harsher than she'd intended and Lily set off at a power walk as her mortification skyrocketed. *Why am I being so awkward and stupid? Why is this hot guy trying to talk to me now? Talk about the worst timing ever,* Lily thought, leaving Alfred in her wake.

Alfred rushed to catch up with her. "I'm a daemon," he said softly.

Lily sighed and her shoulders softened at his remorseful tone. "What does that mean? You said you wouldn't know what to do with the electricity in the city? Can you start there?"

"It's energy I can feed off. I take in man-made electricity, natural sources of electricity, and magic and can use it however I like. Most daemons can only use one type, so when I harnessed all three it became big news. I think the rumors of my range are why Jane was so keen to let me into the Sisters of Salem. She recruited me when I was fifteen. My family was leaving the mosque one day and there she was sitting outside ready to inform my parents how the coven could protect me if I lost control of my power. The years when a daemon is first learning to use his or her powers are the hardest time in their life—much like being a witch, I'd imagine."

The tension and embarrassment in Lily broke. She smiled. "I can't argue with that. I'm in that stage now. And then just when I think I've learned so much there can't be more, someone like you comes along and tells me about daemons."

Alfred beamed. "You can ask me anything you like, Lily. I'd love to talk to you more."

"Are you always so open and out there with girls? It's a tad disarming," Lily admitted.

"Never. But you caught me eye and my father always said if someone catches your eye, do your best to catch theirs."

Lily gaped and Alfred's smile broadened.

"We're closing in. Hurry up, you two, and keep the chatting down." Aoife's sandpaper voice carried through the trees back to where they stood.

Silently, Lily thanked Aoife for her timely intrusion.

What the hell does someone even say to that? she wondered, shooting Alfred another glance as they trudged onward.

"I DID NOT SEE *this* coming. It's huge. How are we going to get past it?" Lily overheard Brigit asking Jane as the manor house sprang out of the tree line five minutes later.

Lily followed Brigit's gaze over the massive lawn but saw nothing abnormal.

"Impressive magical engineering. They must have some truly powerful witches or other magical creatures with them to produce a single shield of that size," Jane exchanged looks with Brigit and Lily sensed they were both thinking of Noro, the elusive fata Nora had mentioned in her letter.

"Much more problematic than the smaller shields we'd been anticipating," Brigit paused and examined the house again. "I think our best bet will be to break the shield from all angles. Here's hoping it cracks fast. Do you think dividing into smaller squads to increase spell surface area would help?"

"I don't think I feel comfortable about anyone entering that monstrosity of a home in a smaller group than we planned for," Aoife jumped into Jane and Brigit's conversation. "It makes us too vulnerable."

Lily squinted and this time she saw what her mother was talking about: the faint fluid-like appearance of the air surrounding the manor. *Damn, that is huge,* she thought, her eyes searching for a crack or seam that usually gave a shield's positions away.

Instinctively she knew this shield had many purposes. Why else would they put so much effort into making it massive when smaller shields on the doors would do?

Keeping intruders out was a no-brainer, but Lily suspected this shield also functioned as a preliminary alarm system to smaller shields or spells. One attack on the shield would sound an alarm and give away the attackers' location before they even touched the manor. Its uniformity suggested it was also being used to keep certain types of magic in check inside. Lily had never seen a shield that performed that function but she knew they existed.

Otherwise wouldn't it be easier to simply piece together smaller shields like a patchwork quilt? I bet they wanted to disable Evelyn's magic and for that the shield would have to be flawless. It's what I would do if I kidnapped her.

"We must be precise in our positioning," Gwenn added. "Forget all earlier plans regarding entry points. It makes more sense for the groups to be at the four cardinal directions and attack each side so that monstrosity falls equally. Undoubtedly, alarms will sound and a front guard will come barreling out. Once the shield has fallen, enter wherever you can and get to your assigned floor as quickly as possible."

The crowd murmured around her, and Lily couldn't help but agree with their concerns.

"What if it doesn't fall?" Jo whispered next to Lily.

"What if it falls too slow and the Acolytes bring out an entire army?" Roger yelled.

"What if we never even get the chance to enter and Evelyn stays a captive?" an elf broached.

Lily glanced at Sara as the crowd debated. She wished they were in the same group. Unfortunately, Lily's niggling feeling they should stick together couldn't argue with Brigit's and Jane's logic.

"You two will be easier to defend if you're in different groups. Besides rescuing your sister, your safety is my main priority. If we have you together in one squad and your squad is under attack, how will your teammates choose whom to defend? Or worse, if you were in the same squad and it got captured, I'd lose two of you in one go. I'm sorry, Lil, I just can't handle that," Brigit had explained when Lily broached the question as they left the safe house.

Maybe I should have fought harder to be in the same group as Sara? With all the uncertainty piling on top of their battle plan, it seemed increasingly important that they remain together.

"It's not perfect, but it's the best plan we have considering the change of circumstance," Jane agreed with Gwenn. "Time is ticking and we have to get Evelyn out. Once the shield falls, rush the building. With any luck we'll be able to find our ways to the areas we studied online. Those of you without magic to break the shield, support your squad in any way possible. Follow me, I'll drop each group at a cardinal point."

The army followed Jane and her compass in a wide circle around the property. It was only when they reached true north where Jane indicated Gamma Squad, Lily's squad, would be dropped that she knew what to do. She rushed over to Sara and threw her arms around her.

"Find me in there, will you? I have a feeling we need to be together," Lily whispered, hoping the short locks of Sara's pixie cut were long enough to hide the movement of her lips.

Sara grabbed Lily's hand, squeezed it tight, and nodded before breaking loose and following Jane to her own squadron's station.

"Hope you two aren't making your own plans there," Aoife whispered, sidling up next to Lily.

Lily turned to her aunt, trying to hide the shock she

felt. She'd been so caught up with Alfred, then thinking about the shield and how to meet up with Sara, that she'd forgotten both she and Sara had received guardians they were to stay close to during the battle.

Aoife was assigned to Lily to make up for Lily's mediocre firepower, and Mary, as a water witch and Sara's elemental opposite, would stick with Sara. Though Lily knew she should feel grateful to have Aoife, a fire witch of renowned power, in her corner, Lily couldn't help but think of Aoife as another obstacle to overcome if Lily and Sara were to find each other.

"Just wishing each other luck. We should keep an eye out for the signals," Lily said, clamping down her mind barriers and turning to avoid the evaluating copper-colored eyes that matched her sister's.

They had been in position less than five minutes when Lily caught sight of a fireball flying high in the air from the west.

"There's the first sign. After my shower of fireballs hit their peak, we begin," Aoife said to the group. "Use the strongest destructive spell or power you can. With any luck our combination of spells and different magics"—she nodded at Eros, the single elf in their group—"will crack the shield quickly. Alfred, you know what to do." Aoife waited until the fireballs from the south and then the east flew up from the trees before shooting a final shower of golden balls high in the sky.

The rush of magic that followed was stronger than anything Lily had ever experienced. She felt as though she had opened a window during a hurricane and would be blown away at any second.

Lily turned to see six wands raised high in the air, spewing streams of light and fire from their tips.

Eros the elf stood with a metal staff at his side, eyes closed and calm as if he were in meditation, while light and wind swirled from the top of his head to collide with the shield.

Lily's eyes sought Alfred's but like Eros, the daemon had his eyes closed. Her gaze darted across his creamy brown skin, taking in the faint yellow light that radiated from it. Though she still wasn't exactly sure how daemon magic worked, she assumed Alfred was harnessing every tiny molecule of errant energy from the witches and elf around him, waiting for the perfect time to strike.

Sylvia, a witch Lily had met this morning, stood in the center of the squad, watching the rest work. Lily wracked her brain trying to recall what Sylvia's speciality was before coming up empty and moving on to the final member of the group.

Quinn, the only other witch in Gamma Squad

besides Lily and Aoife who had no use for a wand shot beams of light from her hands nearly as fast as Aoife.

"Whenever you're done daydreaming, we could really use your help here, Lil," Aoife growled, sweat pouring from her face.

Lily turned to see white hot cracks forming in the shield, small portions of which had already fallen to the ground.

"Shit. Sorry, Aoife. Lascarma!" Lily held her palms to the sky and her shredding spell flew through the air.

"Whoa! Dang girl, did I ever feel that one!" Alfred cheered from behind her.

Lily couldn't help herself. She grinned.

A potent blend of fear and elation rampaged through Lily as her spell hit the shield to mix with the spells of other witches and creatures. Without her meaning to, her body levitated off the ground an inch.

"Stay focused," Aoife instructed, using one hand to push Lily back to the ground as the other continued to shoot an array of spells at the shield.

Oh right. It's that easy. Lily paused in her casting. Besides the obvious distractions of magic flying all around her, the scenario felt off. The diversity of spells and magics being thrown at the shield was beyond anything Lily could imagine, yet it was still standing.

She lowered her hands to a section right in front of her and fired off another shredding spell.

Her eyes widened as the shield mended itself in the exact same spot her spell had just landed. "Aoife, it's fixing itself without any help from a witch or . . . whatever other creature," Lily gulped and a vague image rose in her mind of Noro reclining on a couch and fixing the shield with ease as they threw all they had at it.

"Keep going. It's the only chance we've got," Aoife said, her face purple with exertion.

No witch made shield should be able to hold up to this diversity of spells and magics at once. Lily's stomach sank as piece after piece of the shield repaired itself before her eyes.

The storm of power at her back faltered in waves as her squadmates tired. Lily turned to find three witches bent over at their sides, heaving with exertion. Alfred had yet to release any of the bright yellow energy that radiated off him, and Sylvia was still standing uselessly, hands by her side. Only Quinn and Eros kept pace with Aoife, who had not stopped casting for a second.

Lily cast again, harder this time and in one continuous stream of magic. She raised her arms high, intuitively seeking the top of the shield where fewer spells were directed. Her hands grew warm with a familiar heat as her magic hit the dome and she grinned. Sara's fiery essence was landing there too and mixing with Lily's lukewarm magic.

"Hey! I can feel Sa—what the hell!" Lily exclaimed as the blue light they'd seen from the woods, now bigger and brighter, flew out of the manor upward.

Lily watched, her green eyes bulging as the blue light collided with the shield in exactly the same spot as her magic and shattered it into a million shining pieces.

***

Lily flew backward onto Alfred, who was now a sunshine yellow hue and looked like he was about to burst.

"Can't keep your hands off me already, huh?" Alfred teased, though Lily paid little notice.

Rolling onto her side she gasped as all the pieces clicked into place.

"Aoife! The blue light!"

"Aye, it felt like your sister's magic. I felt it too, the second the light shattered the shield. How she produced such a thing, I have no idea." Aoife's wiry frame stiffened as a howl pierced the calm twilight hour. "Here come the weres."

Across the lawn, a handful of grotesque creatures

charged straight at them. Their bodies rippled and shook as they transformed from man to beast.

Lily's hand flew to her mouth as one man, whose lower half already resembled the four legs of a wolf but whose torso was still resolutely human, covered fifty yards in seconds.

Aoife pressed her hands to her temples, and Lily felt a rush of hot air as her aunt flung her arms wide. "We'll be needing reinforcements with that many. Everyone, get up!"

"Alfred. You're in the lead. The rest of us need a mo' to catch our breath. Use whatever wayward energy you collected and let them have it. The vamps will be here soon to help." Aoife pointed the handsome daemon out into the clearing.

"You're going to send him out there alone? But there's so many," Lily said as Alfred skipped out to meet the weres. Catching sight of an easy mark, the werewolves pushed harder, closing the gap between the pack and Gamma Squad fast.

"Trust me, Lil. Alfred will be fine."

It took everything Lily had not to run out and join the fight—not that she knew how best to fight off six werewolves or even one, a real problem considering her current predicament.

"Aoife! How do I fight a were? What do I use?"

"What do you mean?" Aoife asked, tearing her eyes from the scene.

"Like how do I hurt them? Vampires are fire, but what injures a werewolf?" She glanced at Alfred and moved close to whisper to her aunt. "And daemons. What about them?"

"Shouldn't this have come up a few hours ago? I swear this is all the internet's fault, with its last-minute, instant knowledge," Aoife huffed, unable to keep the tone of exasperation from her voice. "Anything that can kill or injure a witch can kill or injure a werewolf. Daemons are the same. You may have to fight both species longer, though; their hides and skin are imbued with protective properties."

Kill a witch, daemon, or werewolf? Lily's stomach dropped. It went against her very nature as a healer to fight to the death—though she had to admit she had imagined killing vampires, two in particular, and a fata if he was even in there. But killing someone like her, a living humanoid creature with family, was different.

I'm not even sure I could do it to Nora, and I have every right to be pissed at her . . . At least all vamps beside Empusa and Amon are already technically dead, and fata are aliens, Lily stopped trying to reason with herself. *I'll just start with injuring people.*

"Watch this, Lil," Aoife pointed to Alfred, who was vibrating violently.

Ten weres, two hundred feet away mere seconds ago, were now only thirty feet, then twenty, then ten away.

The leader of the pack leapt high in the air above Alfred, who remained stuck in place, seemingly unperturbed by the pack of wolves surrounding him. The leader's jaws were inches from clamping down on Alfred's head when suddenly beams of light flew from the daemon in the direction of the werewolves.

The pack leader exploded, showering the ground with blood and half-intact organs. Two other wolves yelped and rolled in the snow to extinguish the flames that clung to their fur. Another lay dead fifteen feet from Alfred. The ones that had scurried away in time looked hesitant to advance once more.

"Holy shit," Lily whispered as Alfred pulled a dagger from a sheath hidden beneath the bulk of his jacket and slit the necks of the burnt weres as they rolled in the snow.

"And that, wee one, is why we do not worry about daemons," Aoife said, rising from her crouch, a grim smile on her face. "Move out, troops! Let's go help our man!"

The Battle of Peacock Manor
Lily

By the time Lily made it to where Alfred stood, Celestine and the four other vampires were already there, annihilating the werewolves that had been backing away from Alfred. A trail of other were bodies lined the vampires' path across the snow.

It seemed to Lily that despite all their explicit attack training at Fern Cottage, she was going to get a crash course today, complete with blood and guts and all sorts of creatures.

"Good call rounding up the vamps, Aoife," Alfred said as the last werewolf fell at Celestine's hands. "We made fast work of the first wave. Hopefully, whatever else is in that mansion is that easy."

"I wouldn't count on it. Don't let your guard down

because of one easy victory. Absorb whatever wayward magic you can from us and stay next to Lily. Use whatever you've got to defend her."

"With pleasure, sergeant," Alfred said falling into place beside Lily, who felt a flutter in her chest, despite the blood covering the daemon.

They covered the rest of the lawn with ease and Aoife led Gamma Squad along the side of the building abutting the garden and a huge door. Intended as the groundskeeper's entrance, the door would open to a small basement chamber supposedly filled with lawn maintenance equipment. If the photos and diagrams online were accurate, they could then access a discreet staircase built to wind its way up past the kitchen on the ground floor, to a separate quarters kept for the groundskeeper on the second floor.

After seeing the size of the lawn and garden, even Lily, an earth witch and garden lover, could understand why a groundskeeper could demand such privacy. Few would be up for maintaining a property so large.

"Clostium," Aoife said, gripping the knob of the oversized door without hesitation and pulling.

The metal knob flashed red-hot and Aoife snatched her hand away. "Well, they're not as dim as we hoped they'd be. There's an enchantment to repel an unlocking spell. If there's one on this entrance, it's likely the other entrances are under similar spells." Aoife held her singed hand out to Lily.

Lily gripped her aunt's hand. "Salus," she whispered and the burn healed even before it could blister.

"Thanks, Lil," Aoife turned her concentration back to the door. "Well, seeing as we no longer have the element of surprise, we may as well force our way in. Everyone stand back about three meters and cover your eyes." Aoife ushered the group back ten feet before holding her hand out before her.

"Preamporto."

The door shot inward, blowing up a cloud of dust and showering the snow with tiny splinters.

Lily waited, crouched low and hands at the ready for another pack of werewolves to rush out. She sighed with relief when a brisk winter wind blew away the dust to reveal only an empty room filled with riding lawn mowers and a construction crew's worth of shovels.

"Should we grab something as a weapon?" a wizard asked, glancing at Sylvia, who had yet to display any form of magical prowess.

"If you're not already armed that's not a bad idea. Make sure it's something small, and preferably iron if you can identify it, but only if you can still use your wand. Lily, you take this," Aoife said, shoving a rusted trowel into Lily's hands.

Lily ran her thumb over the wooden handle as she stared down at the trowel. The common tool she had used many times when assisting Em and Annika in the garden was now something else.

A weapon. *An iron weapon.*

She recalled Gwenn stating iron, a metal deadly to fairies, was hypothesized in the folklore to also be lethal to the ancestors of all magical beings on Earth, the fata.

Aoife thinks Noro is up there, too. While Lily had thought the same thing many times, she hadn't dared to broach the question out loud. It seemed too crazy to think they might run into a magical alien at any second.

"You alright, Lily?" Alfred asked. He was glowing again, having picked up a little magical energy on their run to the door.

She nodded and followed Aoife up the winding staircase.

The kitchen was huge, silent, and spotless save for the dust that lay thick on the marble countertops. *Have we stumbled upon an unused wing of the house? Does that mean the other squads are being bombarded while we explore?*

Aoife must have had the same idea because she flew up the next flight of stairs.

"Aoife. Should we—?" Lily stopped short when she found Aoife circling the gardener's room.

This room, too, was empty and larger than any other bedroom Lily had seen in real life. Unlike the kitchen the bedroom appeared lived in. Plates of half-eaten fruits and vegetables in various states of decay dotted side tables and the naked mattress nestled in a canopy frame. Piles of paper covered the floor along with a rumpled sheet and a dozen decorative pillows.

Lily bent down to examine a sheet of paper at her feet. Small dots, lines, and words she recognized as astrological names covered the paper's surface. "What is this place?"

"I'm not sure . . ." Aoife said, pausing in her examination of a star chart at her feet. "But if I had to guess, I'd say it's someone's room. Someone who presumably has an obsession with astronomy and astrology." She held up a handful of astrological charts.

"And has magic," Alfred said and Lily noticed his hands cracking and popping like the flash of a camera. "I can sense a residual power, though it's like nothing I've come across."

Lily's eyes met Aoife's, and she knew they were thinking the same thing. This was a fata room.

"Alfred, pick up as much power as you can from here; we may need it. You two," Aoife pointed to Jo and a wizard, "stay with Alfred while he collects power. Lily and everyone else will come with me."

"But I thought we weren't supposed to split up," Lily said glancing at Alfred.

"Plans change, Lil. We may need whatever energy Alfred can collect more than we need three extra people right now. We'll be searching this floor for Evelyn. Alfred, just make sure your group finds us when you're done."

"I'll be fine," Alfred said taking Lily's hand and squeezing it with a devilish wink that made her head swim.

What's come over me? Lily wondered, squeezing Alfred's hand in return before rushing out the door behind Aoife. A clatter of metal, shouts, and cracking of wood hit her ears as she entered the hallway.

"This way," Aoife said, sprinting toward the commotion.

Lily raced after her aunt, her breath tinged with panic. *Closer, closer.* The word repeated over and over in her head as the screams, yells, and moans grew louder.

And then they were there, looking over the edge of an enormous spiraling marble staircase at the fighting below. Lily spotted Brigit and half of Beta Squad, though not the flashing red hair she'd hoped to see, battling their way through two dozen hairy, half-transformed men.

"Should we help?" Lily asked watching Roger, in a surprising show of power, slam a werewolf against the wall with a blasting spell.

"Do you need to ask?" Aoife asked and shot a ball of fire at a werewolf. Flames ate at the were's fur and he rolled to the ground to put it out.

"Mahasoka," Lily murmured and vines shot from her fingertips to bind the same were's feet and legs together.

"Nice! I'll stun the rest and you clean up with the vines? Quinn, you help, too. Everyone else, watch our backs."

Sylvia, Eros, and the rest of their group turned to face opposite sides of the hallway, guarding the witches as they sniped.

Within thirty seconds they had a dozen weres bound on the floor.

The moment the last were fell, Brigit glanced up, mouthed her thanks, and waved them on.

"Now that they have that lot under control, let's search the rooms for Evelyn," Aoife said.

"Down there!" Sylvia said, her usual soft-spoken voice projecting despite the chaos. "The first door on the right, someone opened it and poked their head out."

"You're up then, Sylvia," Aoife said, as they approached the door Sylvia had pointed out.

Sylvia nodded, widened her stance and readied her wand.

"Cover your ears, Gamma Team," Aoife instructed.

"But why—?"

"Do it, Lil," Aoife said, and Lily turned to see everyone else already had their hands over their ears.

Lily's brows furrowed as she covered her ears.

Without further explanation, Aoife planted her hands over her ears, kicked open the door, and jumped back.

An otherworldly shriek sounded, shaking the entire hallway. Lily's legs buckled. *What the hell?*

Then she saw Sylvia, wand raised and mouth open, projecting a soul-shattering scream. Visible sound waves shot from Sylvia's lips, creating a rippling effect in the air into the room beyond the door.

"Brilliant, Sylvia," Aoife said as Sylvia's mouth closed and the vibrations in the air ceased. She stepped over the threshold and examined its occupants.

"Witches, fae, and daemons. No vamps or other. Someone should wait in the hall so Alfred can find us and come mop up. It looks as if they were ready to pounce on us." Aoife gestured to a man who'd fallen to lay half on, half off a luxurious day couch. "There'll be loads of wayward power in here."

"One step ahead of you," Alfred said, running into the room his skin a luminous yellow-orange. He shot Lily a lopsided grin and a sigh of relief escaped Lily's lips. *He's safe . . .*

"Alright, you two, there'll be time for flirting later. Alfred, make it snappy. Lil, bind this lot up and we'll keep moving. I'm going to check the attached room." Aoife approached the door on the opposite side of the room, arms extended, only to find two more passed-out creatures on the other side of the door. "And don't miss in here, Alfred and Lil!"

Lily stuck out her tongue at Aoife then performed eight vine-rope spells in rapid succession. Alfred was still collecting energy when she'd finished so Lily fell into step beside Sylvia. "What kind of supe are you?" Lily asked, trying to pry her mind from Alfred's deep dimples as the squad moved on.

"Half banshee, half witch. Shame is I got the weaker half of both. I'm shit at magic without a wand and have only got three good screams in me before I'm toast," Sylvia shrugged, "Ma always said use what you got, though."

"Are they dead?"

"Knocked out. Witches, fae, weres, and daemons

can't handle the high vibrations. If there'd been a djinn or vamp in here, they'd have been fine more or less. It depends on how close the creatures are to humans. That's why the rest of you had to cover your ears. We can't be hauling around our passed out squadmates."

"That would be a problem." Lily agreed.

"Alright, Gamma Team, it's time to divide and conquer that maze of rooms we talked about. If we clear them all and don't find Evelyn, we move up to the top floor. Alfred, Sylvia, Lily, and Eros, you stay with me. The rest work your way down the rooms on the other side of the hall. Quinn, you lead your half. We'll meet you at the end of the hallway."

Though Lily knew it made sense given the awkward layout and size of the manor, her nerves jangled at the idea of being separated from her squadmates. She hoped that despite their lackluster performance thus far they would surprise her. *Like Roger. Yea, they're all super secret ninja witches like Roger.*

As they moved on, Lily was both relieved and sick to find that while all the rooms on their side appeared lived in, they were also empty. *Have we wasted our time on this floor? What's happening on the other levels? I hope everyone is safe.*

"All clear on this side," Aoife said, sweeping through

the final back room on their side of the hallway unimpeded. "Let's go check on the others."

They arrived in the hallway just in time to see Quinn scramble out of a door, blood pouring from a gash on her arm and a pair of clawed hands reaching out to pull her back in.

"Lotu!" Lily cried.

Her charm hit its mark and the arm flew backward to bind against the body of a muscular man.

"Shut it!" Quinn screamed.

Aoife shot the man back into the room with a spell and slammed the door while the rest of Gamma Squad raced to help Quinn.

"What happened?" Lily asked, pulling the zipper on her healer's fanny pack open and assessing what she had that could help.

"It was a massacre." Tears shone in Quinn's eyes. "Felix and his pack were in there."

"Are they all dead?" A lump rose in Lily's throat as she dabbed Quinn's wound with disinfectant.

"Not all of them. Sally and Todd died fighting, but they captured the rest. Took them upstairs—there's a servant's stairway on the far side of each room on this side. They could be anywhere by now."

"So there's no one in there?" Aoife asked.

"Positive."

We've lost almost half of our team already. Tears sprung into Lily's eyes as she recalled the joy and subsequent spark Jo, the enerkinesis witch she'd met only hours ago, expressed when they'd shook hands. *She wouldn't have been so happy if she knew what was coming.* Lily wiped her eyes and turned her attention resolutely back to Quinn's arm.

"I can't stitch that up, it's too large and the stitches won't hold if you move anyhow, but it's clean now and I can place a benda charm over it so nothing can touch it. A real dressing would probably hinder your ability to defend yourself. I also administered a strong tincture of Shepherd's Purse and yarrow so the bleeding would stop. Try not to hit it on anything," Lily sighed and her hands dropped to her side.

"Let me help." Eros bent down to kneel by Lily. "Elf healing differs from a witch's. I can seal the wound but you won't be healed on the inside and it may still hurt when you move. Is that something you want, Quinn?"

Quinn nodded, her face set into hard lines, "As long as I can fight, I don't care what you two do."

The skin on Quinn's arm puckered and bubbled like a stew over high flame before growing and stretching taut over exposed flesh. Lily glanced at Eros whose hands stopped moving as soon as the skin sealed. *Wish I could heal wounds that quick.*

"Are you fit, Quinn?"

Quinn grimaced but nodded.

"Good. I want us all to stick together until we get up that staircase. We'll reassess once we see what's happening on the next floor." Aoife knelt and helped Quinn to her feet. "Alfred, you look ready to explode; you cover Quinn. Lily, don't leave my side."

<hr>

SCREAMS and the tinkle of breaking glass grew louder as Gamma Squad neared the staircase. Lily peeked over the banister, her eyes sweeping the first floor for a hint of bright red hair but finding none. Brigit and Mary, too, were absent, indicating that Beta Squad had made it to the top floor. *So far, so good,* Lily thought turning and bounding up the stairs with her squad.

Ten steps from the top a strangled scream sounded. Lily started and crashed into Aoife, who had stopped dead in her tracks. Aoife whirled about, righted them both, and extended her hands to fight.

"A fireball." Sylvia shook out a smoking sleeve and pointing to the right, eyes wide with terror.

Lily followed Sylvia's finger to find a spell fly straight for her. She ducked and a stream of magic flew over the banister grazing the end of her ponytail with a sizzle.

"Arma!" Aoife yelled, throwing her arms in a wide circle to encompass them all. "Stay behind the shield. Those were just loose spells. No one's actually seen us yet, but as soon as we crest the staircase, they will. We move forward together until we have to fight."

A clamor of crashing metal, shattered glass, shouts, and mangled screams rushed forth with each spell that hit Aoife's shield. Still, the shield held strong as Aoife pushed more power into it so that it could absorb enemy magic and heal itself in an instant.

As they summited the top of the staircase Lily's eyes widened at the scene before them. They were in a ball-room of sorts.

A ballroom transformed into a battlefield.

An uncountable number of bodies sprawled out across the polished marbled floor, some tied up while others lay gutted or with their eyes wide open. *My tying up and leaving my enemies days are over.* Her healer's fingers curled in instinctive revulsion at the thought and she shook her head. *Toughen up, Lil! It's fight or be a pawn.*

A cascade of fireballs sparked in Lily's peripheral vision. She swiveled her neck to see Brigit flinging fire at a vampire so covered in blood, it made Lily's heart seize.

She found Mary next, her white camo popping out of the mayhem and her blonde hair whipping around her face as she dueled another witch. A few witches Lily recognized from Jane's group had made it to the top floor, too. She was still searching for Sara when a bright ball of light across the room caught her attention.

"What is that?" Lily asked pointing to the neon ball of light.

"No freaking way," Alfred's eyes lit up. "Looks like I have a date with another daemon. This should be fun. I don't get to practice with daemons at my level often." He strode toward what Lily now realized was a glowing man with a vicious smile on his face.

Aoife lifted her shield, allowing Alfred to pass under before resetting it.

"Should someone—?"

"No. Let Alfred do it. That daemon over there has absorbed too much energy. Fighting him would just give him more. It's best that another daemon handle him. Alfred knows what he's doing and if he's as good as Jane says he is, Alfred can absorb whatever the daemon gives off when he defeats him." Aoife squeezed Lily's hand.

Lily nodded, not entirely convinced as she forced her eyes off Alfred's back and into the raging crowd, searching for the smallest hint of red or flashing copper.

And then she saw her. Sara, all the way on the other

side of the ballroom, was like a phoenix, alive with fire, and battling two witches at once. Three huge stained-glass windows framed her small form, the colors within them dancing and flashing with the fire Sara flung about.

"Lift the shield. I have to help Sara," Lily said.

Two more spells hit Aoife's shield precisely where Lily stood and she winced. *Bad timing . . .*

"We'll help her, but you must stay with me. You two are far too important to lose, and we still have to find Evelyn. We'll run to Brigit, grab her, then on to Sara. Everyone else, join the fight where needed!"

Lily nodded. Having Aoife and Brigit with her could only help her chances of saving Sara.

"Shield down on three, two, *one!*" Aoife released her shield and they all crouched low as a dozen incoming spells flew at them, missing them by inches. Aoife grabbed Lily's hand and pulled her into the fray, straight toward Brigit, who like her youngest daughter was now battling multiple adversaries.

"Impingo," Lily cried, deflecting a spell destined to hit Brigit straight in the chest as Brigit went on the offense shooting a stunning spell so strong at one wizard that he fell to the ground like a log.

Aoife tossed a shield between Brigit's back and a black-haired vampire who was creeping up behind her.

The vampire launched himself into Aoife's shield and Lily pumped a fist in the air. They were at Brigit's side seconds later, shoulder to shoulder.

"Ahh," a vicious voice hissed at Lily's back and she whirled about to see a blur of motion come to a stop, revealing a vampire more feral in appearance than Empusa or Amon. The vampire smiled, blood dripping from his cheeks and hands. "Noro will be pleased to see you here. We may get a three for one special tonight."

Noro is here! The hair on Lily's arms stood up.

"Not if we can help it," Aoife said, summoning a massive flame gate around them to close the trio in with the vampire.

The vampire's face fell and Aoife constricted the circle, closing them in tighter and tighter. "Let me out. You'll regret it if you don't. I'm Empusa's favorite son," he begged, all bravado gone as the end of his life flashed before him.

"Somehow I doubt that," Aoife said with a smirk as twenty balls of fire flew effortlessly from her outstretched palms.

Lily's mouth gaped as the flames incinerated the vampire. No wonder the Acolytes had sought other creatures as reinforcement. She hadn't seen her aunt in action last time.

"Nice one, Aoife," Brigit said, slapping her youngest sister on the back with a smirk.

Aoife released her flame gate to reveal the witch whose spell Lily had deflected minutes earlier waiting behind it, her wand pointed straight at Lily.

"Aber-, a . . ." Lily, surprised at the witch's sudden appearance, faltered with the spell.

But Brigit was on it, "Volavari."

The witch's wand dropped from her hand as she flew to the top of the rafters.

"Yea, Brig!" Aoife cheered, grinning as the witch scowled down at them.

"Didn't mean to take that from you, Lil. It was a mom reflex," Brigit said, shooting Lily a sheepish glance.

Lily nodded though her attention had already shifted. She'd spotted Selma, Rena, and Annika, who should have been in the basement, across the large ballroom battling with all their might.

From what Lily could tell, Selma was using her siren gifts to subdue any males within her range while Rena and Annika alternated fighting the females that approached and binding their captives. It was scrappy as all hell and she loved it. Lily watched as Annika shot a well-aimed hex and her worry deflated.

"Let's go help Sara," Lily said, finally assured her

adoptive family could take care of themselves. She took off, leaving Aoife and Brigit in her wake.

Spell after spell flew from Sara's outstretched hands as she whirled about battling a werewolf and two witches. A pile of ash lay at her feet, indicating what had happened to her last opponent. A mere thirty feet away, Lily saw one of the witches Sara was fighting, a pale, petite brunette, lunge at her sister with a dagger.

"Come on, little witchling! Don't tell me you're out of gas already! Is that all you have?" the brunette witch jeered as she deflected Sara's spell and threatened to throw the blade.

Lily screeched to a halt and pointed carefully at the witch, not wanting to hit Sara instead. "Birarazi!"

Her spell hit its target and the witch started to spin like a top, her long brown hair ending in a candle shape above her head. "I'd say she's got one up on you, hag," Lily yelled and sent the witch flying through the stained-glass window.

"That's her. That's the other one," the werewolf roared, and before Lily knew it a terrifying wolf man with enlarged canines and a chest so hairy it rivaled a gorilla's was charging at her.

"Cogerba!" Lily's spell grazed his hide and Lily's mouth fell open as she stood frozen in place while the wolf man kept charging. "Hercapto," Lily tried again, but the grass that rose from the marble grew too slowly to grasp the man-wolf by the ankles and capture him.

The half man, half wolf laughed and gained speed. "The weak one is mine!"

"Like hell she is," Brigit said, sending a shower of sparks at the were as she ran to Lily's side.

The sparks caught on the man's copious body hair. He screamed and fell to the floor trying to pat the fire out. "Go help Sara, Lil. We'll take care of him and those fools" Brigit gestured to a witch and vampire running toward them from the other direction.

"You found me!" Sara said, exhaustion clear in her voice as Lily finally joined her side.

"Of course I did. You're my sister. I'll never leave you." Lily jumped to avoid a curse while simultaneously shooting a freezing hex at the blonde Amazon witch Sara had been fighting. Despite being a wand user, the Amazon was clearly a witch of great skill. That Sara had lasted this long on her own, with this witch, let alone the werewolf and the dagger-wielding brunette, was astonishing.

Spells flew back and forth at a mind-boggling rate and the Amazon deflected or reflected them all. Within minutes it became apparent that Sara and Lily would not be able to beat the Amazon on skill alone. They didn't know enough magic yet, and Brigit and Aoife were still preoccupied with the werewolf, now fully transformed, and the witch and vampire who had come to his aid.

We have to shake things up, catch her unaware, if we're to beat this witch . . . and I think I know just the way.

Lily lifted a corner of her mind barrier and pushed her idea into her sister's head.

Sara's eyes widened and her eyes locked with Lily's.

"Do you trust me? I swear I'll be fast," Lily gasped, hurled a spinning spell at the Amazon who cackled and flung it into the crowd behind her without looking.

Sara nodded, no longer able to speak because she was panting so hard.

With that Lily disappeared into the fray.

The blonde Amazon's laughter rang through the chaos, high and cold. "Your sister decided you weren't worth it, eh?" the witch jeered.

It took all the willpower Lily had to not turn around right then. But she stayed on track sprinting in a wide circle around the ballroom, hoping the witch would write Lily off as she waited for the perfect shot.

As she ran Lily saw Alfred, now a dim yellow, beheading another daemon, and Jane leaping upon the back of a massive wolf pinning Sylvia to the ground. Dashing past the grand staircase, Lily shot a couple fireballs at two weres rushing up the steps. They howled and fell back down the steps as their fur caught on fire.

Her pace slowed as she passed Rena, Annika, and Selma and sent their new opponents into a rousing Celtic jig. Rena gave her the thumbs up and Lily grinned, never breaking stride.

And then she was back where she started, closing in and gaining speed. Lily practically flew toward Brigit and Aoife, who were still battling numerous opponents. But Lily didn't dare act on their behalf. They were moving too fast, dancing around the burnt, furious were, witch, and agile vampire. She couldn't be sure she wouldn't hit them instead of their opponents.

With a final burst of speed she rounded on Sara, bound in a flame gate of her own making with the blonde witch and battling for her life. As she drew closer Lily effortlessly wove a binding spell with water and shot it through the fire, right at the blonde witch.

Sara's flame gate flew back up a second after Lily saw the Amazon witch fall to the ground, her arms and legs clamped to her torso and water streaming off her face.

"Hell yes!" Lily squealed.

"Never thought I'd be happy to see that dirty trick again," Sara wheezed as she dropped her flame gate.

The witch snarled from her position on the floor,

pure hatred in her eyes, "You'll never be able to defeat him. Our master is too great. You don't stand a chance."

"Oh, shove it," Sara said waving her hand and spelling the witch's mouth shut.

Kicking the wand from the witch's grip, Lily stomped on it, cracking it in half with an invigorating snap. "Herbcapto," she said, just because the witch had pissed her off so much. She smiled as grass grew from the smooth marble floor to imprison the witch in long green blades. "Come on. Let's help Brigit and Aoife."

The sisters snuck up behind the vampire dancing dangerously close to Brigit.

"Together?" Sara asked, her cheeks flushed.

Lily nodded. "On three. One. Two. Flampila!"

The vampire never even knew they were there.

Free of her opponent, Brigit shot them a grateful smile. "Dionean! Dionean!" she cried, knocking out the were and witch engaging Aoife with two sneaky stunning spells.

"Great job, girls. And I saw that clever idea, Lily," Brigit wheezed.

"When you should have been focused on your own fight?" Lily raised her eyebrows at her mother.

Brigit shrugged, "You can't blame a mother for looking after her young. I told you, you three are my first priority."

"I bet they're keeping Evelyn down there," Aoife interrupted and gestured down the left fork of the hallway. "I saw the vamp you were fighting guarding the entrance to that wing before he took you on, Brig. Apparently, he couldn't help himself."

Brigit held up her arm to reveal a superficial but profusely bleeding gash, "I think this may have lured him in. Lil?"

Lily grasped her mother's arm. It was riddled with red punctures as if teeth had ripped through Brigit's skin. "Is it a werewolf bite?" Her heart was racing. If it was a were bite, nothing she did could help her mother.

"Goddess be, no!" Brigit said. "A stray spell from that blasted witch who was fighting Aoife."

A breath of relief escaped Lily's lips. She pulled a dried angelica leaf from her healer's pack and placed it over the wound. "Salus," she whispered, closing her eyes and trusting her family to have her back if anyone should rush them.

Even with the added potency of the angelica, the spell took longer than usual to work but Lily was sure that was normal. *I've used a lot of energy fighting,* she reminded herself. *I should just be happy this wound isn't like Quinn's and I can actually fix it.* A final rush of healing magic left her and Lily removed the leaf to find raw, pink skin on Brigit's arm.

Brigit examined the site of injury. "I'll tell Fiona to work on building your stamina when we get back home, but this will work for now." There was no malice in her voice, only honest concern and a certainty they would escape the manor tonight. "Now let's go rescue your sister."

An Ally

Evelyn

"Shield the door! They're on this floor," an athletic witch commanded.

They're coming to save me.

"Drink this, siren," Empusa snarled.

"Again?" Evelyn croaked. She tore her gaze from her emaciated body to find the vampire hovering over her, a glass of blood in her hands. "But I had the other's . . ."

"I am aware you drank my brother's blood this morning. And I'm bidding you to drink mine. In case you're too dense to hear, your wretched family has brought an army down upon us. You must create another portal now and our blood is the only thing that makes you strong enough to do so."

There was no fighting it. Evelyn could barely lift her arms, let alone stop Empusa from pouring blood down her throat. While the sinewy muscles from her last vampire blood cocktail remained, they lay on bones without a smoothing cover of fat. It created the illusion that Evelyn was nothing more than a buff skeleton.

She was sure creating another portal was out of the question. Just two hours prior, when the shield alarms first sounded, Noro had commanded Evelyn to open her second portal, and she'd failed. She was sure this was because it had been too soon after the first portal, which had nearly killed her.

Slowly, she took the glass from Empusa and lifted it to her lips.

"Drink faster, witch," Empusa hissed and tilted the cup up so the blood rushed into Evelyn's mouth faster.

Evelyn's eyes narrowed, though she continued to drink. *Each drop I drink weakens Empusa and Amon. If I can't fight them, it's the least I can do.*

"The shields are on the door, Mistress," a wizard simpered, earning himself one of Empusa's seductive smiles.

"Good. Father, would you add the final touch?" Empusa turned to the navy fata. Noro had been floating near the window for two hours, staring intently into the woods where a handful of Acolytes had guided the rest of the fata through the trees after the shield that covered Peacock Manor fell.

Maybe my family will have caught a few of the escapee fata in the woods and handled them already. Even as Evelyn dared to hope she knew there was no way. Noro would never put Dimia or his kind in danger. The rest of the Acolytes sure but not the fata.

No, he knew someone would come save me eventually. I bet he had an escape route planned the entire time. The fata are probably already on their way to a place where they can hide and absorb magic until they build up the strength to fight.

"With pleasure. Move aside Acolytes," Noro said and the crowd in the room parted wordlessly, creating a path from Noro to the door. A flourish of air—blue and purple and yellow swirls, the likes of which Evelyn had never seen—flew across the room to hit the door shielded with numerous layers of witching magic. The door sparkled, contracted, and then expanded back to normal size once more.

Evelyn's eyes widened, and Noro's mouth grew round with delight. He liked that he'd impressed her. "It's not a charm you'll be learning soon, Eve. We, the fata, use that charm on Hecate only for the highest defense. Any witch or wizard who gets past the superficial spells my Acolytes set will face instant death once they reach my spell. My shield ensures you will not need to rush creating the portal. No one on this planet, save for the fata you brought over yesterday, have knowledge enough to break through my magic."

A flutter of movement pushed against Evelyn's chest and she sighed. She'd discovered in her brief period of consciousness that she had, at best, a moderate amount of control over her pneuma. It seemed she was able to choose when to let it out and ask it where to go but it didn't always listen. If she ignored it too long, the flutter often grew into pain and she ended up letting it out either way. It was infuriating to have something living within her but not have full control over it.

So my family is finally here to save me and you want to abandon me for a little intergalactic mission, is that it? Evelyn's voice was scathing inside her head. *Well, I'm not letting you out until I have to. You're part of me, so why are you on their side?*

The flutter stopped, shot up to her neck, and swayed from side to side.

What the? Are you shaking my head?

The flutter moved up and down.

Holy shit. This is crazy. So you're not on Noro's side?

The flutter moved side to side once more.

Damn. That changes things. Sorry I yelled at you, but we have to talk fast. About that fata charm Noro just used . . .

The Reckoning

Lily

LILY, Sara, Brigit, and Aoife sprinted across the ballroom to the hallway entrance Aoife had seen the vampire guarding. Lily glanced over her shoulder as she ran and her eyes zeroed in on Selma, then darted to Rena and Annika, who fought nearby. She exhaled. All three were still safe—their reactions a bit slower, perhaps, but they were still fighting.

Thank the goddess.

She reached the hallway first, turned, and saw Mary and Gwenn rushing to catch up with their group. Blood smeared Mary's winter camo and Gwenn's dark brown hair was falling out of her hair tie but they, too, appeared uninjured.

"Mary! Gwenn!" Brigit cried after joining Lily in

the relative safety of the hallway. "Where have you been?"

The collective scents of her witchy family members —pepper, ginger, cinnamon, lavender, grapefruit, rain, and holy basil mixed with the blood and sweat from battle—overcame Lily and her head swam.

"We were on the opposite side of the room. We saw Lil race around the ballroom and have been fighting our way across to join you since. Everyone good?" Mary asked, wiping her forehead and smearing blood across it.

"No worse than expected." Aoife nudged them down the hallway, away from the eyes of any Acolytes who might follow. "Now then, does anyone remember where the master rooms are? Evelyn wasn't on the middle floors so I'd wager they're keeping her near Empusa's and Amon's rooms."

"Near the end?" Mary offered, her soprano voice lifting into a question.

They walked down the hall, listening and feeling for shields or magic congregated around the dozens of doors they passed. Twice Lily thought she heard movement behind the sheaths of smooth mahogany, though when she pressed her ear to rich wood the noise ceased. *I wish Sylvia were here. Those last two banshee screams would be useful right now.*

Suddenly, a flash of blue light retreating under a door up ahead caught Lily's eye.

"Did you feel that?" Sara asked, clutching Lily's arm and staring at the spot where the light had been.

Feel it? Before Lily could ask Sara what she was talking about the blue light pulsed again. It extended all the way into the middle of the hall, lingered for a second, and disappeared beneath the crack once more. Lily's heartbeat quickened and she crept toward where the light had just been.

"Something's over here. It's the same shade of blue light that broke the shield. It flashed into the hallway then back under the crack twice." Lily glanced at Aoife. "You know, the light that felt like Evelyn's magic."

Aoife nodded, joined Lily, and pressed her ear to the door. A second later she jumped back, her red hair electrified. "This door's bewitched, that's for sure, and not by any regular shield charm. Strange magic, too, maybe elf?" She lifted her chin and narrowed her copper eyes in question.

Lily couldn't handle the elephant in the room any longer. "What about fata magic?"

Sara inhaled sharply and her hand flew to her mouth.

Lily quirked a brow at her sister's innocence. *She*

must not even have considered Noro would be here. Unlike Sara, I've learned to expect the worst.

However, no one else looked surprised. Least of all Aoife, who didn't pause in her examination of the door.

"Even if Evelyn isn't behind this door, we should check out what is. Any door spelled this heavily, with multiple levels of shields, is hiding something big. Let's hope it's Evelyn so we can get the hell out of here," Aoife said.

"If it's under multiple levels of enchantment, how do we know which spell to use? The wrong one may backfire, right?" Sara's brows knit together.

"Aye," Aoife leaned close and sniffed the dark wood.

A nearby scream broke Lily's contemplation and she turned to find Jane, Quinn, and Alfred at the end of the hallway battling a tall, golden-haired creature that moved with vampiric speed and a transformed werewolf.

"Whatever it is, we better figure it out fast," Lily pointed down the hall. She shot a stunning spell at the were. The spell made it only halfway down the long hall and Lily swore.

"Bloody hell," Gwenn followed Lily's lead and stepped out of the group. "Flampila." A bright blue fireball shot from her hands, missing Quinn by inches, and she swore again. "They're too far away to be accurate. Should I go—"

"No," Brigit said, her tone cutting. "We need you to fight whatever is behind this door. Evelyn is in there. I can feel her. All of this is for naught if we can't save her."

Brigit was right, though that didn't diminish Lily's urge to run and help when the Vikingesque vamp lunged at Alfred fangs bared. Alfred slipped out of the way just in time his dagger extended in his hand. *Goddess, please let that dagger be silver.*

Lily turned back around to concentrate on the door. Surely none of the normal unlocking spells would work, or any spells to force the door open. It wouldn't be anything too obvious.

Lily? Lily . . .

"What?" Lily asked.

Everyone stared at her.

"Who said my name?"

"No one said your name, honey," Brigit said.

"Wait! There it is again!"

It was a whisper of a voice, weak, yet familiar. Whirling about Lily saw Jane, Quinn, and Alfred still fighting tooth and nail to keep the werewolf back. Her heart leapt when she noticed a pile of ash on the floor and fell just as fast when two more werewolves rushed from the ballroom to join the fight. Lily's eyes ran over Alfred once more. While he was stronger and more aggressive than a human, there was no doubt he had weakened. His daemonic glow was no longer the intense sunshine gold of earlier but a light dull yellow. Jane and Quinn also looked spent.

They can barely breathe; there's no way they called out my name.

From the corner of her eye, Lily saw a pulse of blue light, fainter than before, seep out from under the door. *Lily,* the voice in her head pleaded.

Lily gasped and yanked down her mind barriers. "It's Evelyn. She's trying to talk to me mind to mind. She's weak and sounds weird so I didn't realize it was her."

All fidgeting stilled as Lily listened, waiting for the next word, hoping there would be another.

Lil, the light. You. Sara. Grab it.

"I heard her, too!" Sara exclaimed, her eyes wide. "Grab the light? What does that mean?"

"Touch that blue light when it comes through?" Even as Lily said it she knew it sounded crazy. How would touching a light get them through the door to save Evelyn?

"Evelyn must have some insider knowledge. Listen to her," Aoife said, prodding them forward.

They knelt before the door. Lily's lungs were hard and tight as her breath stilled within her. *What if it doesn't come? Or what if this is a trick?*

The blue light flashed again, this time traveling a mere foot beyond the door crack.

Sara clasped Lily's hand and guided their fingers toward the blue glow as one.

White hot pain shot through Lily the instant her fingers brushed the light. A stab to the heart, a burning of nerve fibers up and down her spine, a stilling of all bodily functions. She opened her mouth but before a cry of agony passed her lips, the pain evaporated and in its place there was lightness. She felt good—she felt *amazing,* actually.

"Goddess be," Mary whispered, staring at Lily and Sara with wide blue eyes.

"What?" Lily ran her hands over her face searching for any imperfections.

Sara did the same, starting at her heart-shaped face and moving down to the blue triquetra glowing on her chest.

Hold up. A blue triquetra on her chest?!

Lily gaped at Sara and saw her sister's expression mirrored her own. She looked down. In the center of her chest the same sapphire triquetra glowed. Lily placed her hands over her heart and held still. There was no denying it. It was her, Evelyn, in this tiny light. *But what does it mean?*

"I wouldn't believe it if I didn't see it with me own eyes," Aoife whispered.

"What? What is this?" Sara stammered, pointing to their chests.

"Your sister. She sent you a part of her soul. I'm sure that's what it is, though I've never seen a traveler's soul be so . . . colored. And how she split in three . . ." Aoife trailed off.

Evelyn's soul? Holy shit. Lily clutched her chest tight. *What if it flies out? Evelyn would be so pissed!*

"I just wish I knew what you were meant to do with it," Aoife sighed in frustration.

"Does this remind anyone else of what Seraphina did to her daughter Esther?" Sara whispered and laid her hands gently on her chest. "Seraphina sent her daughter her pneuma, her fata soul, so that their family story lived on as a warning to other witches. Maybe Evelyn remembered the story and figured out how to send some of her soul with information to help get her out. Kind of like you can do with your mind magic, Aoife."

"Aye. That makes sense. If Evelyn is behind that door, there's a chance she knows the enchantments used to keep her in there. Her soul should know them, too, and how to get past the door. It will want to get back to its rightful place, inside her. Souls don't like to stay out of their bodies too long," Aoife said.

Sara nodded as if it all made perfect sense. "We should release them together to strengthen whatever it plans on doing." She grabbed Lily's hand and pulled her to the middle of the large hallway, away from the door.

"But how?" Lily asked, glancing into the group of witches behind them.

"You three are in realms of magic unknown. In a space between witching magic and the magic of our ancestors if I'm not mistaken. I've never come across a manuscript besides Hypatia's book describing the sharing of souls. You'll have to do it by instinct," Mary answered and her sisters nodded in agreement.

"It's like finding the book all over again, isn't it?" Sara asked, grinning at Lily. "Sometimes we just have to listen." Sara released Lily's hand, closed her eyes, and her body fell from its protective stance into relaxation.

I should really start meditating with her, Lily thought before following her sister's lead and closing her eyes. She waited, hoping something, *anything* would come to her.

As if in response a flutter across her heart assured her the sapphire light was still there, waiting. Lily sat with it, feeling it, allowing it to pulse and flow within her. As she settled in with it, the soul grew warm. Notes of courage rose, then defiance. A vision of Evelyn swam up and the light moved upward on its own accord. Its warm pulsations settled between her eyes and pushed hard against Lily's skin.

Her eyes popped open. "Ouch!"

"Is yours pushing against your skull?" Sara asked, opening her eyes and touching the spot between them gently.

Lily nodded. "I think it wants out. It's pushing really hard."

"Try the astral travel spell, girls! Maybe it will be strong enough to expel Evelyn's soul. If she's pushing at your skin, she clearly wants out anyway," Aoife looked thrilled by the prospect that her astral travel students might actually succeed for once, even if it wasn't with their own souls.

Lily shrugged. "Can't hurt."

"Ready?" Sara asked.

"On three." She replied.

"One. Two. Caeliter!" Lily and Sara exclaimed in unison.

Lily gasped as a sudden chill engulfed her head like a brain freeze and a vibrant blue light rocketed out from her third eye. She watched, mesmerized, as the blue light converged with the part of Evelyn's soul that had been inside Sara and flew forth to annihilate the glossy wood door before them.

THE SOUND WAS DEAFENING, the mess monumental, as the witches ran through a cloud of smoke and debris.

"Aberro!" Lily screamed, fingers extended at a figure flailing through the turmoil straight at Sara.

The man flew back against the wall, leaving the stench of filth, sweat, and blood in his wake.

Everyone else in the room stood motionless, their eyes wide and mouths hanging open.

They didn't think we'd be able to get in. Noro himself must have spelled the door. Lily no longer had any question that the fata was here, somewhere. She caught sight of Nora standing tall next to Empusa and Amon, both dressed in pure white, and Lily's eyes hardened. Amon stepped forward and licked his lips at the sight of her but Lily didn't have another second to spare for his lewd gesture.

She'd already moved on to a far more frightening figure: a navy ghost with three dark holes for a face.

Noro.

The fata floated near a bed where Evelyn lay motionless, her chest skeletal and face pale as snow.

Lily whirled to face Nora, her mother's supposed best friend and traitor, eyes narrowed in hate. "How could you? How could you let them kill her?"

Nora opened her mouth to reply, but Noro's voice boomed forth like a gust of wind.

"My Eve is not dead. She's traveling back home to bring her kin to Earth. I admit I did not want her to have to do this again so soon, but your intrusion made it imperative," the fata said through his never-ending black hole of a mouth.

His Eve? What does he mean traveling home?

Only then did Lily notice a small black spot, about the diameter of a juice cup, hovering above the foot of the bed. *What the hell?*

Noro's using Evelyn to create a portal to Hecate, Aoife's voice pushed through Lily's head. *We have to get to her and stop it, but we must be careful not to hurt her. Evelyn's not fully present in her body and very weak.*

Holy shit! Lily stood flabbergasted, watching as the portal grew right before her eyes to the size of a watermelon. *But how? She looks terrible . . .*

Images of Em before she was reborn a vampire flashed in Lily's mind, and she shook her head. Evelyn didn't look *that* bad, but there was no denying she was weak. Lily shuffled forward an inch to get a better look at her sister.

"Stay right there, witch," Empusa hissed. "We wouldn't want you disrupting your silly siren sister, now would we? In fact, I don't think you should be here at all. Let's show our new guests to their chambers, Evelyn's old room will do for the young ones. Put the rest of the witches in adjacent chambers." The vampire snapped her fingers and a half dozen people raised their hands or wands.

The Acolytes stepped forward, all except Nora whose arm remained relaxed on her hip while others did the dirty work for her. Lily was sure they could take the witches and wizards on. It was the vampires, elves, daemons, and fata behind them that gave her pause. *And Evelyn. What if one of our spells hits Evelyn?* She pushed the last thought out to Gwenn, the most skilled at stealth spells in their group, hoping she'd catch it.

A man grabbed Lily's arm. "Get off me, asshole!" she screamed and wrenched her arm from his grasp.

"You heard the lady," the wizard said. He pointed his wand at Lily and nodded to Empusa who winked at him.

"Lady? You think she's a lady?" Lily's fingertips pulsed with power and she took a step closer to the man. Bite marks ran up and down his arm, dotted his neck and crept onto his face. *He's a fang lover. Manipulated by empty promises and a gorgeous smile,* Lily sneered.

"You know she's using you, right? That you'll have no greater status in this new realm than the one you live in? To her you're just a blood bank, nobody important, and definitely not a lover. You're a disposable means to an end." Lily's voice flew at the Acolytes who leaned toward her, many ludicrously poised on tiptoes, listening to Lily and waiting for the McKay witches' next move.

"That's what they said you'd say, but you're wrong. They need wizards and witches, too," The man replied, his face tightening slightly.

"Ha! Then why are you the first line of defense? I'll tell you why: Because it's nothing to them if we injure or kill you. You're nothing to them. You and your little stick," Lily raised her eyebrows suggestively.

Amon sniggered. "Your insults are picking up steam, Lily darling."

But Lily wasn't listening. The second she sensed Gwenn's stealthy shield charm float past her to surround Evelyn, Lily punched the wizard square in the nose.

The McKay clan sprang into action. Aoife laid out two witches with one spell. Brigit bull-rushed Nora, who panicked and ran, bowling over anyone in her way. Mary and Gwenn remained close to Lily and Sara, taking on dozens of others so they could go to Evelyn's aid.

They were almost to the bed when two glowing figures jumped in front of them. *Daemons*, Lily thought glancing at Sara, who also looked unsure. Trusting her instinct, Lily shot the first spell that came to mind, a binding spell, at the daemon nearest her.

The man smiled and leapt in front of the spell, absorbing it.

"Dionean," Sara said, aiming the stunning spell at the second daemon, who followed his partner's lead and drew Sara's magic into his body.

Well shit. Aoife said any spell injurious to a witch would work on a daemon, but apparently she forgot to mention they can absorb spells meant to injure them, too. Maybe it only works if they see it coming? I'll have to be sneakier.

The daemons' malefic grins grew wide on their glowing faces as they inched closer, herding their prey toward the wall.

Lily glanced into the crowd and saw Mary and Gwenn still fighting at least ten creatures while Aoife battled Amon, and Brigit, Empusa. No one even noticed their predicament. Lily grabbed Sara's hand. She was about to make a break for it and hide in the fray where hopefully someone would see their quandary and save them when a pair of hands seized her from behind. Before she knew it Lily was flying backward. She slammed into a wall and heard Sara moan as she landed beside her. Lily scrambled to her knees, arms extended to fight just in time to see a flash of yellow streak by her.

Alfred, glowing bright gold once more, looked ethereal as he fought the daemons with Celestine, whose copious blonde hair whipped around her face as she swirled and kicked.

"Are you hurt?" Lily asked Sara as she helped her up.

Sara blinked, "Fine, just a little dizzy."

"Well, as long as you can walk we should move. This may be our only chance to get to Evelyn without interference," Lily said, spotting an opening to the bedside and taking Sara's hand once more.

The shield Gwenn had cast around the bed for protection kept them from touching Evelyn, but touch wasn't necessary for Lily and Sara to see how much their sister had changed.

Lily held her breath as she stared down at Evelyn, who looked somehow sickly and vibrant all at once. Far thinner than before, Evelyn verged on emaciation, yet muscles popped unnaturally from her biceps and deltoids. Despite the shallow cheeks and visible ribs beneath a thin tank top, something about Evelyn glowed. Her entire appearance was a contradiction.

It's like she's no longer of this world.

"It was her choice, you know." Noro floated out from where he was hiding in front of the black hole, which camouflaged his navy color. He rounded Gwenn's shield slowly and methodically, as if he were not at the center of a raging battle.

"My Eve is nothing if not pragmatic. She knew the truth when she heard it. Her first attempt was more impressive, though. That portal grew larger and faster, but then I *have* pushed her into trying again too early. Eve has already invited dozens of our kin to their new home. I believe you two could do the same, and I extend an offer to create an alliance." Noro's black eyes widened and Lily thought she saw stars shining in the dark depths.

"You would be heroes among fata kind and all our progeny. With your help we could bring magic out into the open and establish a new, rightful world order—one in which the strong rule and the weak follow. Dimia has assured me that as his blood anyone you love will be spared for use in your own households. Personally, you will feel no direct effect of sharing your planet with us and will live in luxury."

Sara stiffened behind Lily as Noro floated closer, his dark eyes serious.

How is it possible I can read the emotions of such a creature? And what's all this "as Dimia's blood" crap?

Lily stood before Sara and Evelyn. Screams, growls, and hisses demanded her attention, yet Lily ignored them, unable to take her eyes off Noro.

"Fear not, Seraphina dear. I do not wish to hurt you. I never did. You made it that way. You always were an impossible creature, strong willed and free thinking. Almost as much so as Lilith."

"Don't call us that. Or Evelyn, Eve. We're not them," Lily growled and backed into Sara, who whimpered and clenched Lily's hand tighter.

Catching the small retreat, Noro swooped in, closing the gap between them in seconds.

Lily gasped at the advance and the intense energy it imparted on her body. She could feel Noro's ghostly shape throbbing and how the air around her vibrated and swirled with his energy.

Noro's eyes latched onto Lily's and he lifted an airy limb, hovering it between them before inching it toward her.

Equal but opposing forces pulled at Lily: Run away or stay and protect Sara, who trembled violently behind her. The protective instinct won out and Lily remained grounded, her eyes boring into Noro's as she wracked her brain for a means of escape.

And then, without preamble or question, Noro was touching her face in a way unlike anything she'd ever experienced. Light, airy, and alluring, nothing like the touch of a human hand, which was hard and brash by comparison. Lily wanted to step closer to him, and she did.

"That's it, Lilith, come closer. We will mend your ways and find a way together, you and I."

Lily nodded, her mind a pleasurable blank. Another caress of her skin from cheek to chest buckled her knees.

"I always liked you best, Lilith. So spirited and free. An explorer, like myself. I thought of you often as my pneuma traveled other worlds, wondering what you were seeing on Hecate."

What is he saying? The question surfaced for half a heartbeat before the bliss of his touch took over once more.

"Now may be our chance. After you have done your duty to fata-kind, perhaps we can get to know each other. I always wished to feast on all three of Dimia's daughters. Perhaps I still will? Perhaps the four of us will be together? Help fill Earth with those worthy of all the power it can give?" Noro smiled, a lecherous round "O."

Behind her, Sara's hand spasmed and suddenly an image Lily had read about dozens of times flashed in Lily's mind's eye. A pregnant woman, half human, half fata screaming beneath the barbaric slashes of Noro.

Two twins, one with green eyes, the other with violet being pulled from her belly and allowed to feast on her blood.

Holy shit! What's happening? Get your head back in the game, Lily chastised herself. *What is he doing to my mind?*

Sara's hand, still clasped with hers behind her back, was now damp and shaking violently as if sending the image to Lily had pushed her over the edge into full-on panic. Sara's terror centered Lily in an instant and she squeezed her sister's hand tightly.

I need to fight him, she pushed her thoughts at Sara, hoping Noro wouldn't catch them.

Not that she had any idea how to fight off this creature. *Maybe if I can make him think I'm still in his thrall? That should buy me a few minutes.*

I'm going to let go now, Sara. Stay behind me.

Lily released her sister's limp hand, which fell and grazed Lily's butt, nearly knocking out the hard object she had stuffed in the waistband.

Lily's hand froze behind her. The iron trowel! *Thank you, Aoife! But I'll only have one shot.*

Keeping up the pretense of being in Noro's thrall, Lily closed the inches between herself and the fata. Slowly, sensually, she reached out and caressed Noro's face with her free hand, repressing the shudder as his mouth grew larger and his eye sparkled.

"What about my sisters?" Lily asked, trying to look slave-like instead of hopeful. "Evelyn . . . Eve is very . . ." She let the sentence trail off as her eyes flickered to the bed and back to Noro.

"Yes, Eve has always been a jealous thing. She will need time to adjust to the new way of life, but I dare say she must get used to it. As second in command on Earth, all three of you shall bear my brand, and we must do our best to populate the planet." Noro shifted his gaze suggestively to the bed.

Lily ripped the trowel from her waistband and plunged it into Noro's airy arm the second he broke eye contact.

The ground shook and Lily crashed into the wall behind her again. But this time she'd expected a blow-back and she jumped to her feet, prepared to fight. A glint of red caught her eye and Lily saw Sara, strong and solid once more, rise behind her.

A sound like the cry of a hawk but longer, more pitiful, and airier met her ears from somewhere on the grounds. Lily stared at where Noro had been seconds before, a faint navy mist the only indication it hadn't been a dream, that she'd really touched an alien being.

Lily whirled on the spot, her eyes searching for the fata.

"He's gone," Sara said gripping Lily's arm, "Whatever you did hurt him and seriously pissed Empusa off. Look."

The room was littered with bodies in various stages of injury. Empusa and her brother were the only Acolytes left fighting and like her brother, Empusa fought three on one, dodging spell after spell with cat-like grace, though it was clear her attention was no longer fully on the fight.

"How dare you!" Empusa shrieked when Lily caught her eye.

"He'll be back! And when my father finds you, you'll wish you'd have listened to his requests."

Lily said nothing. She knew Empusa was right. She may have injured Noro, may have been the first person in thousands of years to do so, but she was sure she hadn't killed him.

Sara pulled Lily back as Empusa lunged at the witches acting as their shield, sending them all staggering five feet backward. But the move was a feint, for the next second Empusa changed tack, running with supernatural vampiric speed toward the far side of the room and launching herself out the window after her father. Less than a second later, Amon disengaged himself from his own duel and followed his sister, leaping forty feet to the ground as the witches shot spell after spell at his back.

Lily shivered as the sound of a crow cawing ominously deep in the forest echoed through the cold winter night and Amon slipped through the trees to safety.

Safe House

Lily

LILY OPENED THE DOOR, circulatio potion clenched in her hand, and saw Rena pointing to Selma snoring in the bed beside her own.

Pushing the door closed gently behind her, Lily wondered how anyone was able to sleep in the middle of the day with all the noise in the Sisters of Salem coven house. *I should just be glad Selma has a knack for it. It must be helping with her miraculous recovery.*

"Hey Mom," Lily spoke in whispers as she claimed the chair usually occupied by Annika. "Drink half and save the rest for when Selma wakes. It will help restore blood flow to your injuries and reduce scarring. Where's Ann?"

"Practicing yoga in the next room," Rena chugged half the potion in three gulps. "I must say, Lil, I've never seen injuries, especially werewolf-scrapes like mine, heal so fast."

Lily smiled. "Fiona is an amazing healer and teacher. We're lucky she finally got her patients covered and arrived in time to take care of all the injured. Only you, Selma, and Evelyn are left. Everyone else has already gone home."

Or at least the ones still breathing have, Lily thought as a vision of the three lifeless bodies their army had hauled out of the manor with the unconscious rose up to haunt her.

"How's Evelyn?" Rena said her voice scratchy.

The ginkgo and chicory root Lily had added to Fiona's potion recipe on a whim filled her nostrils as Rena set her cup on the table between the two beds. Lily shook her head. "Still unconscious. Aoife thinks creating multiple portals took her to the brink of death, and she shows signs of . . . other trauma on her body, too."

Lily tried not to think about the vicious slashes that covered Evelyn's once curvaceous body. Or the strange, ominous marks on her inner thighs. "It's obvious they didn't feed her enough. Fiona says the vast magical output they demanded probably robbed her body of fat and nutrient stores. Evelyn is scary thin and was only gone five days."

Rena's lips tightened and she sighed through her nose.

"We found torture devices in the basement. There was also a flat pile of hay and a bucket that had been used as a toilet. I bet they kept Evelyn there until she needed more care after she opened the first portal," Rena paused. "Lil, what did it look like?"

Immediately, Lily wished she hadn't mentioned the portals. They had been a topic of every discussion since returning to the safe house. The Sisters of Salem were beside themselves, questioning why Evelyn succumbed to making them. Some were practically blaming Evelyn outright for the three deaths the army had incurred the night of the battle. They'd ceased asking only when Brigit forcefully demanded they stop accusing her daughter—who'd been through kidnapping and torture by other magical creatures—of treachery. After Brigit's outburst the debates pivoted and most started questioning how many fata made it over or how fast they would acclimate to Earth.

Lily wished she'd never seen the portal, but she had. In fact, she had been the closest to it besides Evelyn. She shivered. *Three steps and I could have jumped through to Hecate.*

"Like a black hole, which I guess is what it is, though Mary is calling it a wormhole between planets. When we broke into the room it was about the diameter of a doughnut. By the time Aoife helped rein it in, it had grown to the size of a two person kitchen table."

"How did Evelyn open it and how did they close it without her?"

Selma stirred beneath her plaid quilt, and they quieted, neither wanting to be the one to wake her.

Lily considered how to put into words what they'd seen and the theories arising to explain it.

Selma's light snores filled the room once more, and Rena looked at her, waiting.

"We're not sure how she opened it. We think Evelyn sent her soul, the blue light that helped break the shield, into space. No one knows how yet. Aoife said Evelyn's soul looked . . . weird. Not white like hers when she travels, but bright blue. It helped us save her, too, by breaking down the door to the room they kept her in. No one else had a clue how to do that." Lily shook her head. Aoife had said a lot more, but most of it had flown right over her head.

"The door had been heavily warded and Aoife noticed the magic felt off, but Evelyn's soul knew exactly what to do. After we defeated the Acolytes, Aoife put her hands on Evelyn's head. She entered Evelyn's consciousness. Aoife said Evelyn could still communicate with her soul a little inside her head, which really surprised Aoife. Aoife said Evelyn's mind was filled with stars. That led her to the conclusion Evelyn's soul was in outer space. We had to get it back before we left, so Aoife told Evelyn that Noro and the Acolytes were gone and Evelyn was safe, mind to mind, and asked her to bring her soul home." Lily paused, taking in the parting of Rena's lips and shrugged.

"I know, right? It was crazy, Mom—the black hole shrank so fast. The blue light streamed through it right as it closed and flew into Evelyn's chest. When Aoife sensed Evelyn was whole again, she pulled out of her head."

"Amazing," Rena's chocolate eyes widened. "If Aoife hadn't been there." Rena stopped as if unable to comprehend what would have happened.

"We'd have been screwed. Evelyn was so weak and no one but Aoife is a good enough ceremens to communicate like that," Lily paused. "Except Evelyn, of course."

"Of course . . . " Rena trailed off, ran her hand over the wound on her face, and sighed. "You know Lil, I'm pretty tired. Ann bought me some ear plugs this morning, so I can finally get rest. I'll tell Sel about the potion later."

Lily nodded, pulling the covers high over her mother and kissing her on the cheek. She let herself out, knowing Rena would ruminate over the information she'd given her for hours before catching a wink of sleep. They were the same that way.

Lily wondered what to do next. *Maybe go see if Fiona is back from her errands?* Starting back toward the kitchen, she did her best to ignore her rising guilt. She knew what she should do, but it was so depressing. Evelyn was the only one who remained unconscious out of eight people their army had levitated or carried from the manor.

And I'm responsible for all the injuries, not to mention the deaths. If I had told Evelyn I wanted her back at Fern Cottage instead of icing her out, maybe none of this would have happened. Obviously she hadn't felt she could rely on anyone except Sara. She didn't even tell her parents the truth. I should just peek in. Check her vitals.

Lily stopped in front of the door to Evelyn's sickroom. Easing the door open she peered in, hoping to see Evelyn's large blue eyes staring back at her. Instead, Sara's amber, bloodshot orbs drilled into her.

Lily sighed and let herself in. For Sara, she'd face her demons.

"How is she?"

Sara shrugged, her hands dropping from her mala bead necklace to her lap. "Her cuts and bruises are healing well, thanks to your potions, but she's still skeletal and unconscious."

Lily perched on Evelyn's bed facing Sara so that Evelyn lay between them. Her eyes scanned the room, decorated sparingly with impersonal touches. Two queen beds with a trundle beneath one, a mirror in the shape of the sun, a small bookshelf filled with the classics and books of magic, an empty nightstand between the beds, and nondescript white duvets. It was clearly meant to be a guest room and only the IV apparatus between the two beds suggested it was also a sick room.

"She went through a lot," Lily said. "Tortured, starved, who knows what else. Fiona says there's something different about her, but she can't pinpoint it. We'll have to wait until she wakes up to find out what."

"If she wakes up." Sara's voice cracked into a sob.

"Don't talk like that. She'll wake up."

"But how can you be sure?" Sara's voice sounded more like a plea than a question. "No one knows what it took for Evelyn to make that thing. I may be being dramatic, but this has never happened to me before. You have a lot of people who love you, Lil, and you love them. I've hardly had anyone in my life to care about as much as I care about you two." She let out a shudder of a breath.

"No matter how much I want a close family and act

like everything is great, I'm still not used to actually thinking of myself a part of a real family. It's a constant struggle for me to acknowledge that I'm wanted. Now, I can't help but feel as though I'm losing one of the few people I'm meant to love and who's meant to love me." Sara placed her hand over Evelyn's.

Lily's heart wrenched in her chest. *And I didn't make her feel wanted by icing her out. I'm such a dick sometimes.*

She bit her lip. "You know, Evelyn and I have had our differences, but for me, no one can replace the two of you. Even if Mom tells me we're actually quadruplets tomorrow."

A laugh punctuated Sara's sniffles. "I didn't mean it like that. I know you care about us. This is just my own unworthiness issues coming out."

"Still, I know I haven't said it yet, but you should know, I love you both so much." Lily took Evelyn's cold, dry hand in her own warm, moist one and looked Sara straight in the eye.

Sara choked and began crying harder, "I love you two, too. Man does it feel good to say that."

Lily smiled. It did feel good. And far overdue.

If only those words could do more. If only I could do more, she thought, recalling the night after the battle when she'd snuck into Evelyn's room to grasp her sister's hand and pray. It was a move that had been her trump card the night of their unbinding. *Too bad that doesn't seem to work anymore. We're into deeper, darker shit, I guess.*

They sat there like that, Sara's sniffles the loudest noise in the room.

And then Lily's stomach rumbled.

Sara sighed. "I need lunch, too," she said, rising and kissing Evelyn on the cheek. "We can talk to Fiona about new remedies while we eat. She stopped in to check on Evelyn right before you, bags brimming with herbs, plants, and all sorts of healer things."

"Good idea," Lily said, thankful Sara also needed a break. She released Evelyn's hand, placing it under the covers where it would stay warm.

They were halfway to the door when a small, frail cough stopped Lily in her tracks. She glanced at Sara and saw her brows were furrowed and her mouth firmly closed.

"Did you hear that?"

"Did you—?"

"Blood," a third, smaller voice breathed, barely audible over their own.

They whirled to see Evelyn's blue eyes open for a millisecond before closing once again.

"Think back," Brigit instructed, her gaze level. "Is that all Evelyn said?"

"She wasn't exactly in the mood to gossip, Mom," Lily said, trying to keep her annoyance at bay, despite having to repeat herself for the umpteenth time. "She said 'blood.' We ran back to her side and she said, 'Noro and vampires.' Then she blinked a few times and said, 'I drink blood,' and then passed out again. We haven't been able to revive her since."

Sara wrung out her hands and nodded.

"The meaning is pretty clear," Gwenn said pacing around the meeting room. "Noro fed her vampire blood to keep her alive. After such monumental exertion under poor living conditions, I'd wager it's the only reason Evelyn's still with us."

"I agree. But we know how vampires are about their blood. They don't give it up for just anyone, and especially not to strengthen their enemies. I think we're missing something here." Mary stared deep into the fireplace as her fingers twirled the ends of her hair mindlessly.

Lily agreed with Mary, but like so many other things in the supernatural world, she had no idea what the missing piece was. No matter how much she learned, it felt like she never had enough information.

"But Noro is their father and master. Isn't that enough? He could have threatened them with a reduced status in the new world if they didn't," Sara suggested.

"That seems like a threat that would work against a vampire," Aoife agreed. "Most obsess over rank. Have to be top at everything. I bet they hated giving Evelyn their blood even more for that, her being a powerful witch and all."

"All good speculation but there's only one way to find out. Which leads me to something I've been meaning to bring up all day," Brigit interrupted. She'd been unwilling to entertain any theories where Evelyn was concerned, forcing them to deal with the limited facts at hand. "Jane told me last night that there's been a drastic increase in the number of murders in the Meatpacking District. Two bodies were found torn apart so viciously there was no blood left in them. At first I thought it unrelated, but now I'm not so sure. Does it sound like a pair of vengeful, hungry vampires to anyone else?"

Club Life

Lily

"You realize it's up to the local covens and other supernatural groups to rein in any wayward supernaturals, right? None of you have to be here," Jane said as she exited the cab onto Gansevoort Street.

"I know, but your coven has already gone through so much. You lost good people fighting for my girls. And if I'm honest right now, I'd like nothing more than to kick the evil twins' arses," Brigit said, joining Jane on the sidewalk.

Lily and Sara fell into step behind the matriarchs. Lily, too, wanted answers, nearly as much as she wanted to bash Amon's sculpted face in. She never could have imagined her first boyfriend would cause so much trouble. Then again, she would have never imagined him a vampire either.

Jane led the way to their meeting place, down a dark alleyway where Aoife, Mary, Gwenn, and Celestine stood huddled together, steam rising from their mouths. Fiona had begged to come, too, but Brigit insisted she stay with Evelyn in case she woke again, knowing someone needed to be there—and that someone had better be an amazing healer. Celestine offered to go in Fiona's stead.

"I will be able to find the twins more easily anyhow. A vampire can smell the presence of another vampire, especially one that has been on a feeding spree," Celestine had explained to Brigit as they left the safe house for the Meatpacking District.

Lily was glad Celestine was there on their side. The pretty French baker was a killing machine, accountable for a quarter of their enemies' injuries at the Battle of Peacock Manor. To hear Jane tell it, Celestine was also an amazing bodyguard and tracker, both of which they would need in the dark, crowded city.

"We haven't seen or heard anything strange yet," Mary said at their approach, as if by being in New York they would have witnessed ten sketchy scenarios by walking down the street.

"The night is early. The twins are probably still searching for their perfect prey," Celestine said, her nose scrunched up with distaste.

Gwenn grumbled and a whiff of burnt holy basil carried on the cold night air to Lily's nostrils. "We're going clubbing then?" Like Lily, Gwenn had grown irritable during their time in the city with its hordes of people, sparse greenery, and vast expanses of concrete.

If we're not out of commission tomorrow, I'll convince her to walk around Central Park with me. An earth witch date would do us both some good.

Celestine nodded. "Half of us. Half should stay outside. It would be best to have a ceremens or at least a witch capable of some mind magic on both sides for communication's sake. I have a strong hunch I may know where they are. There's a very popular, exclusive club in this area, and it is Saturday night. Beautiful, young bodies enjoying life are what Empusa and Amon delight in feeding on most." She wrinkled her nose again.

Lily thought back to the snippets of news she'd watched this morning. Celestine was right, none of the dead were over thirty, and three of the four had been attractive blondes, the other a green-eyed brunette. It didn't take a genius to figure out who the twins *wished* they were hunting.

Well, I want to hunt them, too. Especially Amon.

"I'll go," Lily stepped forward.

"Me, too," Sara said, locking arms with Lily.

"As much as I hate to admit, it has to be you two," Brigit said. "Four women in their mid-forties going into a hot club would attract attention and we don't want to be noticed."

She paused and gave the group a once over. "I wish Selma had been feeling up to it. This would be the perfect job for a siren. Or even Alfred. He wouldn't stick out and I'm sure he'd love this."

Sara cough-giggled, "Oh I'm *sure* he would, too," she said, and Lily shot her a look.

"Aoife, you're the best ceremens. You should go inside. Celestine are you up for going inside?" Brigit asked.

The vampire nodded.

Jane held out a duffle she'd brought. "Clothes are inside. Borrowed them from my daughters' closets. I guessed on the sizes but they should be close enough since most of the items are spandex heavy."

Aoife, Celestine, Lily, and Sara picked out outfits, threw their jackets next to the duffle, and changed while Jane and Mary guarded the alley entrance and Gwenn pulled up a map of the club Celestine had her google on her phone.

"And you'll be needing a wee bit of this if you're to be believable," Brigit said eyeing Aoife, now dressed in tight faux leather leggings, a chic black top, and wedges.

She pulled a tube of mascara and lipstick from her jacket pocket and aimed them at her sister's lashes and lips.

Sara and Lily smirked at their aunt's deep discomfort. *The woman can battle with the best of them, but confront her with mascara and she nearly cries,* Lily thought holding back a giggle as Aoife's ginger and pepper aroma intensified with her frustration.

"Jane will be the ears outside, so try and listen for her mind, Aoife. I hope you four don't have trouble getting in," Brigit said stepping away from Aoife to reveal a woman Lily had never seen before. The touches of makeup had transformed her face from oddly pretty to gorgeous.

Lily whistled. "We shouldn't have any trouble getting in with Aoife looking like that! Do me, too."

A blush ran over Aoife's cheeks, though Lily thought she looked pleased.

"You four look like you're ready for a grand night on the town," Mary said with a nostalgic sigh. "I bet you have no trouble at all getting to the front of the line."

"Something I could have used magic for anyhow," Aoife grumbled, pulling her top up to hide her cleavage.

"Use magic only when you need to speak with us, at least until you find the twins," Brigit warned, her face stern. "Remember, Celestine told us vampires can sense when magic is being used. Use it too soon and you may scare Empusa and Amon off before you even find them."

"Magic will not be necessary for getting in anyhow —at least not witching magic," Celestine said, touching up her lipstick.

"Here's the map of the club." Gwenn swiped past several photos on her phone. "If Empusa and Amon are in there, try to corral them toward this back door." She pointed to a spot on the basic emergency exit map the club provided on their website. "We'll be waiting in the alley it empties into. Hopefully, we can end this there and avoid chasing them around this city. I doubt you four would make it far in those getups. Even Lily would have trouble and she's the best runner we have."

Gwenn was right. There was no way in hell Lily was running fast or far in her borrowed stilettos.

"Keep the duffel just in case," Lily said, pointing to the bag that carried their regular clothes.

"Do you think we're daft? Aoife will kill us if we leave it anywhere and she has to walk around a second longer than necessary looking like that," Gwenn said, her face splitting into a grin.

"I think we're ready. Let's head to the club. I'll lead," Celestine said strutting down the alley.

HOLY HELL. Lily's head whipped around as she took in the multitude of sensory information the club used to convince people they were having fun. Flashing lights, pounding music, shiny and beautiful people flitting about, all things that would make it difficult to find a vampire. *At least getting in was easy.* The crowd in front of the club had parted as if they were rock stars and the bouncer let them in without a word.

"I said not to use witching magic, but vampires have talents, too, particularly over humans," Celestine explained, smiling down at Lily so seductively her head spun.

"Let's start at the bar. It's elevated so it will be easy to see over the crowd," Aoife said pointing to a long, bustling wall of people vying for the attention of the bartenders.

"Four vodka tonics," Celestine called out to a bartender who zeroed in on her the second Celestine approached the bar.

"I don't like vodka," Sara said.

"We won't be drinking them anyhow." Aoife spun to look out into the sea of people. "Alcohol dulls your senses, normal and magical. Use it as a prop."

They searched the crowd while they were waiting for their drinks. Lily, not having ever been a clubgoer herself, was astounded by the flagrant displays of wealth and open sexual desire.

Ninety-nine percent plastic women fawning over men they wouldn't look twice at on the street. Men buying entire bottles of high-end booze to impress the table. And then there was the dancing. Maybe it was because she had gone to an all-girls college, but Lily had never seen anything like it: Hips grinding hard against other hips, women sandwiched between two men or the other way around, sweaty bodies grasping for other bodies in need. Lily found herself embarrassed for many of the people on the dance floor, though they didn't seem to mind.

"On the house," the bartender yelled over the pounding beat.

"What a surprise. Thank you," Celestine said in a way that indicated she was anything but surprised. She flashed a dazzling smile at the bartender before turning from the bar. "Anyone spot them?"

Aoife, Sara, and Lily shook their heads.

"Well someone's here. I can smell them, and they smell old and full of life. See those high partitions?" She pointed at the other side of the bar. "That's the VIP area. I bet the twins are in there."

That does seem like Empusa and Amon to separate themselves from the masses. If they have to be near humans for something other than feeding, only the richest, most beautiful humans will do.

"It looks smaller and more closed off than the main bar. Won't they see us when we enter?" Sara asked.

Celestine nodded. "They'll likely smell you first. Most witches' scents are different from other humans—more herbal. Once the twins figure out we're searching for them, we must work to corral them to the exit Gwenn pointed out. It should be easier from the VIP section. The front door is much farther away, but still one of us should block it off magically or physically once the twins make their move. Then their only option is the emergency exit."

"If they split, then we'll do the same," Aoife added, her calculating gaze sweeping the room. "Lily and I will take Empusa. Celestine and Sara, you take Amon. Sara, be precise if you use fire around Celestine. In fact, I'd suggest you not release it in here at all; keep it as a small threat in your hands. The vamps will be watching for it but humans may not notice with everything else happening in this place."

"Yes. I'd appreciate it if you waited until we're in the alley before you three break out the fire magic. I'm sure Jane would, too. I don't think our coven could manage wiping the memories of everyone in here if magical fire broke loose," Celestine said.

Lily barely heard the conversation. Aoife's assignment of Empusa stung, though logically she understood it. Amon had too much on Lily. She'd proven herself susceptible to his charms. Still that didn't negate the fact that she wanted to be the one to kick his ass. Her fists clenched and mouth tightened.

He changed Em into an unrecognizable monster and forced me to kill her. If I get the chance, I'm taking him down.

"Empusa had a hand in Em's death too, Lil," Aoife said reading Lily's body language.

Lily nodded and kept her revenge mission to herself.

They made their way through the crowd in a wide circle around the bar, pausing only to deflect the advances of two men and one woman. Lily followed Aoife's lead and deposited her drink on an empty table as they walked by to free her hands. Prop or not, a drink felt like a major obstruction of self-defense.

"Stop!" Celestine hissed and gripped Aoife's shoulder. "Look at that woman. The one stumbling. Does she seem off to you?"

Lily followed Celestine's finger to see a tall blonde in a bandage dress tripping across the dance floor. "She's drunk as he—oh shit!" Lily exclaimed as the woman tossed her hair over her shoulder to reveal two circular marks on her neck, one of which was still bleeding. "How did you catch that?"

"Smelled the blood and followed its trail to the drunkest-looking person in here. Someone took her blood recently."

Their pace slowed as they continued through the mass of bodies around them, each witch now hyper alert.

A man even larger than the bouncer outside stood sentinel in front of the VIP section. "You got friends in there?" The man gripped the velvet rope before him and his eyes lingered on each of them a second too long for comfort.

"Yes," Celestine purred, and the guard's head swung to give her his full attention. "It's a surprise gathering so you won't have my friend's name on a list. She's tall, fit, with auburn hair, brilliant green eyes, and a slight French accent? It's rare that people forget her."

"She's in there." The bouncer pulled the rope to the side without taking his eyes off Celestine. "Have fun tonight, ladies."

One quick glance told them that neither vampire was in the smaller, less-private booths near the front. Those spilled over with people drinking from bottles on ice, looking unconcerned with the fact that two notorious vampires might be in their midst.

Let's hope it stays that way, Lily thought, following Celestine's lead.

As they moved deeper into the VIP section, they discovered it was far smaller than the main club but boasted many more spots for people to sit and socialize, all of which were partially or completely partitioned off for maximum privacy.

"Vampire scent is everywhere in here," Celestine murmured. "If I walk closer to the booths, I should able to pinpoint which one they're in. You three stay here; your scents are too strong. We don't want to tip them off." Celestine strutted to the right side of the room.

Aoife, Sara, and Lily stood as still as possible without appearing unnatural. Their eyes tracked Celestine as she rounded the room methodically. Celestine was nearly halfway through investigating the booths on the right side when Lily heard a noise that raised the hairs on the back of her neck.

It was a noise apart from the thumping base, shrill giggles, and clank of glassware that surrounded them. It was a voice, high, arrogant, and vaguely French. Lily's head swiveled, searching for the body belonging to the voice she knew and hated.

"Empusa's over there," Lily said pinpointing the location of a strangled sound followed by a particularly cruel laugh.

"Lil, wait for Celestine," Aoife said as Lily marched forward twenty feet, cutting the distance between herself and the booth she knew Empusa to be hidden behind in half.

Celestine was at her side in seconds. "She's there, isn't she?" Her voice was low. Lily realized it was because it was possible Empusa could hear them, even with the loud music.

Lily nodded and glanced up at the fifteen-foot-high partitions that would make it impossible for them to sneak up on Empusa. They would have to enter the private booth as all partygoers did: through the tiny entrance that provided the privacy and security people in VIP paid for. *We'll be bottle-necked against one of the most vicious vampires of all time,* Lily thought before turning and motioning Aoife and Sara over so they could discuss a new plan.

Then, the surrounding air shifted.

"Merde," Celestine swore as Empusa soared over the partition with a malicious smile.

A blur of movement high in the air caught Lily's peripheral vision, and she knew Amon had done the same a few booths down. As soon as their feet hit the floor, the twins sped out of the room.

Lily ran through the velvet ropes of VIP and stood

on tiptoes to find Empusa's bright auburn head in the crowd.

But Aoife and Sara, being closer to the VIP entrance and quicker to react, had beat Empusa out to the main bar and Lily glimpsed Aoife zooming around the perimeter of the club in a less-direct but also less-crowded route to the front door. The vampires, who had clearly hoped to lose the witches in the crowd, were a mere twenty feet from the front entrance when Aoife reached the door first, subverting their escape. Empusa and Amon pivoted on the spot, pointing themselves toward the next best escape route: the emergency exit.

They're playing right into our hands! Lily whirled about to follow the vampires and ran right into a wall of human.

"Hey beautiful, how about a dance?" the wall asked, eyebrow raised and breath reeking of tequila.

"Out of my way!" Lily pushed him aside.

"Bitch!" the man yelled.

She would have laughed if she weren't so busy forcing her way through the flailing limbs on the dance floor. A flash of gold in the air caught her eye and Lily glanced up to see Celestine ahead, jumping over tables filled with partiers and martinis. Though she couldn't hear them, Lily saw the collective gasps and screams on the faces of the young, beautiful, and drunk as Celestine flew above them.

She made to follow the flying vampire when Amon's back appeared ten feet away through a slit in the thrashing bodies. *This is my chance!* Lily thought, making a beeline for the vampire who seemed momentarily frozen in place. Five steps, four, three, and then she was there, a long arm's reach away. A small flame ignited in her palm and Lily envisioned herself tapping Amon on the back and the vampire bursting into ash in the middle of the club.

Her dream screeched to a halt when Amon spun to face her, fangs extended, and hissed.

A thin blonde beside Lily screamed, and she made to catch the woman as she fainted.

Amon bolted for the exit, bowling over those in his path.

"Take her," Lily said shoving the girl's body into another woman's arms to chase after him.

The exit sign grew closer and closer as she ran. *Go through the door, go through the door,* Lily repeated the mantra in her head, willing Amon, who was weaving spastically through the crowd in an effort to lose Lily, to swerve toward the door behind which her mother, aunts, and Jane waited.

Her heart leapt when at the last second Amon

veered off course and threw open the emergency exit door to disappear into the night.

Empusa stood, back against a brick wall, penned in by Brigit, Jane, Mary, and Gwenn. Amon was cornered between a dumpster, a building, and Celestine, who was flanked by Aoife and Sara, balls of fire blazing in both their hands.

"Serostium," Lily whispered, locking the club door behind her before directing her hands at Amon ready to fire.

"I see this little operation was well planned. We did not account for spares when we decided to lure the witches out did we Brother?" Empusa's French accent was thick, hinting at her agitation as she glanced at Celestine and then Jane.

Lure us out? All those murders were just a trap to get us out in the open?

Anger bubbled in Lily as she thought of the dead girls' faces splashed across the internet.

"Nothing we can't handle," Amon replied smoothly.

Empusa laughed, high and cold, "True. You witches are so predictable. We knew you would not be able to abide our choice of feeding. Though this time it was surely justified. We gave so much to that weak excuse for a witch. She'd never have been able to survive without us. In fact, I think the McKays are in our debt. Perhaps that it why they are here?"

Lily's face hardened.

Empusa noticed the micro movements and sneered. "Hmm. It is as simple as a mission to avenge the lives of those worthless humans then? How unfortunate to realize you did not catch us off guard. To be told that we desired to meet you once more and take the young ones back to our father. How does it feel to have played right into our hands witches?"

"How does it feel to be so out numbered?" Aoife's growl elicited an unexpected smirk from Empusa.

"It's true, our father did not want us out in the open without him or other Acolytes to act as our shield but we insisted. My brother and I are, after all, unequivocally his best fighters and most devoted generals. Generals, who have failed our father too many times recently and seek to redeem ourselves. I for one, would like nothing more than to bring him the creature that wounded him." Her green eyes leveled with Lily's.

Lily flexed her hands.

Empusa's lips turned up. "A poor idea, witch. Even with your traitor friend here, you are outmatched."

Empusa's gaze shifted to Celestine, pure loathing in her eyes.

"I doubt that! We're going to make you suffer. Like you did to Em, Evelyn, and all those other girls." The words left Lily's mouth before she had a second to consider them.

"As we said before Lily love, if you would have brought Hypatia's book, we'd have had no need to hurt Miss Emily. Speaking of the book, a little bird tells me you've found it? Is that why you're here darling?" Amon's eyes lit up and he grinned charmingly. "Are you bringing me a gift? Then submitting me to a little *suffering*?" Amon's voice grew sultry as he toyed with Lily's words and wagged his eyebrows.

"Why do you want that anyways? It's nothing but a story," Lily's face flushed as her fury soared. *How many people have to die over this damn book?*

"That story is a *treacherous* gospel that must be destroyed," Empusa spat. "When the fata take over they do not want false idols lurking. Human gods give them no pause as they are *nothing* compared to our ancestors. What they care about is fata other than King Dimia and our father claiming godliness over humans, giving their wretched race *hope* as Dimia's traitorous daughters did. We've been searching for the book by the daughter of that blasphemous whore and traitor for centuries. We seek to destroy it. It is the only task our father has given us that we have not fulfilled."

"Seraphina is a whore and traitor?" Lily asked incredulously. "That's a pretty harsh judgement considering Noro was the one to rape her. You'd rather side with a kidnapping, rapist father than a mother who died to bring you into the world?"

She'd expected downright outrage for dissing the vampire's master, but it didn't come. For the first time Empusa, the narcissistic, arrogant, prideful vampire Lily hated, hesitated. Lily's eyes shifted to Amon and saw he too looked uncertain.

"How dare you," Empusa uttered beneath her breath. "How dare you call that traitor to our noble family line our mother!"

Lily glanced at Brigit, her eyebrows raised. *What the hell is Empusa talking about?*

"The book Hypatia left, the one you've been searching for, describes Noro's relationship with Seraphina. He used rape as a means of power, a way to force her to do what he wanted. She never did. But she did give birth to two children. A girl with bright green eyes, and a boy with violet eyes," Brigit said.

Empusa's emerald eyes widened.

"Birthing them nearly killed Seraphina as she was half transformed between a human form and fata. Noro had to pull the babies from her and he nicked her pneuma in the process. Once they—once *you*—were out Noro became ecstatic. You didn't look human or fata; even as babies you were strong and powerful in Seraphina's memory. It's like he was a mad scientist. Noro allowed your mother to die after that. I guess he got what he wanted in you, two powerful beings he could control from birth," Lily worked out the truth as she spoke it.

"Your first meal was of your mother's blood. Your father allowed you to drink her dry as she lay there with her pneuma seeping from her, dying," Brigit finished, sadness clear in her voice.

Empusa shook her head, "*Lies.* Every word. Our mother was no prize by any measure. A lowly human that died as all humans do. It is because of her that we are weaker than our father. Immortal to a point, but with none of the magic of fata. It is because of her I must live in this vile human shell. I detest that I must claim kinship with her, but at least she wasn't a traitor to my father's kind."

"If your mother was human, you'd be witches. Every fata-human mating on Earth has resulted in witches. It's the fata-fata pairings that produced other variations of supernaturals. And you look human because your mother, Seraphina, expelled all her Hecate magic making the portal and had been using magic born of Earth ever since. The human form is ideal for housing Earth's magic. It's evolution," Mary said, her eyes wide with revelation as she dug up the bits of truth hidden in Empusa's words, Hypatia's book, and the hundreds of myths she'd studied in her quest for answers.

"Noro lied to you," Mary whispered. "Used you as pawns against your own blood. The reason you're not full fata is because you weren't born on Hecate. The magic of Earth differs from Hecate's magic, and life had to evolve to match that. I doubt *any* full fata were ever born here or will be even if all the fata come. That's why he's desperate to bring the rest of the fata over. One or even a handful of fata aren't as scary or powerful, but hundreds are. Noro didn't know that then, but I'm positive he does now. And yet, he still didn't tell you. He probably promised someone could change you, didn't he? Give you fata powers? Is that what he said?"

The answer was written across the vampires' stiff faces.

Mary's lips turned down. "You should know, he'll never be able to do that. Fata magic comes from their homeland. They're still powerful as hell once here and acclimated, but in a different way. Fecking hell, they're not even immortal once they arrive here! Seraphina died, didn't she? Lily injured Noro with a trowel and he fled. Why would he run if he were immortal? They may have been immortal on Hecate but on Earth fata can die, just like me, and just like you."

Empusa sprung at Mary fangs bared.

Two massive fireballs shot across the alley. They missed the tip of Mary's nose by inches but saved her from Empusa's bite as the vampire flung herself back into the wall, away from the flames.

"You know, I never realized the irony that the element your mother was master of is the one your kind is most susceptible to? Strange how genetics work out, isn't it?" Aoife said, lifting her arms and calling up two ten-foot-tall flame gates from the concrete to cage in the vampires.

"Fucking witches," Amon bellowed. "You think you're so powerful with your little balls of fire and bag of spells, but what you can't see is that you need us! If what you say is true and the grand fata plan is to rule us all, supernaturals and humans alike, you'll need us. The fata Evelyn let over, they're weak now, but they won't be for long." Amon pulled in a breath of air his vampiric body didn't need and sighed.

When he spoke next his deep baritone was smoother, calmer, less accusatory. "You should know there are more fata that have been here for thousands of years, hiding, biding their time. The ones Eve brought over, they aren't weak at all. My sister and I can hunt them, kill them. Then the new fata will see how powerful the creatures of Earth are. They'll fall in line. Let us go and we'll help. If we work together, the fata won't stand a chance."

Lily's stomach jumped and her skin tingled. She watched the spines of her friends and family straighten as they listened to Amon's words. Brigit and Gwenn lowered their hands slightly. Mary tilted her head in consideration. Aoife frowned, looking like she very much wanted to refute Amon's words but couldn't find a rational way to do so.

It was prudent, smart even, to have the two strongest, most ancient vampires in the world on their side. Spies feeding them insider information and dismantling enemy ranks from within. It was a tempting offer.

Only Lily remained fully on her guard. She remembered all too well how her body responded to Amon's words when they were dating. It responded just as it was now, with her limbs tingling and stomach flopping uncontrollably in response to Amon's smooth, controlling baritone.

But that had all been a lie, too.

"He's lying," Lily said, her eyes locked with Amon's. "I can feel it in my body, the lie. It feels like when we were dating."

Amon smiled smoothly, "That was different, Lily love. I didn't know I was being used then. I didn't know the truth."

Tingle, tingle, flip, flop.

"Still lying, Amon. Try again. Or should I try for you?" Lily quirked a brow.

"If we let you go you may run off and kill a few fata to make sure Noro remembers how powerful you are. Then you'll negotiate a way to remain his right-hand creatures, killing all the new, weaker fata if you have to. There's no way you'll join us. Why be egalitarian, still living in hiding, when you can run the world?" She smirked as his face darkened with the realization that his lies could no longer sway her or save him.

And then Amon soared twenty feet in the air as if it were nothing. Aoife's flame gate followed the vampire's ascent seconds too late. Amon flew straight at Lily, teeth bared and eyes narrowed in hatred. There was another blur in the sky and Lily knew without looking that Empusa had made the leap as well. Flame gates fell and orange fireballs shot high in the sky, following and missing their target by inches. Lily's eyes trained on Amon and she shoved down the fear that fluttered in her gut.

Here's my chance.

Amon landed lightly in front of Lily. A wide smile

split his chiseled face. He, like Lily, realized no one would dare toss fireballs at him for fear of hitting Lily, who stood trapped behind him.

What he didn't know was how she'd hoped for this, prayed for it, and prepared for it. Lily lifted her hands and revealed two fireballs burning red hot in her open palm.

"Flamarba," she whispered enclosing them in a circle of flames.

"Ahh, alone again. Just how I desired tonight would go." Amon started prowling the circle's edge.

Lily mimicked his movements and fired off her first two balls of flame. *I may not be a fire witch but I can do this. I have to do this for Em.*

Amon laughed as the fireballs flew and disappeared into Lily's flame gate, feet from where he was standing. "I see your spell work has improved, Lily love, but you must work on your aim." Then, he lunged at her.

She darted to the side. A searing pain shot through her right leg and Lily looked down to see the skin already puckering up in a blister. Two more fireballs materialized in her hands as if emboldened to act on their own and she hurled them across the circle.

"Herbcasto," she said, reverting to earth magic in hopes of catching him off guard. Grass, green and strong as a rope, shot up from the cement and wrapped around

Amon's legs. *I've got him,* Lily thought as the fireballs stayed on a perfect trajectory for Amon's chest.

But Amon fell to the ground. He ripped the blades of grass like a crazed animal, rolled to the side, and jumped back on his feet.

Dammit! Lily began to call forth fireball after fireball, each taking more effort than the last. Sweat dripped down her face, and her breath shortened as she and Amon stalked around the circle, pouncing and darting to and from one another.

"Mahasoka," she wheezed. Vines flew across the circle at Amon, who hissed and caught them in his hand with ease.

"Oh it's bondage you want, is it? I'll give you bondage, but we'll do it my way." Amon sneered and ripped the strong vines in half as though they were paper.

Shiiiiit.

Let me help, Sara's voice pleaded in Lily's head, alerting Lily she'd allowed her mind barriers to drop. *Circle toward the center of the alley.*

He's mine. I need to do this, Sara.

Lil, please. I can't take knowing you're in there with him. If you're not going to drop the gate, at least let us help.

Fine. I'm losing steam anyway, Lily admitted grudgingly. She clutched two small fireballs in her hand as she circled round, hoping Amon wouldn't make a sudden move and throw her off course.

I'm here.

Raise the gate, Sara answered

Lily raised the gate an inch in the air and watched in horror as both of her fireballs diminished to the size of a candle flame.

I can't, Lily thought letting the gate drop as Amon lowered into a crouch. She didn't have enough fire power to sustain three different spells at once, and what if her sister didn't act in time while her defenses were down?

Do it again! We're all here for you.

Lily glanced over her shoulder, hoping to catch sight of them behind her, but all she saw was a stunning wall of fire two feet deep and ten feet high.

"Trying to escape me, Lily love? Well, we'll see about that!" Amon made to grab her.

With her last bit of magical energy, Lily closed her hands, extinguishing her only means of self defense, and flung the gate up as high as she could. She gasped as a shower of fireballs flew under the two foot gap, filling the space between her and Amon who miraculously jumped back, darted, and swore his way around the flames.

Lily grunted and the gate fell.

Amon was still before her, very much alive.

"You never could get it done yourself, could you? You always needed help," Amon snarled. He circled as far from her as he could, a menacing growl rumbling in his chest. "Pathetic. It's why you'll never be able to forget me, because you can't face me alone."

The truth hit Lily straight in the face. *He's right. I have to do this. It's me and him, it always has been.* She looked down at her trembling hands and tried to draw flame from them.

A flicker died in her palm. She'd expended her fire reserves. Soon, the gate behind her would fizzle and then someone else would finish Amon off.

What a shitty time to have nothing left, Lily thought backing into the flame gate. The heat of the fire threatened to singe her skin, and she inched away, cognizant that she was choosing to face the greater of two evils.

Amon grinned as she moved nearer to him and Lily felt his confidence build.

Then, as though he were a missile on an unstoppable trajectory, Amon's chiseled body shot through the sky toward her. The fire at her back burned and with it an idea sparked in her mind. *It may work. It's so human he won't expect it.* Her skin grew uncomfortably hot as she inched closer to the fire.

Amon flew closer, soon he'd be upon her, ripping into her neck and sucking her life from her.

But she stayed, until Amon was seconds from tearing into her skin. Until his cold fingers grazed her shoulder.

Now! Lily's head hit the concrete as she dropped to the ground, flung her hands to her face, and rolled. *Keep the gate up, keep the gate up.*

Her skin burned as the faux leather of her pants melted to her legs and the fire feasted on skin. What felt like years later, she appeared on the other side and a flurry of hands beat at her. Her vision darkened as flammable material melted excruciatingly into skin.

A collective scream rang in her ears and Lily's eyes popped open to see a storm of snow white ash hurtle through her dying flame gate and land right on top of her.

Secrets Uncovered

Lily

"Do you have the calendula compress ready, Gwenn?"

"Arrgghh." Lily shifted in bed and moaned as her raw skin brushed across the sheets.

"Lil's awake! Get Brig and the others," Fiona instructed.

Footsteps raced across the room and disappeared down the hall.

"Can she move?" a weak, airy, yet familiar voice asked.

Lily shot up, ignoring the intense pain and ripping of burn blisters along the length of her arms.

"Evelyn?" she asked, stupidly looking at her sister, who lay propped upon a mound of pillows in the bed next to her. "You're alive!"

Evelyn smiled a watery smile and looked Lily over. "You shouldn't move much. Your burns look painful."

"When did you wake up? How do you feel?"

"Like hell but I'm fine. Fiona tells me I woke up shortly after they brought you back from the club, but I don't remember that. As far as I know, I woke up late this morning. All I've done since then is call my parents, drink broth, assure the million people that came to check on me that I'm fine, and sleep. I almost wish I hadn't woken up with the guilt trip I got from my parents, but I guess I deserve it."

Lily nodded, unconcerned by Evelyn's issue with her parents. She glanced around trying to determine what time of day it was, a feat made impossible by the lack of clocks and effective blackout curtains in the room.

"It's almost six in the evening. You've been out since last night," Fiona said, reading her movements.

"Here, drink this regeneration elixir. It has goldenrod and aloe to help heal you faster. I added what Indian pennywort I had on hand, but it wasn't much. Celestine said she'd pick up more but she hasn't returned with it yet. I'm hoping she comes back quickly so we can avoid scarring."

Lily took the cup, her hands shaking from the slight weight of it, and lifted it to her lips. It didn't taste good, but it wasn't terrible either, like cucumbers with a dash of wheatgrass and suntan lotion.

"What happened? The last thing I remember is lifting my flame gate and a shower of fireballs." Lily set the empty cup on the night stand.

"You dove into your own flame gate. You were too exhausted to lift it and, as Sara said, 'Too damn proud to drop it.'" Evelyn raised her eyebrows. "Fiona has been telling everyone that while your burns are bad, they'll heal fine. You're mostly in here to rest. Between the battle to save me and the fight at the club you've been going too hard and your magic needs a break."

An image flashed in Lily's mind. Herself, hurling her body against concrete and into a two foot wall of fire as Amon flew through the air after her.

"Oh my goddess! Did it work? Is Amon—?" Lily screeched.

"Oh, it worked," Brigit said striding through the door beaming at Lily. "The twins really should have listened to their father and brought back-up instead of letting their astronomical pride get the best of them because they may still be around. Instead, you clever, brave, stubborn girl of mine, will forever be known as the witch that ended one of the most notorious vampires of all time."

And suddenly, the room filled with people. The

McKay women, Sara, Annika, even Rena and Selma—who still should have been in their own sickbeds—all filed in after Brigit to gather around Evelyn and Lily. Lily listened amazed as Sara described how Amon had barreled right into her flame gate after her, intent on his prey until the last second.

"He burst into a cloud of ash so large it looked like a bomb had gone off," Sara said.

"And his sister wasn't any smaller. I swear all of us in the alley were covered in her after Brigit dealt the final blow. I may have found a wee bit of ash in my hair this morning after my shower," Gwenn scrunched up her nose and stuck out her tongue.

"So they're both gone," Lily murmured.

"Let's not get too excited," Evelyn said, her voice flat. "There are plenty more bad guys to defeat, thanks to me."

Lily turned to look at Evelyn fully for the first time since waking. She still looked skinny, but no longer on the verge of death. The cuts and bruises on her arms, neck, and chest were visible but healing. Lily doubted she would have any marks on her once Fiona finished with her.

"What happened, Evelyn? What did they do to you?"

Evelyn lowered her gaze to the blanket clutched in

her hand. Her eyes flickered up to Rena, Annika, and Selma cautiously.

Maybe I should ask Rena, Annika, and Selma to leave? Telling her story to strangers is probably too much.

"They can stay. Especially now that I know that's who they are. They helped save me," Evelyn whispered, answering Lily's silent question.

Lily didn't care; she was too weary to put her barriers in place anyhow.

Questions threatened to overtake Lily's mind as soon as Evelyn began her story, but with each new twist and turn, she pushed them aside to listen to her sister.

"They forced me to drink vampire blood," Evelyn said, after a moment of silence in which she appeared to be debating with herself.

"Noro said it was making me stronger, and he was right. I opened the first portal later that day. That was when I was in the basement. It nearly killed me when my pneuma made it to Hecate and set down the part of my mind she carried with her. I know some fata made it through then, maybe a couple dozen. They moved me to the room you found me in and kept forcing vampire blood down my throat so I'd become strong enough to try again."

"What do you mean your pneuma?" Sara asked, stopping Evelyn's story for the first time.

"The part of me that can travel now. I assumed it was my human soul at first, but Noro called it a pneuma. It made sense because when I was traveling, I could still think in my head *and* see the stuff around me, and I remember Aoife said she couldn't do that when she traveled. But I could also see my pneuma travel inside my head. It was like being on split screen and very disorienting. My pneuma also seems to have feelings separate from mine. They were pretty weak in the manor but are stronger now and difficult to discern from my own." A pink stain spread across Evelyn's cheeks as she shot a glance at Lily.

"Your pneuma must have been the blue light we saw hovering over the mansion and what helped us enter the room they kept you in. We knew it was a part of you. It felt like you—magic wise, at least," Lily said. "Your pneuma was trying to help us save you."

"I didn't know about the outside shield until it cracked and the alarm sounded," Evelyn said. "Later, though, my pneuma periodically snuck under the door crack into the hallways so she could tell me what was happening. She saw you coming and told me so in her weird pneuma way. It was me yelling for you mind-to-mind while my pneuma—well, a part of her at least— was trying to help you inside. The other part of her I had to send through space so Noro didn't get suspicious.

I remember Noro saying that his spell on the door would kill anyone who tried to open it, that no one of this world would understand the spell."

Evelyn shook her head and snorted. "My pneuma got really excited when Noro said that. She was fluttering around like crazy, so I knew she knew of a way to get through his spell. It was kind of amazing teamwork for two beings who can't really talk to each other."

"She actually split herself into three," Brigit's eyes were wide. "When Lily and Sara touched your pneuma, a part of her rushed inside both of them. And you were making a portal already because we saw it, so that's another portion of her. That's fascinating. I've never heard of a human soul even splitting itself into two."

Evelyn looked thoughtful and then nodded. "That could also be why I couldn't really see what my pneuma was doing in space and why she never made it to Hecate that time. She'd weakened herself and our connection. My pneuma knew I didn't want to make another portal, that I wanted to escape and join you. She promised to do everything possible to put an end to Noro's plans. She must have really pushed herself, literally torn herself apart to make it happen." Evelyn placed a hand over her heart and looked down.

"I knew something was strange as soon as I entered your mind and you were communicating with your pneuma. If you had the ability to think while your pneuma was outside of you, you certainly weren't traveling. At least not in the traditional sense. But my question is where did your pneuma come from?" Aoife asked, studying Evelyn.

Evelyn's cheeks grew red and she looked at her hands. "She showed up right before I opened the first portal. Noro had been doing fata magic on me earlier and it was exhausting, so they forced me to drink vampire blood to prep for opening the portal. As soon as my pneuma flew out of me Noro said that the magic he did released or activated something inside me and Empusa's blood gave it the strength to come out. It makes sense—her coming out wasn't exactly comfortable. It felt like I was generating her or something, and probably took more energy than I had at the time," Evelyn sighed a frustrated sigh.

Lily racked her brain, running through Evelyn's story again and again. *Having a pneuma may come in handy. Like having a helpful familiar stored inside ourselves for when times get rough. Didn't Seraphina describe hers in the book as it floated out of her body? She was dying, and the pneuma was floating out . . . She was scared and then Noro had the babies drink her blood. Holy shit! Empusa and Amon drank Seraphina's, their*

Mother's, blood! I bet it had some of her pneuma in it! And Evelyn drank their blood. Does that mean?

Lily sought out Mary, the only other person who had been as obsessed with the book as Lily had. Her aunt's blue eyes locked with hers at the same instant and Lily's palms dampened. Mary nodded and Lily knew they were thinking the same thing.

"It wasn't whatever magic Noro did. It was the blood," Lily said. "Empusa and Amon's blood wasn't just strengthening you. It gave you a pneuma, or awoke one you already had . . . or something." Two bright emeralds eyes darted to Mary for help.

"If I had to guess," Mary ran her fingers through her blonde hair as the gears turned visibly in her brain, "I'd say Noro realized saving Seraphina was beyond his capabilities. Since he didn't know any better and is an elitist arse, he also would have assumed that any child of his with another fata would be immortal like all fata on Hecate were. He would have wanted to preserve as much of Seraphina's magic as he could. Her pneuma was disappearing into the air, but parts of Seraphina's pneuma still remained in Seraphina's half-transformed body. In her blood."

Mary stopped for a second and squirmed, clearly having a gross revelation.

"Noro saw that his children looked human. Humans drink, so Noro did what was natural. He let them drink. He allowed the twins to feed on their mother's blood not because he divined that's what would become a vampire's sustenance, though of course that did happen, but because it was the only way to preserve some of Seraphina herself in another being. Perhaps he hoped that someone, at some time, would be strong enough to complete the trio. At that point Eve and Lilith lived, and Noro may have held out hope that Lilith would help them. I'll bet he guessed they'd need Seraphina's power to complete the trio. They were special fata, after all. And when the one to complete the power of the three appeared, his children would be able to give them the magic stored inside them, as they were of Seraphina and had also taken in her blood. She was a part of them in every way she could be." Mary took in a shuddering breath, her eyes widening as she verbally worked out what had happened.

"Noro only needed to keep Empusa and Amon close to him for as long as it took. So he lied to them to keep them at his side and working for his purposes, never letting them know their true parentage or that he killed their mother. I wonder if Noro actually cultivated a vampire's taste for blood in those first moments of life? It's as cruel as it is clever, creating the ultimate vessel and killing machine all in one."

Mary ended her soliloquy, released a long exhale, and bit her lip.

You could hear a pin drop in the room.

"So that means Evelyn has Seraphina's magic inside her and it awoke or maybe generated a pneuma from Evelyn's genetics?" Sara asked.

"Evelyn has a bit of Seraphina herself inside her. Her magic, her blood, her soul, all of it. It was pure fata genetic material. I'd wager it did activate something dormant in Evelyn. Something that makes her special and maybe you two as well," Mary lifted her hands in question.

"Thank the goddess," Evelyn choked out and Lily noticed there were tears running down her cheeks. "I thought my pneuma showed up after Noro . . . I didn't want to say this before . . . I was embarrassed, but he kept calling us lovers. He said it was our official coupling that brought out fata instincts. The coupling wasn't like human sex at all, but I could feel him rolling through me. He must have been backtracking after I drank Empusa's blood so I wouldn't suspect the blood had actually done it. I believed him. I thought it, my pneuma, was a part of him or a product of him and I just hadn't been strong enough until then. I'd thought that *I* was a part of him. He even branded me with his and Dimia's marks."

Gasps arose from all around and Selma grasped Evelyn's hand in solidarity.

"Men will always want to claim you because of what you are, beautiful one. Just because he said that does not make it true," Selma said fiercely.

"Are those the symbols I saw when I bathed you? On your upper inner thigh?" Fiona asked, her eyes wide. "Have they changed you in any way?"

Evelyn shook her head defiantly. "I haven't noticed them holding any power over me besides reminding me of my captivity," she said wiping her tears with one hand and gripping Selma tighter with the other.

Sirens really do take to each other well, Lily thought, watching as what she imagined to be a thousand words unspoken passed between Selma and Evelyn.

Evelyn sat up straighter on her bed. "There's more. Noro keeps secrets and lies. He didn't tell any of his followers he fed me vampire blood to help generate my pneuma either. They all thought the blood was making me stronger so I could open the portal, too. I wondered why Nora didn't even know I had a pneuma! She thought I was crazy when I mentioned it!"

Lily caught Brigit's flinch at the taboo name of her childhood friend. That Nora had evaded Brigit, who was the stronger witch by miles, had Lily wondering if

Brigit, somewhere deep inside, had allowed her ex-best friend to escape and was now regretting her decision.

Evelyn took a deep breath. "But I found more marks on my body after I woke from opening the first portal—two triquetras glowing in my palm—so I knew I wasn't crazy. My pneuma showed them to me but they disappeared as soon as Noro entered the room. I don't know what the triquetras mean, but maybe now that I'm awake I can figure it out."

"From what you've said so far, your pneuma reminds me of a familiar," Lily said. "If Sara and I can get one, too, this might help us defeat the fata like yours helped us find you. That could be so useful! We just need to find—" Lily stopped, her stomach sinking.

"Empusa and Amon," Sara finished her tone defeated.

The vampire twins survived for thousands of years, but they die hours before we find out how useful their blood would have been? And I personally killed one?! Why didn't I suck it up for a few more hours?

Lily slumped back in her bed as the excitement of discovery fizzled.

"Maybe we can find one of their children? They had to have ingested some of their parents' blood to change," Gwenn suggested.

"That may take months," Aoife said. "And I'd say

the likelihood of Empusa or Amon's children giving up their blood after we killed their parents is low. Vampires hate donating blood as it is."

"What about Celestine? I bet she'd do it," Lily asked.

"We could ask who her sire was, but there are so many vamps it's unlikely to be one of the twins. I have a hunch closer blood ties would be better. Still, maybe she'd be willing to donate a couple cups and we can see what happens?" Aoife mused.

"What about me?" Evelyn asked.

"You?" Lily asked, confused. *Evelyn already had vampire blood and now she wants more? It must not be as terrible drinking blood as I'm imagining it will be.*

"My blood. I mean, I'm as good as one of their children right? I drank their blood like one of their children would. And we just confirmed I ingested enough of Seraphina's genetics and magic because I have a pneuma."

Lily held back a gag. While drinking vampire blood didn't sound like a great time, the idea of drinking her sister's blood was even more revolting.

Evelyn spoke hurriedly, perhaps in an effort to squash the looks of revulsion cropping up all around her. "It won't be great, but theirs wasn't either. I think it's worth a try. It's easier than going on a wild goose chase to hunt down vampires anyhow."

"Evelyn's right," Brigit said, her lips closing in a tight line. "But it can't happen straight away. You're still too weak. We'll try in a few days. Fiona, do you have any potions that boost blood supply?"

"You may feel a wee poke," Fiona said slipping the needle under Evelyn's skin.

Lily watched, as aghast now as she had been when Fiona started testing Evelyn's blood two days before. Soon, the strange purple liquid Fiona pulled out of her sister's veins would slip down her throat. She supposed it made it a tad bit easier, seeing how alien Evelyn's blood had become, but not much.

It's still cannibalism.

"I don't know why you insist on watching if you're so grossed out," Evelyn sniffed. "You can leave, you know."

It was true. Though Lily's burns wouldn't heal fully for days, Fiona's potions and salves had worked their magic and Lily had been cleared to roam the house yesterday. She hadn't taken full advantage of that privilege yet, content to spend most of her time lying in bed, talking to Evelyn and Sara. Mostly, the triplets spent hours discussing the past few weeks in minute detail.

How could I ever have been mad at her? Am I that vindictive? Lily wondered as she took in the tubes and needles coming out of Evelyn's arms. *Thank the goddess I have Sara to remind me about practicing things I'm apparently terrible at. Like forgiveness.*

"I'm done here. I'll run this to the lab for analysis. I realize it's tough to stay in bed, but keep resting, Evelyn. We need you as fit as possible if you're to give blood soon," Fiona said, sealing a syringe in a biohazard bag and cooler for transport. "I'll be back as soon as I can. Jane made sure her contact at the lab was expecting me today so I shouldn't have to wait again."

They waved Fiona out the door.

"Today may be the day." Evelyn smoothed a bandage Fiona had handed her onto her arm. "I feel great."

"That's good," Lily replied with forced nonchalance. The truth was that Evelyn, despite feeling good, looked terrible. The wounds she'd incurred during her days of torture had healed, a side effect Fiona attributed to the vampire blood, but Evelyn still looked thin and sickly. So much so that when her parents visited, Sonja Locksley had fainted at the sight of her daughter.

"Do you want me to get you anything? You'll need

sugar if you think you're going to give a lot of blood." Lily tried to sound like she wasn't telling her sister what to do.

"Hmm, a juice sounds good, I guess? Green, if they have it."

Lily eased herself off the bed, careful not to brush any of her thin, freshly grown skin against the fabric. "I'll go get it for you," she said, mentally adding a sandwich to the order as she slipped into the hallway.

The safe house had been eerily quiet all day. Celestine and Jane, the coven members who had made a point of being around as much as possible, had jobs and responsibilities to attend to they could no longer put off. Even the onslaught of other coven members venturing into the safe house asking about the Battle of Peacock Manor had slowed yesterday afternoon, after Brigit and Jane announced a conference would be held to answer questions. Everyone except for Fiona, Lily, and Evelyn, who was still too weak to move, had left for the conference earlier that morning.

"If we're going to address the rumors and ask for help, we need to make sure everyone knows the truth of what happened. You should have heard the mad stories people were coming up with. Complete lunacy!" Brigit had exclaimed last night when discussing the conference. "Now that Evelyn is awake and we know for sure there are two dozen new fata running around on the planet in addition to the seven Noro told Evelyn Eve brought over before she died, people will have to be on alert. Thank the goddess Noro blabbed about that because those seven fata at least have had plenty of time to learn how to use Earth's magic. It's a wonder they haven't moved on their plans already, though I suppose Mary's right that seven really isn't too many—or at least not as many as the experts thought, considering the number of magical creatures that live on Earth."

While Lily agreed that they should spread the word, she couldn't bring herself to leave Evelyn. If her grieving over Em had taught her anything, it was that no matter how much a person claimed they wanted to be alone, they still needed someone who cared nearby. And while their experiences weren't the same, Lily felt in her bones that Evelyn appreciated her nearness.

She wondered what kind of creatures would be at the conference. The safe house had been clamoring with witches from all over the world since word of the battle leaked. Even a local pack of weres had come forth wanting to ally themselves with their side. *Too bad we didn't have them a week ago.*

A clatter of metal coming from behind a closed door pulled Lily out of her daydreams with a start.

"Jane? Hello? Anyone there?" Lily called.

The tinny clank of metal on wood answered from behind the door to her right and Lily froze. What if it was an intruder? Was she strong enough to take on another supernatural right now?

A second, louder crash sounded, and Lily sighed. Something was up and she was the only one around to check it out. She crept up to the door and put her ear on it.

A muffled voice floated through the wood.

Placing her hand on the knob, Lily turned it slowly. Once it reached the end of its rotation, she flung the door open and barged through, fingers splayed and ready to fight.

She stopped dead in her tracks.

A man sat on the ground, bound and gagged. A pile of stuff was next to him—metal knickknacks and books he appeared to have knocked off the shelf to get her attention.

Another man lay in a bed on the opposite side of the room, asleep despite the commotion. Lily approached the man on the floor, her eyes taking in his longish sandy hair, excellent physique, and bright blue eyes.

"I'm taking out your gag, but don't try anything funny. I'm a witch and am prepared to defend myself."

The man nodded, his blue eyes wide and earnest.

Lily's hands found the back of the man's skull and a

slight tingle ran through her. *Weird,* she thought untying the gag. As soon as she pulled the cloth from his mouth, the man let out a huge exhale and licked his lips.

"Thanks. My mouth is so dry. It's excruciating," he said.

A bottle of water on the table caught her eye. "Open," Lily said grabbing the bottle and squirting its contents into his mouth.

"Ah, that was heaven," he said.

"Who are you? And why are you here?" Lily asked, unwilling to beat around the bush now that the man's basic needs were met.

"I'm Roman Simons."

Lily inhaled sharply and Roman raised his eyebrows.

"I see you've heard of me. I'll assume it wasn't flattering. Judgin' by your appearance I'm guessing you're Lily. I, too, have heard of you, mostly from Nora. Surprisingly, some of it was flattering—which is sayin' something, because it's hard to impress that woman."

"Enough rambling! Tell me why you're here," Lily said, her frantic tone in sharp contradiction to Roman's mix of relaxed southern twang and straightforward city speak.

"Right. Sorry 'bout that. It feels like an age since anyone has visited. And that guy's not much of a chatter as he's been asleep this whole time," He nodded toward the man on the bed. "I'm here 'cause Rena found me unconscious and locked up in the basement of Peacock Manor. They brought me here with the rest of the injured but once it became apparent no one recognized me, they isolated me. When Brigit found out she interrogated me and here I am."

Why didn't they tell us they'd taken a hostage? Lily barely had time to wonder before she answered her own question. *They're still deciding what to do with him, which means he has a story to tell.*

"Tell me what you told them."

Roman spoke with urgency, as if his life depended on convincing her of something. Lily listened as he told her about his family's debt to the vampires. The celebrated business deal with Locksley Enterprises. The vampire twins' proposal and subsequent threats. The whirlwind courtship with Evelyn punctuated by clandestine meetings with the Acolytes. Finally, the eventual betrayal that led to Evelyn's imprisonment. The story rang true, and tracked with Evelyn's, but it made no sense why Roman was here and unharmed. Then, words spoken by another of Roman's kind, Alistair Levi, the old incubus that had trained Roman came flooding back to her.

"He was grinning from ear to ear and couldn't stop

talking about the girl he was seeing. If I had to guess, I'd say Roman has fallen for Evelyn."

"You told Brigit you love Evelyn, didn't you?"

Roman diverted his gaze to the ground. "Once I was of no use to them, the Acolytes released me, but I stayed. I tried to break her out once but that damn werewolf Felix caught me and locked me up. At first the relationship was all a ploy, a way to protect my family. But within a week I'd started to care about Evelyn. After two I was a goner. I love Evelyn more than anything or anyone, even myself, and if I had to do it again, I'd give up my life for her."

Lily blushed. She didn't know how to respond to such a blatant declaration so instead she turned to the man in the bed. "And who's he?"

Roman followed her gaze. "Oh, he's the groundskeeper at the manor. The Acolytes were not informed he lived there when they rented the place. Apparently, his room is out of the way of the guest rooms. They threw him in the basement because it was easy. Once it became clear Evelyn needed vampire blood to heal, Empusa and Amon used the both of us to feed off of and keep their own blood levels high. Fiona has him in an enchanted sleep so he'll heal faster from the bites. And so he won't remember anything he sees here, of course."

Lily nodded. "I'm putting this back on you. Don't tell anyone I was here. If you do, I'll make you regret it."

Roman sighed, nodded, and opened his mouth.

Goddess be, Evelyn will be pissed when she finds out.

Lily tied the gag tight and walked out of the room without another word.

Some Things Take Time
Evelyn

"Are you sure you're up for doing this? We can always wait another day and do it at home. That way you get a wee bit more rest," Brigit suggested, her face creased with concern.

"Fiona said my labs came back impeccable and I'm tired of waiting," Evelyn replied, unwilling to budge.

"She'll be fine, Brig," Fiona guided Brigit away from Evelyn's bedside to allow herself access to the nightstand on which sat a jumble of tubes, needles, and plastic tubs. "It's better this way. She'll be tired but that's normal after donating blood. This way she may actually get a full night's rest before getting on the plane."

"I'm sure the Locksleys would reschedule the jet if

we said we needed a couple more days," Brigit said, looking desperate for a reason to delay.

"No need, Mom." Evelyn tried her best not to put emphasis on the term that signified bonds of love that she'd been withholding from Brigit since they met. Bonds she could no longer deny, despite Evelyn's tendency to keep new people at arm's length for as long as possible. It felt wrong to call Brigit by her given name when her sisters so openly called her Mom—even more wrong when Evelyn considered how much the woman she'd wanted so badly to blow off when they'd met now meant to her.

We've been through a lot of shit for sure.

Everyone in the room turned to stare at her. Lily's mouth hung open and Sara smiled broadly at Evelyn, like she wanted to wrap her in a bear hug.

So much for not making a big deal about it.

"I already talked to them and they're having Vici meet us at the hangar tomorrow," Evelyn continued as if she'd never dropped the M-bomb. "I still have to tell her I'm a witch, and I don't want to put it off any longer. I got the feeling my parents want to hear the whole story from me, too, and not just Sara. They were so relieved I was alive when they visited and I was so weak that they didn't push it, but I could tell they wanted to know. Especially Dad. These are the best conditions I can leave under, and I'm taking it. It's time for me to get out of the city and back where I belong." A lump rose in Evelyn's throat as she said the words.

Brigit gave a small nod and wiped the tears streaming down her face.

Selma appeared at Evelyn's side and took her hand. *She always knows when I need a little bit of strength.*

It surprised Evelyn how close she'd grown to the siren in the last few days, though Mary and Fiona had both assured her that for those with siren powers bonding strongly was normal. It was an evolutionary hack full-blooded sirens had developed to tamp down other sirens' fierce emotional states and ward off madness that often plagued their kind.

But Evelyn recognized what she and Selma had was more than just a siren bond. Selma had made it a point to sit with Evelyn in the brief periods when Lily was gone or sleeping. In those moments she'd told Evelyn all about Lily growing up. Every story tempted a green-eyed monster within Evelyn that she'd been trying to douse, for Lily had led what Evelyn considered a life full of adventure and love.

But the stories also allowed Evelyn to understand Lily better. It was obvious that was Selma's intent, but Evelyn didn't view it as manipulative. She thought it was nice that Selma loved both of them enough and wanted them to heal together.

"Alright, then. Selma, I need to get in there. Evelyn, arms out. Lily, Sara, come over here," Fiona instructed.

Selma squeezed Evelyn's hand one last time as Lily and Sara gathered round her. Lily, Evelyn noted, already looked queasy.

Without preamble Fiona walked over and slipped a needle into Evelyn's right arm, then her left.

"I still can't get over how strange it looks," Sara said studying the blood flooding the tubes with academic detachment. "Will our blood look like that too, Fiona?"

"Perhaps if you drank enough. But we'll be giving you only enough to release your pneuma. In time, Evelyn's blood should return to normal. It's the raw vampire blood mingling with her own that is giving Evelyn's blood that color," Fiona answered.

"That's a relief," Evelyn said, a smile spreading across her face. "Can you imagine going for a checkup and the doctor drawing this out? How would I ever explain that?!"

Lily swallowed loudly and Evelyn noticed the green tinge of her sister's face had deepened. *She's going to pass out just from thinking about drinking blood. We need to change the subject . . .*

"So, Lil, tell me about this guy Alfred. Sara said he

seemed *very* interested in you during the rescue mission."

Lily's eyes darted to Sara, who had the good grace to look sheepish.

"Sorry, Lil! She wanted to hear the whole story and well . . . It kind of popped out," Sara said with a small grin on her elfin face.

"What a bunch of gossips I have for sisters," Lily grumbled, but Evelyn could see the distraction had worked. A faint stain of pink had spread on Lily's cheeks at the mention of Alfred's name, muting the unattractive green hue from minutes prior.

"It appears so," Evelyn smirked. "But now you have to tell me. Men are, after all, my speciality. You never should have tried keeping something man related from me anyhow!"

Lily's eyes widened, and she bit her lip. "Uh, yea, you're right, silly to keep man related stuff from you. Um . . . well . . . let's see, Alfred is . . ."

Jesus, no wonder Amon was her first boyfriend. He probably charmed the pants off her and manipulated their entire relationship. She can't even talk about a guy she likes.

"Charming?" Evelyn supplied. "That's what Sara said."

"Yes! Yes, he's charming. And a daemon, and," Lily

sighed and Evelyn could practically see her pulse slow, "really, really handsome. I saw him before we left for the manor and thought he was hot but knew it wasn't the time. Then he latched onto me and wouldn't leave me alone when we were trying to rescue you. At first it was weird and a little humiliating."

"The girl blushed more times than a maid on her wedding day," Aoife teased.

"Well, yea! Who expects to be hit on when they're going into battle? And with all their family around! Not to mention how damn honest he was with his intentions of wanting to get to know me . . ."

Evelyn refrained from laughing though the picture in her head warranted it. "Are you two going to keep in touch?"

"We've been texting and he stopped by a couple times while you were still out of it," Lily admitted.

"Did you use any of the tips I taught you, Lil? Tips of how to gain a man's interest forever?" Selma leaned forward, dark red lips curved upward and light brown eyes shining.

"No, Sel! The safe house is hardly an appropriate place to use my womanly charms on Alfred. Especially with all of you noseys around," Lily whacked Selma in the shoulder.

"Well the lad seemed impressed enough as it was.

He requested the cottage address, so Lil may be receiving a few courting gifts soon," Brigit interrupted, her lips turned up slightly.

"You gave it to him?!" Lily asked incredulously.

"He's a lovely man, and so earnest. I didn't think you'd mind," Brigit said with a shrug.

Rena roared with laughter and a slow smile spread on Annika's lips as Lily stared at Brigit, mouth agape and palms to the sky.

Evelyn laughed so hard the needles throbbed in her arms. "Well, I hope it works out for you two, Lil. I'm taking a break from men myself, but I can be your and Sara's wingwoman! I'd help catch you guys all the best men. Hey! We'll go to the Drunken Duck together when we get back to Fern Cottage now that we're out in the open! It will be great flirting practice for next time you see Alfred, and we'll find Sara a burly Irish hottie."

"About that," Sara said with a pronounced cough.

"Don't tell me you picked up man candy at the battle, too?" Evelyn asked. "You guys! You have a siren for a sister and you're not even going to take advantage of it!"

"It's not that. I'm just not sure your magic will work for me." A pink stain spread across Sara's cheeks and her rosebud lips extended in a small smile. "You see, I'm attracted to women."

"What! Why didn't you tell us before? We've shared so much . . . oh my goddess! Did you think we'd react badly?" Hurt flashed across Lily's face.

"No! Not at all! I mean Lil, your mom is gay and Evelyn is so cosmopolitan, and Gwenn had that fling with Rena," Sara shot Annika an apologetic look. "No, I never thought *any* of you would be homophobic about it. I just wasn't ready yet. We've only known each other five months, and to be honest I've only told three other people my entire life—two of whom I was in relationships with. Not even my adoptive parents know, and I don't see telling them anytime soon. Plus, it's a weird thing to bring up. Now was the first time it felt natural," Sara shrugged.

"Some things take time, Lil," Rena said, stepping forward and placing a hand on Sara's shoulder. "You of all people know that."

The distress melted from Lily's face as Rena's words sunk in and she nodded.

"Well, Sara," Evelyn said, her grandiose tone shattering any of the remaining tension. "You'll be happy to know my charms do, in fact, work on women of your tastes. I always got a couple biters when I did siren practice at the bars, so we're all set there!"

"Of course, you did!" Aoife guffawed. "Brig, these

girls are going to turn our quiet little hamlet upside down if Evelyn has anything to say about it!"

"It needs shaking up anyhow," Brigit chuckled. "There hasn't been a real scandal since—"

"Since we were in our twenties!" Mary finished, a mischievous gleam in her eye.

"I can only imagine," Rena remarked glancing at Gwenn with a wicked smile.

"No need to be going into the past. I don't do this often but I'm exercising my eldest sister rights and forbidding any tall tales!" Gwenn held up her hands.

Evelyn leaned back into her mound of pillows listening to the laughter rise and fall all around her, "I can't wait to get back to Fern Cottage. It's been so long since I did magic *I* wanted to do. I was missing it more than I thought I would. Especially when I was stuck in that freaking basement."

"I'll bet," Sara said with a sympathetic smile. "We've been doing mock battles since you've been gone. Lily has these sneaky moves that I won't spoil because she'll definitely try to use them on you. She got me so you better get ready."

"Hell yeah," Evelyn said, her tone impressed. "Can't wait to learn them. She must have loved beating you in something too." Evelyn winked at Sara and Lily grinned.

"Sorry to interrupt, girls, but was this about how much you drank, Evelyn?" Fiona pointed to the glasses now half full with dark purple blood.

"Looks about right," Evelyn confirmed.

"Alright then, girls, you're up," Fiona clamped the tubes attached to Evelyn's arms and lifted each glass to inspect its contents. "Here you are. Try not to waste any. If this doesn't work today, it will be a couple days before Evelyn can give blood again. Do either of you want a nose plug?"

"We got this, right Lil?" Sara asked taking her glass without hesitation.

"I'm so sorry, chicas. I wanted to be here for moral support but I can't watch this," Selma walked quickly from the room, her warm olive skin faded and clammy.

Evelyn watched as Lily's eyes tracked Selma, her face wistful, like she wanted to follow. Instead, she reached out with a trembling hand to take her glass from Fiona.

You can do this. I promise it isn't so bad. Evelyn pushed the thought toward Lily.

Lily smiled a tight, closed-lipped smile and Evelyn knew the message had been received. "Cheers, Sara."

The Blood Drinkers

Lily

THEIR GLASSES CLINKED, sloshing the purple-red liquid up the sides. Lily watched the legs as they ran down again, thicker than molasses. She brought the glass to her lips. Sara was already chugging and Lily heard the glugging of liquid down her sister's throat, the moment she came up for air, and the thunk of her glass on the table.

"It's not so terrible, Lil. Try to focus on the hint of spiciness. Think of it as tea."

Lily glanced up at Sara over the rim of her glass. Her lips, now dark purple, looked ludicrous against the white of her skin, like a child playing dress up.

"Bottoms up, Lil," Evelyn said, leaning forward and tilting the glass up so the blood threatened to spill from it. "Three, three, three right? We need to be on the same page. You can do this," Evelyn lowered her hands, allowing Lily to have the final say.

She could have lowered the glass back down, waited until she was ready, but Lily knew she'd never feel ready. It was better this way, with her sisters urging her on, pushing her to become what she needed to be. Before she could change her mind she tilted the glass upward and hot, thick liquid caressed her lips. It pooled at the entrance of her mouth and Lily commanded her lips to part. They did so infinitesimally, allowing a thin stream of blood to trickle in between her teeth. It tasted like nothing she'd ever had before. Metallic, but also spiced with an undertone of . . . sugar?

Lily allowed her lips to part further, her curiosity piqued. Definitely sugar—hot, syrupy sugar.

OK. I can do this. It's like drinking syrup.

She trained her eyes on what remained in the glass and commanded herself to chug.

But blood, it turned out, was not an easy chugging beverage like the cheap beers of her college days. It stuck to the sides of her mouth and teeth, its cloying sweetness lingering on Lily's tongue like a stalker as she pulled the liquid down her throat as fast as her testy stomach would allow. A bead of sweat trickled down her forehead and off her cheek to land on her collarbone.

After seconds that seemed like hours, the last of the

blood slipped into her mouth and Lily swallowed, grateful the ordeal was over. She set the cup down and wiped her hand across her mouth, wanting to eliminate any evidence that she was a blood drinker.

"You did it! See, it wasn't so bad. Different than I thought it would be. Was the vampire blood spicy, Evelyn? Yours was like drinking over-spiced mulled wine but thicker," Sara said her eyes curious.

"And sweet." Lily groaned as she sat on edge of the bed and bent forward to dampen her nausea.

"Both," Evelyn answered. "I guess that's a way to test when it's all out of my system. I can prick myself and lick a drop of blood every day."

Lily's throat spasmed, and the blood threatened to come back up.

Brigit, intuitive to her daughter's needs, placed a gentle hand on Lily's shoulder and her nervous system calmed.

"It may be awhile before the blood takes effect," Brigit said softly. "We're hoping not to have to do another round back home, but Fiona will have enough supplies if need be. We're flying blind here with an unknown dilution factor. Do either of you feel at all different now? Evelyn mentioned she felt lighter when her pneuma took up residence within her."

Lily and Sara shook their heads.

"I say we let them rest. They need time to absorb it and Lil looks like she should lie down." Fiona shot Lily an understanding smile. "We have plenty of things to be wrapping up before tomorrow anyhow, don't we, Brig?"

"Fiona's right. We can't leave our messes to Jane's coven. It isn't right. The girls are safe here," Gwenn seconded, when Brigit looked as though she was about to protest.

"We'll be just down the hall. All they need to do is ring the bell Fiona bought and we'll come running," Aoife added, taking Brigit by the shoulders.

"And we'll be right next door. We leave early in the morning and Rena still needs to pack for our flight. I'll set my yoga mat up next to the wall while I practice. These walls aren't so thick we wouldn't hear anything strange," Annika chimed in.

Lily wondered if Roman was one of the things the McKay witches needed to wrap up and her stomach heaved whether from the blood or the reminder of the secret she was keeping from Evelyn, she wasn't sure. She closed her eyes and sighed. "I'd like a rest. I do feel a little queasy."

"Well, the blood is doing something then," Fiona said, packing up her supplies. "Ring the bell if you need anything or experience any pain at all. We'll stay close."

Brigit, predictably, was the last to leave. She paused

at the door as she left, checking one last time that they were in fact capable of being left alone, and then disappeared through the door.

Sara pulled the trundle bed she slept on out from under Lily's sickbed. "I'm going to take a nap," she said, lying on the creaky mattress and staring up at the ceiling. "This may be one of our last relaxing days in a while." She closed her eyes and fell asleep within seconds.

"How did she manage that so fast?" Lily whispered, half impressed and half envious as she eased into her own bed.

"I think vampire blood has a sort of draining chemical effect on the body. The first time I took it I bet I would have passed out, too, if I hadn't been so scared and forced to open a portal. I slept for a whole day afterward. As a matter of fact, I think I could sleep that long *now*. Must be from giving blood," Evelyn leaned back into her mound of pillows and closed her eyes.

"I'll turn off the lamp," Lily said, and plunged them into darkness.

Starseeds
Evelyn

Evelyn's pneuma thumped hard against her sternum, waking her from her deep slumber. The first light of day was seeping weakly through the blackout curtains into their darkened room. She glanced over and saw Lily and Sara still snoozing peacefully and a pang of jealousy ran through her.

Why does that always happen when I wake up?

She pushed herself up and nearly fell out of the bed as two lights, one bright green the other a flaming red shot into the bedroom and dove into her sister's chests.

"Holy shit! It worked!" Evelyn screeched. Her pneuma fluttered wildly within her. It occurred to Evelyn that her pneuma had felt the other two approaching and had woken her up for that very reason.

447

"What the hell?" Lily swore, lurching up from the sheets, eyes wide.

Evelyn looked at Lily's hands and saw a faint white triquetra glowing in her sister's palms. "Your hands," she whispered.

Lily's face paled.

A crooked grin spread over Sara's face as she rose from slumber in a less reactionary manner. "It worked. We have pneumas! I can feel her moving inside me!"

"So cool," Lily said without enthusiasm. "Sara, let me see your hands."

Sara turned her palms up to reveal two white triquetras glowing up at them.

"It's the signal Evelyn was talking about! They're letting us know they're here. Though I think that all the fluttering inside me makes that pretty clear," Sara said sitting up and resting her back against the wall.

Another, weaker pang of jealousy shot through Evelyn. They believe it so easily. *Probably because they experienced it together.*

She smothered the emotion before it grew and became the green-eyed monster that had been rampaging through her with increasing frequency since she arrived at the safe house.

Evelyn picked up the tiny bell Fiona kept by her

bedside. "Shall I call the rest of the clan and tell them the good news?"

"GODDESS BE. IT HAPPENED SO FAST," Brigit whispered for the tenth time as Sara showed them her palms once more.

"Far faster than anyone anticipated," Mary agreed, her hands tented in front of her mouth in thought. "So do you feel different? Evelyn, obviously your bodily experience wasn't the same but chime in if what they say resonates with you. I'll need any lead I can get for research."

"Besides the fact that my pneuma won't stop moving inside me, which is pretty weird, I guess I feel lighter, like Evelyn said. More airy," Lily added hesitantly.

"Same," Sara paused. "And older. More than a few years, like I've lived an entire other life."

Evelyn sat up straighter. "Like your pneuma lived a separate life from you? One that came with memories and emotions? I've had these . . . moods since I've been here." She hadn't been ready to talk about them to her sisters. Not when everyone was so concerned over her health. But maybe now that her sisters had pneumas, she could confess.

Sara's brows furrowed. "Maybe? I'm not sure yet."

Evelyn slumped back into her pillows.

"What do you mean by moods, Evelyn?" Mary pulled up a chair next to Evelyn.

"Well, umm, when I wake up sometimes, before I get my head on straight and all, I . . ."

"We won't judge you for what you say," Sara affirmed. "You've awoken or generated . . . whatever, there's a new being inside you. One you can't control entirely. Plus, it may happen to us and we need to know what to expect."

Lily nodded in agreement.

"I've been so envious of you two sometimes!" Evelyn blurted out. "Usually right when I wake up before I get my senses back. And once or twice when you were being all sisterly, too. But I don't think that either of them were from me. I don't really believe you exclude me or anything. My only guess is my pneuma's feelings are taking over my own."

Evelyn's face burned with shame. *My sisters risked their lives to save me, and this is how I repay them? By saying I'm jealous of them?*

"But I've slept in the same room as you for a week and you didn't say anything or seem mad," Lily said, hurt evident in her voice.

"Of course I didn't! We've been getting along consistently for the first time. And I was sure these feelings weren't coming from me. There's no way I'm mad at any of you for anything! What I feel, it's irrational, and I was embarrassed! Getting jealous has never really been a thing for me and I don't feel like I have the right to be jealous in this situation."

"She can't help what she feels, Lil," Sara whispered, though she, too, looked a touch hurt. "It's probably the vampire blood or something."

"What about feeling older like Sara mentioned?" Mary pressed, unwilling to be deterred from her mission. "I'll need any similarities you can tell me that will help with my research. We need to start looking now so we can help train you three and your pneumas when we get home. The Sisters of Salem have a prodigious library I can take advantage of before we fly out tomorrow."

Evelyn cocked her head. "Well, like I said before, I felt lighter, but I attributed that mostly to being starved and depleted of my magic. Older? I don't know if I feel that way but . . . I certainly feel different, like I've lived a lot more. I'm more emotional, less-level headed, especially when I wake up. Wiser? I guess so." Her voice lifted into a question as she contemplated what she'd uncovered.

"We should all meditate on our pneumas!" Sara

jumped in excitedly. "This could be a great chance for us to bond to our pneumas and each other."

"That's not a bad idea," Gwenn said. "Sara has always been abnormally in tune with her body. Perhaps the two of you should join her in a meditation?"

Evelyn groaned. *As if my life isn't woo-woo enough already.*

There was a sudden movement in the corner of the room. Evelyn turned to see Annika had stood and begun pacing in small circles. Four times in a row the tall Swede ran her hands through her long white hair.

Evelyn bit her lip and looked at Selma, who shrugged her shoulders. Annika looked like a woman who'd just had a revelation.

"You feeling alright, Ann?" Lily asked, her brows furrowed in concern.

Annika's gaze shot up from the ground to find the entire room staring at her. "Yes, I'm fine, it's . . . this may not be relevant but I had a thought. What Sara said about feeling older, and Evelyn waking up with those emotions she doesn't think are hers and her pneuma waking her up so she could see the pneumas' return to Sara and Lily, it all got me thinking," Annika heaved a sigh. "I've heard people describe something like this before. Not as profound or abrupt but similar. Anyways, it will sound very strange, but I can't help but feel it might be something."

"Spit it out, Ann!" Rena said exasperatedly.

"You remember that yoga retreat? The one in Costa Rica that you refused to go to?" Annika turned to face Rena.

"How could I not! The stories you came back with from all those wackos had me concerned for the future of humanity. What a bunch of new-age bullshit. And coming from me that's saying something. I bet none of them even live in a commune!"

Annika ran her hand through her hair again. "No, most live in cities. But that's not the point. To be clear, I agree with Rena: I would have called most of what I heard the other yoga practitioners talk about a little too much for my tastes. That is, until right now."

Rena's mouth tightened.

"Since Rena wouldn't go, I was assigned a cabin mate, and mine was a little out there."

"What an understatement! Claiming she was from the moon." Rena shot Lily a look. "Remember I was telling you about the nut jobs Annika met at Thanksgiving?"

Lily giggled but stopped short when Annika scowled at Rena.

"My roommate didn't say she was from the moon.

She said her *soul* was from another planet. That it was an ancient thing, reincarnated in human form on this planet. She called herself a starseed. Apparently there are a lot of people who identify this way. They don't deny that they're human in body but claim their souls aren't. Their souls have adventures and stories of their own. My roommate said her soul always had these feelings that my roommate didn't feel aligned with how she thought."

Many people cocked the heads in confusion and Annika gave them an understanding smile.

"I know, it's different. At first I thought she may have multiple personality disorder or something, but it sounds kind of like what Sara, Evelyn, and Lil said. They're feeling older, odd emotions that aren't theirs and sensations they can't control. Then there's the triquetras that appeared on their palms signifying a triple goddess. That had to be telling us something, else why would it appear? What if they . . . What if their pneumas aren't just a part of them? What if they were a part of someone else? Three someones who have been gone a long time and waiting to reawaken."

Stunned silence shrouded the room.

Sara sucked in a long breath and Lily's hand flew to her mouth.

Holy shit. That's why Noro kept calling me Eve. He

wasn't just being a nostalgic creep. And when he said I shined with the power I had a thousand years ago and that the fata I brought over were still here . . . he was actually talking to her because she was finally there. . . My pneuma. Eve's pneuma. It all makes sense now. Evelyn stared at her blanket. The air became thick, running slower through her airways and feeling muddy in her lungs.

But I can't be. Eve was . . . Evelyn's heartbeat raced as her mind flung about, begging for an alternative that made more sense.

Her pneuma shot from where it had been momentarily resting up into her heart, calming the spasms in her chest.

Evelyn looked down and gasped. Her chest was glowing, a bright sapphire blue triquetra visible in the deep "V" of her sleep shirt. She shot up in bed and her head swiveled violently on her neck.

It's happening to them too, Evelyn thought taking in the deep crimson triquetra on Sara's chest and Lily's emerald green one. *But how can we be sure that we carry the original three sisters' pneumas within us?*

Her eyes darted to Lily—who looked just as concerned as Evelyn felt—to Sara, who sat quietly, eyes closed and searching deep inside. Her gaze moved on to each other person in the room but no one else was paying attention to anyone but Sara.

They're right, Sara knows herself the best of all of us. If anyone can get answers from another soul living inside her, it's Sara. Time seemed to stop as Evelyn waited for her sister to communicate with a being living inside her from another place and time.

Finally, a bright copper penny flashed as Sara opened her eyes, and all breath in the room ceased.

"We aren't just like them in looks and power, not merely less-powerful human imitations. We are the original three sisters *and* us—they can't exist without our bodies to come back to. We're the keepers of their souls and our own," Sara took a shaky breath and released it slowly. "Annika's right. We're starseeds."

Magirattzi

Lily

"Lil, could you help Sara walk Evelyn to the car?" Brigit asked, striding by with a suitcase in each hand.

Lily retreated to their room, pleased to have a task to take her mind off her altered, airy state.

"You two ready?"

"Yup," Evelyn replied sitting up with Sara's assistance.

"If you're good on that side then I'll take this one?" Lily asked Sara who nodded and wedged herself beneath Evelyn's boney shoulder.

They stood together and a profound sense of relief washed over Lily as half of Evelyn's mass fell on her, weighing her back onto the earth. Evelyn was still underweight but apparently it didn't take much to counteract the lightness of Lily's pneuma.

"You don't have anything to take, right?" Lily scanned the room.

Evelyn shook her head and blinked. She looked lightheaded. "My parents are meeting us at the hangar with a few bags. Vicencia let them into the apartment and they packed what I asked them to."

"You don't think your parents let anything slip, do you?" Sara asked.

"I asked them not to say anything to Vici. I want to be the one to tell her. It helps that Dad's her boss; Vici will do what he says without too many questions. She'll be at the hangar because Dad requested it."

That would help, Lily readjusted Evelyn's pokey bones on her shoulder as they walked down the hallway.

They opened the front door and Lily stopped mid-stride. There was a jolt on the other side of Evelyn, indicating Sara had done the same.

"Who are all these people?" Evelyn asked staring into the sea of faces outside the safe house.

Alfred, Celestine, Alistair, and many others looked up at them.

"Everyone's here to see you off," Brigit said bounding up the steps and beaming at them despite her daughters' obvious confusion.

"These are the people who helped save me?" Evelyn asked, a hint of understanding dawning.

"A lot of them," Sara scanned the crowd. "And I recognize even more from the conference we held while you guys were healing. I guess they want to meet you and Lil, make sure we're the real deal."

Lily groaned. Small talk had never been her strong suit—especially not in her new world, where strangeness and things she knew nothing about lurked around every corner.

"So we're networking," Evelyn said, the corners of her lips lifting in self-satisfied smirk. "Leave this to me, girls. Networking is a speciality of mine."

<hr>

ON TO HER NEXT CONQUEST. Lily watched as Evelyn hugged Shefali and the rest of her witchy family goodbye a half hour later. Evelyn hadn't been kidding about her networking prowess. She'd had no trouble winning over any of the masses that came to see them off.

Even more impressive, in Lily's opinion, was that Evelyn always seemed to know what to say, whether it was complimenting Shefali on her gorgeous sari or asking Griselda for a brief demonstration of her powers. The grumpy half leprechaun-half elf had been delighted to indulge Evelyn, who she took to quickly, and created a shimmering rainbow over the triplets.

She's masterful at knowing what people want, Lily thought as her fingers waved through the rainbow. *Why was it so hard for us to get along those first few months? Was it all my fault?*

"I wouldn't say that. I'm not so charming when I'm being competitive, which I couldn't help doing with you two," Evelyn said with an apologetic glance as they shuffled to the next group.

Lily frowned and a look of concentration came over her face as she checked her mind barriers.

"No, you have your barriers up," Evelyn said. "It's just that we're touching now so I can hear pretty much anything you are thinking and some of Sara's thoughts, too. It's the only part of my magic that feels easier than it was before before. I have a hunch my pneuma may be helping somehow. Sorry."

Lily sighed. *Just when I think I have that one thing figured out, Evelyn gets even better at ceremens.*

"Impatient to see me?"

Lily turned to find Alfred and Celestine beaming back at her. She whacked Alfred on the shoulder and smiled. "You wish."

"Oh, but I do!" Alfred's smile widened further.

Evelyn stuck out her hand. "I'm Evelyn. You must

be the one Lily told me about. You're handsomer than she let on."

"So, Lily has been talking about me, has she?" Alfred's tone was full of delight.

Lily couldn't help but grin. "I may have mentioned you a time or two."

"I'm impressed. My sister is tough to please, Alfred. My advice to you: Don't let her slip away," Evelyn leveled her gaze with the daemon's before a charismatic smile spread across her face. "As for myself, I can't thank you enough for risking your life to save me. And joining our cause. If there's ever anything I can do to help, you need only ask. You too, Celestine."

"Just meeting your gorgeous sister is enough thanks for me." Alfred's reply sent a wave of heat into Lily's cheeks.

"More will join the cause once they hear the news. You three will no longer be alone," Celestine added.

"I hope so," Evelyn replied. She shifted her slight weight to rest completely on Sara's shoulder. "I think Lily may want more time with these two. Can you take my weight, Sara?"

Sara nodded, said a quick goodbye, and the pair hobbled off.

Lily threw herself into Celestine's arms first, "I can't

thank you enough. Without your help we'd never have gotten Evelyn out of there. And Sara and I ..."

"You would have found a way out of that jam," Alfred whispered at Celestine's side, and Lily had an inkling he was saying it as much for his own benefit as hers.

"All that matters is you're here now. I'm glad your sister is on the mend. I'll make sure to send Mary a few of my recipes to fatten her up," Celestine said, watching Evelyn and Sara approach the next group with concern.

"I know I'd sure like that," Lily said.

"Then it shall be done. Now if you'll excuse me, Lily, I must go say goodbye to your mother and aunts," Celestine bestowed a kiss on each of Lily's cheeks before disappearing into the crowd.

"Alone at last," Alfred said.

Lily giggled, "If you count being surrounded by a hundred people as alone."

"I get a feeling you and your sisters won't be left alone for a long time, so I'll take what I can get," he lifted her hand to his lips and kissed it.

Lily gasped at the sensation, hot and cold and electrifying all at once. Her body pulled toward Alfred's on its own accord and before she took another breath their faces were inches from each other.

This is crazy. I hardly know him at all and all these people are around.

Alfred grinned. His high cheekbones rose resembling that of a Grecian marble statue, and Lily drew impossibly closer until his breath swept against her cheeks. Lily's skin tightened.

Did she want to do this?

"I'd love to kiss you, *really* kiss you, Lily," Alfred inhaled, and Lily's lips parted. "But I can't. Not here with all these people around."

It felt like a bucket of ice water had been tossed over her.

"What? But why?" It was like someone else was speaking through her mouth. What happened to her private nature? She had been ready to jump on the guy right then and there.

"I want our first real kiss to be special, private," he grasped her hand tighter and Lily's heart thumped against her sternum.

"Oh. I guess that makes sense."

"But I hope you'll settle for this," Alfred said. Leaning in he pressed his lips to hers, softly, sweetly, chastely.

In a second the kiss was over but the fire of his lips on hers remained when he pulled away. *Who knew a peck on the lips could be so damn hot?*

"Perhaps when I come to visit we can learn more about each other?"

"You really are coming to visit, then?"

"You doubted me? Remember I told you what my father said about not letting anything special go?"

Lily grinned and leaned in for their second sweet kiss.

"Well I gotta say, Lil, you sure pick the hot ones," Evelyn said an hour later as they slipped into the fifteen-person van Jane had borrowed to shuttle them to the airport. "And I'll be damned if he's not a gentleman! I saw that schoolboy kiss!"

Lily averted her eyes and grinned. "That surprised me, too. He came on so strong before and I'll be honest I . . ."

"Oh. Believe me. We saw you yearning for more. The tension was palpable, even with thirty people between us," Evelyn finished for her with a wink.

Lily laughed. She still couldn't fathom how she'd been ready and willing to have a full-blown make out session in front of so many people.

Thank the goddess one of us has restraint.

The Truth
Evelyn

"DADDY'S HANGAR IS NUMBER THREE," Evelyn said.

The tall, wolf-like build of James and the short, dark one of Sonya grew larger as the van drew closer. Another woman, about the triplets' age with long brown hair and olive skin, stood with them. *Oh Vici, I'm so sorry.*

"*That's* Vicencia? You forgot to mention she looks like a freaking Italian model," Lily said, her mouth gaping as she smoothed down her hair.

Evelyn gulped. *Can I do this? What if she hates me?*

As if her sister could read her mind Lily turned away from the window and clasped Evelyn on the shoulder. "You got this, Evelyn. Vicencia deserves to the truth."

"What if she doesn't believe me? I can't even do

magic to convince her right now, I'm still so drained. Or worse, what if she believes me and hates me? We've been best friends since we were kids and I hid something so huge from her."

She expected Lily to agree with her, tell her that Vicencia had every right to hate her and that she probably would. Instead, Lily smiled.

"I know it's hard. Shoot, it was hard for me to go home as a witch, really show up as my new self, and my whole family already knew. But you can't keep this from people you love and you can't use the excuse that we're a secret anymore because we're not. And as for Vicencia not believing you, well I doubt that. I'm sure it will answer a lot of unexplained quirks about you." Lily winked and Evelyn couldn't help but grin. "Plus, let's be honest: You may not be able to do any of the flashy fireball stuff Sara pulled with your parents, but you can still read Vicencia's mind. That would convince anyone."

Evelyn nodded, her shoulders tightening into knots as Lily and Sara helped her out of the van and into a wheelchair. The rest of the group started loading bags onto the plane but her sisters stayed with her as they promised they would. "Wheel me over, will you? I want you to meet Vici."

Lily pushed her over to the Locksleys while Sara walked at Evelyn's side. They were less than five feet from the group when Evelyn saw the tears in Sonja's and Vicencia's eyes and the hard set of James' mouth as he scanned her frail body.

"Hi Mom and Dad. Hey Vici. These are my sisters, Lily and Sara," Evelyn blurted out before they had even come to a stop.

Lily and Sara stepped forward. Hugs and greetings flew all around. Sonja was particularly emotional, unable to let go of Sara's hands as she thanked her again and again for helping them. Unlike Evelyn upon first meeting, Vicencia was warm, embracing both Lily and Sara and thanking them for bringing Evelyn back safe and sound.

"It was nothing," Lily bit her lip and Evelyn could tell she was opting to say less rather than accidentally spilling all Evelyn's secrets. *Vici always had a way with getting people to open up around her.*

"Bringing my best friend back is hardly nothing. I mean look at her! What that monster must have done to have her in this state. He better pray he never crosses my path," Vicencia said, her full red lips set in a tight line.

Lily bit her lip and nodded. "I hope you never cross paths either."

Me either, Evelyn thought. *If Roman ensnared me I hate to think what he could do to a normal woman.*

"We should help load the plane," Sara said lightly as

she extracted her hand from between Sonja's and eased toward the rest of the McKay clan. "Thank you so much for letting us to use your jet." She nodded at the Locksleys, who waved their hands at what they considered a nominal contribution.

Evelyn felt the slight pressure of Lily's thin fingers squeezing her shoulder, the faint brush of Sara's dainty ones on her arm, and then they were gone. Leaving her to do what she should have done weeks ago.

Vicencia threw herself at Evelyn, who winced under her best friend's weight. "He seemed so nice. I still can't believe he abducted you! It blows my mind that this happened!"

Evelyn's shoulder was growing wet, signifying that Vici had broken down into tears. Past Vicencia's sleek brown hair, James' and Sonja's eyes bore into Evelyn waiting to hear the words Sara had already told them spill from their daughter's lips. Evelyn knew she'd hurt them by not telling them, by keeping the biggest change in her life from them. *It's time that they hear it from me.*

"About that," Evelyn said, easing out of Vicencia's hug so she could face all three of them. "I have a few more things to confess that you may find hard to believe."

Lily watched out the window as Vicencia's knees buckled under her and James caught her. The second major blow. The first had been less dramatic: an uncomfortable laugh, a step back from Evelyn, and a questioning look at James and Sonja. But then again, claiming she was a witch wasn't as astounding as seeing Evelyn's powers in action. Lily was sure Evelyn had just demonstrated her mind-reading powers to Vicencia, proving without a doubt she was what she claimed to be. That would bring anyone to their knees.

Vicencia's taking it rather well. Definitely better than Evelyn did when she found out she was a witch.

Lily observed the rest of Evelyn's confession, curiosity winning out over the nagging voyeuristic feeling she had as eyes widened, mouths gaped, tears fell, cheeks were wiped, fingers shook, and hugs exchanged.

An entire gauntlet of emotion in under ten minutes. Evelyn works fast.

James grasped the handles of Evelyn's wheelchair and a final flurry of hugs ensued before he pushed her toward the plane. Lily stood to help get Evelyn settled, but by the time she walked to the front of the plane, James was already up the steps with his daughter in his arms.

"Oh. Um. We set up a spot for her over there." Lily

gestured to a pile of blankets as James maneuvered his tall frame through the door and down the wide hallway.

"This good, Evelyn?" Lily asked, motioning to a makeshift bed.

"Perfect," Evelyn said.

Evelyn's lips were blue, and her skin looked clammy. As James set her down Lily heard a weary sigh escape her sister's lips.

"Call us when you get there, Evie," James said, standing to his full height and blushing when he noticed a dozen extra eyes on him. He bent down closer to his daughter so that only Evelyn and Lily, who had taken the seat next to Evelyn, could hear.

"Thank you for telling us and Vicencia. I only wish you would have mentioned it when you first returned, but it doesn't matter. We love you for who you are, no matter who that is." He kissed Evelyn on the cheek.

James rose and addressed the rest of the witches. "Thanks for looking after her. Let me know when we can help with anything. And I mean *anything*."

"Thank you," Brigit said with a small smile. "We appreciate all you've done for us so very much."

James nodded and walked down the aisle, his eyes on his daughter until he exited the plane.

Lily tracked James through the cabin window as he rejoined Sonja and Vicencia, who were huddled together against the winter cold, before retreating to the hangar and their normal lives.

"How'd Vicencia take the news?" Lily asked, turning back to Evelyn. Thick track marks of tears and mascara ran from her closed eyes. Lily wished she had some makeup remover handy for her sister.

Evelyn sighed, sounding exhausted. "Pretty well. I only told her the basics, what Sara told Mom and Dad. None of them realize everything we're up against or what happened with the pneumas, but I'll tell them soon. Once we get home and I've rested more. It was too much to spill all at once. But I've started and there's no backing out now. Vici was a little mad at first. I deserve that."

"She'll warm up," Lily said, sure it was the truth. "The more she learns, the easier it will be for her to accept it. Just like us. Give her time."

The plane pulled back with a jerk. They were halfway down the runway when Evelyn spoke again, her voice soft.

"I hope you're right. I think . . . I want to sleep now." She rolled onto her side, away from Lily.

Lily pulled the blanket up over her sister's shoulders, reassuring her she was still there for whenever Evelyn needed her as the jet rose into the sky to take them home.

About the Author

Ashley lives in Portland with her husband, Kurt, their dog, Flicka, and the house ghost that sometimes makes appearances in her charming, old home.

When she's not writing urban fantasy and portal fantasy novels she enjoys traveling the world, reading, kicking butt at board games (she recommends Splendor and Dominion), and frequenting taquerias.

For all the latest releases and updates, subscribe to Ashley's newsletter, The Coven, today. You can also find her Facebook group, Ashley's Reader Coven and join in on the fun there!

Also by Ashley McLeo

<u>Coven of Shadows and Secrets</u>

Seeker of Secrets

Hunted by Darkness

History of Witches

<u>Spellcasters Spy Academy Series (Magic of Arcana Universe)</u>

A Legacy Witch: Year One

A Marked Witch: Internship

A Rebel Witch: Year Two

A Crucible Witch: Year Three

An Academy Witch: Prequel

The Complete Spellcasters Spy Academy Boxset

<u>The Wonderland Court Series (Magic of Arcana Universe)</u>

Alice the Dagger

Alice the Torch

<u>Standalone Novels</u>

Stealing Maid Marian's Heart (Magic of Arcana Universe)

The Alchemist of Silver Hollow (Magic of Arcana Universe)

<u>Fanged Fae Series - A Bonegates sister series</u>

Blood Moon Magic

Faerie Blood

<u>The Bonegate Series - A Fanged Fae sister series</u>

Hawk Witch

Assassin Witch

Traitor Witch

Illuminator Witch

<u>The Royal Quest Series</u>

Dragon Prince

Dragon Magic

Dragon Mate

Dragon Betrayal

Dragon Crown

Dragon War

<u>The Starseed Universe</u>

Prophecy of Three

Souls of Three

Rising of Three

The Starseed Universe (five-book boxset)

Acknowledgments

Thank you to my husband, Kurt, for always believing in me, even when my drafts were not so great, and allowing the space and time to follow my dreams. You keep me thankful for your love, unyielding compassion, and support everyday. I love you babe.

To Jennifer Roop, my editor, I'd have so many misplaced commas without you! In all seriousness, you brought my work to a new level and gave me valuable, constructive, kind input when I needed it. You're the best!

A huge thank you to all my family and friends. Especially the ones I bugged with strange but pertinent questions to make *Souls of Three* seem more real. Thank you for indulging and always supporting me.

To my critique partners, Kelly Eggleston, April Taylor, and Susan Robinson, I *seriously* could not have written *Souls of Three* to a higher standard without your input. You ladies are amazing writers and I'm so happy we can grow together.

Sometimes an artist author more than critiques on their work, and that is where my Indie Author Business Group came in. Thank you to everyone in the group who helped open my eyes to a whole new world of marketing and promotion that every book needs to be successful. I learned so much in our Friday meetings.

All the magic,

Ashley McLeo